She stood very close, looking up at him as the rain poured down upon them, and Aedan trembled, though it was not from the chill. She placed her hands against his chest. "I saw you coming up here," she said, her voice low and husky. "I followed you. I knew that there might never be another chance. . . ."

Her face came closer.

"I know you want me," she said, trailing her fingers down his cheek.

He knew that this was wrong. He knew that he should push her away, gently but firmly, and flee back down the tower stairs, back to his room, where he could bolt the door and catch his breath and try to convince himself this never happened. But instead, as her lips moved to his, so close he could feel her hot breath against his face, he put his arms around her and pulled her close, crushing his lips to hers.

BOOKS

The Iron Throne
Simon Hawke

Greatheart
Dixie McKeone
Available in 1996

BIRTHRIGHT™ BOOKS

the Iron throne

Simon Hawke

THE IRON THRONE

Cover art by Tony Szczudlo.

First Printing: August 1995
Printed in the United States of America
Library of Congress Catalog Card Number: 95-60305

9 8 7 6 5 4 3 2 1

ISBN: 0-7869-0357-0

TSR, Inc.
201 Sheridan Springs Road
Lake Geneva, WI 53147
United States of America

TSR Ltd.
120 Church End, Cherry Hinton
Cambridge CB1 3LB
United Kingdom

FOR RICH BAKER AND COLIN McCOMB,
who had the vision.

And for Brian Thomsen and Rob King, who expressed an incredible vote of confidence and demonstrated sheer lunacy by asking me to do this book under an impossible deadline and managed to maintain their cool under pressure when I came down with pneumonia in the middle of the project, then recovered only to suffer a gunshot wound to my hand, which necessitated typing this entire book with only four fingers. (Don't ask, I don't want to talk about it.) I pulled it off, guys. That's one for the books. Thanks for hanging in there.

Thanks also to Dr. Arnie Arem, who took care of my injured hand, and Heather Bowman, who came and helped enormously while I was recovering, despite being seven months pregnant and missing her husband, Shawn, who's in the navy.

And special thanks and acknowledgments are due to Margie and James Kosky, Paul Cupal, Robert M. Powers, Sandra West, Bruce and Peggy Wiley, David Foster, Daniel Arthur, Debbie Delisle, and Gypsy Bentz, and all my friends who provided support and encouragement through all this madness. You know who you are, I love you all.

Musical Acknowledgments

For some peculiar reason, one of the questions I'm most often asked is if I write to music and, if so, what is it? Okay, I'm only gonna do it once, so pay attention. The answer is, not always. Sometimes I listen to music just before I write, to get charged up, sometimes while I write, to keep it flowing. Here are the talented musicians who have provided energy and inspiration during the demented hours:

Sisters of Mercy (Britain's coolest export since the Triumph Bonneville), Tangerine Dream, Henry Rollins (poet laureate of the new "Lost Generation"), Bauhaus, Rush, Danny Elfman and Oingo Boingo, AC/DC, Bela Fleck, Eric Clapton, Pearl Jam (Eddie Vedder is the best male vocalist since Morrison), Stevie Ray Vaughan (who will be sorely missed), Ozzy Osbourne, Andreas Vollenweider, Blues Traveler, Yngwie Malmsteen, Billy Idol, Joe Satriani, Steve Vai, Jon Bon Jovi, the Doors, Aerosmith, Melissa Etheridge (the best and most soulful female vocalist since Janis), Roy Orbison, Lita Ford, and the one and only "Hammer of the Gods"—Led Zepplin, played loud enough to crack the sky. I listen to lots of other stuff, but those are the people who do it for me when I write.

(Sorry, Mom, I guess the Mozart didn't take.)

Lands of the Empire

Duchies

- A Avanil
- B Taeghas
- C Boeruine
- D Alamie
- E Mhoried
- F Cariele
- G Elinie
- H Osoerde
- I Aerenwe
- J Dhalaene
- K Ghieste
- L Diemed
- M Anuire City
- N Seaharrow City

Border Nations

- O Mieres
- P Brosengae
- Q Talinie
- R The Five Peaks
- S Thurazor
- T Dhosone
- U Tuarhievel
- V The Gorgon's Crown
- W Mur-Kilad
- X Markazor
- Y The Sielwode
- Z Coeranys

prologue

The Eve of the Dead. The winter solstice. The longest night of the year. It was a fitting night to mourn. Aedan Dosiere, Lord High Chamberlain of the Cerilian Empire of Anuire, stood at the arched window of his tower study in the Imperial Cairn, looking out across the bay at the flickering lights of the city. The palace stood upon a rocky island in the center of the bay, at the mouth of the River Maesil. The city of Anuire lay spread out before him on either bank and spilling over into the bay itself, across dozens of small islands connected by a web of causeways and bridges.

Tonight, every window in the city was illuminated with the glow of candles that would burn till dawn.

It was like looking at the dying embers of a gigantic campfire, spread out across the bay and rising on the hillsides of the banks. A dying flame. An appropriate if rather maudlin metaphor, thought Aedan. He sighed. The weight of his years rested heavily upon him. He was weary and wanted very much to sleep. But not tonight. Only the dead slept on this night.

Each year on the Eve of the Dead, the people of Anuire would lock their doors and light their altar candles, fasting and keeping vigil until dawn, for the constellation of their god had vanished from the sky. On this cold, forsaken night, when the Crown of Glory slipped beneath the southern horizon and Haelyn's Star lay hidden, the Shadow World drew ominously near. And this year, for the first time since the old gods died, the Iron Throne stood empty. The empire crumbles, Aedan thought. The dream has died. And so he mourned, for what was, and what might have been.

Why is it, he wondered, that we never think of growing old? When we are young, we feel immortal. Death is merely something to be challenged, never feared. But one can only challenge death so many times. Depending on his moods, of course. Death was an indifferent gambler. Sometimes, he allowed but one throw of the dice. And sometimes many. He was content to let the dice fall as they may, because no matter how the game progressed, in the end, he would always be the only one left standing at the table.

Tonight, Aedan Dosiere felt very mortal. He had seen many others die, more than his share, their lives snuffed out in battle or by disease or age or blood-theft, and now he felt the spark of his own life guttering like the candles on his altar and his writing desk. Death stood across the table, smiling with anticipation. Not tonight, thought Aedan. And probably not tomorrow, or next month, and perhaps not even this year. But soon. The Reaper was a patient player, and Aedan was growing weary of the game.

At the next autumnal equinox, celebrated in the *Anuirean Book of Days* as the Veneration of the Sleeping, he would be sixty-nine years old. It was appropriate that he should have been born on such a day, though he had never truly understood that until now. There was much that he had never fully understood until now, for all the good it did him. If youth was wasted on the young, he thought, then wisdom was squandered on the aged, for they could no longer profit by it. They could but lecture youth in their frustration, who, being young, would never listen. Michael was like that. He had been born on the Night of Fire, during the summer solstice, which was always marked by a shower of falling stars. And that, too, was appropriate.

A shooting star, thought Aedan. Yes, that was Michael Roele. He had burned brightly from the very start, with an incandescence that was blinding. Everything that Michael was, Aedan had longed to be. Except the royal scion. No, he had never wanted that. His own fate had carried responsibility enough. He was the firstborn of the House of Dosiere, standard bearers to the royal line of the Roeles, and his path in life was set from the moment he first drew breath. It had been his destiny to become the lord high chamberlain to the next Emperor of Anuire, who had yet to be born when Aedan came into the world.

His Imperial Majesty Hadrian Roele IV had married late in life and, up to that point, had sired only daughters. He was in the twilight of his years, and there was a certain amount of urgency to the production of a male heir. The beleaguered Empress Raesa, who was younger than her husband by four decades, had spent most of her married life in almost constant pregnancy. Finally, after gifting him with seven daughters, the emperor's young wife bore him a son. Doubtless, much to her relief. It had been an occasion of great rejoicing and no small amount of trepidation as the empire held its collective breath to see if the child would thrive. However, it had little reason for concern. From the first angry cry that had erupted from his tiny lungs when the midwife slapped his bottom, Michael Roele had stormed into the world with an aggressive energy that would not be denied.

Aedan could still recall that day with vivid clarity. That was another peculiarity that came with age, he thought. His memories of long ago were easily accessible, and yet, for some strange reason, he often struggled to remember something that had taken place just a week before. But that day had been a memorable one. On the day that Michael had been born, Aedan's father brought him in to see the infant prince, lying cradled in his mother's arms.

"This is your lord, my son," his father told him. "Kneel and pay him homage."

Aedan was only six years old then, but he already knew his duty. He had understood that the tiny, wrinkled creature lying nestled in its mother's arms would become the most important person in his life.

He had bowed his head and gone down to one knee before the empress, who was lying propped up by pillows in the large, canopied gilt bed. He could still recall how radiant and beautiful she looked, with her long, golden hair hanging loose around her shoulders.

"What is my lord's name, Your Highness?" he had asked.

The empress had smiled and said, "Michael."

"Michael," Aedan murmured softly to himself, repeating the name now as he had then. Almost as if in answer, a sudden gust of wind blew in through the window and the candles flickered.

Sensing a presence in the room behind him, Aedan turned from the window. In the dim glow of the flickering candlelight, he saw a tall, dark, and slender figure appear in the center of the chamber. His full-length, hooded cloak billowed in the dissipating wind of his arrival, then settled down around him, giving the brief impression of wings being folded back.

"Am I intruding on your vigil, Lord Aedan?"

The voice was unmistakable. It was deep, musical, and resonant, with the old, familiar, lilting elvish accent.

"Gylvain!" said Aedan. "By Haelyn, is it really you, or am I dreaming?"

The elven mage pulled back the hood of his dark green, velvet cloak, revealing handsome, ageless features. His thick, silver-streaked black hair fell almost to his waist and framed a striking face. His forehead was high and his eyebrows thin and delicately arched. His nose was fine and blade straight; his cheekbones high and sharply pronounced, typical of elven physiognomy. The long hair partially concealed large, gracefully curved and pointed ears; the

5

mouth was wide and thin-lipped; the strong jawline tapered sharply to a narrow, well-shaped chin. His eyes, however, were his strongest features, large and almond-shaped, so light a blue that they were almost gray, like arctic ice. With his dark coloring, they stood out sharply, and the effect was magnetic. Aedan stared at him, and the years seemed to fall away.

"The world of dreams is no less real than the waking one," Gylvain replied. "However, I take it your question was rhetorical."

"You have not changed," said Aedan with a smile. "How long has it been? Twenty years? No, by Haelyn, more like thirty. Yet you are still as I remember you, even after all this time, while I . . . I have grown old and gray."

Aedan turned and glanced into the full-length gilt-framed mirror mounted on the wall. Behind him, Gylvain Aurealis stood reflected, looking just the same as he remembered him. By contrast, Aedan had changed enormously. His hair, cropped short as he had worn it since his midthirties, when he began to lose it, was a grizzled, iron-gray stubble. His thick, full beard was streaked in shades of gray and white. His face was lined with age and scarred from battle. The stress of his responsibilities had given him dark bags below his eyes, and years of squinting through a helm into glaring sunlight had placed crow's-feet at their corners. There was a weary melancholy in his gaze that had not been there only a few short years before. Once slim and muscular, he was thicker in the waist and chest now, and in the perpetual dampness of the castle on the bay, his old wounds pained him.

Gylvain's reflection smiled. "You will never seem old to me. I shall always see you as you were when we first met: a shy, ungainly, coltish youth, with the most earnest and serious expression I have ever seen on one so young."

"Your elven vision is far more acute than mine," said Aedan wistfully. "I have looked for that young boy in my reflection many times, but I no longer see him." He turned to face the mage. "Is it too late to ask for your forgiveness?"

Gylvain cocked his head and stared at him with a faintly puzzled expression. "What was there to forgive?"

"Is it possible you have forgotten?"

"I must confess, I have," Gylvain replied. "What cause had I to take offense?"

"Sylvanna," Aedan said.

"Oh, that," said Gylvain with a sudden look of comprehension. "I never took offense. I merely disapproved."

"Of me," said Aedan.

Gylvain shook his head. "No, of the situation, not of you."

Aedan turned, biting his lower lip, and stared pensively out the window. "How is she?"

"Well."

"As beautiful as ever?"

"She has changed but little."

Aedan stood silent for a moment. "Does she ever speak of me?"

"Yes, often."

"Truly?"

"Have I ever lied to you?"

Aedan turned. "No, you never have. You were

always a true friend. But I had thought I crossed the boundaries of our friendship with Sylvanna."

"True friendship knows no boundaries," Gylvain replied. "The only boundaries you had crossed were those of reason. I tried to make you see that, but you were thinking with your heart and not your mind. It was the only time I ever knew you to be just like Michael."

"Had you told me that back then, I would have considered it the greatest compliment," said Aedan. "I wanted so to be like him."

"Be grateful you were not."

Aedan snorted. "There was a time I would have bridled at a remark like that," he said, "but now I understand. Michael and I were like two sides of the same coin. Each stamped differently, but meant to complement the other. I feel my worth diminished by his . . . absence." He shook his head. "But I am being a poor host. May I offer you a drink?"

"Anuirean brandy?"

"But of course." He poured them each a gobletful from a decanter on his writing table, then handed one to Gylvain. "What shall we drink to?"

"Why not absent friends?" said Gylvain.

Aedan nodded. "To absent friends," he toasted. They drank, and as the brandy flowed, the two old friends sat vigil and remembered.

BOOK I

ABDUCTION

ANUIRE

chapter one

"I'm going to be Haelyn; Aedan will be my brother,
Roele; and you, Derwyn, will be the Black Prince,
Raesene," announced Michael in a tone that brooked
no argument. But he got one anyway.

"I don't want to be Raesene! Why can't *I* be Roele?"
Lord Derwyn whined petulantly.

"Because you are not of the royal house," said
Michael in a tone of lofty disdain.

"Well, neither is Aedan," Derwyn protested,
unconvinced by this argument. "Besides, my father
is an archduke, while his is just a viscount, so I out-
rank him."

"Nevertheless, Aedan is my standard-bearer and
his father is the lord high chamberlain," said Michael.

"As such, despite his rank, he is closest to the royal house."

"Well, if I cannot be Roele, then I cannot be Rae-sene, either," Derwyn insisted. "Raesene was Roele's half-brother, so he was also of the royal house."

Michael neatly sidestepped this piece of logic. "When Raesene gave his allegiance to Azrai, he betrayed the royal house and was thereby disinherited. Besides, I am heir to the imperial throne," he added, the color rising to his cheeks, "so I can make anyone anything I want them to be!"

Aedan stepped in to play the diplomat before a minor court scandal erupted. "Why not let me take the part of the Black Prince, Your Highness? I always play Roele, and this would give me the opportunity to do something different for a change. I would enjoy that."

Michael did not want to give in too easily. He tossed his thick, dark hair and frowned, making a great show of considering the matter, then finally relented. "Oh, very well then, since you request it, Aedan, you can be Raesene. Derwyn can be my brother, Roele, and Caelan can be Traederic, the standard-bearer."

He quickly assigned roles to all the other boys, and they made ready to begin the battle. For Aedan, this was sheer torture. At eighteen, armed with a wooden sword and shield, he felt absolutely ridiculous playing with a group of children aged from six to thirteen. However, his duty was to serve his prince, and if his prince wanted to play war, then war it was.

They were playing the Battle of Mount Deismaar, yet again. It was Michael's favorite game, and he stuck to it with a dogged persistence only a twelve-year-old could maintain. He never seemed to tire of it. As usual, Michael took the part of Haelyn, champion of Anduiras. It was just like him to pick Haelyn, Aedan thought. It gave him the chance to die spectacularly and become a god.

Every child in the empire knew the story by heart. Those of noble blood had learned it from their tutors, while commoners heard it from the bards, who sang it as an epic ballad called "The Legacy of Kings." There were several slightly different versions of the ballad, each divided into four main parts, but in all of them, the story was essentially the same. It was the history of the formation of the empire, and like most children of the nobility, Aedan had been taught it early, when he was only six years old.

It began with "The Six Tribes," the ancestors of the humans now settled in Cerilia. The story told how five of the tribes came on a mass exodus from the embattled southern continent of Aduria. The Andu, from whom the modern Anuireans were descended, took their name from their god Anduiras, the deity of nobility and war. The Rjuven had venerated Reynir, the god of woods and streams. The Brechts had worshiped Brenna, the goddess of commerce and fortune, while the Vos had followed Vorynn, the moon lord, who was the god of magic. The last of the five Adurian tribes, the Masetians, had been devoted to Masela, the goddess of the seas. These sea-going traders, whose swift, triangular-sailed sloops had once plied the Adurian coasts, had not survived as a discrete culture in the modern empire, though remnants of Masetian influence could still be found in the Khinasi lands.

The sixth tribe were the Basarji, the ancestors of the people now known as the Khinasi, whose temples were dedicated to Basaia, the goddess of the sun. They were a dark-skinned, exotic-looking people who had crossed the storm-tossed Sea of Dragons from their homeland of Djapar to settle in the southeastern region of Cerilia. Their origins were shrouded in the occult mysteries of their folklore, but it was believed that they had come from the same stock as the Masetians, as there were many similarities between their cultures and, like the Adurians, they had worshiped the old gods, though each tribe had its favored deity among the pantheon.

The Adurian tribes had fled from their war-torn ancestral lands to escape subjugation by their neighbors, who were followers of Azrai, lord of darkness. Their flight took them to Cerilia, across the land bridge that once existed where the Straits of Aerele now flowed.

Before the Six Tribes came, there had been no human presence in Cerilia. However, there were other races who had claimed the land for their own. Chief among them were the elves, who called themselves the *Sidhelien*. Their civilization was ancient and advanced, but they were also capable of fearsome savagery from centuries of competing with the feral humanoids who shared their land. They had carved out their kingdom from territories overrun by goblins, gnolls, and ogres, and in its days of glory, the Elven Court was said to have surpassed in power and pageantry even the Imperial Court of Anuire.

Of the remaining two races living in Cerilia, the dwarves were the most insular. A strong, taciturn, enduring people, they organized their kingdoms around clans, with each clan leader swearing fealty to the dwarven king. Expert miners and skilled fighters, they seldom ventured from their mountain strongholds and lived in peaceful coexistence with the elves. Their only natural enemies were the brutish ogres, who lived deep in the vast caverns that honeycombed the mountains.

Cerilia was also home to a growing population of halflings, though less was known about their history and culture than that of any other race inhabiting the land. Unlike the clannish dwarves, who rarely strayed from their domains, halflings were wanderers by inclination, tending to adapt to customs and conditions prevailing in the territories where they lived. The only permanent halfling settlement in Cerilia, the Burrows, was in the southern region of the Coulladaraight, the sprawling, trackless forest that was home to the reclusive elven kingdom of Coullabhie. The tiny halflings were tolerated by their elven neighbors, but any humans rash enough to venture into those dark woods often did not emerge again.

When the young knights had gathered to begin their game, Michael had decided to cast some of the smaller children as halflings, and an argument had erupted when thirteen-year-old Lord Corwin had insisted that there were no halflings in Cerilia at the time the battle had occurred. Michael had insisted that there were, and his perennial supporters, who had learned the art of sycophancy at a very early age, immediately backed him up, whether they privately agreed with him or not. Corwin wouldn't budge, however, maintaining that it was a fact, and so Michael, convinced that he was right, turned to Aedan to settle the dispute. When Aedan had confirmed that Lord Corwin was, indeed, correct, Michael had snorted with disgust, then shrugged it off and cast the smaller children in the role of dwarves, instead.

It occurred to Aedan that there had been few dwarves at the Battle of Mount Deismaar, but since none of others seemed to know that, he prudently decided to leave well enough alone. Michael had given him a dirty look when he took Corwin's side, and Aedan knew that look too well. Prince Michael did not like to be contradicted, regardless of the facts, but Aedan wasn't going to lie for him.

The truth was that halflings were unknown in Cerilia until about five hundred years ago, long after the Battle of Mount Deismaar. Legend had it that the halflings had fled from their ancestral homeland in the mystic Shadow World to escape some nameless horror that had threatened their existence. Though halflings rarely spoke of it themselves, the bards embellished on this opportunity to whatever fanciful extent their imaginations would allow. They spoke of a "Cold Rider" who appeared one day in the world of faerie, the spirit world, and slowly, it became the Shadow World—cold, gray and foreboding. And the halflings, creatures half of this world and half of the world of faerie, fled the Cold Rider and the darkness he brought with him. Perhaps it was all merely the fanciful imaginings of bards, or perhaps it was the truth. The only ones who really knew for certain were the halflings.

It was said they were the only creatures who could pass between the worlds at will, though exactly how they did this no one knew. It was believed they could "shadow walk," creating temporary portals that would let them slip into the dark domain and reemerge into the world of daylight at another place and time. Yet at certain times throughout the year, the veil between the worlds seemed to part. At such times, unwary humans could stumble through into the Shadow World, and creatures from the dark domain could emerge into the world of daylight.

At the tender age of six, when he first heard about the Shadow World from the older boys at court, Aedan had been plagued by nightmares prompted by the grisly stories he was told around their evening campfires. His young imagination had conjured up all sorts of hideous terrors that had lurked beneath his bed and in his closet, where he was convinced that portals to the Shadow World appeared each night. He would cower underneath his covers as the candle on his nightstand guttered, casting ghoulish shadows on the walls, and when he fell asleep eventually, despite all his efforts to remain awake, he would dream of fearsome monsters wriggling out from underneath his bed to drag him down into the Shadow World and feast upon his flesh.

A few years later, when he was old enough to realize that his closet, even after dark, held nothing more ominous than clothes and that the only things beneath his bed were dust balls, Aedan had regaled young Prince Michael with lurid tales of the horrors that awaited in the Shadow World, perversely hoping to repay the boy for the indignities that Michael made him suffer in his waking hours. But he soon discovered, much to his disgust, that Michael's insufferable arrogance, even at the age of five, persisted in his dreams, where instead of being terrorized by monsters, he merely vanquished them with cool dispatch.

At fifteen, Aedan had felt mortified to act out the *gheallie Sidhe* with a mere child of nine. Back then, that had been Michael's favorite game. Based on the second part of "The Legacy of Kings," the *gheallie Sidhe*, or "Hunt of the Elves," told the story of how the Elven Court resisted the incursion of the human tribes into their lands and how elven knights roamed the countryside, slaying any humans they encountered. This resulted in a war that lasted many years, but the elves were steadily pushed back from their territories because the humans had a weapon they were powerless against, namely, priestly magic.

Elves had mages of their own, but their spells were based upon the natural forces inherent in wood and water, field and air. They had never worshiped deities and could not comprehend this strange new source of power. In the end, the elves retreated to the forests, and the power of the Elven Court was shattered. All that now remained of the vast empire they once ruled were several isolated elven kingdoms scattered across the wooded regions of Cerilia, such as Tuarhievel, Coullabhie, Siellaghriod, Cwmb Bheinn, and Tuarannwn.

At one time or another, during Michael's relentless obsession with the *gheallie Sidhe*, Aedan had played elven warriors from each of those distant kingdoms, dying countless times—and never quite dramatically enough—from the spells of Michael's "priestly magic." Sometimes Michael took the part of elven mages for variety, but that was even worse. He would hide behind the tapestries hanging in the halls and leap out at an unsuspecting Aedan, slaying him with elvish spells.

"*Boola-boola-ka-boola!*"

"What was that, Your Highness?"

"*Boola-boola-ka-boola!*" Michael would yell out again, flinging out his arms and waggling his fingers. "It's an elvish melting spell. You're dead!"

"Elven mages do not cast melting spells, Your Highness. At least, I am fairly sure they don't. Besides, that did not sound anything at all like elvish."

"If I say it's elvish, then it's elvish! Now *melt!*"

"Forgive me, Your Highness, but exactly how am I supposed to do that?"

Michael would stamp his foot and roll his eyes impatiently, as if any moron would know how to melt on cue. "You're supposed to grab your throat and make horrible, gurgling noises as you sink down to the ground into a puddle of stinking ooze!"

"Very well, Your Highness, as you wish." And Aedan would grab his throat and choke, gurgling as hideously as he knew how, meanwhile sinking to his knees and collapsing to the floor, trying his best to look as much like a puddle of stinking ooze as possible. His performance was never quite satisfying enough.

"Aedan, that was terrible!"

"Forgive me, Your Highness, I tried my very best. But I've never melted before. Perhaps if you could show me how?"

Whereupon Michael would demonstrate the proper way to melt, and as Aedan watched his histrionics, he would be forced to admit that Michael did it better.

"Now do it again, and this time, do it right!"

Often, Aedan would have to die at least half a dozen times before the prince was satisfied. It wasn't long, however, before Michael's nonsense syllables and outflung fingers were replaced by the lethal force of wooden sword and shield, and Aedan found miseries anew as he was repeatedly battered into submission by his young prince in the role of Haelyn, champion of Anduiras at the Battle of Mount Deismaar.

The third part of "The Legacy of Kings," and the source of Aedan's current woes, was "The Twilight of the Gods," which told the story of how Azrai, the lord of darkness, had pursued the Six Tribes into Cerilia, determined to subjugate the people and wrest them from their gods.

Azrai first enlisted in his cause the goblins and the gnolls of Vosgaard in the northern regions of Cerilia, and gave their leaders priestly powers. Through cunning and deception, he then corrupted the Vos tribe, who had fallen from their worship of the moon god, and left the path of magic for the way of sword and mace. Next, Azrai sought to seduce the demi-humans, the elves and dwarves, by tempting them through dreams and omens. The stoic dwarves did not fall prey to the blandishments of Azrai, but the elves had burned with the desire for revenge ever since the humans took their lands and pushed them back into the forests. Swayed by Azrai's promises of the destruction of their human enemies and the restoration of their lands, once more, the elves prepared for war.

The kings of the Cerilian tribes were quick to realize the danger and joined forces, setting aside their differences to unite against the common foe. But even as the two armies met in combat, the warriors from the Adurian lands arrived to join the fray on Azrai's side. Realizing that Azrai's victory was within his grasp, the old gods appeared to their besieged followers at the land bridge between the continents of Aduria and Cerilia, where the mortals were trapped between their enemies' forces.

Each god had chosen a champion from among his or her followers to lead in the final battle. Anduiras, the god of the Anuireans, chose Haelyn, who best exemplified all the virtues of a noble knight. Together with Roele, his younger brother, and their standard-bearer, Aedan's ancestor, Traederic Dosiere, Haelyn led the tribes in one last, desperate assault against their enemies. Arrayed against them were the armies of the southern lands, in addition to the humanoids, the treacherous Vos, and the warriors of the elven kingdoms, all led by Azrai and his champion, the traitor, Prince Raesene, half-brother to Haelyn and Roele, whose ambition led him to betray his people and sell himself to the dark god.

Michael, indisputably, was always Haelyn when they played the game, but no one ever wanted to be Prince Raesene. The casting of the role of the Black Prince would always be the occasion of an argument among the young nobles of the Imperial Court, and depending on his mood, Michael would either settle things by force of royal prerogative or else stand back and watch his playmates settle it themselves. At such times, Aedan would be forced to step in and break it up while Michael watched with glee, delighting in the bruises that his future chamberlain received as he tried to separate two homicidal eight-year-olds armed with wooden swords.

This time, the matter had been settled peaceably, thanks to Aedan's diplomatic skills, but it still left Michael in a surly mood. He had been denied his halflings and had revealed his lack of knowledge, due to his indifference in his studies. Now his choice for the Black Prince had been successfully disputed, though Aedan had tried to smooth things over as best as he knew how. Still, the future chamberlain had seen that stubborn set to Michael's jaw before and knew exactly what it meant.

Someone was going to catch it when the "battle" started. It wasn't likely to be Derwyn, who had whined about being picked to play Raesene, because now he was on Michael's side as Prince Roele. Corwin, however, had been chosen to play the goblin general, which meant he was a likely target, despite being a year older and almost twice the size of Michael.

Aedan sighed with resignation. He would have to make a point of staying close by Corwin's side so he could interpose himself if things got out of hand. As the Black Prince, it would be logical for him to challenge Haelyn, and he could thereby step in to take the brunt of the assault. It would mean more bruises, because Michael never held back on his blows, and though he was only twelve, a wooden sword could still raise a nasty welt, especially since Aedan wore no armor save for a light skullcap. Being older and much bigger, he had to take care to control his blows, which was more difficult while wearing armor. Meanwhile, his armored young opponents would flail away at him for all that they were worth, and he would once more wind up black and blue. However, better that than risk the chance of Corwin ringing

Michael like a gong. Aedan didn't want to think about the problems that could cause. By all the gods, he thought, I *hate* this game.

Once the cast had been agreed upon and sides were chosen, the two "armies" retired to draw up their battle lines. The opposing generals formed up their troops and proceeded to inspect them. When they were satisfied, they stood before their warriors and addressed them, exhorting them to bravery in dying for a noble cause. Michael stood before his soldiers and his earnest, high-pitched tones rang out across the field. Aedan, as Raesene, was obliged to do the same, feeling like an utter fool.

When he was sixteen, Aedan had tried appealing to his father, pointing out how ludicrous it was for him to play with children half his age. However, it had been to no avail.

"Son, you must learn to do your duty by your liege," his father, Lord Tieran, had said.

"But, Father, he is not the emperor yet," Aedan had protested. "He is a mere child, and a spoiled one at that!"

"Watch your tongue, boy! It is not your place to speak so of the prince."

"Forgive me, Father," Aedan had said, sighing with frustration, "I meant no offense, but must I continually suffer the laughter and the taunts of all my friends? Why must I be his nursemaid? It simply isn't fair!"

"Who told you life was fair, boy?" his father had replied sternly. "When it comes to duty, fairness does not enter into it. One of these days, you shall take my place as lord high chamberlain, and when that time comes, you will have need of all the skills that you are only now starting to learn. A few years from now, you will understand and thank me. Prince Michael does not need for you to be his playmate or his nursemaid, but you need Prince Michael . . . for your training."

Now, two years later, Aedan understood just what his father had meant, but understanding did not make his task any easier to bear. His friends no longer taunted him, except to chide him gently on occasion in good humor, for by now they too understood more about duty . . . and about how difficult the prince could be. The emperor was old and ailing and could not take a hand in Michael's rearing, even if he had the inclination, and the empress was overly indulgent of her only son. Even Michael's older sisters gave him a wide berth, a luxury Aedan was denied.

He surveyed his "troops," standing all abreast in their little metal helms and suits of armor, looking like toy soldiers as they fidgeted in place, anxiously awaiting the attack. Their eyes followed him as he strolled up and down the line of his army, almost a dozen strong, improvising his speech as Prince Raesene.

"All right now, men . . ." he said, barely able to suppress a chuckle. "The time has come for us to seize the day and destroy the enemy once and for all!"

His young knights cheered the words of their commander, banging their little wooden shields with their blunt wooden swords. The "goblins" snarled, the "gnolls" howled like wolves, the "elves" responded in an ululating chorus, and the "Vos" growled and looked appropriately menacing.

"There he stands!" said Aedan, pointing with his

wooden sword. "My brother, Haelyn!" He spat out the word "brother" as if it were a curse. "The favored of the gods! The champion! What monumental arrogance!"

His words were laced with heavy sarcasm, and he was surprised to discover how much he enjoyed saying them. He had never been Raesene before, and it suddenly occurred to him that in this role, he could say things about Prince Haelyn that he would never dare say about Michael.

"Look at him out there, parading before his troops and strutting like a silly peacock! The great and noble Haelyn! All my life I have had to suffer his sanctimonious self-righteousness, his smug superiority, his annoying, squeaky little voice—" He caught himself, realizing that he was getting a bit carried away. "Well, the time for reckoning has come! You gnolls and goblins, today you shall strike a blow for the glory of your people!"

The "humanoids" responded with a chorus of snarls and howls.

"You elves, today you shall savor the sweet taste of revenge!"

The "elves" raised the swords and gave their war cry.

"You Vos, today you prove once and for all which tribe deserves to rule!"

The "Vos" struck their shields with their swords and stamped their feet.

"Today we shall soak the field with the blood of our enemies!" Aedan glanced over his shoulder and saw that Michael was still gesturing expansively and pacing back and forth before his restive troops, giving his long-winded speech. Well, thought Aedan, there was no reason why the "enemy" should wait for him to finish it. He raised his sword.

"For Azrai and for glory!" he shouted. *"Charge!"*

The young knights gave voice to their battle cries and with weapons held aloft raced toward their opponents. Caught in midgesture, Michael turned with an expression of surprise and saw the "enemy" surging toward him. Without hesitation, he raised his wooden sword and gave the command to charge.

The two armies collided on the slopes of Deismaar, and it was the greatest battle the world had ever seen. They fought from sunrise until sunset, and the air reverberated with the clashing of steel against steel, like countless hammers ringing upon anvils. That sound alone was enough to almost deafen those in the center of the fray, but added to it were the cries of men and beasts, goblins screeching, gnolls howling like the hounds of hell, elves giving voice to their unearthly, ululating war cries, humans yelling, horses neighing, the wounded of all races calling out for aid and moaning, all amid the choking dust raised by countless thousands milling on the field of battle.

Aedan found himself face-to-face with Lady Ariel, a grimly determined girl of twelve with long blonde pigtails hanging out from underneath her helm. Her eyes burned with intensity as she raised her sword and launched herself at him, screeching with all the fury and abandon of a berserker seized with battle lust. Oh, gods, he thought, not Ariel. He backpedaled from the ferocious assault, taking a rain of blows upon his wooden shield. In her fierce determination to prove herself the equal of the boys, Ariel struck as hard as any of them, and Aedan still had bruises from the last time they had squared off against each other.

With the boys, he could always deliver a carefully controlled whack against the side of a helm to slow them down a bit or "kill" them when they got too carried away, which was almost always, but with little Ariel, he could do little more than block her blows, because he was afraid that even with her armor on, a light blow could hurt her. And he couldn't simply tap her, because Ariel did not acknowledge such light strokes. Nothing short of a blow that knocked her down would make Ariel admit that she had "died." The other boys had no such scruples and would bash her hard enough to make Aedan wince, but he was much bigger and much stronger and did not wish to cause her any harm. As if she knew this, she always sought him out when they played war, as if it were a personal vendetta. He did his best to defend himself from this diminutive amazon.

Aedan glanced around the battlefield, searching for Michael and Corwin in the melee. Corwin had been right next to him when they began the charge, but now he was nowhere in sight. He could only risk quick glances, but could not spot him anywhere among the two dozen or so mingling bodies and, worse yet, he could not see Michael, either.

"*Ow!*" Ariel had scored a telling blow upon his thigh. It stung, and Aedan knew that it would leave a nasty bruise.

"Down!" she shouted. "Down to one knee! I've crippled you!"

"You have not; it was a glancing blow, merely a scratch." He could not afford to be crippled at this stage; he still had to find Michael and Corwin and make sure they didn't take each other's heads off.

"Liar! I say you're crippled!" Ariel shouted, smashing away at him with a flurry of blows as she kept up the litany with each furious stroke. "Crippled . . . crippled . . . crippled . . . crippled . . . crippled!"

Aedan backed away and tripped. Ariel immediately pressed the advantage as he tried to regain his feet, but managed only to get up to one knee before she was upon him.

"Die . . . die . . . die . . . die . . . die!"

She's out of her mind, thought Aedan, cowering behind his wooden shield as he warded off the rain of blows. And then, miraculously, she struck a blow that hooked his shield and sent it flying out of his grasp as he watched in stunned disbelief.

Thunk!

"*Ha!* Dead!" Ariel cried out triumphantly.

The blow had come down squarely on his metal skullcap, and Aedan's vision swam. The sound reverberated inside his head like a ringing gong. The ground came up to meet him as he fell and everything went black.

Toward sunset, it seemed certain Azrai's forces would prevail, but as the sun sank beneath the horizon and darkness descended on the field of battle, the elves suddenly crossed over to join the forces led by Haelyn, and the tide began to turn.

No one knew precisely what occurred to make the elves change sides. According to some versions of the story, as darkness fell, the elves saw Azrai revealed for what he truly was and realized they had been duped. Other versions had it that the elven generals discovered that at the close of battle, when the humans were defeated and the elves were at their weakest, Azrai would betray them and have the gnolls and goblins eliminate the last potential threat to his dominion. But whatever the true reason may have been, Haelyn's embattled forces were in no position to refuse their help. Elf and human, who for years had tried their utmost to destroy each other, turned and faced the greater enemy, fighting shoulder to shoulder against the troops of Azrai.

As the moon began to rise, the champions of the gods, led by Haelyn and Roele, managed to break through a weak point in the ranks of Azrai's troops. Haelyn led the charge straight up the slopes of Deismaar to where the lord of darkness himself stood upon the higher ground, flanked by his generals and priests. Beside him stood Raesene, the traitor, and at Azrai's signal, the Black Prince led his troops down in a countercharge to meet the attackers. The brothers met midway up the slopes, each determined to destroy the other, while Azrai and his priests retreated to still higher ground. And it was then, at the climax of the struggle, that the gods themselves appeared in human form and joined the battle, uniting all their powers in an all-out effort to annihilate the lord of darkness and his priests.

Never before had god battled against god. The ground shook on the battlefield below, and the slopes of Deismaar trembled. The sky was cracked with lightning, and thunder drowned out every other sound. The earth heaved, and men and beasts fell screaming to the ground. All eyes turned toward the summit of the mountain, where the skies were lit up with a blinding glow unlike anything ever seen before.

It was the Twilight of the Gods, and it lasted only a few brief moments, but those who had survived the conflict never forgot the sight as long as they lived. The light grew brighter, and then brighter still, until the upper portions of the mountain where the gods were locked in combat was totally obscured from view. Then an incredible, thunderous explosion shook the sky, leveling the mountain and everything else for miles around.

The blast of the cataclysm washed down the mountain with the force of a hundred hurricanes, and no one was left standing. The ground cracked and split and swallowed up whole regiments as smoke and flames shot up from the fissures. Of all the hundreds of thousands of combatants who had clashed from dawn till dusk upon the blood-soaked battlefield, only a few survived, and later, when they looked back on what had happened, they counted it a miracle.

The final part of "The Legacy of Kings" was called "The Birth of the New Gods and the Abominations," and it told the story of what happened when the old gods died, having given up their lives to destroy the evil that was Azrai. The cataclysmic explosion that had leveled Mount Deismaar in an instant and reduced it to a smoking crater had released the cosmic essence of the gods. Those who had stood closest to the holocaust caught the full brunt of this searing wash of divine essence as it radiated from the epicenter of the blast like an incinerating wind. The champions of the gods, who had followed Haelyn in his bold assault up the mountain slopes, were closest, bathed in the full force of this raging wind of divine essence. Their bodies were discorporated in an instant, and in that same instant, their souls rose up to become new gods.

Haelyn became what Anduiras had once been, the noble god of battle. Aerik the druid took the place of Reynir, the patron of the forests. Seramie inherited the goddess Brenna's role as the deity of fortune, and Avanalae took the mantle of Basaia, goddess of the sun. Nesirie supplanted Masela as the lady of the seas, and Vos, the moon lord, was succeeded by the new god, Ruornil, who became the god of magic. But the dark essence of Azrai had been released as well, and it imbued two of his grim champions among the Vos, the warriors Kriyesha and Belinik, who became the Ice Lady and the Prince of Terror.

These were the new gods, created from the old, and in time, the people of Cerilia would learn to worship them, erecting new temples to their glory and passing on this story of the new creation to the succeeding generations. But those days were yet to come when the survivors of the cataclysm rose, astonished to discover not only that they were still alive, but that they had changed in ways that would forever make them different from ordinary mortals.

The god essence the cataclysm had released had been much dissipated when it reached them, but the remaining energy had still imbued them with abilities no humans had possessed before. In the coming years, these wondrous powers would be passed on to their descendants, who would be called "the blooded," those who had inherited blood abilities bestowed on the survivors of that battle where the gods themselves gave up their lives.

Among these comparatively few survivors were

Roele and Traederic, who were not as close as Haelyn when the earthshaking blast occurred. They had
turned to pursue Raesene, who fled when the old
gods joined the battle, and though he made good his
escape, he too was changed.

As smoke and flames rose up from the fractured
battlefield, the earth began to groan and tremble.
Slowly, the land bridge started to sink. Even then, the
survivors turned upon each other. As Azrai's minions
struggled to fight their way clear before the land
bridge sank, Roele marshaled his remaining troops to
stop them from escaping. Many were killed on both
sides, but soon they realized that they had to look to
their own lives if they did not wish to sink beneath
the waves that threatened to inundate them. In their
battle frenzy, they did not notice the strange new feelings surging through them, and it was only later that
they discovered they had inherited the powers of
those whom they had slain in the cataclysm's aftermath. They found that god essence could not be destroyed, but could be ripped or drained from those
who had possessed it, and this dreadful practice soon
received a name—"bloodtheft."

Bloodtheft soon became a way of life for those of
Azrai's minions who had escaped, for outnumbered
as they were, they realized their vulnerability and
sought every opportunity to kill those who were
blooded, the better to insure their own survival and
increase their powers. And as their powers grew
from the blooded men they'd slain, they gained the
ability to transform themselves with the god essence
they had seized. In their greedy quest for greater
power, they became abominations, travesties of their
once human form, and the elves, who were the first

to learn of these perverse new creatures, gave them a new name—awnsheghlien, "blood of darkness."

The traitor Prince Raesene became the mightiest of the awnsheghlien, a fearsome and grotesque creature who was called the Gorgon. Among others of his kind were the Ghost, the Kraken, the Serpent, the Sinister, the Hydra, and the Hag. Still others were in the process of their transformation, and once the metamorphosis became complete, more power gained through bloodtheft enabled them to create others like themselves and, in this manner, a new race came into being in Cerilia—a race of monsters who bore only a faint resemblance to the humans they once were.

However, this took many years. While the soon-to-be awnsheghlien went into hiding in Mount Deismaar's aftermath, those few who had fought Azrai's evil and survived returned to their own kingdoms to recuperate and rebuild what had been lost. Haelyn became the new god of the Anuireans, and his brother, Roele, became their king, founding the dynasty that bore his name. In time, through conquest or alliance, he unified the disparate human kingdoms under his rule, and the Anuirean Empire was born.

Over the years, the sons of Roele became known as the Emperors Roele, ruling their domains from the Iron Throne in the Imperial Cairn in the capital city of Anuire, built on the shores of a large bay in the Straits of Aerele, tens of leagues from the shattered islands where Mount Deismaar was destroyed and sank beneath the waves.

As Aedan came to and shook his aching head, he looked up to see the bodies of the "dead" lying all around him, craning their necks or sitting up to watch the next occupant of the Iron Throne battle the goblin general. Oh no, thought Aedan as he sat up, rubbing his sore head. Michael and Corwin were hard at it, bashing away at each other with grim determination. The survivors of the battle stood around them in a loose semicircle, watching for the outcome. Most of them cheered on the future emperor, but a few brave souls were shouting out encouragement to Corwin as the two opponents flailed away at one another.

Aedan's practiced eye saw that the older boy was holding back a bit, taking care to avoid injuring the younger warrior, but Michael was laying on for all that he was worth and, despite his smaller stature, was giving Corwin lots of trouble. Aedan tried to get up, but dizziness overcame him, and he sat back down again with a groan. Suddenly, Corwin knocked Michael's shield from his grasp and, sensing victory, raised his wooden blade and moved in for the kill.

As his stroke came down, Michael parried it, holding his wooden sword in both hands. He launched a devastating kick at Corwin's groin. Had Corwin not been wearing a codpiece, he might well have sung soprano for the remainder of his life. As it was, he grunted and doubled over from the blow, dropping his shield and clutching at the source of his acute discomfort, while Michael, instead of moving in to deliver the coup de grace, stood back and broke out laughing at the older boy. It was a bad mistake.

Corwin came up out of his doubled-over crouch, eyes blazing, and with a cry of rage, unleashed a hail of blows at Michael as if he were purely determined to kill him. Aedan jumped to his feet and started running toward the boys, but before he'd covered half the distance, Michael's sword went flying and Corwin brained him on the helm with all his might. Michael jerked and stiffened, then went down like a felled tree.

As Michael lay motionless upon the ground, a shocked silence descended on the battlefield. Aedan came running up and crouched beside him. "Michael! Michael!" he repeated with concern, forgetting in his anxiety to address him by his title rather than his name.

Michael did not answer. Carefully, Aedan removed his helm. He sighed with relief when he saw there was no blood, but that was still no guarantee he wasn't seriously injured. He patted Michael lightly on the cheeks, but there was no response.

"Michael!"

Corwin stood over them, eyes wide, shocked as the realization of what he had done sank in. The pain of Michael's kick to his essentials, evidenced by his awkward stance, was completely overwhelmed by the thought of what he'd done.

"I—I didn't mean it!" he stammered in a small voice. His lips continued to move, but no sound came out.

Aedan could spare no thought for Corwin. He gazed down at Michael, slapping his cheeks lightly. "Michael? Come *on*, Michael. . . ."

There was no response.

"My god," said Aedan, glancing skyward. "Haelyn, help me!"

Michael made a small moan. His eyelids twitched, then fluttered open. His gaze appeared unfocused. He groaned.

"Michael! Michael!" Aedan said. "How many fingers am I holding up?"

He held up two. Michael tried to focus. "Four?"

"Lie still," said Aedan. "You may have a concussion." He glanced at Corwin. "Pray that it is nothing worse."

Corwin's lips were trembling. He had gone completely white.

Aedan gently picked up Michael in his arms and started carrying him back toward the castle. Behind him, the young warriors of Mount Deismaar trooped silently with their wooden swords and shields. The war was over.

ANUIRE

chapter two

Seaharrow stood upon a cliff overlooking Miere Rhuann, the Sea of Storms, roughly two hundred miles from the capital city of Anuire. The castle's crenelated towers dominated the broken landscape for miles around, its machicolated battlements gave a commanding view of the surrounding country-side, and its thick, massive walls defied assault. Situated on a high and craggy rock formation, with the sea and a sheer wall of granite at its back, Seaharrow was a virtually impregnable fortress that a small body of men could easily hold against an army.

Archduke Arwyn of Boeruine had rather more than a small body of men, however, which was one of the reasons he was an archduke and one of the most powerful nobles in the empire. Seaharrow was his holding, and his ancestors had held it before him for hundreds of years.

Below the castle, the town of Seasedge lay spread out upon the rocky coastal plain. It was the capital and seaport of the nine provinces governed by the archduke. It was not a very large town, but it boasted a hardy population. Only the Northern Marches were less settled than the windswept western coastal region, which reached from the waters of the Tael Firth to the Straits of Aerele and east to the Seamist Mountains. During the winter, fierce storms battered the coast and strong easterly winds howled through the castle battlements. A visitor to Seasedge at this time of the year would wonder why anyone could possibly wish to settle on this desolate, storm-lashed stretch of coast.

In the summer, however, the climate was more temperate, and each year, at the end of spring, the Imperial Court of the Empire of Anuire traveled en masse in a heavily armed convoy to the Archduchy of Boeruine, to take up residence at Seaharrow. The brisk northern breezes coming in off the Sea of Storms at this time of year provided welcome relief from the hot and humid winds that buffeted Anuire during the summer season, bringing with them the monsoons that boiled up from the Adurian coast. But the monsoon season at the beginning of the summer was not the only reason the emperor came to Seaharrow each year.

The Archduchy of Boeruine had strategic significance by virtue of its geographical location. On its northeastern borders lay the Aelvinnwode, the thick pine forest that covered most of the territory known as the Northern Marches, and the hostile goblin kingdom of Thurazor, as well as the lawless, mountainous region known as the Five Peaks, which was home to goblins, bandits, gnolls, and renegades of all description. To the north of the Five Peaks and east of Thurazor lay the elven kingdom of Tuarhievel, ruled by Prince Fhileraene, whose great-grandfather was the only elven chieftain who had remained loyal to Azrai at the Battle of Mount Deismaar.

Rhuobhe Manslayer had remained with Azrai not out of any love for the dark lord, but out of a fierce hatred of humans. After the battle, he became awnsheghlien, and together with the renegade band of elves who followed him, he had seized a small portion of the Aelvinnwode on the northeastern border of Boeruine, where he still relentlessly pursued the *gheallie Sidhe*, for which he had won the appellations of Manslayer and Foresttaker, both of which he had defiantly adopted as his own.

The Prince of Tuarhievel did not seem to share his great-grandfather's belief that the only good humans were dead ones, but it was difficult to tell precisely what Fhileraene believed. His mother, Queen Ibeicoris, was still the ruler of Tuarhievel, but Fhileraene held the actual reins of power in the elven kingdom. Though he traded with the humans, he still maintained good relations with his great-grandfather, the Manslayer, whose followers were made welcome at his court. Though he outwardly condemned the *gheallie Sidhe*, there were still sporadic outbreaks of it in his kingdom, and human traders who did business with Tuarhievel did so at their own risk.

With hostile territory abutting more than half its

borders, Boeruine was a vital outpost of the empire, and the emperor took pains to ensure that Lord Arwyn was always kept aware of the important role he played in the interests of the Iron Throne. Summer Court at Seaharrow, therefore, was more than merely a holiday for the nobles of Anuire. It was also a time for important business of the empire to be conducted and for political alliances to be reaffirmed.

Arwyn of Boeruine was well aware of his important position in the empire, and he took it very seriously. Each year, before the Imperial Court arrived, he took on an additional staff of servants from the town, in addition to court pages, an honored and coveted function fulfilled by children of Seasedge. Seaharrow was swept and scrubbed from top to bottom, an enterprise that took up the entire spring season, and the kitchen larders were freshly stocked with game from the nearby forest and produce from the outlying farms. Visiting nobles and dignitaries arrived from all the nearby provinces, doubling the population of the town and filling its inns to overflowing. It was a busy time for Seaharrow and the town of Seasedge, and the Archduke Arwyn went to great lengths to make certain everything ran smoothly.

Consequently, he became extremely agitated when word reached him that Aedan Dosiere was coming up the path to the castle, trailed by the survivors of the reenacted Battle of Mount Deismaar and carrying the injured young heir to the throne in his arms.

So great was the archduke's consternation that one might have thought it was his own son who had been gravely injured. His shouts roused the entire castle into a flurry of activity. He sent for the physicians and gave loud orders for the doubling of the guard at the gates and on the walls. He ordered water heated in case the prince's wounds needed to be bathed, and he had servants running in a dozen different directions. In fact, the archduke was overdoing it a bit, purely for the sake of appearances, because secretly a thrill of excitement had run through him at the news.

Prince Michael was Emperor Hadrian's only heir, and if anything happened to him, Arwyn himself, who was descended from the bloodline of Roele, would be the successor to the Iron Throne. At least, so he believed.

None of this impressed itself on Aedan, however, for he was worried to the point of panic over the young prince, who had been his responsibility. After being confronted by the archduke himself and informing him what happened, he had been dismissed with a rather ominous, "I shall deal with you later." Then Lord Arwyn had personally taken Michael from his arms and carried him upstairs.

Had Aedan been a few years older and somewhat wiser in the ways of Imperial Court politics, he might have had second thoughts about turning Michael over to the man who stood to gain the most if anything should happen to him; but fortunately, Aedan's father was on the scene, having been alerted by all the commotion, and did not leave Michael's side even for one instant.

The fact that his father had not said a word to him made Aedan still more miserable, certain it was contempt that silenced him. However, that was not the case at all. The lord high chamberlain knew perfectly well that Arwyn was within one twist of his powerful wrists from possibly becoming next in line to assume the throne, not that Lord Tieran suspected the archduke of treachery. He simply had a healthy respect for the foibles of humanity and so would make sure Lord Arwyn was not unduly tempted. Under such circumstances, he could not spare any thought at all for his own son.

Fortunately for everyone, except perhaps Lord Arwyn, Michael's injuries were no more severe than a mild concussion and nasty bruise on his forehead. The physicians bled him just a bit and ordered bed rest for a couple of days. Meanwhile the archduke took out his frustrations first on young Viscount Corwin, whom he ordered confined to the dungeons, and then on Aedan, whom he would also have thrown into the dungeons save for the fact that he did not wish to antagonize the lord high chamberlain, who was closer to the old emperor than any other man. He was therefore forced to satisfy himself with mercilessly browbeating Aedan until he ran out of breath, then dispatching him to clean the stables.

It was there that Lady Ariel found him, several hours later, shoveling manure and cursing his existence.

"Aedan?"

He looked up and saw her standing there, looking nothing like the screaming, armored banshee who had knocked him senseless earlier that day. She had changed into a simple, dark green velvet gown that fell to her feet, which were shod with dainty black slippers. She was bareheaded, her long blonde pigtails hanging down on either side of her chest. She looked like a perfectly normal little girl rather than the roughhousing tomboy that she was.

Aedan grimaced as he scraped horse droppings off the dirt floor and shoveled them into a wooden wheelbarrow. "What is it, Ariel?"

"Aedan, I just . . ." She hesitated. "I just came to say I am sorry."

He merely grunted and resumed his work. "Well, think nothing of it."

"I know that it was all my fault," she said in a small voice. "What Corwin did, I mean. If I hadn't struck you down, perhaps you could have stopped it."

"It was my own fault," said Aedan. "It serves me right for allowing a mere slip of a girl to knock me down. I should have been paying more attention. Frankly, I'd just as soon you didn't mention it to anyone."

"Well, I just thought that if I told your father what I did, he would know it was all my fault and wouldn't blame you."

Aedan froze, bent over his shovel. He glanced up at her with disbelief. "You *told* him?"

She nodded. "I did not wish to see you get in trouble. I went to him and said it was I who was to blame, and I would take whatever punishment was meted out, and he should not fault you for something you could not possibly have prevented because you were lying senseless on the ground when it occurred."

Aedan shut his eyes and groaned inwardly. "Wonderful," he said.

Ariel did not quite catch his sarcasm. She smiled and said, "I thought you would be pleased. And your father was very understanding. He said I was a brave girl for coming forward and telling him about it, and told me not to worry about being punished since no real harm was done. He also spoke with Lord Arwyn, and Corwin's been released from the dungeons. So, you see? Everything's turned out all right."

"Just great," said Aedan with a sigh of resignation.

"I only hope you're not too angry with me for knocking you down," said Ariel.

"No, Ariel, I'm not angry."

"I never meant to hurt you."

"You didn't hurt me, Ariel. I'm fine."

"Because I would never wish to hurt you, Aedan. I'm afraid I got a bit carried away. Sometimes, I just don't know what gets into me."

"Can we please forget about it, Ariel?"

"So then you're not angry with me?"

"No, I'm not angry with you!" he shouted in frustration.

She flinched and took a step back. "You *are* angry."

He took a deep breath and exhaled slowly. "I'm not angry, Ariel. Honestly. I just don't want to talk about it anymore, all right? I have a lot of work to do, so if you don't mind, I'd like to get on with it."

"I only wanted to say I was sorry."

Aedan closed his eyes in silent suffering. He counted ten, then said, "Very well. You've said it. It's over and done with now. We shall speak no more of it. Agreed?"

She brightened. "Agreed. Well then, I shall leave you to your work."

"Thank you."

She turned and started to leave, then paused. "Oh,

and your father said he wanted to see you as soon as you were done."

"Of course," said Aedan with a sour grimace. "Thank you for delivering the message."

"You are most welcome." She gave him a quick, bobbing curtsy, then turned and left the stables with a spring in her step.

Aedan moaned, leaned on his shovel, and hung his head in misery. One of the horses whinnied.

"Oh, shut up!" he said.

* * * * *

A couple days' bed rest was more than sufficient for Michael to be up and about. After the first day, he was already complaining that he didn't want to stay in bed, demonstrating he was as hardheaded as he was stubborn. But for a change, the empress put her foot down and gave Aedan orders to make sure he remained in repose, even if he had to tie him down. Aedan delighted in the opportunity to take these orders literally, and the first time Michael tried to disobey, he tied him to the bedposts. This brought on a royal tantrum of epic proportions, but after several hours, Aedan succeeded in getting Michael's grudging word that he would not try to get out of bed if he untied him, and though he complained about it bitterly, the remainder of the recuperation period passed without further incident.

To his credit, Aedan thought, when Michael found out that Corwin had been sent to the dungeons on his account, even though it had only been for about two hours, he was deeply chagrined and immediately sent for the older boy.

45

Corwin arrived looking pale as death. When Lord Arwyn had ordered him thrown into the dungeons, the poor boy had been convinced that he would never see the light of day again. However, when he was released a mere two hours later, though it had still felt like an eternity to him, it was without any explanation. Consequently, when the jailer came to take him from his cell, Corwin had felt sure he was on his way to meet the headsman's axe.

Aedan was there when Corwin came into Michael's chambers and fell to his knees to plead forgiveness. Michael immediately told him to get up and come over to the side of his bed, whereupon he told the older boy that, by rights, it was *he* who should be asking *his* forgiveness.

"What you gave me I had coming," Michael told him. "I got no more than I deserved. And it was a well-struck blow, whereas mine was most unseemly. I am truly sorry, Corwin, that you had to spend time in the dungeons on my account. I promise I shall try to find a way to make it up to you. Will you forgive me?"

Corwin was so flustered, he did not know what to say.

"Corwin, please say you'll forgive me, or Aedan will be very angry with me and I shall never hear the end of it."

"But . . . Your Highness, it is not my place to—"

"Corwin, if I say it is your place to forgive me, then it is your place to forgive me, so forgive me and let's have done with it, shall we?"

Corwin accepted Michael's apology, and then Michael accepted his, remarking how it was the first time Haelyn had ever lost the Battle of Mount

Deismaar, and to a goblin general, at that. "Next time, there shall be a reckoning," he cautioned.

Corwin looked dismayed. "Next time?"

"Of course," said Michael. "After all, I have a score to settle with the goblins now."

Corwin swallowed nervously. "Perhaps, Your Highness, next time I might have the privilege of fighting on the side of the Anuireans."

"No, no, I want you on Azrai's side," said Michael. "Everybody else always holds back a little when they fight me, because I am the prince. But you did not hold back. And that's just what I want. I will never get any better if everyone always holds back and lets me win. Next time, Corwin, I want you to make me work for it."

"As you wish, Your Highness," Corwin said, with a bow, though he was clearly unhappy with the whole idea. The thought filled him with dread.

"And another thing," said Michael. "I'm tired of everybody calling me that all the time. Your Highness this, Your Highness that. . . . Nobody ever calls me by my name except my sisters and my parents, and I hardly ever talk to them. What is the point in having a name if no one ever uses it?"

"It would not be proper for people to address the heir to throne by his first name, Your Highness," Aedan said, not bothering to comment on the fact that the reason Michael's sisters rarely spoke to him was because they were spoiled rotten and detested him, and most parents had better things to do than spend time speaking with their children, anyway. Besides, the emperor was in poor health and rarely spoke to anyone these days, leaving most matters of state to his royal chamberlain, and the empress was too busy with her daughters, trying to get them married off, which was no easy task considering their lofty rank and still more lofty dispositions, to say nothing of the fact that there were seven of them.

"Well, I don't care. I'm tired of it," the prince maintained. "Can't they at least call me 'my lord Michael' or something?"

"Hmm," said Aedan. "As it is a point of royal etiquette, I shall have to consult my father. Perhaps, since you wish it, he may allow it in informal circumstances, but only among your intimate friends at court."

"*He* may allow it?" Michael said, bridling. "Why should it be his decision? I am heir to the throne, while he is only the royal chamberlain."

"That is very true," admitted Aedan, "but the matter does not rest with him alone. There is the question of precedent, and the etiquette of titles and so forth, which may have to be researched. It is a complicated matter."

"Well, have him look into it as soon as possible," said Michael. "My name is not Your Highness, it is Michael Roele, and I want people to use it."

"I shall speak with my father at the earliest opportunity, Your High—uh, my lord Michael," Aedan promised.

"When I am emperor," said Michael, petulantly, "I shall make such decisions on my own, without having to consult all sorts of people. It is foolish. Suppose we are in battle and someone is coming up behind me? By the time you call out, 'Your Highness, look out behind you,' I'll be dead."

"In such an event, my lord," said Aedan, suppressing a smile, "in the interests of brevity, I shall be sure to call out your name."

"Good," said Michael. "I should hate to die of royal etiquette."

That evening, when Aedan repeated the conversation to his father, Lord Tieran responded with amusement. "I see no reason why the prince's intimates cannot address him as 'my lord Michael' or 'my lord' in informal circumstances," he said, "though use of his first name alone would be highly improper, of course. Unless it were in battle, in a situation such as he described," he added with a smile. "And as emperor, needless to say, he will certainly be free to make all such decisions on his own, without consulting anyone." Then he grew serious. "And I fear that he may get his wish much sooner than he thinks."

Aedan frowned. "Is something the matter with the emperor?"

His father nodded. "His health is rapidly failing. It is generally known that he has not been well, and that he is old and tires easily, but I have taken pains to conceal just how weak and frail he has become. I do not know how successful I have been in keeping his true condition secret, but I am seriously concerned that he may not last out the summer. And if he were to die before we returned to the Imperial Cairn, we could all find ourselves in a rather precarious situation."

"Why?" asked Aedan.

"The Archduke of Boeruine is an ambitious man," his father said. "A powerful man. Prince Michael is much too young to rule unguided. He will need a regent. Ordinarily, the empress would fulfill that role, guided by myself as royal chamberlain, but she

too is young and Boeruine could easily claim that
the empire required a stronger, more experienced
hand. With the court at Seaharrow, it would be a
simple matter for him to take control and appoint
himself as regent. And once he had done that, he
would be but one step away from the Iron Throne
itself."

"But . . . Prince Michael is the heir," said Aedan.
"Surely, Lord Arwyn could not entertain notions of
displacing him. That would be high treason!"

"You still have much to learn, my son," Lord
Tieran said, shaking his head. "Once he was regent,
Boeruine could wed the empress, and whether she
wished to marry him or not, she would be in a poor
position to refuse while in his hands here at Seaharrow. Once he had brought about the marriage, if
some unfortunate accident befell Prince Michael,
Lord Arwyn would become the next Emperor of
Anuire."

"And I always thought Lord Arwyn was loyal to
the emperor!" said Aedan.

"He is," his father replied.

"But . . . if he is loyal, how could he contemplate
committing treason?" Aedan asked, uncomprehend-
ing.

"Because he would not see it as treason," his
father explained patiently. "He would see it as a
responsible and entirely reasonable act taken to safeguard the security of the empire."

Aedan simply stared at his father with disbelief.

Tieran saw that he didn't understand, so he elabo-
rated for his benefit. "Arwyn of Boeruine is not an
evil man," he said, "but he *is* an ambitious one. In
many ways, an evil man is easier to deal with,

because you always know what to expect. An evil man knows what he is and accepts his nature. As a result, he has no need to justify his actions. An ambitious man, on the other hand, is a far more slippery creature, and highly unpredictable. He often fools himself as well as others.

"Boeruine is not an evil man," Lord Tieran continued, "but he could easily convince himself that the empire was in danger with a mere child on the Iron Throne, and that the empress was herself too young and inexperienced to rule as regent. In that, at least, he would be correct. She could certainly do so with my guidance, but Lord Arwyn would doubtless feel that his guidance would be superior to mine. And he may even be right at that—who knows? He certainly is capable of governing the empire. Either way, he would tell himself that, as a widow, the empress would be vulnerable to unscrupulous suitors seeking to gain power, so by marrying her, he would only be protecting her and safeguarding the empire from greedy and ambitious men.

"And as a descendant of Roele," he went on, "who better than himself to guide the empire and provide for the emperor's widow? The empress is a beautiful woman, so I suppose it would not be very difficult for Lord Arwyn to convince himself he loved her. He is a strong and handsome man, and he might even be able to convince her. After all, the only man that she has ever known has been the emperor, and a man of his age and constitution does not really stir the fires in a young woman's heart. But whether he courted the empress or coerced her, Lord Arwyn would convince himself that he was acting out of the best possible motives. And that is why ambitious men are dangerous, my son. I would rather have an evil man to deal with any day. At least evil men are honest with themselves."

"But how could he possibly justify doing anything to Michael?" Aedan asked.

"Well, perhaps he wouldn't really need to," Lord Tieran replied. "Ambitious men often do not work in obvious ways, and they tend to surround themselves with underlings who know how to carry out their wishes, even if they are not obviously expressed. Lord Arwyn might decide to go out hunting with some of his knights one day, and that evening, over the campfire, he might choose to share some of his concerns about the empire. He might expound, in a casual sort of way, about how difficult it was to govern with a temperamental child on the throne, whose abilities were unproven and whose disposition was not conducive to instilling confidence in his subjects. He might sigh wearily and muse about how much easier things would be if only he didn't have to worry about Prince Michael all the time. . . ."

"And his knights would take that as an order for his murder," Aedan said in a low voice as understanding dawned.

Lord Tieran shrugged. "No direct order would be given, of course, but his men would understand his meaning, just the same. And when Prince Michael turned up dead, no one would be more outraged than Lord Arwyn, who would vow vengeance on the regicides, whoever they may be. He would decree a period of mourning throughout the empire, during which he himself would mourn sincerely, and following which, for the good of the empire, he would reluctantly allow himself to be persuaded to ascend the throne."

Aedan shook his head, stunned. "How is it you can even think of such things?"

"Because it is my duty to think of them," his father replied. "I do not say that this is what Lord Arwyn *will* do, merely that it is something he *may* do. It is a possibility, and it is my duty—as it shall be yours someday—to consider such possibilities and determine just how likely they may be. And in Lord Arwyn's case, I think it is a very likely possibility, indeed."

"Then we must leave here and return to Anuire as soon as possible!" said Aedan.

"What reason would we give for our abrupt departure?" asked his father. "My unfounded suspicions based on my personal dislike for our host? Thus far, he has done nothing to warrant our distrust. We are barely halfway through the season and the entire court is here, so we cannot pretend that some urgent business of the empire has arisen that requires our presence in Anuire. Moreover, we cannot simply pack up and steal out in the middle of the night. For one thing, there is the matter of Lord Arwyn's men-at-arms, and for another, we could not risk the journey without an escort. Even if we did not take the wagons and left most of the court behind, it would still take at least a day or two to organize the party, and the emperor is in no condition to travel at present."

"Then at the very least we must get the prince to safety," Aedan said. "With a small escort, I could take him to Anuire myself and then we—"

"No, that is out of the question," said Lord Tieran,

shaking his head. "Your courage is commendable, as is your initiative in suggesting such a course, but it would be far too great a risk. For a small party, the journey would be dangerous in itself, and the moment he discovered that the prince was gone, Lord Arwyn could send a party of knights after him, which he would doubtless lead himself, citing concern for the prince's safety. Suppose he overtook you on the road, with none to see what would transpire? It would be a simple matter for him to return and claim he found the prince's party ambushed by unknown marauders and slain to the last man . . . and boy."

"Then what are we to do?" asked Aedan with chagrin.

Lord Tieran sighed. "For the moment, there is nothing we can do. Our situation may indeed provide a great temptation to Lord Arwyn, but we do not know for certain that he shall give in to it. These are all merely suppositions, after all. He may surprise us and prove he is a better man than I suspect he is."

"And if he is not?" said Aedan, with concern.

"Then he must still take care about appearances. He cannot seize the throne in a way that would be obvious to everyone. That could easily provoke a war. He would have to take his time and manage things very carefully. That factor, at least, is in our favor. And we must pray for the emperor's recovery . . . or at the very least, for him to survive the summer. I do not think Lord Arwyn would dare to act while the emperor still lives."

"It was folly for us to come here in the first place," Aedan said. "If Lord Arwyn cannot be trusted, why have we honored him by holding summer court at Seaharrow? Why have we placed ourselves into his hands?"

"Because we need him to safeguard the Western Coast provinces from incursions by our enemies in the Northern Marches," said his father. "Political alliances can be very complicated things, very delicate and tenuous. A leader must often ally himself with men he does not like or trust. Such things are less important than whether or not such men can be controlled. Do you recall when you first learned to ride?"

Aedan blinked, surprised by the sudden change of subject. "Yes. My horse threw me and I landed so hard I had the wind knocked out of me."

"And you were afraid to get back on," his father said. "Do you remember what I told you then?"

"That my horse threw me because he sensed my fear," said Aedan. "And that if I did not conquer my fear and get back on again at once, I would never learn to ride because I would always be afraid and the horse would always sense it."

"Exactly," said Lord Tieran. "In some ways, men are much like horses. If a strong hand controls the reins, they may be spirited but will respond to commands. However, if they sense fear . . ."

Aedan nodded. "I think I understand," he said. He took a deep breath and exhaled heavily. "There is still so very much I have to learn."

His father smiled. "It is a wise man who knows he has much to learn. It is a foolish one who thinks he knows it all. Take care of the prince, my son. See to it he is not left alone. My concerns may prove groundless in the end—and I pray they do—but remember that it is not wise to place temptation into the path of an ambitious man."

* * * * *

That night, Aedan couldn't sleep, so he made his way up to the parapet of the tower in the west wing of the castle, where the royal party was quartered. This tower, one of four at each corner of the castle, was toward the rear, looking out over the sea. No guards were stationed here, so he could enjoy some peace and quiet in which to think, with nothing to distract him save for the pounding surf on the rocks far below.

For the moment, he was not concerned for Michael. Two men-at-arms from the Royal House Guard were posted at his door. Soldiers also guarded the rooms of the emperor and the empress, and they were within sight of one another in the corridor. This was normal procedure, and as such, would not serve to reveal Lord Tieran's suspicions to Lord Arwyn. What the archduke didn't know was that Lord Tieran had posted two additional guards inside both Michael's and the emperor's rooms, as well. Castles were often built with secret passages, and though Lord Tieran did not know if Seaharrow had such hidden corridors behind its walls, he wasn't taking any chances.

As Aedan stood on the tower parapet and looked out at the sea and the surrounding countryside, he could see most of the castle, as well. Lord Arwyn's quarters were in the east wing, and Aedan wondered if he were asleep right now or if he were awake, considering what to do. Lord Arwyn was not a fool; he knew the emperor was ailing. Hadrian was old, and at his age, even a slight illness could easily turn fatal. If he died, Michael would become the emperor, and he was not yet ready. Nor was Aedan ready to assume the role of royal chamberlain.

Michael's ascension to the Iron Throne would not mean Aedan would immediately assume that post, however. His father would continue in that role until he felt Aedan was prepared to take his place. But tonight, Aedan felt a long way from being prepared. He had never even considered the possibility that Lord Arwyn might harbor ambitions to sit upon the throne himself, and after speaking with his father, he felt woefully inadequate.

What his father had said about considering possibilities had made him think more about his role in being Michael's "nursemaid," as he had always thought of it. When he was a few years younger, he had resented having to perform that task, but then he came to understand that its purpose was to help him develop patience and form a bond with the young prince, so that when the time came for Michael to assume the throne, he would feel trust for his royal chamberlain and, in turn, Aedan would have learned how his sovereign thought. Now, however, Aedan realized that there was much more to it than that.

Without knowing it, he had also been training him to consider possibilities. The role that he had played in the young nobles' reenactment of the Battle of Mount Deismaar had, in a sense, been similar to the role his father played in the political maneuverings of the Imperial Court. He had learned enough of Michael to know how he was likely to respond in given situations, and when young Corwin had shown him up, he had considered the possibility—correctly, as it had turned out—that Michael would take out his anger on Corwin in the game. He had also considered the possibility that the bigger boy might hurt Michael if things got out of hand. He had been equally correct in that assessment, too, though he had failed to anticipate that Ariel would interfere with his ability to step in and stop it at the proper time.

Children's games. Yes, they were that, and he had been both frustrated and embarrassed to be forced to play them at his age. But now, for the first time, he understood why his father had insisted on it. On a smaller scale, he was learning how to consider possibilities, how to assess the personalities and idiosyncrasies of the players, how to gauge their reactions and deal with them appropriately. Now, however, he would have to learn how to apply those skills on a much higher level. For the first time, he began to understand just how difficult his father's duties really were.

In the distance, dark clouds roiled over the sea. He saw a flash of lightning and a moment later heard the distant roll of thunder. The wind picked up. A storm was moving in. In more ways than one, he thought grimly.

"It appears I was not the only one who could not sleep," a young female voice said from behind him.

He turned and saw Princess Laera standing on the parapet behind him. At nineteen, she was the eldest of the emperor's seven daughters, and next spring, she would be the first to wed. Ironically, she was to marry none other than Lord Arwyn, who was twice her age. However, if his father's fears were realized, thought Aedan, there was a possibility Laera might lose her intended to her own mother. Strange were the ways of imperial politics, indeed.

"Good evening, Your Highness," Aedan said, bowing to her.

"Good night, you mean," she said. "It is almost the midnight hour."

"I had just come up to get some air and think awhile," Aedan said. "However, I shall not intrude on your privacy."

"Nonsense. It is I who am intruding on yours," she said. "Stay, Aedan. I would be grateful for the company."

"As you wish, Your Highness."

"Must you be so formal?" she asked. "We have known each another since we were children, yet you have never called me by my name."

What, Aedan wondered, was this peculiar penchant in the children of the royal family to want to be acknowledged by their names? It was as if being addressed by their proper titles, as was their rightful due, somehow failed to acknowledge their individual existence. And even as the thought occurred to him, he realized that perhaps, from their viewpoint, that was precisely what the protocol of court accomplished: they forced people through law and custom and tradition to acknowledge *what* they were rather than *who* they were. No one had ever acknowledged their individuality, only their positions. It had to make them feel rather lonely.

"Well, since we are alone, I will call you Laera, if you will allow me the rare privilege," he said.

"I do allow it," she replied with a smile. "It would be nice if you could see me as a woman and not only as a princess of the royal house."

It was difficult not to see her as a woman, Aedan thought, with her dark hair hanging loose and billowing in the breeze, which also plastered the thin material of her nightgown against her body. She looked altogether too much like a woman and not enough like a princess. Self-consciously, and reluctantly, Aedan averted his gaze and looked out to sea.

"A storm is coming," he said uneasily.

She came up beside him and rested her arms on the parapet wall. "I love summer storms," she said. "The way the sheet lightning lights up the whole sky, the way the thunder rolls, as if the gods were playing at ninepins, the way the rain comes down so hard and fast and leaves everything smelling so fresh and clean. I love walking in the rain, don't you?"

He glanced at her. The wind was blowing her long, raven tresses back from her face as she inhaled deeply, taking in the moisture-laden sea air. Aedan could not help noticing the way her chest rose and fell with her breaths. She was leaning forward against the wall, and her posture accentuated her breasts, which threatened to tumble out of her low-cut nightgown. She glanced at him, and he quickly looked away. Had she caught him staring? Aedan felt himself blushing and turned his head so she wouldn't see.

It wasn't all that long ago that Laera was a gangly, coltish little girl, proud and haughty, with legs too long for her torso, but since she turned fifteen, she had begun to blossom and seemed to become more beautiful with each passing year. Her once reed-thin figure now possessed lush curves, of which Aedan was all too uncomfortably aware with her standing so close, barefoot and wearing nothing but a sheer white nightgown.

It struck him that they really shouldn't be alone like this, especially with her being dressed the way she was. Or barely dressed, he thought. She was promised to Lord Arwyn, after all, and if someone saw the two of them together in such circumstances, it could easily be misinterpreted. It wasn't right.

"Well . . . I think perhaps I should be going," he said, rather awkwardly.

"No, stay awhile," she said, reaching out and putting her hand on his arm. Her touch lingered. "We never have a chance to talk anymore. Why is that?"

Aedan's lips felt very dry. He moistened them. Did she feel completely unselfconscious standing before him in her nightclothes? "I suppose we never talk because I am usually kept busy with Prince Michael, and you are kept busy with . . ." He actually had no idea how she spent her days. ". . . whatever it is a princess does," he finished lamely.

"Learning courtly graces, sewing and embroidering, dancing, riding, lessons on the lute . . . all those things meant to prepare a girl to be a noble's wife. I am sure you would find it all quite boring. I know I do."

"We could trade," Aedan offered with a smile. "Then I could learn to sew and play the lute while you could spend the day reenacting the Battle of Mount Deismaar with Prince Michael and his little friends."

"No, thank you, very much," she said, making a face. "I concede you have the worse of it. I cannot imagine how you stand it. Michael is an absolutely horrid child. It must be awfully trying for you."

"Oh, it's not really so bad," said Aedan, though privately, he could not agree with her more. "It is good training for my future role as royal chamberlain. It teaches discipline and patience."

"It must," said Laera. "I don't know how you can put up with him. He may be my brother, but he is an insufferable little monster. When I heard that Corwin knocked him senseless, I thought it was just what he deserved. To tell the truth, I wish I'd done it myself."

"That was entirely my fault," Aedan said. "I should have prevented it, but I fear I was not quick enough."

Laera smiled. "Yes, I heard that Lady Ariel slowed you down a bit."

Aedan blushed again. Damn that Ariel. The story must be all over the castle by now and everyone was probably having a good laugh at his expense. "Yes, well, that was my fault, too. I wasn't paying attention. I was trying to keep an eye on Prince Michael, and she managed to get in a lucky blow. I really should have known better. She always comes after me during the games. She knows that I won't strike her, so she takes advantage."

Laera smiled again. "That isn't why she does it."

"Oh? Why, then?"

Laera chuckled. "You mean you don't know?"

He frowned and shook his head. "No. What other reason could there be?"

"She is in love with you."

"*What?* Ariel? Oh, that's absurd!"

"It's true, you know."

"But she's just a child!"

"A child on the verge of becoming a young woman," Laera said. "In many ways, a girl of twelve is more mature than a boy of the same age. She is certainly old enough to feel romantic inclinations. And among the peasantry, it is not at all uncommon for girls to marry at her age and start having children soon afterward."

"Well, among the common folk, marrying young is often a necessity," said Aedan. "They are poor and need more children to help them work the fields. Besides, they age quickly from their toil. It is hardly the same sort of thing. I am much too old for Ariel."

"I was only a year older than Ariel is now when I was promised to Lord Arwyn, and he is more than twice my age," said Laera.

"That is hardly the same thing," Aedan replied. "You are of the royal house, and your betrothal was arranged to cement a political alliance. Besides, you did not marry at thirteen. You were merely promised. You shall be a grown woman when you take your wedding vows."

"I am already a grown woman, as you have surely noticed," she replied with a mocking little smile.

Aedan flushed with embarrassment and silently cursed himself. She *had* caught him staring, after all.

"It will not be long before Ariel grows into a woman, too," Laera continued. "And there is much less of an age difference between the two of you than there is between Lord Arwyn and myself. In only a few years, she will not seem too young for you." She sighed and looked off into the distance. "Whereas Lord Arwyn. . . ." She sighed again. "I think I understand now how my mother must have felt when she was promised to my father."

"I was told that women find Lord Arwyn handsome," Aedan said.

Laera shrugged. "Perhaps, if they like that brutish sort. But he seems very coarse to me. He's like a great big bear, with those large eyebrows and that great, thick, bushy beard. I'll bet he's hairy all over." She grimaced with distaste. "The thought of him lying on top of me makes me shudder."

Aedan was dumbstruck at her remarks. He would never have imagined that a woman could talk that way, especially a princess of the royal house. He could not think how to respond.

"Do I shock you?" she asked, seeing his dismayed expression.

"I . . . uh . . . well . . . I have never heard women speak of such things before," he said, feeling flustered.

She cocked her head, curiously. "You think we are so very different? You think that only men think about such things? Would you wish to lie with a woman whom you found repulsive?"

"We, uh . . . we really should not be speaking of such matters," he said awkwardly.

"Why not?"

"It is . . . well, it . . . it is simply not proper!" he said with exasperation.

"Oh, I see," she said. "And you, Aedan, are so very proper in all things. I suppose that is why you have been stealing glances at my bosom every time you look at me before you so quickly and properly avert your gaze."

Aedan gasped and blushed deep crimson. "I never did any such thing!"

"Liar," she said, meeting his gaze.

"I really should be going," he said, and turned to leave, but she grasped him firmly by the arm.

"I did not dismiss you."

He moistened his lips, took a deep breath, and turned back to face her. "Forgive me, Your Highness. Have I your leave to go?"

"No, you do not," she said. She cocked her head and raised her eyebrows. "So, you wanted to look? Well, then . . . look."

She stood back from him and spread her arms out slightly from her sides. The lightning flashed overhead and, an instant later, was followed by a sharp crack of thunder. The wind picked up, blowing in off the sea, and it blew her nightgown back, pressing it close against her skin and outlining her figure clearly. As she turned slowly for his benefit, the lightning flashed again, the thunder boomed, and it began to rain, pelting down hard and fast. In a moment, they were both drenched, and as Laera's nightgown became soaked, it clung wetly to her skin, revealing everything. She might as well have been standing before him naked.

His breathing quickened. She stood there, facing him now, her long, dark hair plastered against her forehead and the sides of her face, and he could see the goose bumps on her flesh and the way her nipples stood out. He was unable to look away. She was breathing heavily, and her lips were parted slightly, glistening as the rain ran down her face, like tear tracks. She licked at the moisture, holding him immobile with her intense gaze.

"I shall be forced to marry a man I do not love," she said as she approached him. "A man I do not want. That is my duty as a princess of the royal house. But is it so very wrong of me to have . . . just once . . . a man I can desire?"

She stood very close, looking up at him as the rain poured down upon them, and Aedan trembled, though it was not from the chill. She placed her hands against his chest. "I saw you coming up here," she said, her voice low and husky. "I followed you. I knew that there might never be another chance. . . ."

Her face came closer.

"I know you want me," she said, trailing her fingers down his cheek.

He knew that this was wrong. He knew that he should push her away, gently but firmly, and flee back down the tower stairs, back to his room, where he could bolt the door and catch his breath and try to convince himself this never happened. But instead, as her lips moved to his, so close he could feel her hot breath against his face, he put his arms around her and pulled her close, crushing his lips to hers.

Her tongue slipped between his lips and found his and his head swam with the overwhelming, new, and utterly intoxicating sensation. She rubbed up against him as her fingers trailed down his cheeks and his hands seemed to move down of their own volition, pressing her still closer as they kissed, hungrily, sinking to their knees into the water pooling on the parapet. She helped him pull her soaked nightgown over her head, and as he removed his shirt, she fumbled with the wet laces on his breeches, loosening them just enough to pull them down and, without waiting for him to remove them, she pulled him down on top of her. They made love in the pouring rain as the wind whistled through the battlements, and thunder rolled and lightning split the sky.

ANUIRE

chapter three

Aedan's concerns about the emperor's health soon paled in the face of new anxieties. He was racked with guilt over his affair with Princess Laera and filled with dread of being discovered, for contrary to what she had said that night, it was not enough for her to have, "just once," a man she could desire. She had to have him again. And then again, and again, and again.

Aedan felt helpless in the grip of conflicting new emotions. He knew it was madness to continue the affair, but at the same time, he just could not resist her. And he understood only too well that he was the one who had the most to lose. Laera was a princess of the royal house, and he doubted she would suffer very greatly if knowledge of their secret trysts came to light. The marriage with Lord Arwyn would surely be called off, but that would be just what she wanted. He, on the other hand, would take the full brunt of Lord Arwyn's wrath, and under the circumstances, his father would be powerless to help him.

He could be thrown into the dungeons, or else challenged by Lord Arwyn, and he did not think much of his chances in such an event. The Archduke of Boeruine was one of the most powerful knights in the empire, whereas, Aedan reminded himself painfully, he hadn't even been able to stop little Ariel's assault. True, he had not really been fighting or paying very close attention for that matter, but he knew his skills as a swordsman were nothing compared to Arwyn's. He had been training for only a few years, while Arwyn had won countless tournaments in addition to proving himself many times in actual combat. But for that very reason, Arwyn might decide he was not worth challenging. He could simply have him tried and executed. It would certainly be his right. What if, in a careless moment, Laera allowed something to slip? What if they were caught together? Or what if, anxious to escape the marriage, she were to reveal their affair on purpose?

Every possible scenario for disaster went through Aedan's fevered mind, but when Laera's eyes met his during dinner in the great hall, and she gazed at him with that conspiratorial, knowing look, his knees went weak, his heart pounded, and he wanted her all over again, despite the guilt and fear. Sexual awakening had come to Aedan with a vengeance, and one smoldering glance from Laera was enough to bring him to immediate, acute, and uncomfortable attention.

They met several more times on the tower parapet where they had begun their affair, and then Laera accosted him in a castle corridor one evening and pulled him into a niche behind a tapestry, where they made love while, several times, people passed by in the corridor. The fear of being caught had added a dangerous excitement to their lovemaking, but afterward, Aedan never wanted to go through anything that nerve-racking again. Laera, on the other hand, had enjoyed it so much that she became emboldened to take still greater chances.

The next time, she found him in the stables, putting up the horses after he and Michael had gone riding, and they coupled in an empty stall, with the grooms brushing down the horses only yards away. It had been necessary for Aedan to cover Laera's mouth so that he could keep her cries of pleasure muffled, lest anyone should hear. She didn't seem to care. The risks they took only seemed to excite her all the more. And she would not be put off. She seemed to delight in the control that she exerted over him, and kept finding new ways to tempt fate.

She would tell him to meet her in the castle courtyard after dark, and they would make love in the shadows while the guards stood posted at the gate, less than a stone's throw away. When a tournament was held in the fields below the castle, she took him underneath the stands, and they made love beneath the royal box, where the empress sat with all of Laera's sisters and with Prince Michael and Lord Tieran at her side.

It was as if Laera *wanted* to be caught, thought Aedan, and the worst part of it was that he seemed to have lost all sense of reason and self-control. It was as if she had some sort of strange power over him. Each time he resolved to end it, to insist that it was wrong and could not possibly go on, she would look at him or touch him or press her lips to his and his will would simply evaporate in the rush of hot blood through his veins.

And then she started coming to his room at night.

He was preparing for bed one night when Laera came in, dressed in nothing but her robe, which she opened as she entered. He stared with disbelief. She slipped the robe off her shoulders and let it fall to the floor, and stood naked before him, like a beautiful sculpture unveiled, her creamy skin illuminated softly in the candlelight. His breath caught as he stared at her, drinking in her beauty. She had a way of looking at him that was at the same time seductive and possessive. And, as usual, he was unable to resist her.

After that first time, she came to his room almost every night, sometimes staying nearly until dawn. Her appetite was insatiable, and Aedan felt worn out. On a number of occasions, he had tried bolting his door when he retired for the night, but no sooner had he thrown the bolt than a stab of anxiety went through him and he thought, what would happen if she found herself locked out? What would she do? He was afraid to find out. And at the same time, he wanted her to come. And so his door remained unbolted.

He cursed himself for being weak, and for being afraid of refusing her, but on the nights she didn't come, he found himself waiting for her with tense anticipation, feeling frustrated and disappointed when she failed to arrive. She neither told him that she would not be coming, nor did she offer any explanations or excuses. It was maddening, but there seemed to be nothing he could do about it. She enjoyed keeping him off balance. It was as if he were her plaything, to be used or disregarded subject to her whims.

Aedan was certain disaster was at hand when one of the house guards winked at him as they passed in the corridor one day. With horror, Aedan thought, he *knows!* And of course he knew, for the guards stationed in the corridors could not have failed to notice when Laera left her room each night, dressed only in her robe, not to return until at least several hours later. The guards were supposed to remain at their posts, but in the middle of the night, with everyone else asleep, it would have been a simple matter for one of them to follow her discreetly and find out where she went. By now, thought Aedan, with a sinking feeling, the entire house guard must know!

Fortunately, because they were the Royal House Guard and not the men-at-arms of the Archduke of Boeruine, their first loyalty was to the royal house, which meant the princess, and by extension Aedan as well. They found it quite amusing that the royal chamberlain's son was not only having it off with a princess, but doing it right under the nose of her future husband, the proud and imperious archduke. It was just the sort of thing to strike a chord of manly empathy in any self-respecting guardsman's heart.

However, Aedan reasoned that if the house guard was aware of what was going on, it would only be a matter of time—and not much time at that—before all the servants knew, as well. He knew he simply had to break it off somehow before disaster struck, but he did not know how, or even if he could. Laera had initiated their relationship, and now Laera controlled it. Aedan was afraid that if he tried to end it first, she would take it as a rejection, and that might give her all the excuse she needed to reveal their affair.

She was haughty, wilful, stubborn, and domineering, and the few times he had tried to tell her that what they were doing was wrong and dangerous, she had simply refused to listen. And even if, somehow, he *could* break it off, it really made no difference in the end, because the damage had already been done. Laera would not go to her wedding bed a virgin, and Lord Arwyn would thereby have the right to dissolve their marriage on the spot. It would disgrace the royal house and, after that, no self-respecting nobleman would want Laera for a wife, regardless of the political advantages.

It was an intolerable, nerve-racking situation, and Aedan did not see how he could possibly get out of it. It was all that he could do just to get through each successive day. With the exuberant energy of youth, Michael kept him on the go all day, and then at night, Laera wore him out with an altogether different sort of exuberance. And what with the attacks of guilt and self-recrimination that he suffered every night after she left his room—though she drove all such thoughts out of his mind while she was there—he wasn't getting enough sleep. The anxiety was beginning to take its toll.

Worst of all was the thought of what this would

do to his father. In all his life, Aedan had never disobeyed him, and what he was doing now was much worse than disobedience. He would bring dishonor and disgrace down on his family, and the thought of it made him sick at heart. It might have been easier if he could have told himself he loved her, but he did not, and he was certain Laera did not truly care for him. No tender words of love had ever passed between them. It was physical desire, pure and simple, nothing more than wanton lust, and that made it absolutely indefensible.

The trouble was, when she came creeping to his room at night and slipped her robe off her shoulders, and he would see her naked body gleaming in the candlelight, all reason simply left him. He could not control himself at all and, afterward, he would lie alone in bed, so overwhelmed with guilt that his chest would ache as if a huge weight were upon it. He had been raised to cultivate self-discipline and patience, yet he had become a slave to his own baser instincts. He could see no way around it. He was doomed.

After several weeks had passed since their first tryst on the tower, Aedan was a nervous wreck. He would flinch if someone merely called his name, expecting that at any time his treachery would be revealed. For it was treachery: he was conducting an illicit affair with a princess of the royal house in her future husband's home. It preyed on his mind to such an extent that he was beginning to feel as if he would welcome being caught.

One morning, as he was saddling up the horses in the stables for himself and Michael to go hawking, he felt a light touch on his shoulder and practically jumped out of his skin. He spun around as he heard a throaty giggle and saw that Laera had sneaked up behind him in the stall.

"Laera! By Haelyn, you scared me half out of my wits!"

As he tried to catch his breath and make his heart stop hammering, she began to loosen the laces on her bodice. "I see the grooms have changed the straw," she said, with a sultry little smile. "It's nice and fresh."

"Are you mad?" he said. "Michael will be here any moment!"

"He slept late this morning and is still getting dressed," she replied as she slipped out of her gown. "We have time for a quick one."

"Laera, for pity's sake, the grooms!"

"Are all outside, exercising the horses," she said, pulling him into an empty stall. "We are all alone. So hurry, get your clothes off. I want you." She reached for his breeches.

He somehow found the strength of will to back away. "Laera, please! I beg of you, listen to me! This cannot go on! It would be worth my life if we were caught!"

"Then that should make it all the more exciting!" she said, reaching for him. "Besides, it is your duty to serve the emperor and his family. So . . . serve." She put her arms around him and kissed him passionately.

"Aedan?"

It was Michael! Aedan quickly pulled Laera down inside the stall. She giggled and he pressed his lips to hers, desperately trying to silence her.

"Aedan, where are you?"

Laera loosened the drawstring of his breeches and started to pull them down. Her eyes were alight with excitement. Michael was but a few feet away, just outside the stall. The only thing separating them was a five-foot-high wood partition. Aedan stared at her with alarm, soundlessly mouthing, "*Stop!*" He tried to pull his breeches back up, but she grinned and fought him, pulling them back down. He was certain Michael would hear the rustling sounds they were making in the straw.

"Aedan, are you there?" Michael called out. "I see you have the horses saddled. Well, I am ready to go!"

So was Laera. She was squirming underneath him, wrapping her legs around him to prevent his escape. "Laera, *please,* I beg of you!" he whispered frantically into her ear.

"Make love to me," she whispered back, a wild look in her eyes. "Make love to me right now or else I'll scream!"

"*No!*" he whispered harshly. "Laera, this is insane—"

She took a deep breath and opened her mouth to scream. He hastily covered her mouth with his own and she chuckled deep down in her throat.

"Aedan! Aedan, I'm going! I'm not waiting any longer!" Michael called out.

Neither was Laera. She was breathing heavily, moaning as she moved beneath him. Aedan did not see how Michael could possibly fail to hear. Panic-stricken, he covered her mouth with his hand, looking over his shoulder and expecting Michael to open the stall door at any second. In his anxiety, he failed to notice that he had covered not only Laera's mouth, but her nose, as well.

Unable to breathe, she struggled to remove his hand, but he held her down with determination, pinning one arm with his free hand and the other with his knee as he watched to see where Michael was. Laera bucked and thrashed beneath him, but Aedan cursed her silently as he looked over his shoulder and gritted his teeth, watching the stall partition.

He heard footsteps, then the clip-clopping of hooves as Michael took his horse out of its stall. Pressing down on Laera in an attempt to keep her still, he continued to watch the stall door, holding his breath and listening. He heard Michael's horse snort and wicker just outside the stable doors. Then came the soft creak of the stirrups as the boy mounted up and hoofbeats as he trotted off.

Aedan closed his eyes and let out a long sigh of relief. However, he wasn't safe yet. The grooms could return at any moment. He had to get Laera dressed and out of here. "Laera—"

She had stopped her struggles and lay still beneath him, her eyes closed.

"Laera?"

With a shock, he suddenly noticed that he had been covering both her mouth and nose. He jerked his hand away.

"Laera!"

She gasped for air, reflexively, and Aedan almost sobbed with relief. For a dreadful moment, he had thought he might have killed her. Her eyes fluttered open, and she coughed, gasping for air.

"Laera! Laera, forgive me! I didn't realize—"

His head jerked as she slapped him hard across the face. "You bastard! I couldn't breathe!"

"Laera, I'm sorry, I—"

"You might have killed me, you miserable wretch!" she said, shoving him away and getting to her feet unsteadily. He tried to help her, but she pushed him back again and he fell onto the straw. She stood over him, naked, her eyes blazing with fury. "How dare you! I ought to have you whipped!"

"Laera, lower your voice, for mercy's sake!" he said, pulling up his breeches and brushing off the straw. "The grooms—"

"The grooms! The grooms! It would serve you right to have the grooms come in here and find us like this! What do you suppose they'd think?"

He got to his feet. "And just what would you have them think?" he asked with an edge to his voice. Even as he spoke, he realized that suddenly everything had changed.

"I could tell them that you'd lured me to the stables and then choked me so you could remove my clothes and have your way with me!" she said spitefully. "And *then* what would you do? What do you think Lord Arwyn would do when he found out?"

"He might find out considerably more than you intended," Aedan countered angrily.

"Oh, and do you really think that he would take your word over mine?" she asked contemptuously.

"No, I rather doubt he would," said Aedan. "But he might take the word of the house guards, who saw you leave your room each night for the past few weeks and come to mine."

"They never saw where I was going!" she said, but a look of uncertainty came into her eyes. For the first time, she seemed to realize she was no longer completely in control.

"Didn't they?" Aedan said. He shrugged. "Well, perhaps not. Perhaps one of them didn't follow you to see where you went each night. Perhaps he never saw you go into my room. Perhaps there is some other reason why they all wink at me and smile each time I pass them in the corridors."

"Even so," she said, "they are the Royal House Guard, and their first loyalty will be to me, the princess, and not the lowly chamberlain's son!" She tried to say this with conviction, but a note of doubt crept through.

"The lowly chamberlain," said Aedan, echoing her words with heavy sarcasm, "is the man who has always seen to it that they were paid on time and well, and who has made certain their families were properly provided for, and given comfortable quarters and the care of court physicians whenever they were ill. It is just possible that they might also feel some loyalty toward him, and not wish to see his son falsely branded as a rapist when the truth is that the princess is a wanton slut."

She stared at him with shock, then struck him across the face with all her might. He saw it coming, but he took the blow, not even trying to avoid it. "You insolent pig!" she said, spitting out the words. "You'll pay for that! And to think I gave myself to you!"

"Indeed," said Aedan, wryly. "It was a gift I never asked for and was a fool to have accepted in the first place, considering its questionable worth."

With a cry of rage, she launched herself at him, arms raised, fingers hooked like talons, ready to claw his eyes out. He caught her by the wrists and pivoted, using her own momentum to throw her down. She fell, sprawling, into the straw.

"Enough!" he said. "By all the gods, enough! Whether in anger or in lust, you have laid hands on me for the last time! Now get up and put your clothes back on! You are still a princess of the royal house, so try to act like one! And henceforth, I shall try to act as befits my proper place and station, which I had forgotten, like a fool. As for the rest of it—your threats, your wounded pride—do what you wish. Whatever it may cost me, I am past caring one way or the other."

Aedan turned and left the stall, leaving her lying there with an incredulous look on her face. He crossed the aisle and took his horse out of its stall. Michael already had a good head start, and he had to catch up to him. It was not safe for the prince to be out riding alone, and it was past time he started thinking once again about his duties and responsibilities—for however long they would remain his duties and responsibilities. Perhaps only until this afternoon. It would not surprise him if he were seized by Arwyn's men-at-arms the moment he returned. He didn't care. He felt, at least for the moment, marvelously free.

Laera's words had been like a bucketful of cold water dashed into his face. Whatever spell he had been under was finally broken, and he saw her for the selfish, spiteful, spoiled girl she really was . . . and himself for an utter fool. One way or another, however things turned out, at least it was finally over and he could try to regain, if at all possible, some vague semblance of his self-respect.

He truly didn't care about what would happen to him now, except for how it would affect his parents. His disgrace would become theirs, as well, and for their sake, he hoped Laera had enough wits about her to leave well enough alone. Perhaps he had convinced her she would not come away unscathed if she made any accusations against him, that if she chose to reveal their affair or claim he had forced himself upon her, it would be her disgrace, as well. Perhaps it would not be very chivalrous of him to reveal a lady's indiscretions, even in self-defense, but neither was it very ladylike for a woman to salvage her own questionable virtue by accusing her chosen lover of rape. Either way, he knew Laera would not forget or forgive. He had made an enemy for life. And it was his own fault for becoming involved with her in the first place.

However things turned out, Aedan was past feeling guilty. Now, he felt only anger, not so much at Laera as at himself. Once again, he had received a painful lesson in the foibles of human nature—in this case, his own. Belatedly, he understood the true meaning of self-discipline. Laera had excited him, and he had wanted her. He would not take refuge in choosing to think she had seduced him, for even though she had initiated their affair, he had been a more than willing participant right from the start. He had known full well what he was doing, as he had known the consequences, and yet he did it anyway. He could blame no one but himself, and whatever punishment would come his way now, he would certainly deserve it. If only, somehow, his parents could be spared the disgrace of their son's folly.

Torn between anger at himself and agonized concern over his family, Aedan rode quickly down the trail leading from the castle, reining in at a bend on a promontory that gave a commanding view of the town of Seasedge and the spreading fields of the coastal plain. As his gaze swept across the wide expanse of gently rolling, grassy fields, he searched for a lone rider. Finally, he spotted him, galloping across a meadow to the east, not far from the edge of the forest. He had flown his hawk, and the bird had already stooped to make a kill.

Aedan urged his horse into a canter down the serpentine trail, and when he reached the more gradual incline of the lower slope, he kicked his horse into a gallop. Michael would be angry with him, and to make things worse, he had not brought his hawk. He tried to think of what he would tell the prince, what excuse he could make for his tardiness. He felt a brief pang of guilt at the thought of lying to him, but if Laera talked, Michael would learn the truth soon enough. If not, it was just as well. He was too young to understand about such things, and there was nothing to be served in causing him undue distress. Aedan had neglected his duties long enough in thinking only of himself. Now he would have to think about the prince, which he knew he should have been doing all along.

He lost sight of Michael when he reached the plain, and he used the ends of his reins to whip up his mount as he galloped in the direction he'd last seen him. He should have brought a guard escort with him, as he usually did, but it was too late to worry about that now. As he topped a small rise, without slacking pace, he scanned the fields ahead of him. No sign of the prince. Perhaps his hawk had stooped upon its prey in a slight depression and Michael had dismounted out of sight. He continued riding in the same direction, heading east, toward the edge of the pine forest.

He didn't like the idea of Michael's being out alone, and he liked even less the idea of his being so close to the forest. The province of Boeruine was not Anuire. They were on the frontier, and there could be brigands in the forest, or bears, or some equally dangerous creature. Renegade elves were also a possibility, though Aedan didn't think it likely they'd risk coming so close to Seaharrow. Still, Michael should have known better than to go riding off alone. And, he immediately thought, he should have known better than to be distracted from his duties.

He topped another rise and reined in briefly to look around as his restive horse pawed the ground and snorted. Still no sign of Michael. Where could the boy have gone? Surely, he would not have been foolish enough to ride into the forest? But then, Aedan reminded himself, this was the fearless Prince Michael Roele, conqueror of imaginary elves and goblins, slayer of monsters from his dreams. Michael simply didn't know enough to be cautious. And if he had gone into the forest. . . . Aedan swallowed nervously. A grown man could easily get lost in there. He urged his mount into a gallop once again.

As he rode, he scanned the sky, thinking he might spot Michael's hawk, but there was no sign of the bird, either. He glanced back toward the castle. He was pretty sure he had reached roughly the same spot where he had seen Michael from the trail leading down from Seaharrow. The boy could not have ridden very far.

"Michael!" he called out. "My lord!"

He waited. There was no response. Aedan felt a

knot of tension in his stomach. Suppose the prince had fallen from his horse and was lying injured somewhere nearby, unable to respond? Aedan called out again. No answer. He searched for tracks.

After a while, he found them. They were leading toward the forest.

Aedan swore softly to himself and followed the tracks of Michael's horse. As he approached the tree line, he heard an unmistakable screech and looked up. It was Slayer, Michael's hawk. He had helped Michael train the bird himself. He whistled loudly, calling the bird. With an answering cry, it came flying out the trees just ahead. He held his arm out, and the hawk came down to roost. Aedan winced as the sharp talons dug into his forearm. He had neglected to put on his hawking glove. He looked around. There was still no sign of Michael.

"Where is he, girl?" he asked the bird. "Where did he go?"

The hawk looked agitated. It swiveled its fierce little head sharply back and forth, fluttering its wings. Aedan gritted his teeth at the pain in his forearm as he felt blood moisten his sleeve. He had lost the trail. He turned his horse, looking down at the ground as he tried to find the tracks again. Suddenly, something came hissing through the air, and he felt what seemed like a sharp, strong blow to his shoulder. The hawk took wing with a screeching cry as Aedan tumbled from his saddle.

He fell hard on his side and cried out with pain. He rolled onto his back, clutching at the shaft protruding from the wound. A bolt from a crossbow. Bandits! He reached for his sword, and it was only then he realized that he had left it behind in the stables in his rush to get away from Laera and catch up with the prince.

He cursed himself for an idiot and fumbled awkwardly with his left hand for the dagger in his right boot, realizing with a sinking feeling that even his sword would have been an inadequate defense against crossbows. The dagger would be nearly useless. Still, it was all he had. But even as his fingers closed around the hilt of the dagger in his boot, another crossbow bolt struck the dirt scarcely an inch away from his foot, and he froze. He heard a low, nasty sound that was halfway between a chuckle and an animal growl, and looked up to see four small figures emerge from the brush.

They were no more than about four and a half feet tall, but they were very muscular and lean, armed with short swords, long knives, spears, and crossbows. Each of them wore chain mail, greaves, and peaked, open-faced, spike-topped casques. They carried small, round war shields strapped to their backs, and two of them held spears pointed down at Aedan, while the other two aimed crossbows at him. All four had sharp, swarthy features; feral, golden yellow eyes with snakelike pupils; dark, coppery skin; flat faces and sloped foreheads. Their arms were unusually long, and their teeth were sharp and pointed, the canines shaped like fangs. Haelyn help me, Aedan thought. Goblins!

He had never seen a goblin before, but he had heard stories about them, and he knew their small stature did not make them any less dangerous. They were extremely strong and possessed preternaturally quick reactions, with excellent night vision. They were a seminomadic, warrior culture who used slave

labor extensively, and it was said that they sometimes ate human flesh as a ritual to take the power of
their enemies. There were goblin kingdoms spread
throughout isolated regions of Cerilia, in the lands of
Thurazor, Urga-Zai, Kal Kalathor, the Blood Skull
Barony, Markazor, and the Five Peaks. However,
Aedan had never dreamed that goblins would dare
to venture this far south, so close to Seaharrow.

They were probably part of a raiding party from
Thurazor or the Five Peaks. He could not imagine
only four of them would have risked such a journey,
penetrating so deeply through elven lands to reach
Boeruine. All this flashed through his mind in an
instant as he desperately tried to push his fear aside
and think clearly, for he knew his survival would
depend on what happened in the next few moments.

"Get up, human, if you wish to live," one of them
said, speaking Anuirean in a guttural, heavily ac-
cented voice.

Aedan slowly struggled to his knees, wincing
with pain, then rose unsteadily to his feet, clutching
at the crossbow bolt protruding from his shoulder.
He saw another goblin try to seize his horse, but the
stallion reared up and neighed, then bolted from the
creature. Run, Windreiver, Aedan thought. Run
swiftly back, so they will know at the castle that
something has gone amiss.

One of the goblins bent and snatched the dagger
from Aedan's boot, and then a spear point in his
back prodded him into the trees. As he walked,
Aedan tried to ignore the pain in his shoulder. His
mind raced feverishly. Had they taken Michael?

They approached the remainder of the party, waiting under the cover of the trees. There were about a

dozen of them, in addition to the four who had captured Aedan. Two of them held Michael between them, gagged, with his hands tied behind his back. The rest were mounted on large, gray wolves that growled threateningly as Aedan approached. Wolf-riders, he thought. That clinched it. A raiding party out of Thurazor.

He realized that if they had meant to kill Michael and him, they would undoubtedly have done so already. What then? Take them as slaves? Hold them for ransom? The latter seemed a likely possibility. He and Michael were obviously not peasants, so the goblins must have naturally assumed they were nobility from Seaharrow. If the creatures planned to hold them for ransom, at least he and Michael had a chance of getting out of this alive. So long as they didn't know who Michael was.

"Listen," Aedan said to his captors, "if you mean us any harm, then know that my father will pay handsomely for the safe return of my little brother and me."

One of the goblins chuckled as he sat astride his wolf. His laughter was an ugly, rasping sound. "Brothers, is it?" he said with a sneer. "Funny, I seem to recall that the emperor had only one son."

Aedan tried to keep his alarm from showing. They knew! But perhaps there was a chance he could still convince them otherwise. He glanced at Michael, who apparently didn't even know enough to be afraid. Instead, he looked angry—furious, in fact—and was making noises into his gag, which fortunately were completely unintelligible.

"The *emperor?*" said Aedan, trying to look surprised. "What in Haelyn's name makes you think our father is the emperor? He is but a lowly viscount who—"

"Save your breath, boy," said the goblin leader. "The prince has already told us who he is. He has promised to have us all drawn and quartered and then boiled in oil for daring to lay hands on his royal person." He chuckled. "No one but a prince could possess such arrogance at so young an age."

Aedan silently cursed Michael for a fool. If only he'd known enough to keep his mouth shut! "What did you tell them that for, you little idiot?" he said to Michael angrily. "If they think you are the prince, they'll only demand a higher ransom, more than our father could ever hope to pay!" He turned back to the goblin leader. "Don't listen to him; he's just a child! He must have hoped to frighten you into releasing him. He didn't know that goblins would not fear the power of the emperor, as we do!"

The goblin leader smiled. "A good attempt, young lord," he said. "And I might even have believed you had I not had the prince described to me in detail, nor seen the royal signet graved in gold on his left hand." He held up the ring. "I shall keep this as a trophy. Our quest has gone far more easily than I could ever have expected. Who would have thought that our quarry would come riding straight into our waiting arms?"

The goblin leader's words sent a chill through Aedan. They had not merely stumbled onto a raiding party. These wolfriders had come *specifically* for the purpose of kidnapping the prince! They knew the royal seal, and they had a description of the prince, as well. They must have been waiting in the forest for an opportunity to seize Prince Michael as he was out hawking or riding, and they had come prepared to do battle with an armed escort that, Aedan realized miserably, he should have brought along with him as he usually did. All that could only mean one thing—someone had given them that information. There was a traitor in the Imperial Court! But who?

Who stood to gain the most from some tragedy befalling Michael? Arwyn of Boeruine, of course. Aedan's father had considered the possibility of Arywn's ambition leading him to treachery, but he had not considered that Arwyn could be so bold and black-hearted as to ally himself with goblins. But then, if Arwyn wanted Michael dead, why go to such lengths? Why not just hire some brigands or some mercenaries to perform the task, or else entrust it to some of his own men, whose loyalty to him was beyond question? Why involve the goblins? And why, for that matter, would goblins enter into any plot with a human warlord? There had to be some reason that would benefit both parties. Aedan tried to think clearly. If he could reason out their motives, it might help him figure out what to do.

If the goblins planned to hold the prince for ransom, as seemed likely from their behavior and what the goblin leader said, Arwyn of Boeruine would be the logical choice to deliver that ransom. And since the emperor was at Seaharrow and not Anuire, he had no immediate access to the treasury, which meant Lord Arwyn would have to raise the ransom himself. And that would put the emperor—and more significantly, the empress—in his debt. But what would be in it for the goblins? Well, the ransom itself, obviously. That could be enough. The only heir to the imperial throne would bring, literally, a princely ransom.

However, if no ransom was forthcoming, Michael would probably be killed. The goblins would get all the blame, and no suspicion would ever fall on Lord Arwyn. All he had to do was fail to deliver the ransom, or claim the goblins had killed Michael anyway, in spite of the ransom being paid. And that, of course, would mean war.

That had to be the answer, Aedan thought. A war would benefit both Lord Arwyn and the goblin prince of Thurazor. If the Archduke Boeruine declared a war of retribution against Thurazor for the murder of the prince, the empire would surely unite behind him, for any noble who refused the call to arms would appear to be taking the side of the goblins. And the same thing would unite the goblin kingdoms behind Thurazor. The elves living in the Aelvinnwode would be caught squarely in the middle, and it would be impossible for them to remain neutral in the conflict. They would have to choose one side or the other. There would be no question of their siding with the goblins, their age-old enemies. Even at the height of the *gheallie Sidhe*, the elves had hated the goblins just as much as they had hated humans, if not more. Besides, since then, the elves of Tuarhievel had established tenuous trading ties with the outposts of the empire.

It was a foregone conclusion that, caught between two warring armies, the elves would take the empire's side. Regardless of which side they chose, however, they would be the losers in the end, for the war would be fought upon their lands, which lay between the goblin kingdom of Thurazor and the empire's northern frontier. It would mean the end of Tuarhievel's independence. Because of geographical factors alone, the elves would suffer the greatest death toll, and when, at length, the war was concluded with a negotiated peace that would allow both sides to claim victory, the elven lands would be partitioned between the empire and the goblin kingdom, and any elves who had survived would either be forced to flee or else live in subjugation under the goblins or the humans.

It all fit together and made perfect sense, but reasoning it out gave Aedan little satisfaction at this point, for it meant Michael almost surely had to die. And if Michael's death was a foregone conclusion, so was his. Well, Father, he thought, it seems I've learned how to consider possibilities, for all the good it's done me. And I thought my worst worry would be Laera.

Several of the goblins dragged over a crude litter they had lashed together from pine boughs and branches. They harnessed it to two of the larger wolves, so that one end dragged upon the ground, and tied Michael to it. The goblin leader then rode over to Aedan.

"I perceive you are a noble's son," he said. "Therefore, you should be worth something, as you attend the prince. Well, you may continue to attend him, provided you do not slow us down. You are too big for the wolves to draw upon a litter, so you shall have to run. Keep up, and you shall live. But if you cannot keep pace . . ." The goblin made a slashing motion across his throat.

Aedan gulped. "I shall do my best," he said.

"We shall soon see if your best is good enough," the goblin said with a sneer.

Aedan's arms were tied behind him securely, and a rope was looped around his neck, the end held by a wolfrider who grinned at him maliciously, showing his pointed teeth.

"Let us go," the goblin leader said. "Before long, these two shall be missed and a search party will be sent out. I intend to be deep in the Aelvinnwode by then."

The wolfriders moved off, with Michael drawn on the litter, bound and gagged securely. Aedan had to run to keep up and keep slack in the rope around his neck, which he soon realized had been tied with a slip knot. If he allowed any tension, it would choke him. Unlike Michael, he had not been gagged. The goblins were not concerned about his calling out, since it was not likely anyone would hear. Besides, one jerk on the rope would cut off any cry he made, and they had Michael as a hostage for his silence. It occurred to him that Michael might have been spared his gag, as well, had he possessed the sense not to lose his temper with his captors and annoy them.

Aedan was amazed at Michael's lack of fear, but then, the prince had never had any real reason to be afraid before. Perhaps his young mind simply did not grasp the danger, or the fact of his own mortality. In any case, Aedan soon forgot all about Michael as his attention became occupied with trying to keep up with the wolfrider who held his rope. The wolves were trotting through the thick forest at a good pace, but fortunately, they were not running all out, otherwise Aedan would never have been able to keep up with them. Clearly, the wolves drawing Michael's litter could manage no more than a trot, for which

Aedan was profoundly grateful. As it was, it wasn't long before his lungs were burning and his legs aching and he was gasping for breath.

Several times, he faltered as he tripped over a rock or an exposed root, and the rope tightened around his neck. To his relief, he discovered that the slip knot was tied in such a manner that it would loosen once again after he got some slack back in the rope, but it still took some time before the tension eased and there were periods when he found himself struggling to draw breath while having to run harder to catch up and gain more slack. His entire world became simply putting one foot in front of the other and avoiding any obstacles that could trip him up and bring about disaster. It was sheer torture.

After a while, they stopped to rest, just when Aedan felt he couldn't run another step. He had lost all track of time as he had tried desperately to keep pace. As they stopped, he fell gratefully to the ground, sobbing for breath. His clothes were drenched with sweat and his legs felt as if they were on fire. They still had a long way to go to reach Thurazor, which Aedan assumed must be their destination. He tried to recall his geography lessons. He seemed to remember that Thurazor was at least three or four days' travel from Boeruine, through the Five Peaks region covered by the Aelvinnwode. He did not see how he could possibly last that long. He already felt completely worn out.

Still, he could not afford to think about his own exhaustion. His first duty was to the prince. Gasping for breath, he dragged himself to his knees and looked up at the wolfrider who held his rope.

"May I please see to the prince?" he asked hoarsely.

The goblin grunted and released the rope, jerking his head toward the litter. Aedan knew there was little reason for them to fear he would run away. With his hands tied behind his back, and exhausted as he was, he would not have gotten ten steps before the wolves brought him down. He struggled to his feet and made his way over to the litter, while the goblins sat cross-legged on the ground, munching on some sort of dried jerky they had taken from their bags. Aedan didn't want to speculate on what sort of meat it was. He crouched beside the litter, then glanced at the goblin leader. He could not loosen Michael's gag, since his own hands were tied. He knelt beside the litter.

"I am deeply sorry about this, my lord," he said. "If I had met you at the stables, as I should have, none of this would have happened."

Michael simply shook his head. It was evident that the seriousness of their situation had finally sunk in, but as his eyes met Aedan's, there was no reproach in them.

"We are in very desperate straits, indeed," said Aedan, keeping his voice low. "We must try our best to keep our wits about us."

Michael nodded that he understood.

Aedan hesitated. Should he share his suspicions with the prince? He had no proof that Lord Arwyn had a hand in their abduction, and he could hardly make such a serious accusation without evidence, although he wasn't sure how much it really mattered now. Still, he felt he owed it to Michael to be honest with him about how precarious their plight truly was. He took a deep breath and then continued.

"I doubt there is much hope for rescue," he said. "At least we are still alive. It would seem they intend to demand ransom for us. There is, however, another possibility. They might intend to sell us into slavery. A goblin lord who held the Prince of Anuire as his personal slave would gain immeasurable status, and as such, you would bring a considerable price. Aside from that, Thurazor and all the other goblin realms would greatly benefit from instability within the empire."

Aedan paused and swallowed nervously, then plunged on. "And if the heir to the throne were killed . . . it would almost certainly lead to war, which could be of benefit to certain factions within both the empire and the goblin realms. The succession would be placed in doubt, and any number of powerful nobles in the empire would intrigue to gain the throne. In such a climate, armed conflict would be inevitable, and the goblins would be able to increase their territories and gain strength while the empire was torn by civil war."

Michael's gaze was somber. He shook his head slightly, his eyes asking the question.

"What are we to do?" said Aedan, guessing what he meant.

Michael nodded.

Aedan sighed wearily. "For the moment, there seems to be nothing we can do. We shall have to bide our time and wait for an opportunity to escape, if we can. I shall be honest with you . . . our chances are very slim. Still, we must try. In the meantime, we must not antagonize our captors, as you did before. We must act frightened and submissive, and hope for the best. There is no shame in showing fear in a situation like this, and it could work for us. Let them think they have broken our spirits. Then they may get careless, and we may get lucky."

Michael nodded once again.

"You, there!" the goblin leader called out. "What are you whispering about?"

"I was merely trying to reassure His Highness," said Aedan. "He is frightened and having trouble breathing. Can you not remove the gag, at least? I promise he will not trouble you."

The goblin leader jerked his head at one of the wolfriders. "Remove the boy's gag," he said. "But if he does not keep his mouth shut, it goes right back on again."

"Could we please have some water, too?" Aedan pleaded.

"Give them water," the goblin leader said curtly.

"Thank you. You are most gracious," Aedan said, bowing his head slightly.

The goblin leader chuckled. "Gracious, am I? Well, no one has ever said that to me before. You hear that?" he said to the others. "I am most gracious. How do you like that?"

They all laughed maliciously.

One of the goblins removed Michael's gag and cut Aedan's bonds, but left the rope around his neck. He handed him a waterskin and said, "I will leave your arms untied, but mind that if you try to run, we shall set the wolves on you. We have the prince. We do not need you."

"You think I would leave my prince?" said Aedan.

"You might to save your own skin," the goblin said.

"If you believe that," said Aedan, "you know nothing of honor and duty."

"I know you've a rope around your neck," the goblin said, sneering, "and you would dangle nicely from a tree, so mind your mouth, boy!"

Right, thought Aedan. Don't antagonize them. He would do well to take his own advice. He offered the waterskin to Michael, but the prince shook his head. "No, you drink first, Aedan. You have been running, and you must be exhausted."

Aedan was in no mood to argue. "Thank you, my lord," he said, and drank greedily. He then held the skin to Michael's lips so he could drink, as well.

"I do not blame you for this, Aedan," Michael said when he was finished drinking. "It is all my fault. I should have waited for you instead of riding off alone."

"And I should have been doing my duty, instead of. . . . Well, I suppose it really doesn't matter now. We shall get through this somehow, I promise you."

"I am not afraid," said Michael.

"I am," Aedan confessed.

"Haelyn will not let us die," said Michael with conviction.

Aedan sighed. "I wish I shared your faith, my lord."

"Right now, I am lord of nothing," Michael said, "so you may as well call me by my name. After all, it is not as if we are at court."

Aedan had to smile. "Very well, Michael." He patted his shoulder. "With any luck, we may live to see court once again."

"Aedan, listen . . . if you have a chance to escape without me, you must do so."

"Absolutely not," said Aedan.

"I insist. I order it."

Aedan smiled. "As you said, we are not at court now. When we return, you can have me punished for my disobedience. But I shall not leave you."

"I will have you lashed for your impertinence."

"As you wish."

"I will make you marry Lady Ariel."

Aedan grinned. "That's a bit harsh, don't you think?"

"Would you rather marry my sister?"

Aedan stared at him, completely taken aback.

"I heard you, you know," said Michael. "In the stall. Why do you think I left? I knew what you were doing."

Aedan was stunned. "But . . . what would you know of such things?"

"I'm not stupid, you know."

"I . . . I don't know what to say," said Aedan, blushing with embarrassment and shame.

"You could certainly do much better," Michael said. "Laera may be my sister, but she is selfish and mean-tempered. She cares nothing for you. She cares nothing for anyone except herself. She will only bring you trouble."

Aedan snorted. "You mean, this isn't trouble enough?"

"You may have a point, there."

Aedan shook his head ruefully. "Well, if it makes you feel any better, it's over. I finally came to my senses, though a bit too late, I fear. I am truly sorry, Michael. And deeply ashamed. I've let you down."

"You certainly have," said Michael. "I see I shall have to choose your wife for you. You seem to have no judgment in such matters."

Aedan could not help smiling. "And you, of course, are vastly experienced."

"I did not say I would choose her now," said Michael. "Besides, experience and judgment are not the same thing."

"No, they're not," Aedan admitted. "But it usually takes the one to acquire the other. And sometimes, as I have recently discovered, the lessons can be rather painful."

"Enough!" the goblin leader said, approaching them. "Time to move on."

Aedan groaned as the wolfriders mounted up again. The banter had momentarily lifted their spirits, but now grim reality sank in once more. Fortunately, they proceeded at a slower pace this time. They were obviously less concerned about pursuit. They were deep in the Aelvinnwode now, and fast pursuit would be impossible. If a rescue party from Seaharrow had been sent out, it would have been difficult for them to pick up their trail, and even if they had, they would have been unable to proceed quickly through the thick forest of the Aelvinnwode.

Aedan held out little hope for rescue now. If they were going to get out of this somehow, they would have to do it on their own. And he held out little hope for that, as well.

He had long since lost all sense of direction, and the thick canopy of branches overhead meant he could not orient himself by the stars. Even if they could manage to escape somehow, he could not see how they could hope to elude the wolves. As he followed along, led on his leash by the wolfrider, his spirits sank lower and lower. He could not share Michael's optimism, yet he marveled at the boy's attitude in the face of their dire predicament. Perhaps it was just his youth. Maybe he really didn't know enough to be afraid. Or perhaps he had underestimated Michael all along. In many ways, he was a stubborn, willful, spoiled child, but at times such as now, he seemed older than his years. Most boys his age would have been reduced to abject terror by their situation, but Michael did not panic. Even at twelve, he was keeping his wits about him, which was certainly more than Aedan could say for himself.

They did not stop again until well after dark. The goblins did not pitch camp or light a fire. They were in elven territory, and clearly did not wish to draw attention to themselves. Besides, they could see in the dark, and had their wolves for protection from predators. They simply stopped, unharnessed Michael's litter, and leaned it up against a tree to rest the wolves pulling it, then sat down and ate some jerky from their packs. Afterward, they gave some to their captives. Aedan had no idea what it was, but the meat was quite tough and very salty. Knowing what unsavory creatures goblins were, it was probably some sort of rodent. Still, he was so hungry he would have eaten saddle leather. After they ate, the goblins settled down to sleep, either curled up on the ground or leaning back against the trunks of trees, their weapons close at hand. Aedan noted that two of them remained awake to stand watch.

After he ate and fed Michael some jerky and some water, they had tied him up again, both his hands and feet, so that he could do little more than squirm along the ground like a caterpillar. Still, at least he had been given a brief amount of freedom. Michael had remained tied to the litter ever since their capture, and when Aedan asked repeatedly if they couldn't untie him for at least a little while, if only while they ate, one of the goblins cuffed him and told him to keep his mouth shut. It infuriated him; there was no reason for it other than pure meanness. They were punishing him for his earlier outburst. But Michael did not complain. At least they had removed his gag and left it off because he had stayed silent.

Feeling utterly exhausted from the long journey, Aedan curled up beside the litter to which Michael had been tied, and as he shivered with the cold, he became overwhelmed with despair. He saw absolutely no chance for escape. What bothered him most was his uncertainty about their fate. At worst, they would be killed in the end, and at best, they would wind up slaves, thralls to some goblin lord in Thurazor for the remainder of their lives. Better to die than live like that, he thought.

He felt sure he was right about Lord Arwyn. Someone had certainly betrayed them, and he could not imagine who else it might be, who else could benefit from Michael's death or disappearance. But if the plan called for him and Michael to be killed, why had the goblins bothered keeping them alive this long? Perhaps because some sort of proof that they were alive would be required when the demand for ransom was delivered. Or perhaps because they really did intend to sell them into slavery. It was even possible the goblins had some other plans for them that he could not foresee. His imagination started to come up with all sorts of lurid possibilities, which only increased his anxiety and made sleep difficult, despite his exhaustion. There was no sound from Michael, and Aedan assumed he was asleep until he heard his name whispered softly.

"Aedan? Are you awake?"

"Yes," he whispered back. "I'm dead tired, but I can't seem to get to sleep."

"I think I've almost got my hands free."

Aedan craned his neck to look up at him in surprise. "*What?* How?"

"When they tied me up, I tensed my muscles," Michael whispered. "It was a trick I learned during our games. It gave me just a little bit of slack in the ropes when I relaxed, and I've been working at them ever since. Now I think I've almost got my right hand free."

Aedan was astonished. Michael hadn't been untied ever since their capture, which meant he had enough presence of mind right from the beginning to think about escape and he'd been working on the ropes all day long while they had traveled.

"I got a little worried when you asked them to untie me," Michael continued, whispering softly. "They would have seen I'd been working on the ropes and would have only tied me up tighter." Aedan heard Michael grunt softly. "There! Hold on. . . ."

A few moments later, Michael had untied the ropes holding his feet and crouched beside him.

"Lie still," whispered Michael, as he worked at the knots on Aedan's bonds.

A short while later, Aedan's hands were free. He sat up and glanced around quickly to see if the goblins standing watch could see. He felt Michael's hands working at the ropes around his ankles.

"I'll get these," the prince whispered. "You keep watch."

Aedan marveled at the boy's composure, but then he realized they were still a long way from being truly free. The goblins standing watch were actually sitting underneath a tree about fifteen or twenty yards away, playing some sort of game with dice. He could barely make them out, but he could see the motions they made as they tossed the dice and he could hear their voices. They were absorbed in their game and not watching them at all. But the guards were not their greatest worry.

As Michael got his feet untied, Aedan whispered, "What about the wolves?"

"I think they're sleeping," Michael whispered back, jerking his head toward where the beasts had all curled up together a short distance away. "They've come a long way, bearing riders, and they were fed just before the goblins went to sleep. If we're very quiet, we might have a chance to slip away."

"But the moment they realize we've escaped, they'll wake the beasts and set them on us," Aedan replied. "We'll never be able to outrun them!"

Michael's face was close to his. "We have to try," he whispered. "If we can reach that stream we crossed a while back, we can follow it and they will not be able to pick up our scent."

"That's good thinking. But it's several miles, at least," Aedan replied. "We'll never make it!"

"Aedan . . . do you want to escape or don't you?"

He bit his lower lip and nodded.

"All right, then. Come on."

Slowly, they started to crawl away from the camp, taking great care not to make the slightest noise. It was agonizing progress and, at any moment, Aedan expected to hear shouts of alarm behind them and the growling of pursuing wolves. His heart raced and his stomach felt tight as he crawled behind the prince, trying to breathe steadily and evenly. He had never felt so afraid in his entire life. The thought of being brought down by wolves and torn to pieces was foremost in his mind as he carefully placed his hands and knees down, dreading to make the slightest rustling sound. Once, a twig snapped softly underneath his knee and he caught his breath and froze, but as loud as the sound had seemed to him, it went unnoticed. After what seemed like hours, they were finally far enough from the camp to risk getting to their feet.

And then they started running for their lives.

chapter four

They plunged through the forest with Michael
leading the way, his smaller size making it easier for
him to dart among the trees and pass below low,
overhanging branches. Aedan's longer legs were not
much of an advantage in the heavily overgrown terrain, besides which, he had been on his feet all day,
running for miles, and he was dead tired. He tried
not to think about the burning pain in his over-
worked leg muscles as he ran, concentrating only on
putting one foot in front of the other. And it seemed
to take all his concentration.

They could not have run more than a hundred
yards when he was already gasping for breath and
stumbling. In the darkness, with the thick forest

canopy blocking the moonlight, he could not see more than a few yards ahead of him, and he strained to keep up with Michael, whom he soon lost sight of and was only able to follow by the sounds of his running footsteps somewhere just ahead. And to make matters worse, his leg muscles started to cramp.

He did not know how much longer he could keep it up. He knew it wouldn't be long before his muscles cramped so badly he could not go on. If he could only make it to the stream . . . but he did not see how he could. Already, his left leg was starting to fail him, and he slowed as he was forced to trot with a limp in Michael's wake. The important thing was for the prince to get away, he told himself. It would not be long before their escape was discovered and the wolves would be on the trail. There was no hope of outrunning them. None at all. However, if they caught him first, it might give Michael enough time to reach the stream and lose them. Then he might get away, if he were lucky.

Aedan winced with pain as his left leg cramped so badly that he could not take another step. He stumbled to a halt and supported himself painfully against a tree trunk. It was no use. He would never make it. Go, Michael, he thought. Go, run for it!

In the distance, he heard the howling of the wolves as they picked up their trail. It felt as if a giant fist had suddenly started squeezing his gut. It was all for nothing. But maybe not. There was still a chance he could buy Michael some time. At least he would give his life in the service of his prince. Perhaps it would compensate for his dereliction of his duty in his affair with Laera. It was certainly no more than he deserved for having acted like a fool.

There was a sudden rustling ahead of him and he straightened, breathing heavily, prepared to meet whatever new threat could be facing him, but it was only Michael. He had doubled back.

"Run!" Aedan shouted at him. "They have discovered our escape! Run for your life! I will try to hold them off as long as I can."

"With what?" asked Michael. "Don't be stupid. Come on!"

"I can't," said Aedan, wincing with pain. "My legs . . . cramped. . . . I can't go on. Save yourself."

"I am not going to leave you," Michael said. "Now come on, Aedan, lean on me. . . ."

"Forget about me! I'll only slow you down!"

"We go together or not at all," insisted Michael, taking his arm and putting it around his small shoulders. "Now lean on me. Come on, you can do it!"

"It's no use. We'll never make it. You must go on without me."

"Shut up and move!" said Michael.

They started off at an awkward, shambling trot, with Aedan leaning on Michael for support, but he knew it was hopeless. The stream was still at least a mile or two away. The wolves would catch them long before they reached it.

"Michael . . . please . . ."

"Shut up and run, Aedan," Michael said, through gritted teeth.

"I can't. The pain . . ."

"Forget the pain. Pain is only a sensation."

If their situation hadn't been so desperate, Aedan would have laughed at the sheer lunacy of such a statement. And yet, somehow, it helped. He grimly set his teeth and increased his pace, trying not to lean too hard on Michael, who barely came up to his chest. The howling had stopped now, but that was only more ominous. It meant the wolves were on the stalk. They would be gliding almost soundlessly through the forest, following their scent, their jaws agape, their tongues lolling, goblin riders on their backs. Death was racing toward them on padded paws. They would undoubtedly spare Michael, at least for a time, but they did not need Aedan and there was no question in his mind he would be killed as an object lesson to the prince to prevent further escape attempts. If only Michael hadn't stopped. . . .

He thought he could hear faint rustling sounds behind them, but he wasn't sure. They were no longer trying to move quietly. There was no longer any point. They were trying to move as quickly as possible, but even if they could run at full speed, it still would not be good enough. It would take nothing less than a miracle to save them now.

Haelyn, help us! Aedan thought. Don't let it end like this! If not me, at least save Michael.

They came to a small clearing, overgrown with a carpet of moss and lacy ferns, strangely illuminated by the moonlight filtering through the trees. Aedan did not remember their passing this way before. He thought they were headed back roughly the way they came, but he was no longer sure of anything except that they would never reach the stream. He cursed himself for not being stronger and having more endurance, for having succumbed to Laera's charms, for having failed his prince.

If Michael had not stopped to help him, he might have made it and the wolves would have lost his scent as he splashed through the shallow water, following the streambed for a distance before jumping out on the opposite bank and heading back the way they came. The goblins would know, of course, which way he was headed, but the forest was thick, and there was a chance he might have been able to elude them, or meet a rescue party, if one had been sent out. . . . In any event, it was all pointless speculation now. They had tried, and they had failed, and Aedan knew it had been all because of him. They began to cross the clearing, but before they could get more than a dozen yards, a low growling froze them in their tracks.

A pair of lambent eyes appeared in the darkness ahead of them. And then another. And still another. Aedan's heart sank. The wolfriders. The wolves had not only caught up to them, they had passed them, and now they stood surrounded, in the center of the clearing, the threatening growls of the wolves coming from all sides.

"We are undone," said Aedan with bitter resignation. "Forgive me, my lord."

"Well, we shall simply have to try again another time," said Michael.

Aedan snorted as the wolfriders moved into the clearing, hemming them in. "I fear there will be no other time for me."

"I shall not let them kill you," Michael said firmly.

Aedan shook his head. "Whatever happens, you must not try to interfere," he said. "You must try to live, for however long you can. Perhaps there is still hope."

But he did not really believe that. For him, at least, it was over. Eighteen years, he thought. A short life, but a good one. He could not really complain. He drew himself up, ignoring the pain in his leg, and decided that no matter what, he would do his best to make a good end. The prince would not see him die like a coward.

As the wolfriders approached, a cold wind blew through the clearing. And, unfathomably, the wolves appeared to hesitate. They raised their heads, nervously sniffing the air, and several of them gave uneasy little whimpers. The goblin leader glanced all around, sharply.

"Bows!" he commanded.

By all the gods, thought Aedan, they are going to shoot us both! But then he realized he had misunderstood the command. The wolfriders had unlimbered their crossbows and drawn their swords, but they were looking all around them, not at Aedan and Michael, but at the brush on the outer borders of the clearing. The wolves were acting skittish. Several of the riders were having difficulty controlling their feral mounts.

Suddenly, the wind came once again and all the wolves began to howl. It was a bloodcurdling sound, but it was not the baying of wolves about to move in for the kill. There was a tone of terror to their cries. And then one of the wolfriders cried out and clapped his hand to his cheek. Another one cursed, and also brought his hand up to his face. Aedan could not understand what was happening. Then the air above the clearing was full of soft, hissing noises, and rain began to fall.

The goblins were shouting and batting at the air around them. The wolves were dancing about, darting to the left, then to the right. Several of them had thrown their riders and bolted into the trees.

"What's happening?" asked Michael.

Aedan shook his head, mystified. "I don't know."

It looked as if rain were falling, sheeting down, but inexplicably, they were not getting wet. Whatever it was that was coming down from the sky was not touching them, but was falling on the goblins and the wolves, coming down very, very fast. . . . Aedan crouched and touched the ground before him.

Pine needles!

Thousands of them, hundreds of thousands, were raining down from the trees, but they were not merely falling, they were *hurtling* down with incredible speed and force, hissing through the air like a storm of tiny arrows. The upper arms and faces of the goblin wolfriders, wherever there was bare skin, resembled pincushions as the pine needles struck them with such force that they became embedded in their flesh. The wolves were howling and squealing with pain, and in moments, they had all thrown their riders and bolted off into the trees. And yet, miraculously, Aedan and Michael had remained untouched. All around them in the clearing, the moss was covered with a thick carpet of pine needles, and the ferns were beaten down . . . except for a three- or four-foot circle where they stood.

The goblins had all dropped their weapons and were crouching on the ground, crying out and snarling with pain, trying to cover themselves up, and then, as abruptly as it began, the rain of pine needles stopped.

Aedan and Michael stood motionless, frozen with astonishment, holding their breath. Everything was quiet, except for the moans and curses of the goblins.

Aedan was completely at a loss to explain what had just happened. And then Michael said, "Aedan, *look!*"

From the underbrush at the edges of the clearing all around them, tall, slender figures in dark, hooded cloaks appeared. Each of them carried a short, powerful, double-recurved bow to which long arrows had been nocked.

"Michael, get down!" Aedan said, dropping to the ground and pulling the prince down with him and covering him with his body.

The arrows whistled through the air all around them and each one found a mark. In seconds, the goblins all lay dead. Aedan raised his head as the hail of arrows stopped. The elves standing around the clearing remained where they were, but they had lowered their bows. And then the wind returned. It blew through the clearing, then came back and began to swirl roughly in the center, forming a rapidly spinning vortex, and as it dissipated, a tall and slender figure stood revealed, his long cloak swirling around him and then settling to drape around his shoulders.

For a moment, the figure simply stood there, gazing at the bodies of the goblins, and then he turned toward them. Aedan realized this was the explanation for the mysterious rain of pine needles. An elven mage.

Now the elven archers who had killed the goblins moved into the clearing, as well. Several of them began to pick up the weapons the wolfriders had dropped, while others stripped the bodies of their daggers and armor.

"What are they doing?" Michael asked him softly.

The mage overheard him. "The goblins have no further need of their armor and their weapons," he said to them in a deep, resonant, lilting voice that seemed almost musical. Aedan wished he had a voice like that. "We can make good use of them, however. We are not a rich kingdom, you see, as is your human empire."

"But they are much too small for you," said Michael with a frown.

Aedan was still trying to get over what had just happened, but Michael's impetuous curiosity asserted itself even at a time like this. Apparently the boy was simply incapable of feeling fear.

"Indeed, they are too small for us," the mage replied, "but not for our children. We start their training at an early age."

He pulled back his hood, revealing long, raven-black hair with silver streaks running through it, gracefully curved and sharply pointed ears, and a sharp-featured, youthful-looking face that was strikingly handsome.

Aedan drew himself up and gave him a slight bow. "Greetings, Sir Wizard," he said. "I know not what you intend to do with us, but allow me to thank you for saving us from the goblins."

The mage gazed at him speculatively for a moment, a faint trace of a smile at the corners of his mouth. He returned the bow. "You are welcome, young lord," he said. "But in truth, we were less concerned with saving your lives than in taking theirs."

"As that may be," said Aedan, "you could still have shot us down along with them, but you chose to spare us. And for that, we are both grateful."

"Indeed," said Michael. "I shall see to it that you

are well rewarded when we return to Seaharrow."

Aedan winced inwardly. Would the boy never learn when to keep his mouth shut? There were still elves within the Aelvinnwode who pursued the *gheallie Sidhe*, and though these elves had spared their lives, at least so far, they could still be held for ransom . . . which Lord Arwyn would be in no great hurry to deliver.

"What he means, Sir Wizard," he said, hastily, "is that we will do our utmost to persuade our families to compensate you to the best of their abilities for rescuing us from our captors." He shot Michael a quick warning glance.

The elven mage watched them with bemused interest. "Knowing what I do of Arwyn of Boeruine," he said, "he is much more likely to repay us in steel rather than in gold."

"I would never allow that," Michael said emphatically.

"*You* would not allow it?"

Aedan nudged him, but it was already too late.

"I give you my word that you shall always be treated fairly, and with respect, at Seaharrow and throughout the empire," Michael said, oblivious to the warning.

"Indeed?" the mage said, raising his thin, sharply arched eyebrows. "I take it, then, that I have the distinct honor of addressing the Prince of Anuire?"

"I am Prince Michael Roele, heir to the Iron Throne of Imperial Anuire, and this is my standard-bearer and chamberlain, Lord Aedan Dosiere."

The mage bowed to them both. "A rare privilege, Your Highness," he said. "And your lordship," he added to Aedan.

"And whom have we the honor of addressing?" Michael asked.

"I am Gylvain Aurealis, wizard to the elven court of Tuarhievel," the mage replied, inclining his head slightly.

"How did you make those pine needles come down like arrows from the trees?" Michael asked him.

"It was done with magic, Your Highness, as you have doubtless surmised. However, as to the precise method, I fear I cannot tell you that."

Michael frowned. "Why? Is it an elven secret?"

"No, it was an elven spell, Your Highness," said Gylvain. "But having used it, I have now forgotten it. So even if I wished to, I could not tell you just now how it was done."

"You mean a spell, once used, is always forgotten and must be learned anew before it can be used again?" asked Aedan.

"Such is the nature of magic," the mage replied. He raised his eyebrows in surprise. "They do not teach you such things?"

"Our mages teach only their apprentices," Aedan replied. "Such knowledge and power is closely guarded."

"Indeed?" said Gylvain. "Pity. We teach all our children about magic. They do not all choose to become wizards, of course, for the path is a long and arduous one, but they can all use magic in small ways, to add depth and meaning to their lives. Magic is a part of nature, as are we, and to understand it is to understand the world around us and become attuned to it."

"Well, I have learned something new," said Michael, nodding. "That is useful."

Gylvain smiled. "Knowledge is always useful, Your Highness. And you will soon have an opportunity to add to your store of it. You shall be my guests at the court of Tuarhievel."

Aedan was about to protest that they could not go to Tuarhievel and needed to return to Seaharrow as soon as possible, but these elves had saved their lives. They were in their debt, and it would be dishonorable to refuse their hospitality. Aside from which, Aedan was not sure if he *could* refuse. He was still far from certain as to the elven wizard's motives.

Gylvain was being very civil, even courtly in his manner, but Aedan knew there was just no telling what an elf would do. The elven kingdom of Tuarhievel was officially at peace with the empire, but humans had nevertheless been their enemies for generations. The *gheallie Sidhe* was not a distant memory in these parts. For Rhuobhe Manslayer, it was still a way of life, and it was impossible to tell which elves in the Aelvinnwode gave their allegiance to Fhileraene and which followed the Manslayer. In many cases, it was said, they followed both.

Either way, the miracle they'd prayed for had been delivered and they were in Haelyn's hands now, though unlike Michael, Aedan's faith in their god was not quite as simple and unquestioning. He did not regularly pray to Haelyn, as devout Anuireans did each night, and he had only been to temple a few times in the last year or so, during official functions on the holy days. He swore by Haelyn in his speech, but that was more from habit than from faith. When it came to that, Aedan had his doubts.

In part, this was no more than a function of his age, for he was at a stage in life when young people questioned everything they had been taught. To a large degree, however, his doubts had grown as a result of his exposure to the Fatalists, a group of young people who believed that when the old gods died at the Battle of Mount Deismaar, the storm of dissipated god essence gave birth to the bloodlines, but no new gods were created.

What proof was there, the Fatalists asked, of their existence? The priests claimed to speak *for* them, but what proof was there that *they* spoke to the priests? None. The new gods were a fiction, they maintained, devised merely to give the people hope and the priests power. Haelyn and the other champions of Deismaar had simply died from being too close to the explosion, and that was all there was to it. There were no more gods. The people of Cerilia were on their own, and their fate was their own responsibility.

When Aedan first heard this philosophy expounded in the tavern known as the Green Basilisk, back in the capital city of Anuire, he had been deeply shocked. It was sacrilege to speak so, nothing short of outright blasphemy. And politically dangerous, as well. But at the same time, the rather shocking nature of the patrons who frequented the tavern was the reason he kept going back there. The Green Basilisk was a bit disreputable, and known to be the gathering place of some unsavory types, but that only added to its allure.

During the day, the only breaks he had from Michael were those hours in which the prince was forced to spend in study, during which time Aedan had to be with his own tutor. At night, however, his time was more or less his own, and he was anxious for some stimulation in the company of people his own age. He had found that in the Green Basilisk.

The tavern was little more than a hole in the wall in the artists' quarter, a square room with a bar in the back and no windows in the walls, which made the atmosphere inside quite dark and stuffy. The Green Basilisk catered mostly to a younger crowd, a mix of artists and bards, craftsmen, students, and the more adventuresome children of the noble class and merchant guilds, who saw themselves as daring nonconformists. They all dressed down when they came to the Green Basilisk, in plain tunics, demicloaks and breeches of dark gray or black, though Aedan noted that the material and cut of the clothing worn by the children of aristocrats was markedly superior to those of all the others. During his first visit, shortly after he had turned eighteen, he had been attracted by a girl seated with a group at one of the tables and had wandered over to join their discussion.

The young nobles among them had naturally recognized him, for his father was prominent at court, and a few of them he knew, although not very well. They introduced him to the others, whom he had never met before. The girl who caught his eye was Caitlin, the pretty blonde daughter of a farrier. Aedan was very much attracted to her, though he knew a serious relationship would have been out of the question. As a tradesman's daughter, she was of the peasant class and not descended from a bloodline. A serious liaison between them would have been frowned upon, as any offspring such a relationship might produce would dilute the powers of the bloodline. Nevertheless, Aedan had started frequenting the tavern and often met there with the others for long discussions over ale, bread, and cheese, late into the night.

Initially, Caitlin was the main attraction, but Aedan soon discovered she was interested in another member of the group, a young bard named Vaesil, who was the chief exponent of the Fatalist philosophy. For a short while, Aedan allowed himself to nurse the hope that Caitlin might eventually come to prefer him, but he soon realized that he could not compete, either with Vaesil's handsome looks or his sharp wit and musical talents. The two of them always sat together, and Caitlin hung worshipfully on Vaesil's every word.

With a wistful resignation, Aedan had eventually accepted that Caitlin saw him as no more than a casual acquaintance, merely one of the crowd, and he began to entertain the thoughts of other possibilities. Caitlin was not the only pretty girl who came to the Green Basilisk, and the Fatalists always attracted a good deal of attention. For the young aristocrats, the Green Basilisk was a place they could go slumming, mingling with the lower classes and getting a taste of common decadence. For the others, the tavern was a stimulating gathering place for freethinkers and rebels, albeit the rebellion was mostly in the form of dress and conversation. Young women went there to meet interesting young men, hopefully someone from a well-off merchant family or, better yet, a blooded noble, and young men, whether of the aristocratic class or not, went there to meet young women.

For the blooded young aristocrats, it was fairly easy pickings, for there was no shortage of young women from the common classes who nursed the dream of marrying a nobleman. Most of them, however, were doomed to disappointment. Though it occasionally happened that a blooded aristocrat took an unblooded commoner to wife, weakening the bloodline was the sort of thing that could get a man disowned. Most of the young men of the Anuirean aristocratic class had their marriages arranged for them by their families, often at a very early age.

Still, that did not stop many of them from dallying with young girls from the lower classes, most of whom were more than eager to accommodate them. They knew that even if such a liaison did not lead to a marriage, if a child resulted, the child would be blooded and would, in time, possess the blood abilities, albeit diluted, of the father. Because of this very fact, many aristocratic fathers lectured their sons sternly on how to conduct such casual affairs, stressing the importance of breaking off the act of lovemaking at the crucial moment so that a pregnancy would not result. However, this was not always successful, and on those occasions when blooded bastards did result, they were often taken into the service of the father's family and, on rare occasions, even recognized. Consequently, there were many female commoners who went to great lengths to entice a blooded young aristocrat.

For Aedan, however, it had never been as easy as it was for the others. While he had made many new acquaintances, he had not really found any close friends. Part of this was due to his natural reticence in conversation. He could not hold court the way Vaesil did, and had always felt awkward around girls, especially attractive ones. Aside from that, he was Lord Tieran's son, and while most girls had no reservations about flirting with young viscounts or baronets, they always took a different attitude when they found out who Aedan was. Even with the other young nobles, Aedan was always aware of a certain forced deference in their manner.

It took a while before he realized the reason for it. As the future royal chamberlain and the young prince's friend and confidant, he was practically a member of the royal family as far as they were concerned. No one ever took issue with him over anything, except perhaps only in the mildest way, and he soon understood it was because of who he was and his position. He could never be sure if they would tell him what they really thought. Still, he didn't mind that so much. He had enjoyed the company of the group and found their discussions very stimulating. He felt a certain daring recklessness in associating with them.

Now, just a few months later, it struck him he had not previously even had the barest inkling of what true recklessness could be. Laera had certainly taught him that. He doubted he would ever again feel quite so intimidated by a pretty face or shapely waist. And the recklessness he had displayed in going after Michael had been unforgivable. Ordinarily, they went out hawking with a party of armed men from the house guard, even when they stayed relatively close to Seaharrow. Not only had he neglected to assemble such a party, which was what he should have been doing instead of rolling in the hay with Laera, but he had allowed the impatient prince to go off on his own and then compounded his offense by going after him alone, forgetting his sword in the stables. Not that it would have done him a great deal of good, he realized. Still, if he had immediately assembled an armed party and then gone after Michael, there was a chance that none of this might have happened.

Had he simply been so distracted by what occurred with Laera that he wasn't thinking, or was he too concerned about the questions that would have been raised, such as why he had allowed the prince to ride off by himself in the first place, and what had he been doing? Either way, he had acted stupidly, and even the risks involved in his affair with Laera seemed like nothing now compared to what they had gone through. And there was still no way of knowing how it would turn out.

Although Gylvain and his elves had rescued them from the goblins and did not seem to mean them harm, now they were going to Tuarhievel, in the northernmost section of the Aelvinnwode, even farther from Seaharrow than Thurazor. And though Gylvain seemed favorably disposed toward them, once they reached Tuarhievel, it would be Fhileraene who would decide what to do with them.

If Haelyn had truly ascended and become a god at Deismaar, Aedan hoped he was watching over them. But if the Fatalists were right, he and Michael were completely on their own. However, as the saying went, there were no atheists in a melee, and while the goblins had them, Aedan had discovered that when his own life was at stake, he could become as devout as the Patriarch, himself. In the comfortable safety of a tavern, it was one thing to question faith and argue the virtues of self-reliance. In the Aelvinnwode, it was another thing entirely, and now Aedan found himself fervently hoping he could rely on a greater power than himself.

Gylvain had left them for a few moments to confer with the other elves, who had finished stripping the bodies of the goblins they had slain. Michael watched with interest. He had never seen elves before. Neither, for that matter, had Aedan. They were certainly getting more than their share of new experiences. They were dressed unlike the wizard. Gylvain wore a voluminous, ankle-length, dark cloak, with several unusual-looking amulets hanging on silver chains over an indigo-blue tunic, which was belted at the waist with a wide, black leather belt studded with silver ornaments. He had on black hose and short, ankle-high, black shoes made from leather with the rough side out. The other elves, like Gylvain, all wore their hair extremely long, but they were dressed in green and brown, with rough-out leather doublets and short cloaks. They all wore soft, rough-out leather knee-high boots fastened with crisscrossing rawhide thongs and fringed at the tops. It was perfect dress for woodsmen, Aedan thought. They would blend in easily with the forest all around them.

Aedan closed his eyes and concentrated, drawing on his blood ability of healing to restore himself. There had been no time before, and he had no energy, in any case. Now, he used what little energy remained to heal his wound and make his leg muscles relax. Unfortunately, it left him in an even more weakened condition, and he had no idea if there would be enough time to recuperate.

"I don't see any horses," Michael said after a moment. "Do you suppose they were all traveling on foot?"

"Except for Gylvain, perhaps," Aedan replied. "I wonder what it's like, being able to travel on the wind." And then the significance of Michael's observation struck home. They would have to walk all the way to Tuarhievel.

He estimated that they were probably somewhere near the southern border of the Five Peaks region. On foot, it would be at least a three- or four-day journey to Tuarhievel, probably more, depending on the terrain. The thick, old-growth forest of the Aelvinnwode was not conducive to easy travel.

"It is said that elves have great powers of endurance," Michael said, "and that they can run like deer."

"I do earnestly hope they have brought horses," Aedan said anxiously. "I have done quite enough running. I have healed my wounds, but it has left me with almost no strength at all. I am not sure I could walk another twenty yards, much less all the way to Tuarhievel."

"There are still a few hours left till dawn, I think," said Michael. "Maybe they will camp awhile and you can rest up for the journey."

Aedan sighed wearily. "A week's rest would not be enough for me, at this point. I am absolutely exhausted."

"I am tired, myself," said Michael, "and I have not suffered nearly as much as you have. I shall tell the wizard we must rest here awhile before we can go on."

"Perhaps it would be better if you *asked* him," Aedan said. "He has been most respectful, but remember he is still an elf and owes you no allegiance."

"True," said Michael. "Thank you for reminding me. I must learn how not to take such things for granted."

Aedan glanced at him curiously. The boy was full of surprises. When it came to Michael, Aedan himself had taken much for granted. He had always considered Michael a spoiled child, which he certainly was in many ways—arrogant, willful, petulant, and stubborn. Yet whatever Michael's shortcomings were, cowardice was apparently not among them. He had proved himself brave, steady, and resourceful. In the face of adversity, he had comported himself more ably than Aedan had, despite being six years younger. He truly did have the makings of a king. The fate of Imperial Anuire was in good hands—provided they ever got back.

The wizard finished speaking to the others and returned to them. Michael looked up at him curiously, and though Aedan tried to keep the concern he felt from showing on his features, judging from Gylvain's expression, he was not entirely successful.

"Allow me to reassure you that there is no need for concern," the wizard said. "I have said you shall be my guests at the court of Tuarhievel, and guests you shall be, treated with all due respect and courtesy. And as soon as possible, you shall be returned to your own land, and under proper escort."

"I thank you, Sir Wizard," Michael said, "both for your offer of hospitality and again for saving us from our captors. Rest assured, we shall not forget."

"I am pleased to hear that, Your Highness," Gylvain replied. "And I would be pleased if you addressed me simply by my name, rather than 'Sir Wizard.' I am neither titled, nor a knight. And we elves do not stand on such formality."

"Very well, Gylvain," said Michael. "Then you must call me Michael."

The elf smiled at that.

"And as I am in no position to presume upon your allegiance," Michael continued, "I would humbly request a favor of you."

"Ask, and I shall grant it, if it is within my power," Gylvain replied.

"We are both tired, but Aedan is utterly exhausted. The goblins forced him to run after their wolves for the better part of the day. His legs are cramping and causing him pain, and he is weary from healing a wound he sustained. You may be anxious to return to Tuarhievel, but for my friend's sake, I would plead with you to allow us time to rest."

"That was well spoken," Gylvain replied, nodding with approval. "Never fear, however, I shall not trouble you to walk all the way to Tuarhievel."

"You have horses, then?" said Aedan, brightening.

"Elves can move more quickly through the forest on foot than they can on horseback," Gylvain replied. "However, there is no need for us to travel through the forest when we can go above it."

"*Above* it?" Aedan said.

Gylvain smiled. "Observe," he said. He lifted up his cloak and spoke a phrase in Elvish. As he did so, he stepped close to them and wrapped the cloak around them both, embracing them within its folds.

Unable to see within the dark folds of the cloak, Aedan suddenly felt his feet leave the ground. He grew light-headed and dizzy as he felt himself turning around and around in midair, faster and faster, until he was whirling like a child's top and, at the same time, rising higher and higher. He wanted to cry out in alarm, but his breath caught in his throat.

As they spun within the vortex, he heard the whistling sound of wind, rising rapidly in pitch, like a storm blowing through the treetops, then lost all sense of his body. It wasn't as if he had gone completely numb; it was as if his body had somehow simply ceased to exist. He tried to bring his hands up to his face, to feel if he still *had* a face, for there was absolutely no sensation of the wind upon his skin, or the chill of the night air. However, when he tried to move his arms, he realized with an abrupt stab of panic that he had no arms to move, nor legs, for that matter. He couldn't feel anything because there was nothing there to feel. And then, abruptly, the blackness faded and he could see. It would have taken his breath away if he'd had lungs to breathe with.

They were high above the forest clearing where they'd stood a moment earlier, and the treetops were falling away rapidly beneath them. He heard the rush of wind, though he was not sure how, since he was not aware of having ears. Nor was he sure how he could see, with no eyes to squint against the swirling wind.

It was still dark, and yet, below him, he could clearly make out the elves moving through the forest, appearing and disappearing once again as they ran through the open spaces between the trees and then were once again obscured from view by the forest canopy. At first, he thought there were more of them than the dozen or so he had first seen, but then he realized he was seeing the same ones, only they were moving with astonishing speed. He could not believe how quickly they were darting through the trees. It was, indeed, true what they said about elves' being able to run like deer. If he were on the ground with them, even if he were fully rested, he knew he could never have hoped to keep pace. No human could ever run that fast.

His perceptions had changed completely. They were high above the forest now, and yet he could see perfectly, despite the darkness. In fact, he realized, he wasn't really seeing, because his human eyes did not possess the night vision of the elves. Moreover, he could see all around him without moving his head. Indeed, he had no head to move. His physical body had melted away somehow, vaporized like the morning dew, and what he was perceiving was registering not upon his senses, but directly upon his awareness.

The only time he had ever felt anything like it was on those occasions when he was asleep and dreamed he had somehow left his body and was hovering above it, looking down and seeing himself lying there in bed. He did not know why he had such dreams and was grateful they did not come more often, for they were profoundly unsettling. They always seemed so real, it was as if he could actually *feel* himself floating in midair, just below the ceiling, and there was always that strange, alarming, vertiginous sensation of his body falling away from him.

The feeling he had now was very similar, only this time, it persisted and there was no ceiling to stop him. They kept rising higher and higher, and now he had no sense of spinning, just an eerie sensation of floating, of feeling completely weightless and free, like a bird soaring high above the forest. At that moment, it suddenly occurred to him that maybe he had died, and the realization struck with absolute terror, the more so because he felt completely helpless, unable to do anything about it. Panic gripped him as he thought of himself rising forever, never to return to earth.

Have no fear, Gylvain's voice came from somewhere very close. *You are not dead. You have merely been transmogrified by magic. You have become one with the air currents upon which we soar. There is no reason for alarm. We are the wind, and here in the skies, we are in our element.*

It's wonderful! Michael's excited voice came to him as if he were shouting gleefully right into his ear, except it didn't feel as if he actually heard him, more as if Michael were a part of him, within him somehow. *It's fantastic! Oh, Aedan, look! We're flying, just like birds! We're flying!*

Have no fear? thought Aedan. How was it possible that Michael could not be afraid? Was it just his youth, or was the emotion of fear something he completely lacked? Despite Gylvain's reassurances, it seemed they'd died and their souls were rising up into the heavens! It was the most frightening experience Aedan had ever known, and yet to Michael, it was a joyous thing, a new adventure, and Aedan felt his wild exhilaration. Felt it! It was only then that Aedan realized he was not actually hearing their voices; he was somehow privy to their thoughts, as they were aware to his. Transformed into the wind, they were all one, together, mingled with each other in the swirling air currents that swept above the forest.

Yes, we are all one, Gylvain replied to his unvoiced thoughts, *one with the wind. One with the power of nature. This is the true kingdom, one that is not subject to the rule of emperors or princes. It is the kingdom we are all a part of . . . the kingdom of the elemental forces that shape the world and shape us all.*

They swept over the treetops with a speed unlike anything Aedan had ever imagined. *But how?* he thought. *How is this possible?*

Magic, Gylvain's thoughts replied. *Magic makes all things possible to those who apprehend the possibilities.*

But did you not say that once a spell was used, it was forgotten? Michael asked.

That is so, Gylvain replied. *But there are no fewer than a score of different spells for windwalking, and I devote myself to constant study of my arts. I am forever learning spells and losing them and learning them again. That is the way of magic, as indeed it is the way of all things in the world. To pursue the ways of knowledge is to forever be a student, learning the same lessons over and over again. It is a never-ending process, and the reward of it is the process itself. We forget too easily, and must always learn again. The study of magic is an apt metaphor for life; when one stops learning, one begins to die.*

Between the reassuring presence of the wizard and Michael's boundless joy and exhilaration at their flight, Aedan's fear began to ebb, to be replaced by a growing sense of awe. He did not feel the wind of their swift passage through the skies: he *was* the wind, and far below him, the Aelvinnwode was like a vast green carpet stretching out across the land. In the distance, he could see the mountains of the Five Peaks region, and to the northwest, he could make out the rapidly approaching forest highlands of the goblin realm of Thurazor. But for the elves, that would have been their destination. Now, however, they swept past the land of their late captors and continued in a northeastern heading, past the rugged Stonecrown Mountains toward the elven kingdom of Tuarhievel.

It did not seem possible that they could have covered so much distance in so short a time, but when Aedan saw the first gray light of dawn appear over the horizon, he realized much more time had passed than he had thought. Hours had somehow seemed like only moments as he was caught in the fascination of the spectacle unfolding far below him, seeing the world the way a hawk would see it, or an eagle.

From the sky, he watched the sunrise, its rays casting an expanding band of light over the forest and the rolling, rugged country of the Northern Marches. His initial fear became forgotten as he was mesmerized by the beauty of the land waking up to a new day.

The forest seemed to slowly rise up toward them, and he realized they were descending. They were still moving forward with great speed, but they were gradually angling down, and soon he was able to make out birds flitting among the uppermost tree branches, oblivious to their presence. As they went lower still, a flock of doves rose up out of the trees, ascending toward them. Aedan could not get over the experience of birds flying *up* toward him. The flock flew closer with a fluttering of white wings in the early morning sun and then, amazingly, the doves passed *through* them! They were all around him, and even within him, soaring on the wind currents, and Aedan could actually *feel* their hearts beating.

Then the doves were above them, and they descended lower still, barely skimming the treetops, which bent with their passage. It was dreamlike and surreal as they swept over the forest, rushing smoothly through the sky above the forest canopy. Not even in his dreams had Aedan ever experienced anything like this. Surely, he thought, this was what it felt like to be a bird. As a child, he had often watched birds and wished he were capable of flight. Now he was doing it. And for a moment or two, while the doves had flown with them, he had experienced their feelings and sensations, too.

He had always thought that wizards lived their lives in dark and musty rooms, dimly illuminated by candles set in skulls, that they spent all their time puttering about with ancient manuscripts and arcane scrolls and breathing in the sulfurous fumes of their mystic potions while they squinted in the smoke from their incense burners. This, however, was magic of a different sort. Elven magic.

It made him wish his course in life had not been predetermined from his birth, for if this were what elven magic could accomplish, he would have become an eager student of it. He wondered if elven mages would accept human apprentices, and even as the thought occurred to him, Gylvain responded.

Elven magic is for elves alone, the mage replied. *If we were to teach it to humans, it would no longer belong only to us, and the possibility for its misuse would be too great. Just as no human wizard would ever take an elf as an apprentice, so no elven mage would ever teach a human.*

But are not the principles of human and elven magic the same? asked Aedan.

Indeed, they are, Gylvain responded. *However, the disciplines are different, as are the spells. And we are not yet so trusting of each other that we may reveal all our secrets. Someday, perhaps.*

But not today, thought Aedan, realizing the wizard's reply served as a pointed reminder of their situation. Elves and humans were far from friends, and the peace between them was still a fragile one. It would be a long time before elves and humans were able to trust one another, if that day ever came. The memory of how the humans had invaded elven lands and took them for their own was still painfully fresh among the elven kingdoms, and with the Manslayer still actively pursuing the *gheallie Sidhe* in these very woods, the days of humans falling to elven blades and arrows were far from over.

Nor are the days of elves falling to human blades and arrows, Gylvain replied, reminding him once again that while they were joined in the spell of windwalking, he was privy to their thoughts, while his own, unless he wished them known, were somehow guarded.

When I am emperor, I shall decree an end to that, Michael replied.

Would that our problems could be solved so simply, the wizard responded. *You may find when you ascend the Iron Throne that there can be vast differences between what a ruler wishes to do and what he is able to do. I wish you luck in those days to come. But for the present, I bid you welcome to the elven city of Tuarhievel.*

And suddenly there it was, directly ahead of them, appearing out of the forest as if out of thin air. Accustomed to the way human cities were constructed, Aedan was unprepared for the sight that greeted him as they came upon Tuarhievel.

When humans built cities, they chose sites for favorable terrain features and then cleared vast areas of land in preparation for the construction of the roads and buildings and market plazas. The defensive walls and fortifications required clear approaches so that potential attackers would be exposed as they advanced. Nature, in other words, made way for human cities.

Elves, on the other hand, followed an entirely different philosophy of building.

Tuarhievel simply rose up out of the forest. The clear-cutting was minimal, and wherever possible, the trees had been left standing so that the forest and the city were all one, a melding of natural features and construction. From a distance, it would have been impossible to spot the city, and Aedan thought it likely that unless a traveler knew the way exactly, he could easily pass within a hundred yards of Tuarhievel and never even see it.

Wooden thatch-roofed homes were constructed among the trees, shielded from the elements beneath their canopy. The streets of the city—little more than dirt paths, really—wound in serpentine fashion among the trees and natural clearings had been utilized as small, shaded plazas where the people drew water from wells and market stalls were erected. In many cases, homes had actually been built around the trees so that the trees themselves became part of the construction, with the upper stories of the homes situated in the thick lower branches.

From overhead, the forest masked to some degree the density of the construction, which increased as they approached the center of the city. Many of the structures had open platforms built in the branches above them, often on several levels, with wooden catwalks running from tree to tree, connecting them. Tuarhievel had streets upon the ground and in the air, as well. But one structure towered above all others, its graceful, intricately carved and fluted wooden spires rising high above the treetops. They were approaching the forest palace known as Tuaranreigh, where Prince Fhileraene ruled from the legendary Throne of Thorn.

As they circled the palace, Aedan marveled at the sculpted spires, carved from hand-rubbed and -oiled wood, a figured ebony with swirling, golden-yellow highlights running through it. The spires were of unequal height and clustered close together as they rose from the central structure of the palace, which was built of wood and mortared stone that must have been quarried generations earlier in the mountains to the north, beyond the Giantdowns. The steep-pitched, gabled roof below the spires was tiled in rosy slate. Stone gutters for the run-off of melted snow or rainwater led to spouts carved in the shapes of screaming gargoyles.

Tuaranreigh was not a proper castle, at least not by human standards, since it had no outer walls or battlements. However, Prince Fhileraene had little reason to fear a siege. The Aelvinnwode itself was a far more effective outer defense than any walls or moats or barbicans could be. An attacking army would have to penetrate through miles of dense forest and thick underbrush, which made the march of massed formations virtually impossible. And long before such an army could even reach Tuarhievel, it would be destroyed piecemeal by elven archers and warriors who could attack from cover and then quickly disappear into the trackless forest.

Aedan remembered from his lessons that back in the days of the Great War between the humans and the elves, no human warlord had ever been foolish enough to pursue the elves once they had retreated to the forests. No invaders would ever reach the palace of Tuaranreigh, except as captives.

The wind on which they sailed circled round and round the spires of the palace, gathering speed and forming a swirling vortex that descended slowly to the ground. Aedan once more felt that strange, unsettling sensation, as if he were floating away, and the light-headedness returned as he became aware of his physical senses. He felt himself spinning rapidly inside the swirling wind funnel, his hair whipping around his face. He gasped, struggling for breath within the vortex, then felt the ground beneath his feet as the wind slackened to a breeze and dissipated, leaving them standing on the pathway to the palace.

Aedan brushed his hair out of his face and looked around, but everything still seemed to be spinning. He had difficulty remaining on his feet. He felt dizzy, and when he tried to take a step, he almost fell. He saw that Michael was no better off. The prince staggered and went down to one knee, swearing softly. Aedan closed his eyes and waited for the world to stop spinning. His body felt extremely heavy and clumsy. Small wonder, he thought. A moment earlier, he had been lighter than air.

"The effects will pass within a few moments," Gylvain said. "You may find it helps to close your eyes, stand still, and breathe deeply until the dizziness subsides."

Aedan opened his eyes after a few moments and tried to focus them. As the dizziness ebbed, he looked around. They were on a pathway that wound through a long and narrow clearing flanked by rows of ancient poplars, a sort of natural, tree-lined corridor leading up to the palace. The sound of water running over rocks drew his attention to a stream that ran down the center of this natural corridor. On either side of the stream were winding pathways leading to a gracefully arched stone bridge that gave entrance to the palace gates.

Unlike the castles of the empire, which had dirt roads wide enough for several horsemen riding abreast, the pathways leading to the gates of Tuaranreigh were clearly meant for foot traffic only, for they wound through lush rock gardens planted with lacy green ferns, flowering shrubs, and wildflowers. Benches made of split sections of tree trunks were placed at irregular intervals along the pathways, on both banks of the stream.

At first glance, it seemed to Aedan that the stream flowed around the palace, making a sort of natural moat. Then he realized it was actually coming out through an archway in the wall beneath the bridge, apparently flowing out of the palace itself!

Through the trees, Aedan could make out some of the buildings he had spotted earlier from above. They resembled peasant cottages with their thatched roofs and wooden shutters, but they were larger, and had the open platforms constructed in the trees above them, with interconnecting catwalks suspended at different levels high above the ground. Everywhere he looked, Aedan saw the perfect union of nature and architecture. The city was part of the forest, and the forest an integral part of the city.

As they walked toward the stone bridge leading to the gates of Tuaranreigh, a number of elves stopped to stare at them. Aedan knew human traders sometimes visited Tuarhievel, but judging by the looks they got, humans were still not a common sight. He noticed that everyone they passed bowed his head respectfully.

"They seem to know me," said Michael.

Aedan frowned, momentarily puzzled by his remark, and then sudden comprehension dawned. "They bow to Gylvain, not to you," he said.

"Oh," said Michael. "I see." He sounded a bit annoyed, or perhaps disappointed.

"Remember, you are not a prince here, save by rules of courtesy alone," Aedan told him softly. "Fhileraene rules in Tuarhievel, not Emperor Hadrian."

Michael frowned. He was accustomed to being treated as befitted the royal scion, and the fact that he would enjoy no such status here was a bit difficult for him to grasp. However, the goblins had already done much to advance his education, and Michael was learning not to take such things for granted. He nodded to show he understood.

Aedan felt relieved, though he was still apprehensive about their situation. It would certainly not do to have Michael putting on airs in front of Fhileraene. From all that he had heard about the elven prince, Aedan did not think he would be amused.

They followed Gylvain up the path as it curved away slightly from the riverbank, around a moss-covered rock formation, and then back toward the stone bridge. Elven warriors armed with swords and spears stood guard upon the bridge and by the two massive, arched and studded wooden doors. They did not challenge Gylvain as he approached, but made no effort to hide their curiosity about his two young human companions.

As they passed through the doors and entered the great hall of Tuaranreigh, both Aedan and Michael stopped dead in their tracks, staring wide-eyed at the tableau spreading out before them. They had crossed an entry hall and suddenly stood at the entrance to a forest clearing. But that did not seem possible. They were indoors . . . or were they?

For a moment, Aedan felt totally disoriented. They should have entered into the great hall of the palace, but this was a hall unlike any he had ever seen. It was open to the sky, with flagstones forming pathways between well-tended plots of giant ferns and colorful bromeliads, moss-covered rocks with trickling fountains, small trees and flowering shrubs. There was an arched opening in the wall through which the stream flowed, with a small wooden bridge spanning the spring from which it bubbled.

It was, in fact, an atrium that served as a great hall. The palace had been constructed around a forest clearing with a pool fed by an underground spring. Archways in the walls led to the east and west wings of the palace, as well as to the keep at the far end. But the main feature of the atrium was just in front of the vaulted entrance to the keep, surrounded by a stand of oaks.

Aedan had heard stories about the legendary Thorn Throne of Tuarhievel, but he had never known if they were truth or fancy. Now, he saw it for himself. It was a rose tree, the largest he had ever seen. Its multiple trunks curved sharply outward, forming a natural throne before they branched off into a spreading canopy of blue-green leaves and spectacular blooms of ivory white and bloodred. And seated on that throne, flanked by his ministers and surrounded by his court, was Prince Fhileraene, ruler of the last elven kingdom in the Aelvinnwode.

As they were announced, Gylvain escorted them toward the throne, his hands resting lightly on their shoulders. Their arrival caused a considerable stir among the elves present at the court. All eyes were upon them as Gylvain stepped forward, went down to one knee, and bowed deeply to his prince. Aedan followed suit, but Michael remained standing, perfectly calm and composed as he gazed curiously at the elven prince.

Fhileraene appeared to be in his midthirties, but then physical appearances were very deceptive with immortals: Fhileraene had ruled Tuarhievel since before Michael's grandfather was born. He was tall and slender, with harsh, angular features and straight black hair that hung down well below his shoulders. His mouth was wide and thin-lipped, with a touch of cruelty about it. His eyes were dark brown and hooded, giving him a brooding aspect, and his nose was prominent and hooked. It was said he was the very image of his renegade great grandfather, the awnshegh, Rhuobhe Manslayer.

Aedan wondered if any of the elves present at the court were Rhuobhe's warriors. It was a decidedly unpleasant possibility. Killing the Prince of Anuire would be a mark of tremendous status among those elves who had sworn eternal enmity to humans. Of course, not all the elves were like that, but here, there would be no way of telling which was which . . . until it was too late.

"Rise, Gylvain," Fhileraene said. "And you, as well, Lord Aedan." He glanced at Michael with a flicker of amusement in his eyes. "And of course, princes do not kneel, and that is as it should be. You honor us with your presence, Prince Michael. I am pleased to see you are alive and well."

"Thanks to Gylvain," Michael said. "We are in debt to him for rescuing us from the goblins."

"Then you are in debt to me, for it was I who sent him," Fhileraene replied with a smile. Seeing their confused expressions, he went on to explain. "Little goes on within my realm of which I am unaware," he said. "Intelligence had reached me that goblin raiders out of Thurazor had been spotted traveling through the Aelvinnwode, heading south. They were taking a great risk going through my lands. I wondered what could justify such a risk. Now I know. They had captured quite a prize."

"Well, we are very grateful to you, Your Highness," Aedan said. "Thanks to you, that prize has been denied them. And as soon as we return to Seaharrow, we shall make certain—"

"You shall not be going back to Seaharrow," Fhileraene said, cutting him off. "At the moment, I do not think that would be prudent."

Aedan simply stared at him. Had they been rescued from the goblins only to be held for ransom by the elves? "Forgive me, Your Highness," Aedan said, "I . . . I fear I do not understand."

Michael was more direct. "Are we your prisoners?"

"Why, not at all," the elven prince replied with genuine surprise. "You are honored guests, free to move about Tuarhievel as you please. However, I feel myself responsible for your safety, as you are now in my domain. And if you were to return to Seaharrow right now, chances are that you would almost certainly be killed."

"*Killed!*" Michael said in a tone of outrage. "*By whom?*"

"By the man who even now is in the process of seizing the Iron Throne," Fhileraene replied calmly. "Lord Arwyn, the Archduke of Boeruine."

ANUIRE

chapter five

"You lie!" Michael shouted angrily before Aedan could stop him. "Lord Arwyn would never dare attempt such treason, not while my father lives!"

Aedan grabbed him by the arm and squeezed hard, causing Michael to gasp with surprise and pain. Fhileraene's face clouded over, but he kept his calm.

"You would do well, Your Highness, to remember that you are not in your own empire here. In fact, at this point, it does not even appear as if you may even have an empire. However, thus far, you have been treated with the respect due to your rank and station. If you wish that to continue, I expect you to return the courtesy."

Aedan held on to Michael's arm and gave him a warning look, then turned to Fhileraene and said, "Please forgive the outburst, Your Highness. It is just that you have given us some shocking news, if indeed your information is accurate."

Fhileraene nodded. "You may rest assured it is," he said. "Emperor Hadrian has died, and the Archduke of Boeruine has not wasted any time putting his plans in motion."

Michael looked stricken at the news. He shook his head and softly murmured, "No . . . It cannot be!"

"I am sorry for your loss, Your Highness," said Fhileraene, "but surely, you must have been prepared for this eventuality. After all, your father was very old, by human standards, and has long been in poor health. You see, I make it my business to know which way the wind blows in the Aelvinnwode and the surrounding territories. This move by Arwyn of Boeruine does not really come as a surprise. There have long been rumors of his intriguing with Thurazor, and there are other forces at work in these events, powerful forces of which you are not yet aware. You are at the heart of a situation not of your own making, but it shall be up to you to make the best of it."

"Meaning no disrespect, Your Highness, but why should you care what happens to the throne of Anuire?" asked Aedan. "Or to us, for that matter?"

"A fair question," Prince Fhileraene replied, nodding. "It is true I have little reason to love your human empire, but of necessity, I have had to learn to live with it. With Hadrian on the Iron Throne, elf and human were able to regard one another with some tolerance. The peace between us has not always been an easy one, but with the exception of isolated incidents, it has been kept. I labor under no misapprehensions that this would continue with Arwyn of Boeruine in power."

Those "incidents" to which he was referring so disingenuously, Aedan thought, involved none other than his own great-grandfather, Rhuobhe Manslayer, whose bitter hatred of humans ensured he would never tolerate them, much less keep peace with the empire.

"The Archduke of Boeruine's ambition is boundless," Fhileraene continued, "and that makes him dangerous to us. He treats with our enemies and conspires against us. We have no desire to see his bid for power succeed."

"So then you help us merely to bring down Lord Arwyn?" Aedan said.

"That alone would be no mere thing," Fhileraene replied. "However, there are still other factors that would serve my interests in this situation."

It all suddenly became clear to Aedan. If what he said were true, and Aedan could think of no reason Fhileraene would lie, Arwyn of Boeruine had committed himself, and now there could be no turning back. He probably would never have dared go so far if he had not already mustered up support for his claim to the throne. Apparently, Lord Arwyn had been intriguing with more than just the goblins of Thurazor. How many secret alliances had he already forged among the nobles of the empire? How long had this been going on? He must have been planning it for years, waiting only for the right opportunity. Now, with the emperor dead and Michael out of the way, his path was clear, and he had wasted no time.

The emperor must have died around the same time as their abduction, Aedan thought. For Fhileraene to have learned the news so quickly, he must have spies in Seasedge capable of communicating with him through magic or perhaps carrier pigeon. But that was not at all unlikely. There were halflings in Boeruine, and it was quite conceivable some of them could be in the pay of Fhileraene. For that matter, the spies could also be humans. Arwyn of Boeruine was not universally loved. He had made his share of enemies.

Either way, when Aedan and Michael did not return from hawking, Lord Arwyn must have realized the goblins had succeeded in capturing them, especially after Windreiver had returned. And Michael's horse must have made its way back to the stables without its rider, as well. Lord Arwyn must have quickly and immediately moved to take advantage of the opportunity. This was exactly what his father had feared, thought Aedan. Lord Arwyn must have seized the court the moment Emperor Hadrian had died and Michael's disappearance was discovered.

Aedan felt a tightness in his stomach as he thought about his parents. What had become of them? His father would never have stood idly by while Arwyn tried to take the throne, and Arwyn had to know that Lord Tieran would oppose him to his last breath. With a feeling of despair, Aedan realized his father would undoubtedly have been among the first to be eliminated.

However, Lord Arwyn had no way of knowing he and Michael had been rescued. He had acted on the belief that they were safely on their way to Thurazor to be enslaved. He must have claimed Michael was dead, otherwise he could not have justified assuming the regency of the empire, and eventually, the throne itself. If Michael suddenly appeared now, his life would certainly be in danger unless he were able to rally support among the other nobles of the empire. And if Arwyn refused to yield at that point, it could mean only one thing.

There would be war. The empire would be split in two between those loyal to Prince Michael and those who would support Lord Arwyn. And without knowing how much support Arwyn could muster, there would be no telling how long it would last, nor what the cost would be. And if it came to war, no matter which way it turned out in the end, the empire would be left weakened. That would certainly serve Fhileraene's interests.

"So where does that leave us, with respect to you, Your Highness?" Aedan asked. "And what has become of the Imperial Court?" he added nervously, afraid to hear the answer.

"For the present, it leaves you as my guests," Fhileraene replied. "The last word I received, only this morning, reported only that Lord Arwyn had declared a state of emergency upon the Emperor Hadrian's death and Prince Michael's disappearance and had imposed martial law upon the province of Boeruine. And, by extension, one supposes, whatever portions of the empire he can induce to go along with him. Beyond that, there has been no further information. As you must have guessed, I have agents in Boeruine, and under current circumstances, they must remain especially circumspect. As soon as I know more, I shall send word to you. Gylvain has extended his offer of hospitality to you, and you shall remain welcome in Tuarhievel until it can best be determined what our course of action should be."

"If the Imperial Court is being held hostage at Seaharrow," Aedan said, "we must reach Anuire as soon as possible and raise a force to rescue them. We must make certain word is spread that Prince Michael . . ." he paused, significantly, ". . . Emperor Michael, I should say, is still alive. The longer we delay, the more time Lord Arwyn has to strengthen his position."

Fhileraene smiled. "You shall make a good minister to your liege," he said. "Very well. Let Prince . . . Emperor Michael compose a message to his subjects, while you prepare a list of those to whom it should be sent, and I shall arrange for messengers to be dispatched. In particular, is there someone you may depend on in Anuire whose loyalty is beyond question and who may accurately report to you on the state of matters there?"

Aedan thought only for a moment. "My tutor, Baladore Trevane, the librarian at the College of Sorcery in Anuire."

Fhileraene nodded. "I know of him," he said. "A man worthy of respect, by all repute. Very well, it shall be done. And the other messages shall be sent out as soon as you have prepared the list. Gylvain will see to it."

"I am very grateful for all your help, Your Highness," Michael said to Fhileraene, with a slight bow. "I shall not forget."

"Rest assured we shall remind you if you do, Majesty," Prince Fhileraene replied with a wry smile. "From this day forth, it shall be known that the elven kingdom of Tuarhievel was the first to recognize the Emperor Michael Roele and declare an alliance against those who would disrupt the peace between us."

"It shall be so," said Michael, drawing himself up proudly. For the first time since he had heard the shocking news of his father's death, he seemed to accept the fact that he was now no longer Prince Michael, but Emperor Michael.

At the moment, an emperor without an empire to command, thought Aedan. But as to whether or not it would remain that way, there was no way of knowing until word had been sent out that he was safe and they heard responses to their messages. Would the nobles of the empire line up behind Michael, as was their duty, or would they transfer their allegiance to Arwyn of Boeruine? And if some nobles did defect, would there be enough to make the eventual outcome certain?

Too many questions, Aedan thought, and not a single answer. Yet. It was a difficult way for Michael to begin his reign, and for him to begin his duties as lord high chamberlain. They were both too young, and far from ready. But fate did not wait on the convenience of individuals, as Aedan recalled his tutor saying often. As they took their leave of Fhileraene and once more made their way outside, escorted by Gylvain, Aedan said a silent prayer to Haelyn. He thanked the god for their deliverance, and he prayed for guidance in the days to come. They had been saved. Now it would be up to them, two boys, to try to save the empire.

* * * * *

Baladore Trevane was out of breath. He was no longer a young man and was unaccustomed to running. He was a short man, about five-and-a-half feet tall, and his considerable girth did not permit him to move very quickly, but nevertheless, he had trotted all the way to the docks from the College of Sorcery, panting with each labored step. His hair was white, merely a fringe that went around his head like a laurel wreath, and he carried a red kerchief as he ran, using it to mop the perspiration off his bald pate, so that the sweat wouldn't run into his eyes. As he huffed and puffed his way onto the docks, he wished he could have used a spell to transform himself into a bird and flown to the Imperial Cairn. However, at his age, he had to be careful of his spells.

For one thing, he would have made an exceedingly stout bird. A pelican, no doubt, a great, big fat one. And as a pelican, he would still have expended considerable energy in flapping his wings to fly. Assuming he could even get off the ground. It was easier to run, all things considered. At least that way, he didn't have to worry about whether or not he got the spell exactly right.

His memory just wasn't what it used to be. He no longer trusted his recall. He had to look everything up. Some things he remembered with no difficulty. He could, for example, still recite the history of the empire without getting a single date wrong, but when it came to spells, sometimes he simply wasn't sure anymore. There was nothing more ludicrous or pathetic than an absentminded sorcerer, he thought. But then again, he was almost seventy years old. All in all, he was in remarkably good health for his age, even if he did get a trifle vague from time to time.

On this occasion, however, there was nothing vague about his state of mind at all. A halfling messenger had arrived at the college, carrying a dispatch all the way from Tuarhievel from Prince Fhileraene himself. Of course, the fact that the messenger had been a halfling meant that he had almost certainly not traveled all the way from Tuarhievel the way normal people would. Doubtless, he had shadow-walked, creating a portal into the Shadow World and passing through it, emerging in Anuire. A handy little skill to have, thought Baladore, going from Point A to Point B without passing through the distance in between. Too bad humans couldn't learn to do it. Still, he understood that passage through the Shadow World, even for a halfling, could be very dangerous, so the message that this halfling brought had to be important. When he learned it was from Prince Fhileraene, he knew it was. But when he saw whose hand had written the message, his heart leapt, and he ran straightaway for the Imperial Cairn.

Young Lord Aedan was alive! And Prince Michael was alive, as well! It was wonderful news, and he rushed to bring it to the palace. He hailed a boat captain and had the man take him out to the island where the palace stood. With the sail up and the rowers assisting the boat's passage through the bay, it was much faster than traveling along the causeways, and even though boat travel made him seasick, this news simply couldn't wait.

Baladore had not gone to Seaharrow with the Imperial Court. He had remained in the city of Anuire, as he always did, because his duties as librarian of the College of Sorcery required his presence there at all times. The college was the repository of all the magical knowledge of the empire, and it was one of the few places in Cerilia where students could come—if they were fortunate enough to be accepted—to study the mystic arts. The college numbered some of the finest adepts in the empire among its teaching faculty, and many wizards from realms as far off as Zikala or Kiergard made annual journeys to the capital to study and do arcane research in the library of the college in exchange for teaching some of its students. Consequently, Baladore could not afford to be absent from his post and so he always remained in Anuire throughout the summer season while the Imperial Court repaired to the cool ocean breezes of Seasedge in the province of Boeruine.

Baladore's first inkling that something had gone drastically wrong at Summer Court came only when he heard that Lord Tieran had arrived at a gallop back at the palace with the empress and the house guard. Rumors had flown wildly all over the city and, what with his duties, it was a few days before Baladore was able to make his way to the palace to ascertain what had really happened.

That was when he had discovered that the emperor had died at Seaharrow, which was tragic news, of course, but not nearly as devastating as the news that Prince Michael and Lord Aedan had disappeared, apparently the victims of foul play. They had apparently gone out hawking in the morning and their horses had returned to the stables by themselves. There had been blood on Aedan's saddle, too.

Why they had gone out by themselves, without taking an escort of the house guard with them, was anybody's guess. It was certainly not like Aedan to be so irresponsible. He had even left his sword behind in the stables. Clearly, his mind had been elsewhere than on his duties. Questioning of the guards posted at the castle gate had resulted in the information that Prince Michael had gone out hawking by himself, and that Aedan had followed alone, shortly thereafter. Lord Arwyn had reportedly flown into a rage at his guards for allowing the prince to go out by himself, but the guards had insisted that Prince Michael had commanded them to let him through, saying Aedan would be following right behind. They had naturally assumed Aedan would follow with an escort, but when Aedan came galloping through the gates alone, they had seen no reason to stop him. Perhaps the guard escort would follow on his heels. When they didn't, however, it was reported to the captain of the watch, who supposedly should have delivered the information to Lord Arwyn, who in turn claimed he had never heard a thing about it. When the boys' horses returned by themselves, Lord Arwyn had raged that heads would roll and had immediately set out with a squad of mounted men-at-arms in search of the two boys.

What Lord Tieran had done then must have been the hardest thing he had ever done in his entire life. As soon as Lord Arwyn and his knights had passed through the castle gates, Lord Tieran had assembled the Royal House Guard and immediately had horses saddled for the empress and her daughters. Without stopping to bring anyone else along except his wife, the Lady Jessica, Lord Tieran had made haste to depart before Lord Arwyn could return with his knights. He had left the rest of the court behind and immediately set out for Anuire on horseback with his female charges and the entire house guard for an escort.

They had ridden hard, covering the entire distance from Seaharrow to Anuire, about two hundred and fifty miles, in a mere three days. It must have been a brutal pace, thought Baladore, for he had heard that when they finally arrived at the Imperial Cairn, the empress and her daughters had to be lifted from their mounts and carried inside. It was a miracle they hadn't killed the horses.

Lord Tieran had set a fast pace during the day, and then a walking pace during most of each night to allow the horses to recover. They took only short rest periods, sleeping for only a few hours at a time while the guards took turns standing watch. More than anything, Lord Tieran had been afraid of being overtaken on the road by Lord Arwyn and his knights. They had to reach the capital at all costs, even though Lord Tieran knew absolutely nothing of what had become of his own son.

As the sea breeze ruffled Baladore's cloak, he bit his lower lip and tried not to think about the pitching of the boat in the choppy waters of the bay. Instead, he thought of how Lord Tieran had looked when he had seen him last—tired, drawn and haggard, pale, with a haunted, tortured look about him. To have left Seaharrow as he did, with his own son's fate uncertain, must have taken a supreme act of will and self-sacrifice. As a father, he must have wanted desperately to set out on Aedan's trail. As lord high chamberlain, however, his first duty was to the empress and the empire, and he had to act quickly to safeguard both.

As the boat drew up to the jetty at Cairn Rock, the windswept island from which the imperial palace rose almost like a natural extension of the rock formations, Baladore stepped onto the dock, assisted by the boat captain. He swallowed hard, thanked the man, paid him a bonus for making the journey under full sail, then hurried up the jetty toward the palace gates, grateful to be on dry land once again. Well, relatively dry, at any rate, he thought. He squinted at the sea spray coming off the rocks as the waves crashed against the island. The wind had picked up, and the swells were coming in harder and faster.

Why Haelyn, in his mortal days, had ever wanted to build the palace on this rock out in the middle of the bay was something Baladore had never been able to discern. Its natural defensive position was the only thing that argued for the site. It was as safe from any attack as possible, except a protracted siege by sea, and an enemy's ships would have had a hard time maintaining a blockade, given the unpredictable swells and currents of the bay in the Straits of Aerele. Unless a captain really knew these waters, he could easily wind up on the jagged rocks that ringed the island like a deadly necklace.

Admitted through the gates, Baladore hurried to find Lord Tieran. The lord high chamberlain was in his private quarters in the tower, standing at the window and staring out across the bay at the city of Anuire. He turned as Baladore came in. Lord Tieran appeared to have aged at least ten years since he had returned from Seaharrow. The strain of worrying about the empress, who had sunk into despair at the loss of her son and husband, and the stress of losing—or so he thought—his own son, added to his concerns about the fate of the empire now that the succession was in doubt. It all had turned his hair completely white, and there were new lines etched into his face. His eyes looked dark and sunken from lack of sleep, and he had lost weight, as well.

"Baladore," he said, greeting him in a weary voice. He frowned. "By the gods, you look red as beet, and you are all out of breath. Please, sit down, old friend. Here, have some wine and tell me what brings you out to the Cairn in such a state."

"Great news, milord," said Baladore, sinking down gratefully into a chair. "Wonderful news! Miraculous news! Prince Michael is alive and well, as is your son!"

Lord Tieran stared at him with disbelief, as if he weren't sure he'd heard correctly. "By Haelyn! Can it be true?" he said, his voice barely above a whisper.

Baladore took a quick gulp of wine before replying. "I have just this morning received a message from your son," he said, "written in his own hand, which your lordship is aware I know as well as I do my own. And there is an added postscript from the prince, with his signature appended. Here, see for yourself."

"A message?" said Lord Tieran, his eyes lighting up as Baladore passed him the scroll. "But how? By what means?"

"Delivered by a halfling, milord, sent from Tuarhievel by Prince Fhileraene himself," Baladore replied. "What transpired is all contained therein, in your son's own hand." And he waited, slaking his thirst with wine while Lord Tieran read the message, which was an account of how the boys had been captured by the goblins and then rescued by the elves, led by the mage, Gylvain Aurealis, and how they had been received by Prince Fhileraene.

"Bless you, Baladore, for bringing me this news!" Lord Tieran said. "I must bring this to the empress at once! She was convinced that Prince Michael had died, as I fear I was as well. I had dared hope they still lived, but I did not really think we would ever see them again. This message will restore her spirits." He paused as something else occurred to him. "Baladore, this note makes no mention of any ransom," he said, uncertainly. "Surely, Prince Fhileraene must want something for their safe return?"

Baladore shook his head. "If he does, milord, neither the message nor the messenger made mention of it."

"Hmm. Does this halfling messenger wait for word to be sent back?"

"He awaits back at the college, milord, where I have seen to it he shall be fed and rested well."

"It is good," Lord Tieran said. "Oh, it is so very good, indeed. I feel, good Baladore, a tremendous weight has been lifted from my chest, a weight that had been crushing me. Come, come with me. We must go tell the empress together. I am certain she will want to see the message and read it for herself. Then we must compose a reply and send it back to Tuarhievel with this halfling. Prince Fhileraene must know the empire will be grateful for the safety of Prince Michael. . . ." He paused. "No, by Haelyn, *Emperor* Michael! The succession is no longer in doubt."

He clenched his fist around the scroll. "Arwyn of Boeruine will find he has gravely overreached himself. Claim regency, will he? Well, he shall have a hard time justifying his claim to power now. And if he persists, all will see his bold ambition for what it truly is. Come, Baladore, let us go tell the empress the great news. And my wife, of course. She has cried tears of grief for long enough. She will now cry tears of joy, and it will do my heart no end of good to see it."

* * * * *

"Is that the best you can do?" the elf girl said as she easily parried Aedan's attack. "You will surely never slay your enemy if you come at him so gingerly."

"I did not wish to hurt you," Aedan replied.

Sylvanna raised her thin and gracefully arched eyebrows. "Indeed? And what makes you think you could?"

"The fact that I might, even though unintentionally, is enough to give me pause," said Aedan. "I owe my life to Gylvain Aurealis, and it would be a poor show of gratitude if I were to injure his own sister."

"Ah, I see," Sylvanna replied. "So a sense of obligation to my brother makes you exercise caution and hold back, is that it? Well, in that case, perhaps I should seek another opponent to help me in my practice, for you are not providing any challenge."

"As you wish," said Aedan. He swept his borrowed sword out to the side and bowed to her, then turned and left the practice ring to sit by Michael while another opponent, an elf, stepped up to take his place.

"I think you have annoyed her," Michael said as Aedan sat down on a log beside him.

"Better that I cause her some annoyance than an injury," said Aedan. "We are guests here, and I do not need to shore up my pride or endanger our position by besting a female in a practice match."

"You may be rating yourself too highly, and her not highly enough," Michael replied as he watched Sylvanna cross swords with her next opponent. "She knows what she's about."

As other elves watched, they moved around each other inside the practice circle. Each held a dagger in one hand and a sword in the other. They used no shields, and the blades were sharp. Sylvanna's new opponent did not share Aedan's hesitancy about engaging her. He darted in quickly and did not hold back in the least. The blades clanged against each other, and the daggers flashed, steel striking upon steel; then both combatants sprang apart and started circling once again.

Aedan frowned as he watched the contest. "Someone will get hurt if they keep that up," he murmured. "The blades are unprotected, and they are not even wearing full armor."

"That does not seem to cause them much concern," Michael replied, his gaze intent on the circling combatants.

Aedan shook his head as he watched them engage, blades flashing, then spring apart again. "It is foolhardy to take such risks," he said. "What are they trying to prove?"

"Perhaps they are not trying to prove anything," said Michael without taking his eyes off the match inside the ring. "The intent may simply be to recreate the conditions of real combat as closely as possible."

"Which increases the possibility of a very real injury," said Aedan.

Even as he spoke, Sylvanna parried an attacking stroke, deflected a knife blade with her own, pivoted, and brought her sword around in a tight arc, opening a cut on her opponent's upper arm. He gasped, and Aedan sprang to his feet as he saw the blood flow.

"Well struck!" the male elf said, and bowed to his opponent.

Sylvanna inclined her head toward him, acknowledging the compliment, but displaying no alarm or even any regret over having wounded him.

"Let me help you," Aedan said. "I have healing ability."

The elf simply shrugged. "It is of no consequence," he said. "A minor cut is all it is. It will remind me to keep more on my toes the next time. But I thank you for your offer, just the same."

Aedan stared at him as he walked away. What sort of people were these elves? The way they had been going at each other with no protection other than steel breastplates, one of them could easily have been seriously wounded, even killed. However, he saw what Sylvanna had meant when she stated without rancor that he had provided her no challenge. He had held back, because she was a girl, but now he saw that Michael had been absolutely right. He had rated himself too highly and her not highly enough. She was better than he was. Much better.

He watched as another opponent moved into the ring to take her on. Sylvanna stretched a few times and swung her blade about, then took her stance. She was about as tall as Aedan, with a typically elvish build—wiry and lean. However, her shoulders were broader than those of most young women Aedan had known, and the muscles of her back gave her a figure that tapered to her narrow waist. Like her brother, Sylvanna had long black hair streaked with silver highlights. She had gathered it in a ponytail for weapons practice, to keep it out of the way. Elven women were not buxom as human females often tended to be, and Sylvanna was no exception. She was long limbed and small breasted, but Aedan did not find that unattractive. Sylvanna was not as voluptuous as Laera, but she moved with the smooth litheness of a cat, and Aedan liked the way she bore herself.

He was surprised to find himself suddenly comparing her with Laera. They were completely unalike in almost every way. Laera was beautiful, while Sylvanna was merely pretty at best, and took no pains at all to enhance her appearance. Laera was flirtatious and seductive; Sylvanna was unassuming and direct. Laera was soft, with smoldering dark eyes; Sylvanna was lean and muscular, with striking gray eyes so light that they seemed like cut crystal. But as he found himself comparing the two, Aedan realized Laera was found wanting.

The clang of steel against steel filled the clearing as the two opponents circled each other in the practice ring. The elves who waited their turn at practice, or simply watched, clapped their hands and called out encouragement at well-struck blows. If he hadn't known better, Aedan might have thought the two were fighting in earnest. However, as he watched, he realized they took care to aim no cuts or blows at the face or neck, or at the legs. The target areas were the protected chest and the unprotected arms and shoulders, but any cuts aimed at the latter were carefully controlled. The blades were lighter than those used by most humans, and consequently quicker in action. A first cut ended the combat, but it was clearly not the object of the exercise. The idea was simply to penetrate the opponent's defense. A light hit upon the steel breastplate was counted as a killing stroke and ended the match.

Sylvanna was not the only female who came to practice. Among humans, females did not generally participate in combat. Sometimes tomboys like Ariel played at war while they were young, but as they grew older, they usually followed more ladylike pursuits. Among the elves, things were apparently quite different. The women trained along with the men, and though most of them would have lacked the upper body strength to wield broadswords effectively, they seemed equally adept with the men in the use of the lighter, faster elvish blades.

Sylvanna defeated her second opponent with a touch to his breastplate, and he saluted her in acknowledgment as the next opponent stood up to take his place. Aedan marveled at Sylvanna's strength and endurance. A short, unsatisfactory, aborted match with him, then two matches with full-grown male opponents, and she hadn't even cracked a sweat. She used the blade as if it were a part of her and was clearly commanding of respect among her peers.

"I would not have thought a woman could fight as well as that," said Michael as he watched her with admiration. "She is at least the equal of the best swordsmen in the house guard."

"Yes, she is very good, indeed," Aedan agreed, nodding emphatically. "After watching her, I feel foolish for holding back. On my best day, I would stand no chance against her."

"The lesson here, I think, is not to underestimate a female just because she is a female," Michael said. He glanced at Aedan and grinned. "I should have thought you would have learned that one before, with Ariel."

Aedan scowled. "Apparently, I shall never hear the end of that," he said. "If it weren't for you, I might have been paying closer attention that day."

"You mean it was all my fault?" asked Michael innocently. "It wasn't *my* shield she hooked, nor was it *my* skull she nearly cracked."

"As I recall, it was someone else's skull that was very nearly cracked," replied Aedan dryly.

"Yes, well, I will concede that we both took our share of lumps that day," said Michael with a grin.

Sylvanna finished her third match by beating her opponent, scoring a light cut on his forearm. They saluted one another, and both left the practice ring. As two other fighters took their places, Sylvanna came back to where the two boys were sitting. There was a slight flush on her face from her exertions, but otherwise, she looked none the worse for wear. Aedan had grown tired merely watching her.

"I owe you an apology," he said as she came up. "I held back because you were a woman, but even at my best, I would have proved a poor match for you."

"Well, you are young yet," she replied. "Doubtless, if you practice diligently, your skills will improve with time, as mine have."

Aedan frowned. "You cannot be much older than I."

Sylvanna curiously cocked her head at him. "I don't know. How old are you? It's difficult to tell with humans."

"I am eighteen," he replied.

"Ah. Well, I am somewhat older."

"Indeed? You do not look it."

"Let me think. . . ." she said, frowning slightly. "By human reckoning, I believe I would be in my fifties."

Aedan's jaw dropped. "Your *fifties?*" he said with disbelief.

"By elven standards, I am still a mere child," she replied with a smile. "And most of the people you saw practicing today were younger still."

"You said 'by human reckoning,' " said Michael as they started walking back to Gylvain's home. "Do elves reckon time differently?"

"It is not that we reckon time differently," Sylvanna replied, "for being immortal, the reckoning of time does not concern us as much as it does you. But the difficulty lies in the fact that time often passes differently for us than for humans."

Aedan frowned. "How can that be?"

"I cannot say," Sylvanna replied with a shrug. "I once asked my brother that same question, but he was not able to account for it, either. It seems no one can. But in the elven lands, time appears to pass differently for humans. What may seem like a few hours to you while you are in Tuarhievel may actually be days on the outside, and what may pass for weeks while you are here may actually be years in human lands. This effect on humans seems to increase the longer they remain with us, so it is difficult for us to reckon time in your terms. At best, we can but estimate its passage."

"You mean that if we remain here for a week or so, a year or more may pass back in the empire?" asked Michael with astonishment.

"It is possible," Sylvanna said, "though by no means certain as far as anyone can tell. We once had a human trader remain with us for several weeks, studying our crafts. When he returned to his village beyond the Black River, he discovered that eight years had passed, and everyone had thought him dead. On the other hand, when traders have remained with us for only a few days, there has been no noticeable difference when they returned, except for one man, who found that he returned a mere hour after he had left."

"It sounds like magic!" Michael said.

"Perhaps it is," Sylvanna replied. "Gylvain seems to think so. He believes something happens when enough elves gather together in one place, but he cannot say how or why. It may have to do with our being immortal, or with the way we practice magic, or perhaps there is some other reason. Anyway, no one knows for sure what causes it."

"So then the longer we remain here, the more likely that a great length of time will pass back in the empire?" Aedan asked in a worried tone.

"That would appear to be the case," Sylvanna said.

"Then the longer we remain here, the more time Lord Arwyn has to strengthen his position, if I understand correctly," Aedan said with concern. "I did not realize this before. Why didn't someone tell us this?"

Sylvanna shrugged. "Doubtless because you did not ask. But there is no reason for alarm: there is a way this effect may be counteracted. My brother explained to me once. It is not without some risk, of course, but it has been the way your message has been sent back to Anuire."

"How?" asked Aedan.

"Through the Shadow World," Sylvanna said. "A halfling took your message back to the capital city of your empire. In this same manner, when it is time for you to leave, a halfling guide will take us. He will open up a portal to the Shadow World and we shall travel through it to reemerge into the world of daylight at another place and time."

"You said, 'a halfling guide will take *us*,' " Aedan said. "Will you be coming along with an escort to take us back?"

"No, I shall be returning with you," she replied. "Gylvain and I are both going with you to Anuire. Prince Fhileraene wishes to be kept apprised of how events unfold back in the empire."

"You mean he wants someone with us to look after his interests," Aedan said.

"Does that seem unreasonable to you?" she asked.

"No," Aedan replied, "of course not. We owe Tuarhievel much, our lives included, though it is your brother who personally holds that debt as far as I'm concerned. But even if that were not so, I would still be pleased to know you were going back with us." He blushed, then quickly added, "The both of you, that is."

"I am looking forward to it," said Sylvanna. "I have lived all of my life in the Aelvinnwode and never been outside Tuarhievel. I would like to see the human world and find out what it is like."

"It is different," Aedan said. "Our cities are not

much like yours, nor are our villages. Our streets are not as clean, I fear, nor do we live among the trees, as you do. We build our houses and our palaces differently, and we live behind stone walls. There is much to recommend your way of life. It is more peaceful and calming to the spirit. Perhaps that is why time seems to pass more slowly here."

"Still, I would prefer to be back in Anuire," said Michael. "After all, I am emperor now, and I must claim my throne."

"As I must serve you and the empire," Aedan said. "Duty calls. But," he added sadly, "except for that, there is little for me to go back to now."

Sylvanna frowned. "What makes you say that? You would not wish to see your family?"

Aedan swallowed hard before replying. "My parents were my only family," he said. "I had no brothers and no sisters, and now I fear my parents are probably both dead. Perhaps my mother survives, but my father would have been too great an enemy to Lord Arwyn for him to have been left alive."

"But . . . your father lives," Sylvanna said.

Aedan stopped and stared at her. "What?"

"A message was received from him this morning," she said. "You mean you did not know?"

Aedan could not believe his ears. "My father is alive? There has been a message from him? Are you sure?"

"My brother mentioned it to me this morning when he had word from the palace and was summoned to the prince's presence," she replied. "Perhaps he meant for me to tell you, but I thought you already knew."

"This is the very first I've heard of it!" said Aedan,

his heart giving a leap.

"What was the message?" Michael asked eagerly. "Did Gylvain say?"

"Something about how Lord Tieran had safely reached Anuire along with the empress and her party," said Sylvanna. "There was more, but that is all I can remember now."

"You have remembered the most important thing," said Aedan. Impulsively, he grabbed Sylvanna and gave her a hug. "Thank you! Thank you! This is the best possible news!"

Taken aback, Sylvanna stiffened, and Aedan released her and stepped back, feeling a bit flustered. "Forgive me," he said.

"No, it is I who must ask your forgiveness, Aedan," she said. "Had I but known you thought your father dead, I would have told you right away. I had not realized. . . . How awful it must have been for you!"

Aedan closed his eyes as an immense feeling of relief surged through him. For a moment, he was so overwhelmed, he simply couldn't speak. He felt his lower lip tremble and was afraid that he might start to cry. Sylvanna's arms went around him and held him close. Then Michael's hand settled on his shoulder, and they were all three holding each other for strength and support. For a few moments, no one spoke. Aedan took a deep breath, and they stood apart, looking at one another.

"It must have been so very lonely for you," said Sylvanna, "thinking you were the only one of your family who was left alive."

Aedan nodded, struggling to compose himself. He glanced at Michael, reached out, and squeezed his shoulder reassuringly. "You realize what this means?" he said. "Lord Arwyn does not hold the empress hostage and cannot enforce his claim upon the regency. He has failed. The moment he learns you are alive and well, he must either give up his bid for power or brand himself a traitor."

"He has already done that," said Michael firmly. "And what is more, he knows it. He cannot simply be brought to heel. He must be brought to justice."

Aedan gazed at him, and for the first time, he saw not Prince Michael, but Emperor Michael. "Yes, you're right, of course," he said. "One way or another, there will be war, and there is no avoiding it."

Michael nodded. "The empire is my birthright," he said, "and if I must fight to keep it together, I shall fight to my last breath."

"We both shall . . . Sire," Aedan said. They clasped hands. "Come, Sylvanna," he said. "Let us go and find Gylvain and see how soon the emperor and I may start for home."

BOOK II

BIRTHRIGHT

ANUIRE

chapter one

The Southern Coast, with its vast, rolling, grassy
plains, gradually gave way to the patchwork farm-
lands of the Heartlands, roughly one hundred miles
inland from the Straits of Aerele. The two regions en-
compassed all the territory from the province of Osoerde to the east, on the shores of the Gulf of Coeranys,
to the tangled woodlands of the Erebannien and its
coastal marshes to the southeast, to the forests and
lush meadows of Mhoried and Markazor in the
north, and west to the provinces of Taeghas and Brosengae, on the shores of the Sea of Storms. Located at
the southern end of this whole region, which covered
the lower half of the western portion of the Cerilian
continent, was the capital city of Imperial Anuire.

When the land bridge connecting the continents had still existed and the first humans had crossed over from Aduria, it was in Anuire that they had established their first settlement. Over the succeeding years, that settlement eventually grew into a thriving town, and the town into a teeming city, and the city, as the people spread throughout the land, into the seat of government of the Anuirean Empire. As the oldest and most populous human city in Cerilia, Anuire was a vibrant center of trade, learning, and entertainment, a bastion of the arts and of political intrigue. Each time Aedan left the city, he always felt as if he were leaving civilization behind to venture out into the wilds of the outlying provinces, and he could not wait to return. This time, in particular, he was eager to get back . . . not only to Anuire, but back into the world of daylight.

As they rode through the cold and misty woods, he knew that they would soon be approaching the lands of Diemed, roughly sixty miles from the city of Anuire, which lay just across the River Maesil. The river marked the boundary between the provinces of Diemed and Avanil, where the capital was located, and Aedan was extremely anxious to see it once again. He knew they would be there soon, and he kept trying to reassure himself with that knowledge, while at the same time forcing himself to remain constantly on the alert. He could not afford to become preoccupied. Not here.

They had journeyed this way several times before, and Aedan had learned, over his last few reluctant and uneasy expeditions to this foreboding, chilling land, to recognize some of the natural features of this most unnatural place. Even though some of it had begun to look familiar here and there, other parts of it kept changing, and he knew he would never, as long as he lived, truly grow accustomed to the Shadow World.

As they rode their horses slowly through the thick, dark woods, past grotesquely twisted and misshapen trees choked with hanging moss that resembled the gray hair of old women, Aedan thought about the first time he had traveled through the Shadow World, eight years earlier. He hadn't liked it then, and his tolerance for the world between the worlds had not increased with time. It was, after all, the world of his worst childhood nightmares and, unlike most things in dreams, in this case, the reality was worse.

Eight years ago, he and Michael had set off from Tuarhievel together with the elven mage Gylvain Aurealis and his sister, the elf warrior Sylvanna, on their return journey to Anuire. They had traveled with an escort of elven fighters and a halfling guide named Futhark. From the elven city, they had traveled on foot for two days through the Aelvinnwode until they reached the foothills of the Stonecrown Mountains to the south, near the lands of Markazor.

Even back then, Aedan had known that they were venturing into dangerous territory. Markazor had goblins living in its forest highlands, and the Stonecrown Mountains sheltered gnolls and ogres and desperate human renegades who had fled from persecution by the law in their own lands. Yet, this was where Futhark had brought them, because for some unknown reason, as the halfling had explained, the veil between the worlds was thinnest in those regions where chaos reigned over order.

Futhark was unable to explain why this was so. Perhaps, he had said, it had something to do with the energies generated by negativity and evil. Perhaps those places where people had descended into depravity were brought closer to the Shadow World, which became more and more permeated with evil with each passing year. Or perhaps, he theorized, the awnsheghlien rendered their domains temporally unstable by their massive expenditures of dark power and the profligate bloodtheft required to support it. The halfling didn't know for certain, and Aedan found it difficult to follow even his theoretical explanations. All the halflings really knew, said Futhark, was that it was easier to cross over in certain areas than in others. And those "certain areas" were definitely not places Aedan would have visited by choice.

This time, as in the previous few journeys they had made through the foreboding Shadow World, the place where they had crossed over was the Spiderfell, but that first time, returning from Tuarhievel, it was a little-known mountain pass in the Stonecrowns, near the border of Markazor. Aedan thought back to how it was then, and the memory seemed as sharp as ever. Even though it had occurred eight years ago, when he was just eighteen, it seemed as if it had been only yesterday.

Aedan had always wondered about the reputed ability of halflings to create dimension doors so they could shadow-walk. While he had dreaded actually crossing over into the world of his childhood nightmares, at the same time, he had been perversely curious to see how it was done. As they had moved up the path leading to the mountain pass, Futhark had gone into the lead, a bit out in front of all the others, but not so far that they lost visual contact.

As he walked, the halfling seemed to sense the air, almost as if he were an animal, stopping on the trail every now and then and sniffing the wind to detect the presence of any predators. There were halflings in Anuire, but Aedan had never really spent any time with one before, so he watched Futhark closely, with fascination.

The halfling looked like a more-or-less normal adult human male, except for the fact that he was about three-and-a-half feet tall. Everything about his proportions was in proper scale, unlike dwarves, whose legs and arms were smaller and out of proportion to their heads and torsos.

Futhark's hair was thick and black, rising in a crest on top and descending to the middle of his back almost like a horse's mane. His features were angular and sharp, similar to those of elves except that his eyebrows were thick and lacked the pronounced, delicate arch that elves had, and his ears were not as sharply pointed. In fact, one had to look closely to notice that they were pointed at all. City halflings, Aedan had heard, tended to adopt the dress styles of whatever locality they lived in. Futhark, however, dressed in leather hides. His arms and chest were bare beneath a dark brown leather doublet laced together with rawhide thongs, and his breeches were made of soft, natural buckskin with the rough side out. On his feet, the halfling wore leather moccasins that came up to just above his ankles and were likewise fastened with rawhide thongs. Perhaps, thought Aedan, he dressed this way because most elves in Tuarhievel wore similar attire.

As they walked, Futhark kept stopping and looking around, head cocked as if he were listening for something. Occasionally, he would stretch out his arms, his hands held palms out, fingertips splayed and extended, as if he were feeling the air. And then, abruptly, as they started on a slight downward slope entering the rocky pass, the halfling stopped and made a pass with his hands, as if clearing cobwebs from before him, and a gray, swirling mist appeared on the trail just ahead.

It was as if a fog had suddenly risen, but in only one small area, an arched space in front of them no larger than a portal. And it was a portal . . . a doorway into another dimension, a bridge to the world between the worlds.

Aedan recalled how his stomach had suddenly tensed and a sharp pressure had started in his chest. His mouth had gone completely dry, and he found it difficult to swallow. His breath began to come in short, sharp gasps, and cold sweat trickled down his spine. His curiosity had been fully satisfied. He had seen a halfling make a dimension portal. He did not quite understand *how* he did it, but that was something he could pursue another time. He had seen the door to the world between the worlds opened. However, he did *not* want to find out what was on the other side.

Anyone with half an ounce of sense would have known enough to feel at least *some* trepidation at passing through that swirling mist and into the unknown, especially since people had been known to pass into the Shadow World and never emerge again. Anyone in his right mind would have thought twice about entering that misty portal that had suddenly appeared like a low-flying cloud upon the trail. Anyone except Michael Roele. Michael was positively thrilled and could not wait to go through. It was then, seeing the eager expression on his young face as it lit up with enthusiasm, that Aedan became convinced the new and not-yet-crowned young emperor was not merely fearless; he was crazy.

With Futhark leading the way, they had gone through the swirling cloud into the Shadow World, emerging in a place that looked, in many ways, much like the world they had just left . . . except, at the same time, it was different.

They could recognize the trail they were on. The path ahead of them looked much the same as it had back in the world of daylight. The countryside was similar, as well, and so far as Aedan could tell, they were still in the foothills of the Stonecrown Mountains, heading into the pass that led to Markazor. Only after that, things were not quite the same.

For one thing, the *light* was completely different. Even though it had been a clear and sunny day when they passed through the portal, when they came through into the other side, everything was dark and gray and damp, as if on a foggy, heavily overcast day out in the coastal marshlands. Tendrils of mist rose up from the ground, over which hung a perpetual fog that came up almost to their knees. Vision was limited to no more than a dozen yards or so, except for brief periods when the mists parted from a sudden gust of bone-chilling wind. And it was *cold*. Numbingly cold. The kind of cold that seeped into the bones and made them ache. It was a mirror image of the daylight world, only this mirror was a dark one, reflecting only . . . shadow.

At first glance, the surrounding countryside looked similar to the place they had just left, except that everything was gray and mist-shrouded, but on closer examination, the trees turned out to be twisted into macabre shapes and choked with hanging moss that trailed down from the branches and raised unpleasant shudders if it contacted the skin. The underbrush was different, too. It was more sparse and spiky, with thorns large enough to cut the flesh like daggers. The ground was mostly bare and rocky, save where a strange silvery-blue moss grew in widespread tufts, like a diseased carpet. And there were nervous scurryings in that tangled thorny underbrush, creatures stirring that Aedan didn't really want to see. He found out about some of those creatures soon enough.

"Aedan, stop! Don't move," Sylvanna said, as they headed down the trail.

She had spoken calmly but forcefully, and something in her tone had made Aedan freeze at once. "What is it?" he asked uneasily.

"Just don't move," she replied. "Not even a muscle. Don't even twitch. Stand very, very still."

Out of the corner of his eye, he saw her draw her dagger from its sheath on her belt. He frowned in confusion, then felt something moving across the back of his neck. He swallowed hard and clenched his teeth as he fought down the shiver that threatened to run through his entire body. Something was crawling on him . . . something hairy.

Sylvanna stepped forward quickly, and her blade flashed at the back of his neck. He felt just the faintest scratch as the tip of the blade barely brushed his skin, then saw Sylvanna stomp her thick-soled moccasin down on something white and multi-legged. A violent shudder went through him, running down his spine all the way into his feet.

"What was it?" he asked, uneasily.

"Albino spider," she replied. "A small one, just a baby. They grow as large as your head, and that's just the body. Sharp fangs, deadly poison. One tiny bite, even from a little one like that, and you would have died in horrible agony within moments, beyond the help of any healer or magician. The poison simply works too fast."

Aedan had paled. "Thank you," he said. "It seems you've saved my life."

"Just be careful of that hanging moss," she replied. "They like to make nests in it, and they can't tell the difference between the moss and your hair. If you let one get into your hair, even if it doesn't bite you, it might still lay eggs."

Aedan still felt rather queasy whenever he thought about that. Since then, he had fought in many battles, and had faced several of the horrors the Shadow World had to offer, but nothing had ever made his skin crawl like the thought of tiny eggs hatching in his hair, releasing a horde of little white spiders with sharp fangs dripping poison. He had avoided the hanging moss ever since, as if contact with it would be lethal. And, he thought, when one considered what it sheltered, it easily could be.

"What are you thinking?" Sylvanna asked, riding up beside him on the trail through the misty woods. Her voice brought him sharply back to the present once again, and he realized he had been preoccupied with reverie. That was entirely too dangerous to be countenanced under present circumstances, but he was exhausted—they all were—and his mind had simply started drifting of its own accord.

"I was thinking of spiders," he replied to her question. "Little white spiders, hatching from a score of tiny eggs."

For a moment, she stared at him, frowning with puzzlement, and then her face cleared as she suddenly made the connection. "Ah, you were thinking back to the first time we journeyed through the Shadow World."

He nodded. "In some ways, it seems as if it were only yesterday. But in others, it seems like a lifetime ago."

"It was about five years ago, wasn't it?" Sylvanna asked. "Or was it longer?"

"It was eight years," he replied, smiling to himself. Elves were not good with the concept of time. Being immortal and consequently having all the time in the world, they found little significance in time, unlike humans, who had less of it and therefore paid it more attention. "Eight years in which a great deal has happened."

For one thing, he thought, as he glanced at the emperor riding a short distance in front of him, Michael had grown up. At twenty, he was still young, but physically, he was a full-grown man. He had shot up to over six feet and was now taller than Aedan. He outweighed him, too, by at least forty pounds. Michael had taken his training very seriously, working out with the weapons master every day. As a result, he had developed a husky, muscular build, with a thick chest and large, powerful arms able to swing a two-handed broadsword with great speed and strength.

Many young men of the empire were little more than boys at his age, but Michael had done a lot of living in the eight years since Tuarhievel, and those years had been fraught with unrest in the provinces and heavy responsibilities at home.

Boeruine had been only the beginning. When they had returned to Anuire after their abduction by the goblins and their brief stay in Tuarhievel, they discovered that a little over a year had passed on the outside. That was the difficulty in traveling from the elven lands, where time's flow was affected in peculiar, inexplicable, and unpredictable ways. One was never certain how much time would have passed when one came back to human domains, even when going through the Shadow World.

Shadow-walking was not Aedan's preferred mode of travel by any means, but Michael had employed it many times since that first journey. By creating a portal into the Shadow World, a halfling could at least temporarily suspend the flow of time. As Futhark had explained it, if they had a desperate need to travel from Anuire to Kal Kalathor, clear on the other side of the continent, and they absolutely had to be there as soon as possible, if they were to travel on horseback, even at a fast pace, changing mounts on the way, it could still take as much as a month. It would mean covering a distance of at least a thousand miles, even more if they went out of our way to avoid traveling through such potentially dangerous territories as the Coulladaraight and the Tarvan Waste.

On the other hand, if they were to shadow-walk through the world between the worlds, their journey would take roughly the same length of time . . . but they could emerge back into the world of daylight almost at the same time as they had left to go into the Shadow World. In other words, for them the same long span of time would have passed, but little time in the daylight world. With one exception. Elven realms.

In the same mysterious way that the laws of time were twisted in the Shadow World, so were they affected in the elven realms, which to Aedan suggested a correlation of some sort, though he could not venture to guess what it could have been. The point was that while time within the Shadow World seemed almost to stand still, in elven realms, it was completely unpredictable. It either "expanded" or "contracted," and there was no way of predicting which way the effect would go. As a result, traveling from the elven realms into the Shadow World and emerging in human domains could have some interesting effects.

"I have never forgotten our first journey through this dreadful place," Aedan said as he and Sylvanna rode side by side, holding their horses at a walk. Galloping or even trotting through the forests of the Shadow World was risky. There was no way of knowing what you were likely to run into—unless, of course, the unknown was preferable to the risk of facing whatever was behind you. "As if it were not enough that we faced death by choosing to come this way, to discover that a year had passed while we were in Tuarhievel for merely a few days. . . ." He shook his head and sighed. "Well, at least we have not had to repeat that particular experience, even if the emperor does insist on saving time by traveling through the Shadow World whenever we need to cover a lot of distance. I used to suspect he didn't fully understand the risks involved. Now I realize he simply doesn't care. But that first time . . . I shall never forget it. I never truly understood the strain my father had been under until I saw him. Only a week or so had passed for me, but it was a year for him. A year in which he was never really certain what the next day would bring. One year in which he had aged twenty."

"You still miss him very much, don't you?" Sylvanna asked.

Aedan nodded. "More than I can say. I miss his wisdom and his guidance. It was my mother who sustained the greatest loss, of course, but in another sense, she merely lost her mate, while I lost not only my father, but my teacher, too. There was so much more I could have learned from him, if only he could have lived at least a few more years. . . ."

"I sometimes think it must be terrible to be human," said Sylvanna. "All your accomplishments, your dreams and passions, are so ephemeral. Your life spans are so very short, I often wonder how you stand it."

Aedan smiled. "You mean to say you pity us?"

"Well . . . no, not quite," she replied. "Pity implies a sort of condescension, and in the last few years, I have learned a great deal about you humans and what you can accomplish if you set your minds to it."

"Perhaps we do so precisely because our time is short," Aedan told her. "Knowing we are but mortal is what gives us our drive to live life to its fullest. If we seem a bit desperate to you, maybe it is because, in a sense, we are. You elves, by virtue of your immortality, do not possess that desperation. To humans, elves seem . . . well, not desperate, like us. That is why our passions burn so brightly. When you know from the outset that your time is limited, then each day becomes precious."

Sylvanna studied him curiously for a moment as they rode side by side, rocking gently with the gait of their mounts. "That makes sense, I suppose. I have noticed that you humans seem to feel things very intensely." She frowned and shook her head. "I don't mean to say that we elves are not capable of intensity of feeling, for we are . . . it is just that humans seem so much *more* intense. And uncontrolled."

"It's that edge of desperation," Aedan replied with a smile. "It comes from our mortality, as I said. We live hard, work hard, play hard . . . love hard."

Sylvanna glanced at him. He met her gaze steadily. She did not look away. "By extension of that argument," she said, "I suppose one could claim that mayflies would be the most passionate creatures in the world, since they live only one day."

"And note how very violently they beat their little wings and fly always toward the light," said Aedan. "They are so attracted to the flame that they will fly into it and allow it to consume them. If that is not a suitable metaphor for unbridled passion, then what is?"

"I thought those were moths," Sylvanna said.

"Well, mayflies do the same thing, don't they?"

She frowned. "I'm not sure. Do they?"

Aedan shrugged. "Even if they don't, it does not invalidate the metaphor."

Sylvanna smiled. "You may have missed your true calling," she said. "Instead of a royal minister, you should have been a bard."

Aedan winced. "Oh, anything but that," he said.

Sylvanna raised her eyebrows. "Oh? I seem to have touched a nerve."

"I knew a bard once," Aedan said. "In fact, I knew a number of them and they were all insufferable, but this one was the worst. Most bards are in love with the sound of their own words, which makes them merely conceited, but this one was also in love with an idea, which made him dangerous."

"Why would idealism make someone dangerous?" Sylvanna asked.

"Ah, now there's a question for the emperor's chief minister," said Aedan with a grin. "In my capacity as lord high chamberlain, I should tell you that *all* idealists are dangerous, because they are individuals who hold ideas in higher esteem than any emperor or king or noble. An idealist's first loyalty is to the morality of the idea that he champions . . . or she, as the case may be. As a consequence, there is no room in such an individual for compromise. Personally, however, I find that there is a certain type of an idealist one can live with."

"And what sort is that?" Sylvanna asked, taking the bait.

"One who agrees with you," said Aedan with a chuckle.

"I should have seen that one coming," said Sylvanna with a wry grimace. "You'd think by now I would have learned better."

"Elves are notoriously slow learners," Aedan said teasingly. "That is yet another disadvantage of your immortality . . . you never really feel pressed to do anything quickly."

"Some things are best done slowly," she replied with a sidelong glance at him.

"You mean . . . like courtship?" Aedan asked.

"And other things, as well."

Aedan cleared his throat uneasily. Over the past eight years, he and Sylvanna had grown very close, something he had not imagined would be possible when they first met. For one thing, he had not expected to know her long enough, but she had returned to Anuire with them, accompanying her brother, Gylvain, and they had both stayed, together with the halfling, Futhark, and the elven escort that had brought them from Tuarhievel, a group of about a dozen warriors.

It was part of an alliance concluded between Lord Tieran, acting on behalf of the then still-uncrowned Emperor Michael and Prince Fhileraene of Tuarhievel. The elves were to act as the emperor's personal guard, initially to ensure his safe return to Anuire and, later, to demonstrate to all that the elven kingdom of Tuarhievel had formally allied itself with Anuire and thrown its support behind Emperor Michael.

It was an unprecedented agreement and one that from the outset had been certain to arouse the ire of extremists on both sides, such as Rhuobhe Manslayer and Lord Kier Avan, Duke of Avanil, who had about as much use for elves as the Manslayer had for humans. Since Avanil and Rhuobhe, the renegade province the Manslayer had carved out for himself in the southern region of the Aelvinnwode, shared a common border, there were frequent raids back and forth by the Manslayer's warriors and Lord Kier's knights, and the skirmishes were as constant as they were violent. Indeed, if not for Kier on the south and Arwyn of Boeruine on the north of Rhuobhe's borders, the Manslayer would have spread his violent hatred much farther through the empire.

Why then, Aedan had wondered at the time, had his father negotiated this unusual alliance? And why had Fhileraene agreed to it? The answer lay, as his father had always taught him, in a consideration of the possibilities.

For Fhileraene, there were certain advantages to the alliance that were not immediately apparent on the surface, but became clear upon some consideration. Fhileraene knew that he could not hope to stand alone against the humans *and* the goblins of Thurazor, as well. His great-grandfather, the Manslayer, did not share that particular problem. While Rhuobhe was beset on both sides by the Duke of Avanil and the Archduke of Boeruine, he was separated from the goblin realm of Thurazor by the province of Boeruine and the Five Peaks region. He could afford to concentrate on waging his war of constant skirmishes solely on the humans.

Fhileraene, on the other hand, was virtually surrounded by his enemies—the goblins of Thurazor to the west, the savage giants of the Giantdowns to the north, and the feral minions of the awnshegh Raesene in the mountains of the Gorgon's Crown, to the east. He enjoyed good relations only with his neighbor to the northwest, the province of Dhoesone, which needed its alliance with Tuarhievel because it was an isolated outpost of the empire that was surrounded by demihuman realms. Fhileraene understood full well that such alliances were imperative to keep his borders secure against his enemies. In order to help ensure the survival of his realm, Fhileraene had to be adroit in his political maneuverings. The alliance he had agreed to with Lord Tieran was a case in point.

By his signing of the treaty, Fhileraene had clearly signaled the elven kingdom of Tuarhievel's formal recognition of Michael's birthright as successor to the Iron Throne, and this had turned out to be no small thing, as Lord Arwyn had taken steps to consolidate his own position in the year they'd been away. He had managed to induce the provinces of Talinie, Brosengae, and Taeghas to recognize his claim to regency.

Lord Rurik Donalls governed the windswept province of Talinie, and with the goblin realm of Thurazor abutting his northeastern borders and both the Aelvinnwode and the lawless Five Peaks region to his southeast, the Earl of Talinie desperately needed the protection and support of a strong warlord like the Archduke of Boeruine. His northern province was sparsely settled, with the only city being the well-fortified capital at Nowelton, situated on the coast and to some degree protected from the fierce storms of the Miere Rhuann by the rocky cliffs of Dantier Island. Most of Talinie was covered by thick forest, except for the narrow band of rocky plain along the coast. There were no teeming cities like Anuire in Lord Rurik's domain, nor even large villages like Seasedge, but the residents of Talinie were a tough and hard-bitten lot, mostly hardy woodsmen and rough miners who carved the coal out of the highlands. The Earl of Talinie could not muster a large army of warriors, but the men he had were tough and seasoned fighters accustomed to frequent skirmishes with goblin raiders and the bandits of the Five Peaks region. Together with the knights and men-at-arms of Lord Arwyn, they made a formidable force.

Then there was the province of Taeghas, which had gone over to Boeruine. Lord Davan Durien, the Count of Taeghas, ruled a relatively poor province from his hold at Stormspoint, on the coast just south of Boeruine. Taeghas possessed a wide variety of terrains, from coastal plains to moors, from lowland forests to the Seamist Mountains, which separated the province from Avanil. The small seaport town of Portage at the tip of Finger Bay was devoted primarily to fishing, and the remainder of the residents of Taeghas were tenant farmers and herdsmen. The periodic raids by trolls who came down from the Seamist Mountains, attracted by the produce of the farms and the sheep and cattle of the herdsmen, meant that Lord Davan, like Rurik of Talinie, needed a protective alliance with a warlord like Arwyn of Boeruine.

Finally, there was Brosengae, situated where the Straits of Aerele flowed into the Miere Rhuann. Brosengae was cut up with large bays and swampy bayous that opened onto lush and fertile coastal plains that gave way, in turn, to wooded foothills and forest highlands. Like Taeghas, Brosengae had the Seamist Mountains on its borders, which meant that its populace was vulnerable to raids by trolls. However, unlike Taeghas and Talinie, Brosengae was a wealthy province, headquarters to several powerful guilds. Its sheltered bays provided good anchorage for merchant ships, smugglers, and corsairs, all of whom found welcome in equal measure from harbormasters who were not too particular whom they admitted, so long as they could pay the docking and the mooring fees.

Lysander Marko, Duke of Brosengae, shared a common border with Avanil, the province where the empire's capital city of Anuire was located, and so far as Aedan could see, his alliance with Boeruine was nothing less than opportunism. He could easily afford to maintain a force of men-at-arms and mercenaries to keep the predations of the trolls under control, and he had no worries about goblin raids or massed bandit attacks, since his province was far to the south of Thurazor and the Five Peaks, and sheltered by Boeruine, Taeghas, and Avanil.

No, thought Aedan, Marko did not enter into his alliance with Boeruine as a result of intimidation by Lord Arwyn. He did so because he saw a chance to undermine his rival, Lord Kier Avan, Duke of Avanil. Everyone had his own personal agenda, Aedan thought, and Arwyn had exploited each of them for his own gain. Promises were made, bargains concluded, tribute paid—when the commoners of the merchant classes received such "tributes," they were generally known as bribes, thought Aedan wryly—and the upshot of it all was that Arwyn of Boeruine had essentially united the provinces of the entire Western Coast region under his own banner.

All that had happened in the year they had been at Fhileraene's court in Tuarhievel—a year that had actually been only about a week or so for them—and no one had suspected then that Prince Michael could still be alive. No one save Lord Tieran, who had kept that information to himself until Michael had returned safely to Anuire, the better to ensure he *could* return safely. By then, however, Lord Arwyn had long since reported his death and sent dispatch riders throughout the empire to spread the word and announce his assumption of the regency.

Talinie and Taeghas had formally given their support to him right from the outset, which made Aedan wonder if they had simply judged which way the wind was blowing and acted to safeguard their own interests, or if they had received some advance notification of Lord Arwyn's plans. Either way, they were the first to grant their recognition. Brosengae followed, but not until Avan had refused, questioning Boeruine's right to the regency and declaring for Lord Tieran and the empress. The Baron of Diemed had announced support for Lord Tieran and the empress, as well, but not until Kier of Avanil had declared himself. With Avanil across the river from Diemed, Baron Harth Diem had wanted to see which way the more powerful Duke of Avanil would go.

And so it went throughout the empire, each province and each ruling noble waiting for as long as possible to declare allegiance either to Lord Tieran and the empress or to Arwyn of Boeruine, for no one wished to be premature in his formal recognition of either party. They first wanted to see how their neighbors would declare, especially if those neighbors were wealthier and more powerful.

This, however, was precisely what Lord Tieran had gambled on, for he knew it would buy him time—time in which the young emperor might return and assume his rightful place on the Iron Throne of Anuire. And he had needed as much time as he could buy, because he had no way of knowing when Michael and Aedan might return. He knew about the strange way time flowed in the elven realms, and he had also known it was completely unpredictable. For Michael and Aedan, a few days could go by while for him and the rest of the human world, it could be weeks or months or even years.

It had to be incredibly difficult for him, thought Aedan, trying to manipulate the political situation to his best advantage—insofar as he was able—while at the same time knowing the strongest weapon he could use against Lord Arwyn was one he did not dare reveal. If he had announced Michael was still alive and safe within the borders of Tuarhievel, Arywn and his allies could have taken steps to prevent his return and see to it he never left the Aelvinnwode alive.

It must have been a terrible strain for him, thought Aedan. And it had certainly taken its toll. His father had died a year ago, while Aedan was out on a campaign with the emperor. And those campaigns had been virtually unceasing almost since the time they had returned.

Eight years, he thought. Eight years of almost constant warfare, trying to hold the empire together. Michael was doing a good job of it, however. And with each campaign, he had improved significantly as a general. In the beginning, the campaigns had been planned by Lord Korven, commanding general of the Imperial Army of Anuire, who had been adamantly opposed to the idea of Michael going out into the field with the troops. At the time of the first campaign, Michael had just turned thirteen, and Lord Korven had believed it was much too risky for a mere boy—and the only heir to the imperial throne, at that—to accompany the army into battle. However, Michael had insisted on it, and, to Aedan's surprise, his father had supported his choice.

"It is true he is young and would expose himself to risk," Aedan's father had said to him when he protested. "However, those very things also work for him. The troops shall see the boy emperor riding with them, leading them beneath his standard, and it shall both invigorate and motivate them. If they see that a boy is unafraid to fight for a cause, then they, as grown men, shall take courage from his presence."

"But what if he should be killed?" Aedan had asked.

His father shrugged slightly. "That is the risk that every true leader must take. If he wants his men to be willing to die *for* him, then he must also be willing to die *with* them. A ruler who simply sends his troops out while he remains behind in the safety of his castle will never command the same loyalty and respect as one who leads his armies into battle. More than anything else right now, Michael must gain the respect and loyalty of the troops and of his vassals. And respect and loyalty are never freely given. They must be earned."

So at the age of thirteen, Michael had led the Imperial Army of Anuire into the field, which sounded much more impressive than it was in fact, since a great deal of the army's strength at any given time depended on troops sent from the empire's provinces. And in the beginning, all they had were the troops quartered in the capital and those sent by Kier of Avanil. Messengers had been dispatched to all the other provinces with an imperial command for a troop levy, but while no one had refused outright, neither had anyone except the Duke of Avanil hastened to comply. They all waited to see in which direction the wind would start to blow. And, at least in the beginning, it had blown against Emperor Michael.

When word had been sent out that Prince Michael was alive and well and had returned to Anuire to claim his birthright, Arwyn had responded by accusing Lord Tieran of trying to palm off a pretender on the people of the empire. An entire year had passed, he said, in which there had been no word from the missing emperor and now he had returned? From where? If it were truly the prince, what had he been doing all this time? How had he escaped his goblin abductors? And why had the elves, the old enemies of humankind, chosen to help him? What did Prince Fhileraene have to gain?

What Lord Tieran had to gain was obvious, Arwyn had maintained. He was after power and sought the regency for himself. What other possible reason could there have been for his cowardly flight from Seaharrow with the empress at a time when not only the prince's fate but that of his own son was uncertain? Arwyn even went so far as to suggest that the high chamberlain had taken the empress from Seaharrow against her will—for what mother would leave when her son was missing?—and was now holding her at the Imperial Cairn in Anuire as hostage for his claim to regency. Arwyn manifested considerable outrage over this, despite the fact that it was probably exactly what he had planned himself.

It was a believable claim to many and not really an unexpected move. The Archduke of Boeruine had, after all, declared that Prince Michael was dead.

When Michael had returned, Arwyn really had only two choices—back down from his claim to regency, swear fealty to Michael, and hope the new emperor would not hold a grudge, or else declare him an imposter foisted off upon the people by Lord Tieran, aided by the elven magic of Prince Fhileraene. Aedan was not at all surprised when Arwyn chose the latter option.

Since then, it had been one campaign after another, and not always against the forces of Boeruine, which had become considerable. Lord Arwyn had recruited mercenaries and bandits from the Five Peaks region to join his army and he had even gone so far as to openly ally himself with the goblins of Thurazor. His rationale for doing so was astonishingly bold. Lord Tieran, he claimed, had betrayed the empire by allying himself with the elves. And rather than face the possibility of their old enemies overcoming them with the aid of the Anuirean troops, the goblins had decided to throw in their lot with the forces of Boeruine, the rightful regent, in exchange for Arwyn's support against the elves. What was more, in his dispatches from Seaharrow to the other provinces of the empire, Arwyn had actually *bragged* of this alliance, invoking the memory of Mount Deismaar and comparing himself to Haelyn, who had made an alliance with the elves against the dark forces of Azrai for the common good. And incredibly, there were many who took him at his word.

As soon as it became evident that Arwyn would not recognize the emperor, insisting he was an imposter, and would not give up his claim to regency, a number of other provinces also rebelled. At first, it was not open rebellion; they simply failed to respond to Michael's call to arms. Coeranys sent no reply to Lord Tieran's dispatches. Suiriene, far to the east on the shores of the Sea of the Golden Sun, likewise failed to respond, as did the province of Alamie in the Heartlands. The Baron of Ghieste, whose walled city was located in the Heartlands to the north of Anuire, sent regrets and claimed that all his troops were needed at home to secure his borders against gnoll raiders from the Spiderfell.

The implications of this were all too clear. A good number of the late emperor's vassals were sitting on the fence, unwilling to declare for Michael and against Boeruine because they were afraid to choose the losing side. Arwyn's strength and prowess as a warlord were well known throughout the empire, while Michael was just a boy and had yet to prove himself. The Viscount of Osoerde had even gone so far as to demand proof that Michael was not the pretender Arwyn claimed he was. And despite Michael's coronation in the capital, the empire was plunged into an interregnum. Thus Michael had been forced to begin his reign by fighting for what was rightfully his. And unless he moved decisively, the empire was in danger of disintegrating.

Aedan's father and Lord Korven had concurred that given their present strength—or rather, lack of it—they could not hope to successfully mount a campaign against Lord Arwyn, who'd had a year of preparation to solidify his position. Consequently, they had been forced to mount campaigns against those provinces that had not responded to the call to arms. They had marched on Ghieste first, since it was the closest capital, with its borders adjacent to Avanil.

Lord Korven led his troops on a forced march to Ghieste, with Michael riding at his side and Aedan bearing the Roele standard of a red dragon rampant on a field of white. Lord Richard, Baron of Ghieste, was taken completely unawares. He awoke one morning to find the Royal House Guard and the Army of Anuire, augmented with the troops of Avanil, encamped before his castle, prepared to conduct a siege. It was the last thing he expected. Nor was he given time to think. No sooner had he realized that there was an army camped just beyond his walls than an envoy was dispatched to him with an imperial summons to come out and meet with the emperor in his tent. A refusal would have been tantamount to open rebellion, and he could not have withstood a siege. Lord Richard had no choice but to comply.

He had ridden from his castle to Michael's tent with only a token escort, and it was at that meeting that Michael began to prove himself worthy of his birthright. Lord Tieran had advised him beforehand, but Michael had conducted the meeting all by himself, which had taken Lord Richard by surprise. He had expected to deal with the high chamberlain, but instead found himself facing a very self-assured boy of thirteen, who comported himself with a confidence well beyond his years.

He had greeted Lord Richard warmly and expressed sympathy for his problems with the raiders. He had assured him of his support, promising that the next time there was a raid upon his city, he would send a force on a punitive expedition against the gnolls to show them that the emperor would not countenance incursions into his lands. He further reassured him that he would not dream of leaving the Barony of Ghieste unprotected by taking all its troops away on a campaign, so he would only take a third of them. And to demonstrate the high esteem in which he held Lord Richard, he would grant his eldest son the singular honor of a knighthood, so that he could lead Ghieste's troops in the campaign under Lord Richard's standard.

Lord Richard knew he had been adroitly out-maneuvered. He was in no position to refuse, with Lord Korven and his troops on the scene, and once they had departed, he could not once more become recalcitrant, because the emperor would have his eldest son with him as a hostage. By knighting young Viscount Ghieste, Michael would also be able to keep the viscount with him at court, which would please young Ghieste, for life at the Anuirean court was much more stimulating and vastly preferable to an unattached young man than the quiet, rural life in an outlying province. At the same time, it would ensure Baron Ghieste's loyalty, and by having a third of Ghieste's troops with him, even if it wasn't a significant addition to his forces, their marching with the emperor under Ghieste's standard amounted to a formal recognition of Michael's birthright. And so the city had been "retaken" without a single blow being struck. It had been a masterful piece of armed diplomacy for which Lord Tieran was responsible, but Michael had done his part and handled himself flawlessly, leaving Lord Richard very much impressed.

Unfortunately, things had not gone quite so easily with some of the other provinces. Coeranys was over three hundred miles from Anuire, and there was no way of surprising the Duchess Sariele with a forced march across the Heartlands. Eugenie Sariele had ruled the province since her husband had become crippled by disease, and for years, she had done so more or less independently of Anuire. The lands of Coeranys, out in the Eastern Marches, were sparsely populated, and their inhabitants subsisted primarily on guild trading and raising livestock. The landrunners, nomadic herdsmen of Coeranys, were fiercely independent, ranging far and wide across the grassy plains, and many of them had gone tribal, setting up their own nomadic governments without feeling the need to answer to the duchess, who left them pretty much alone.

Much of the terrain was swampy, particularly the southern region of the province, where waters from the gulf made considerable inroads through the bayous, streams, and marshes of the lowlands. The storms that swept down regularly from the rocky highlands of Baruk-Azhik kept the land inundated with almost constant rain and much of the central lowlands of the province were peat bogs that were not easily traversed by an armed force. Unless one really knew the territory, it was easy to get lost in the swamps or stumble into a soft, deep bog and get sucked down.

The capital of Coeranys was the city of Ruorvan, built upon the banks of the River Saemil, which flowed into the swampy marshes from the foothills of the Sielwode. To the south and east and west of the city, the land was all bogs and bayous, which rendered it practically unapproachable from those directions. The only reasonable overland approach to Ruorvan was from the north, through the province of Elinie, across a narrow band of high ground

running through the marshlands into the open
plains to the north of the city. There was, consequently, no way that an army could approach the
capital of Coeranys by stealth—unless it came
through the world between the worlds.

Lord Korven had tried twice to lead his force into
Coeranys to bring the Duchess Sariele to heel. Both
times, he had failed. Aedan and Michael had been
with him each time, and both expeditions had
proved disastrous. The first one had floundered in
the marshes to the northwest of Ruorvan as they
tried to cross the River Saemil. Heavy rains had
raised the floodwaters and reduced the roads to a
sea of mud in which horses sank almost to their
withers and foot soldiers bogged down to their
knees. After weeks of battling such impossible conditions, the army had been forced to turn back.

The second expedition fared no better. While the
weather had not been nearly so severe, by the time
the second campaign had been mounted, the duchess had been warned by the failure of the first one
and had mustered not only her troops, but the nomadic landrunners as well to repel the emperor's
forces.

The narrow strip of high ground between the
swamps and marshes on the eastern borders of
Elinie, the only practicable overland route into Coeranys across the River Saemil, was only about twenty
miles wide, and much of that territory was taken up
by soft and grassy peat bogs across which an army
could not march. There were only a few miles of
passable ground, and this narrow strip could be easily defended by a much smaller force against a larger
one, especially when the defenders were intimately

familiar with the terrain. Faced not only with the knights and men-at-arms of the Duchess Sariele, but with the fierce and savage landrunners as well, the emperor's forces found themselves fighting for every inch of ground as they attempted their approach.

Lord Korven's fighting tactics had been seriously hampered by the fact that he was not only forced to wage conventional warfare against the troops of Coeranys, but also fight constant defensive actions against the landrunners, who pursued hit-and-run guerilla warfare against the advancing army. They would strike at night or during a heavy rainstorm, inflict heavy casualties with their powerful longbows, then retreat into the swamps, where every effort to pursue them had only resulted in the loss of more men. And once again, the emperor's army had been forced to turn back in defeat.

Meanwhile, Lord Arwyn had not remained idle. With his army considerably strengthened by troops from Taeghas, Talinie, and Brosengae, he had attacked Avanil. He had waited until his spies informed him that the Army of Anuire was marching on Coeranys and after calculating how long it would take the emperor and Lord Korven to reach the River Saemil, he launched a devastating two-pronged attack on Avanil. He had split his army, sending part of his forces through the forest east from Seaharrow and across the border into western Alamie, then south to Avanil, while the rest of his troops marched east from Brosengae, crossed the border into Avanil, and attacked the capital city of Dalton, where Lord Kier of Avan had his stronghold.

With a good part of his forces on the march with

the Army of Anuire, Lord Kier was left with only half his normal complement of troops. He had anticipated the possibility of an attack from across the border of Brosengae and had concentrated most of his defensive garrisons along the twenty-mile stretch of open plain between the southern tip of the Seamist Mountains and the coast. What he had not expected was an attack through western Alamie, which was not only a lengthy route, but also entailed marching an army around the outer borders of the territory claimed by Rhuobhe Manslayer.

The temptation for the Manslayer to conduct hit-and-run tactics against the rearguard of an army marching around his territory would have been irresistible, or at least so Lord Kier had thought. Besides, an army on the march from Seaharrow through western Alamie would have had to cover some four hundred miles to reach Dalton, with at least one hundred and fifty of those miles through thick, old-growth forest that would leave them likewise vulnerable to guerilla tactics. What the Duke of Avanil failed to take into account was the possibility that Rhuobhe Manslayer might be perfectly content to let such an army pass around the borders of his territory unmolested, if he knew they were en route to attack other human forces. If such an advancing army was defeated and found itself forced to retreat, he could then attack it on its return march, when the troops were weakened. On the other hand, if they were successful, he could wait until they had departed and attack the losers.

And that was precisely what he had done, though there had been no way for Arwyn to know that for sure in advance. As Aedan's father had told him so many times before, considering the possibilities was everything in life. Arwyn had simply assessed the possibilities and gambled on the odds. Successfully, as it turned out. While half of Arwyn's army moved against the garrisons protecting the border between Brosengae and Avanil, the other half had marched through the forests of Boeruine, around the northern tip of the Seamist Mountain range and Rhuobhe's territory, then crossed the border into western Alamie to slash and burn their way south toward Dalton. It was his way of making Duke Flaertes pay the price for sitting on the fence and failing to declare for him.

Michael's third expedition against Coeranys was delayed by the necessity of having to conduct forced marches all the way across the Heartlands to come to Lord Kier's rescue. En route, they passed through the Duchy of Alamie, marching through the capital of Lofton in a show of force to induce Lord Deklan Alam, Duke of Alamie, to declare himself for the emperor. Naturally, with an army marching through his capital, Lord Deklan had hastened to reaffirm his loyalty to the empire, whereupon Michael resorted to the same ploy he had used with the Baron of Ghieste. He had ceremoniously knighted Lord Alam's eldest son and appointed him to command a portion of Alamie's troops on the campaign to western Alamie, thereby making certain Lord Alam would not experience a change of heart once the army had departed.

In western Alamie, they found only the devastation left behind by Arwyn's army as they had marched south on Avanil. Farms and villages were burned, livestock slaughtered, fields of crops razed and trampled to the ground. Western Alamie would not soon forget Lord Arwyn, and when the Army of Anuire reached the capital of Haes, Duke Flaertes did not need any prodding to declare in favor of the emperor. The Army of Boeruine had not paused in their march to lay siege to Haes, but they had laid waste to every town and village in their path, and the capital was jammed with refugees and wounded who had lost their homes and come to their lord to seek refuge and redress. What Lord Tieran had not been able to accomplish by diplomacy, the Archduke of Boeruine had accomplished with the sword. Duke Flaertes acknowledged Michael as the rightful ruler and gave him half his troops.

They had then made haste from Haes toward Dalton, and when they crossed the border into Avanil, they found even more destruction. Scouts had been sent on ahead and they returned to report that the two halves of Arwyn's army had reunited and had laid siege to Avanhold, Lord Kier's castle. When Arwyn learned that the emperor's army was on the march to Dalton, he had given up the siege and crossed the border into Brosengae. He had declined to offer combat to the emperor, but his purpose had been accomplished. He had punished Flaertes for failing to take his side against "The Pretender," as he referred to Michael, and though he had been forced to give up his siege of Avanhold, he had destroyed much of the city and had decimated Lord Kier's inferior forces.

Michael had chafed to pursue him into Brosengae, but Lord Korven had convinced him that it would be unwise. Their troops were tired from slogging through the marshes on the failed campaign in Coeranys and the long forced marches across the Heartlands. Moreover, Arwyn had torched the fields and killed all the livestock at the crofts around Dalton, much of which was still in flames, thereby rendering the emperor unable to reprovision his forces. And to make matters still worse, the Manslayer had waited until the Army of Anuire had crossed the border into Avanil and then launched a series of savage raids against the beleaguered Duchy of western Alamie. Michael had to send out parties of rangers to scour the countryside for available provisions, then turn back to give aid to Duke Flaertes in his attempts to stop the Manslayer's depredations.

When the army finally returned to Anuire after the long and disastrous campaign, the troops were utterly worn out. Many had fallen in combat with Rhuobhe's elves, while others had succumbed to sheer exhaustion, hunger, and disease. It was then that Michael had vowed he would never again fail to come to the aid of loyal vassals because his troops could not arrive in time. And remembering their journey from Tuarhievel to Anuire, he had struck upon the idea of marching through the Shadow World.

Ever since, the Army of Anuire had fought almost continuously as Arwyn's forces struck out across the Heartlands and sporadic rebellions broke out throughout the empire. No sooner would the emperor's army have to respond to one of Arwyn's forays than another outbreak of warfare would erupt elsewhere in the empire. The goblins of Markazor launched an assault on the human holdings in that embattled province. Osoerde was attacked by sea raiders from Ghamoura. The gnolls of Chimaeron, emboldened by the internecine conflict in the empire, launched repeated raids against Coeranys, causing the recalcitrant Duchess Eugenie to appeal to the emperor for help in repelling the invaders.

"Let her stew in her own juices," Lord Korven had responded when the dispatch rider from Coeranys arrived in Anuire, bearing the call for aid. "We lost a lot of good men in those miserable swamps, and now she wants our help? The gnolls may gnaw on her bones for all I care!"

"No, Lord Korven," Michael had replied. "I understand how you must feel, and I must confess that under other circumstances, I would share your views. However, I must think first of the empire, and if we could not bring the Duchess Eugenie back into the fold by marching against her, we shall do so by marching to her aid. Recriminations will not serve our purposes, however justified we feel they may be. In the long run, it is the end result that matters. The empire must be whole again."

So they had marched to relieve Coeranys, only this time, they had taken a portal through the Shadow World. Futhark, who had led them through the Shadow World on their return trip from Tuarhievel, was once again their guide. For a time, he had incurred the resentment of the troops, for they had mistakenly thought at first that marching through the Shadow World was his suggestion. Futhark had not complained, but Aedan had noticed that the troops were surly and abusive toward him, which had prompted him to correct their misapprehension.

When they found out that it was the emperor's idea, they were still unsettled by the notion, but no one questioned it thereafter. By then, Michael had turned fifteen and had been on each and every campaign in the field with his troops. He had fought with them and suffered the extremes of weather with them. He did not eat until they ate; he did not sleep until they slept, and he eschewed luxurious accommodations to live in the field exactly as they did. Physically, he was still a boy, but in every other respect, they had come to regard him as a man. He had won their loyalty and admiration, and they would have followed him anywhere—even into the dreaded Shadow World.

The campaign to relieve Coeranys had marked a new beginning for the Army of Anuire. They had driven the raiding gnolls back into Chimaeron and thereafter, the Army of Anuire became known throughout the empire as Roele's Ghost Rangers for their seeming ability to be in two places almost at the same time. Michael had employed halflings as long-range scouts and messengers, so that they could pass quickly through the Shadow World and deliver intelligence about enemy troop movements and raids by gnolls and goblins and depredations by the forces of the awnsheghlien, who took advantage of the empire's instability, seeking to increase the size of their domains and pursuing bloodtheft with an unprecedented vengeance. And with each new outbreak of violence, no matter where or how far away, Michael and his troops would be there to deal with it.

One day, Roele's Ghost Rangers would be seen marching in Osoerde, and merely hours later, they would be engaged in Mhoried, two hundred miles distant. They would fight a battle with some of Arwyn's forces on the plains of Alamie, then pass into the Shadow World and reappear the same day to subdue Baruk-Azhik, over four hundred miles away. Stories of their exploits were at first greeted with disbelief, but in time, the facts became incontrovertible.

Magic was initially held to be responsible, but those who spread such tales were soon countered by those with some knowledge of the thaumaturgic arts, who pointed out that no living mage, regardless of how powerful, could summon up enough magic to transport an entire army. In time, the only other possible explanation was accepted—the Ghost Rangers traveled through the Shadow World. And that was when the Army of Anuire began to acquire its fearsome reputation. Men brave enough—or crazy enough—to travel through the Shadow World were men to be feared.

It was a reputation that aided them in battle, Aedan thought, and it was far from undeserved, for quite aside from the risks involved in any military campaign, the Shadow World posed dangers of its own. Safety was certainly increased by their numbers, but they were still subject to attacks by the undead in the world between the worlds, or by the strange and lethal creatures who inhabited the misty plane. And now, after eight long years of hard campaigning to hold the empire together, the army had acquired a fine edge, like a sword forged by a master armorer. The troops were now tough, seasoned campaigners, hard-bitten and weather-worn, and though the aging Lord Korven still served as their general, Emperor Michael now made all the decisions about strategy and tactics.

We've come a long way, Aedan thought as he rode behind his emperor through the gray and misty realm, but there is still much to be done. After eight years, though they had fought his forces many times, they had still not managed to subdue Lord Arwyn. Seaharrow was a virtually impregnable fortress, and over the years, Arwyn had established well-fortified garrisons on all approaches to his holding. He did not travel through the Shadow World, but his army was just as strong and equally well trained, besides which, he had the tactical advantage. Michael had to protect the entire empire and respond to each outbreak that occurred throughout its borders. Arwyn had only to protect the Western Marches, most of which he had brought under his domain, and there was never any way of telling where or when his troops would strike.

Despite that, a great deal had been accomplished. Save for occasional raids across the borders from Boeruine and Brosengae, the Heartlands had all been won back to the empire, as had most of the Eastern Marches. The Southern Coast had been secured, save for periodic outbreaks of fighting on the borders of Avanil and Brosengae. The Northern Marches of the empire and the territory still farther to the north remained wild outlands, and there had been no opportunity to campaign for the lands of far eastern Cerilia, where the Khinasi held sway in the south and awnsheghlien and other demihumans controlled the north.

In eight years, Michael had taken an empire that had been plunged into an interregnum and was disintegrating into warring states and brought most of it back together. All that remained now was to deal decisively with Arwyn of Boeruine. And that, of course, was much easier said than done. Boeruine had always been one of the strongest duchies in the empire and Arwyn the empire's greatest warlord. His forces and the empire's were fairly equally matched, and he had the advantage of terrain. All approaches to his holding at Seaharrow were covered by thick forest through which an army could not march without rendering itself vulnerable to destruction.

The only other approach, the one always taken by the court when it had traveled to summer in Seaharrow in the past—and that seemed so long ago now, thought Aedan—was the southern approach through Brosengae, through a narrow band of coastal plain about twenty miles wide between the southern tip of the Seamist Mountain range and the Straits of Aerele. There were several small passes through the Seamist Mountains, but taking an army through them would be an invitation to disaster. They would have been trapped like rats in a maze. And attempting an invasion along the southern route, through Brosengae, entailed all sorts of knotty problems.

Arwyn was an experienced commander, and he had anticipated every possible invasion route. He had strong fortifications built along the twenty-mile stretch of land between Avanil and Brosengae, south of the Seamist Mountains and north of the southern coast. And those fortifications had been tiered in several ranks. If the first line of garrisons happened to fall, the forces holding them could retreat to the second line, and then to the third and fourth, meaning that an attacking army would have to advance repeatedly against well-fortified positions.

Even if the garrisons all fell, the forces holding

them could continue to retreat into Brosengae, fighting holding actions all the way. Their supply lines would grow ever shorter, while those of the attacking army would extend farther as they fought for every foot of enemy ground. Despite that, Michael had attempted to advance along that route repeatedly over the years. Each time, he had been forced to turn back. It took the entire strength of the Army of Anuire to assault the garrisons along the border, while only a portion of Arwyn's troops were needed to hold them.

Each time they had advanced, Arwyn had forced them to turn back by employing the same tactics—as Michael attacked the garrisons south of the Seamist Mountains with his full strength, Arwyn detailed the troops of Taeghas and Brosengae to hold them, meanwhile using his own Army of Boeruine, augmented by troops of Talinie and goblin battalions from Thurazor, to advance along forest trails he knew well to attack western Alamie.

The situation had seemed virtually insurmountable, no matter how Aedan looked at it. Attack Arwyn in the south, and he would send the troops of Boeruine and Talinie to attack the empire in the north. Counter the attacks in the north, and the troops of Brosengae and Taeghas would attack in the south, advancing into Avanil. Back and forth it went for years, with a steadily mounting body count, and nothing was resolved. There was only one possible alternative, but it was highly dangerous.

If they could find a route through the Shadow World into the coastal region of Boeruine, then they could bring the war to Arwyn's doorstep. However, finding portals into the Shadow World was easier in regions like Thurazor, Tuarhievel, or the Spiderfell, where confluences of ley lines occurred. These lines of force that ran beneath the earth were what enabled halflings to open portals to the Shadow World. Somehow, the halflings tapped into the energy that flowed through these "underground conduits" and used it to break down the barriers between the world of daylight and the world of shadow. No one knew for certain exactly how they did it. Aedan had seen Futhark create these portals many times, but watching it gave him no clue. It seemed to work like magic. And there was a limit to how much Futhark would explain.

He had explained, however, that portals into the Shadow World could be created more reliably at or near points of ley line confluence than elsewhere, and exiting the world between the worlds in similar regions, such as Markazor, the Sielwode, or the Erebannien, was likewise more easily accomplished. In a region like Boeruine, however, where ley lines did not meet, exiting the Shadow World would be more difficult and unpredictable.

They could enter the Shadow World through a portal created just within the borders of the Spiderfell, the nearest point of ley line confluence, and then march through the Shadow World in a northwesterly direction until they reached the region that corresponded spatially with Boeruine. But with no confluence of ley lines in Boeruine, there was no sure way of predicting exactly where they would come out.

Sending halfling scouts through an exit portal first would not address the problem, since if the ley line on the other side was weak—in other words, too far away from the point at which they intended to leave the Shadow World—the area in which the scouts came out might not be accessible again.

"I don't understand," Michael had said when he and Aedan had discussed the plan with Futhark. "Do you mean the scouts would be unable to return, or that we would not be able to follow them out?"

"No, we could send scouts through," Futhark had explained, "and they could come back and report to us what they had found beyond the portal, but the portal would not necessarily open out onto the same place twice. It is conceivable, even probable, that we could come out in a different location altogether, and accidentally wind up surrounded by the forces of the enemy."

That was not exactly an encouraging thought. Nevertheless, Michael had decided to attempt it. They had gone in near the Spiderfell, which was risky in itself, as it was the domain of one of the more powerful awnsheghlien. It was said that the Spider could see through the eyes of all the arachnids in his domain and thus knew everything that went on within the Spiderfell. If this were true, and Aedan had no idea if it were, the Spider had thus far refrained from taking on the entire Army of Anuire. However, he could decide to send his creatures against the emperor's forces, and Aedan did not relish the thought of being attacked by millions of poisonous arachnids. The very thought made him shudder with disgust and fear. Nor were lethal spiders the only danger in the Spiderfell.

The awnsheghlien had the ability, empowered by bloodtheft, to create other creatures like themselves, less powerful, but still quite dangerous. And awnsheghlien also had human and demihuman troops at their command, some of which the emperor's forces had engaged on previous occasions. It was bad enough to have to face the combat-seasoned forces of Lord Arwyn without also having to do battle with gnolls, monsters, and human predators along the way.

Regardless, Michael had decided that the attempt was worth the risk. Futhark and his halfling scouts were highly dubious, but they agreed to try. They had taken on ample provisions and marched from Anuire into the Spiderfell, then gone through a portal into the Shadow World. Once they had crossed over, they turned east and marched for about three hundred miles, across the region of the misty world that spatially corresponded with the Heartlands, heading toward Boeruine.

Unfortunately, as Futhark had feared, they had failed to find a portal that would lead them to Boeruine. Instead, they had emerged on the high slopes of the Seamist Mountains, where they had fought a battle with a savage tribe of ogres into whose territory they had blundered. The hulking, brutish demihumans had been greatly outnumbered, but they had fought hard to protect their domain against what they had thought was an invasion. Reasoning with ogres was impossible. They were only slightly above the level of beasts. The army had been forced to kill them all in order to defend themselves, and despite being outnumbered, the ogres had inflicted heavy casualties. When it was over, there was no question of continuing the campaign. Michael had been forced to give it up and retreat.

So they had trudged back through the misty Shadow World, having failed in their objective. On the way back, several men were lost to poisonous snakes and the voracious albino spiders, and three of the advance guard had blundered into a sinkhole as they crossed a marsh and disappeared in an instant. The morale of the troops was low, and Michael felt responsible. He had fallen into a sullen silence and not said a word for days. Aedan had tried to lift his spirits, but it was no use. He had known the emperor all his life, and he had seen his sullen moods before. At times like these, it was best to leave him be.

Talking with Sylvanna as they rode before their troops helped Aedan keep up his own spirits, for which he was very grateful. In the past eight years, they had grown close, and with his heavy responsibilities as the lord high chamberlain, it was a great help to have someone he could talk to without having to weigh every word he said.

Aedan was not sure when he first realized he had fallen in love with her. He had guarded himself carefully against such feelings ever since his ill-considered affair with Princess Laera. However, with Sylvanna, there had never been a time when passion simply struck and overwhelmed him. His feelings for her had grown gradually, almost unnoticeably, until one day he realized she meant more to him than anyone else in the entire world, except perhaps Michael.

Michael was his liege lord and his friend, and he had a duty toward him, a duty to which he had been born. He loved him as a friend and as his sovereign, but he loved Sylvanna with all his heart and soul. He had never told her outright, but he was sure she knew. And he was sure she felt the same way, too. It was something that neither of them had ever acknowledged openly, for there were many reasons it would be unwise. They served different sovereigns, allied for the present, but still with a long history of enmity. Aside from that, Sylvanna was immortal, and though she looked younger than he did, she was many years his senior. By elvish standards, she was still quite young, but in human terms, she was old enough to be his mother. And then, of course, there was Gylvain, who had become both a friend and mentor to Aedan and the emperor. And Aedan felt sure he would not approve a match between them. So he kept his peace. He had learned his lesson with the Princess Laera.

She was still at court, for with Arwyn in rebellion, the marriage had never taken place. And though she was still unwed, her beauty had only increased with the passing years. However, things between them were extremely awkward. Aedan had made an enemy for life, and he knew that if she were given the slightest opportunity, Laera would not hesitate to take revenge for his having spurned her. Her eyes seemed to burn with hatred whenever she saw him, and Michael took pains to keep the two of them apart as much as possible. Marrying her off to a noble in a distant province might have solved the problem, but Laera's disposition had driven off a number of likely suitors. Nor were the whisperings about her at court likely to attract a husband desirous of a faithful wife.

Laera had been a mistake, thought Aedan, and he could live with it. But he did not wish to make a similar mistake with Sylvanna. The two women were as different as night and day, thought Aedan, and Sylvanna was easily ten times the woman Laera could ever hope to be, but that was no reason to do his thinking with his heart and not his mind.

"What?" asked Sylvanna.

"I said nothing," he replied.

"No, but you were looking at me very strangely just now," she said. "Is something wrong?"

"No, nothing," he replied, shaking his head. "I only wish we were back home already. I have had about as much of this dreary place as I can stand."

"It will not be long now," she replied. "We should reach Anuire tomorrow."

"I wish it were today," said Aedan uneasily. "We have had nothing but misfortune on this journey, and I have never seen the emperor's spirits so low." He glanced back at the marching lines trudging wearily behind them on foot. "It cannot help but affect the troops."

"They have experienced setbacks before," Sylvanna said. "They are veteran campaigners. They can handle it. A few weeks of unwinding in the taverns and brothels of Anuire, and they'll be ready to go out again."

Aedan glanced at her curiously. "And what about you? How do *you* unwind?"

"I am an elf," she replied. "Unlike humans, I am not a slave to my emotions."

He could not read her tone or her expression. For all the years that he had known her, it was still sometimes difficult to tell when she was joking and when she was serious. Elves had a rather peculiar sense of humor, different from that of humans, and he had never quite grown accustomed to it. Was she simply stating what she believed to be a fact, or was she directing a subtle barb at him?

"If you expect me to believe that," he replied, "I'm

afraid you will be disappointed. I know you too well."

She cocked an eyebrow at him. "You think so?"

"No one can control her emotions all the time," he said. "Not even you elves, for all your smug superiority. I have seen what you are like in battle. And I have also seen how you respond afterward, when you find out how many of your people fell. We are not so very different, after all. You only like to think we are."

"I suspect it is you who likes to think we are more similar than our natures warrant," she replied. "We *are* different, Aedan. And wishing otherwise won't change that."

She had spoken flatly, in a matter-of-fact tone, as was her manner. However, Aedan thought he had detected a trace of wistfulness in her tone. He chose not to pursue the subject.

Ahead of them, the emperor suddenly reined in, then leaned over to address Lord Korven, riding beside him at the head of the formation, some distance behind the scouts and the advance guard. Aedan and Sylvanna reined in as well, then turned their mounts and rode off to the side, as had the emperor and Lord Korven, so as not to halt the troops coming up behind them.

"What is it, Sire?" Aedan asked as they rode up beside the emperor and his general.

"I don't know," Michael replied, frowning. "Look there, on that rise." He pointed.

At first, Aedan couldn't make out what he was pointing at, but a moment later, he saw it. To their right, several hundred yards away, the land sloped up to form a rocky hogback ridge. The lower slopes of this ridge were shrouded with a thick fog, with here and there some of the scrubby, twisted trees and sparse undergrowth showing through. The upper portion of the ridge was devoid of trees or growth of any kind and rose up from the fog like rocks protruding from the sea. There was something moving along that ridge, paralleling the course of the army.

Aedan stared intently, trying to make out what it was. The shape that moved across the ridge was black as pitch and amorphous. From this distance, it was difficult to gauge its size with any accuracy. It seemed to flow, undulating in a peculiar way, extruding projections that seemed almost like legs, but did not quite hold their shape. Aedan counted four of them. It was as if an inky black cloud were *cantering* across the ridge, thought Aedan, though of course that was impossible. Or was it? In the perpetual twilight of the Shadow World, there was much that was different from the world of daylight. Was this some sort of strange creature they had not previously encountered? And if so, what was it?

Aedan recalled how, as a boy, he had watched clouds roll across the sky and had searched for shapes within them. If he looked at them long enough, some would appear to take on the shapes of animals, or faces, or birds. So too, he now watched this bizarre apparition and began to see an approximation of a form. The four leglike extrusions that flowed from its main body seemed like a horse's legs, and after a moment, he began to see the rough shape of a horse's head, even a mane, which streamed like dark and misty tendrils from the horse's neck. And the lower part of the strange black cloud looked rather like the horse's body, while the upper part seemed to take on the appearance of a rider with a cloak streaming out behind him.

"It looks like a small storm cloud," Korven said, and then echoing Aedan's thoughts, he added, "and the way the wind is blowing it across that ridge, it almost resembles a mounted knight."

"I feel no wind," said Michael with a frown.

"That's because we are below it," Korven said, then shrugged. "It is nothing. Just a cloud, that's all."

"That is no ordinary cloud," said Aedan. "It looks too small. And there is no wind propelling it. Look closely, my lord. It moves as if of its own accord."

"Nonsense," Korven said. "With all due respect, Lord Aedan, you are allowing your imagination to run away with you."

And as they watched, the cloud suddenly stopped, directly opposite them on the ridge.

"Nonsense?" asked Aedan tensely. "Look again. If the wind has ceased to blow it, why does it not drift? It's stopped. And now it's watching us."

Up on the ridge, the shape of the black cloud shifted. It seemed to solidify before their eyes, and it unquestionably took on the distinct form of a horse and rider, except the two seemed to be one form.

"That is no cloud," said Michael. He turned to young Viscount Ghieste. "Davan, ride ahead and bring me Futhark."

Young Ghieste set spurs to his mount and galloped off, returning shortly with the halfling guide seated on his horse behind him.

"You summoned me, my lord?" asked Futhark.

Michael nodded and pointed to the ridge. "Look there," he said. "See that dark form on the ridge?"

The halfling looked, then paled, and his eyes grew

wide as he beheld the shadowy form. "May all the gods protect us!" he said.

"What is it, Futhark?" asked Sylvanna.

"Doom, my lady," the halfling guide replied fearfully. He swallowed hard. "It is what I feared the most each time we came this way." He turned to Michael. "We must flee, my lord! We must leave this place at once!"

"Flee?" Lord Korven said. "From what? What *is* that thing?"

"That which has driven my people from this once sunlit world to yours," said Futhark. "It is the Cold Rider."

ANUIRE

chapter two

"What manner of creature is this Cold Rider?"
Michael asked, curious at Futhark's reaction. In all
the battles they had seen, with either humans or
demihumans, the halfling had always displayed
crafty survival instincts, but he had never shown
any fear. Until now. The dark form on the ridge had
not moved since he—or it—had stopped to watch
them. Yet there appeared to be movement *within* the
form. Watching from a distance, they could not
make out any facial features or other details, if
indeed there *was* a face, but like a reflection cast
upon a pond that rippled when a stone was tossed
into the water, the outline of the dark figure on the
ridge appeared to shift, as if unable to retain solid

form for more than a moment or two.

"He is the Usurper," Futhark said, averting his gaze from the dark form on the ridge. "Many years ago, he first appeared in our world, no one knew from where, and wherever he rode, the green plants withered, the animals died for lack of forage, the numbing cold spread and the gray mist followed. Hence the appellation he was given, the Cold Rider. As to what manner of creature he may be, I cannot say. I know only that where he passed, our world was blighted until it became the dismal place you see about you now."

"Is he dangerous to us?" asked Aedan. "However powerful a creature he may be, surely he would not attack an army."

"The Cold Rider has never been known to attack directly," replied Futhark. "It is enough merely to see him. Those who have the misfortune to lay eyes upon that evil apparition soon experience some awful tragedy, and many do not live to tell the tale. He is a harbinger of doom, a manifestation of evil itself. We must make haste to get away from here, my lord, before some evil fate befalls us."

"It all sounds like a lot of superstitious nonsense to me," Lord Korven said scornfully. "Such things as weather and the climate change purely of their own accord, and not because some ghost decrees it so. For all we know, that shape upon the ridge is nothing more than swamp gas or some strange trick of the light."

"With respect, my lord, there is much about the Shadow World that you have yet to learn, despite your travels here," said Futhark. His voice had a hollow ring to it. He was clearly frightened. "Before the

Cold Rider came, this was a world of sunlight and bountiful beauty. Brightly colored birds sang in the trees; the meadows bloomed vividly with wildflowers in profusion; faeries flitted in the forest clearings like playful fireflies; and there was game aplenty. Now look about you and tell me what you see.

"And there is much here that, thankfully, we have not yet seen or experienced. Wherever that ghastly apparition rides, the undead are sure to follow. Monsters such as your world has never seen are presaged by his appearance. Whether he commands them or they simply follow in his wake, no one can say, but it is not for nothing that my people have fled this world for yours and only return here for brief periods, and often at great risk."

"Why come at all then, if this Cold Rider poses such a danger?" asked Lord Korven, still skeptical of the halfling's claims.

"Why have you come?" Futhark countered. "Sometimes necessity entails acceptance of great risk. Shadow-walking is something only we halflings can do, and in the case of my scouts and myself, we are being well paid for the risks we take. This world is wide, and there is only one Cold Rider. The odds against encountering him are great, but this time, they have turned against us. If we do not leave this place as soon as possible, there is no telling what may happen, but I fear we may not even live to regret it."

Michael shook his head. "If you were to create a portal back into our own world now, it would bring us out well within the borders of the Spiderfell. We could easily get lost there, and I have no wish to make my weary troops do battle with the Spider's minions. We must go on, at least until we can emerge in Diemed."

"As you wish, my lord," Futhark agreed reluctantly. "But I would strongly advise that we make all haste and do not camp for the night. I know the troops are tired, but they can rest far better and more safely once we have reached Diemed than they shall here."

Michael pursed his lips, considering the halfling's suggestion. "I am loath to push the men more than necessary. They have already marched a long way after a failed campaign in which they lost many of their comrades." He fell silent for a moment, and Aedan could tell that those losses weighed heavily upon the emperor. "But if you feel strongly about the matter, we shall press on."

"I do, my lord," the halfling guide replied. "The appearance of the Cold Rider bodes us ill, very ill, indeed, and I shall not rest easy until we are well quit of this place."

Michael nodded. "So be it, then. We shall press on. Inform the men. Tell them we shall march tonight and make camp in Diemed tomorrow, where they shall have two days to take their ease. I am anxious to reach home, but that is the very least that I can do for them. Haelyn knows, they all deserve a rest."

"Look," Sylvanna said, glancing back at the ridge. "He's gone."

They turned back to the ridge. The shadowy horseman had disappeared, as if he were never there.

"An ill omen," Futhark grumbled. "An ill omen, indeed."

* * * * *

Night within the Shadow World was not much different from night in the world of daylight, at least insofar as appearances were concerned. It was the days that were different. During the day, the sun never showed itself in the world of shadow. It was like a heavily overcast and foggy day back in the world of light, with gray skies and mist perpetually floating just above the ground. At night, however, with the twisted trees and scrubby undergrowth camouflaged by darkness, one could almost think that it was any other place in Cerilia, save for the ghostly silence, occasionally broken by the cry of some . . . *thing* . . . out in the darkness. And despite having journeyed through the Shadow World on previous occasions, Aedan could never quite grow accustomed to those sounds. Or to the deathly silence when they ceased. No crickets, no night birds . . . nothing. He did not know which was worse.

On previous expeditions through the Shadow World, they had always made camp at night, for the curious suspension of time in this unearthly place meant that there was no reason to conduct forced marches through the night. They could remain within the Shadow World for days or even weeks, and when they came back out into the world of light, only minutes or hours would have passed. However, that was no reason to tarry. There were too many dangers in the Shadow World for that, and the longer they remained there, the more they risked.

When they made camp in the Shadow World, they kept bright fires burning and posted sentries around the perimeter of the camp, more than they would have in their world. And in the Shadow World, there was never any temptation for sentries to sleep on the watch. While the others warriors slept—always very lightly—the sentries on duty would remain wide awake, eyes always scanning the darkness just beyond the camp perimeter. These were lessons they had learned the hard way.

Once, Aedan recalled, during their first excursion into the Shadow World, a sentry had fallen asleep on watch. The others had been alerted by his frenzied screaming. The nearest sentries to his post were merely a score of yards away, but by the time they reached his picket, there was no sign of him. They never found him. He had simply disappeared without a trace, dragged off somewhere into the darkness. No one knew by what. After that, there were never fewer than three sentries at any one picket, and the memory of what happened to that poor soul who had disappeared kept a fine edge on their alertness. No one ever fell asleep at his post again.

This time, however, the Army of Anuire, the famous Ghost Rangers of Emperor Roele, did not make camp. They kept marching through the night, lighting their way with torches. They would be visible for miles in the darkness, but that was less cause for concern than the inability to see whatever was around them. A good number of them had seen the ominous figure of the horseman on the ridge, and it had not taken long before word of the Cold Rider spread throughout the ranks. Many of the troops had become friendly with the halflings that marched with them, and by nightfall, there wasn't one of them who did not know what the Cold Rider represented. Aedan supposed there was nothing that could have been done about that. Though it was cause for unrest among the troops, at the same time, it would keep them on their toes. With men that were as tired and dispirited as they were, that was perhaps only for the best. They could not afford to relax their vigilance until they had passed back through the portal and reached Diemed.

They kept moving at a steady pace, with the emperor and his retinue leading the formation on their mounts, Aedan bearing Michael's standard, and Sylvanna riding by his side just a few yards behind them. The advance guard had been strengthened and pulled back, so that they were only a short distance in front of the main body, their torches clearly visible. The archers marched with arrows nocked in their drawn crossbows, and almost every man had his hand upon his sword hilt. The tension in the air was palpable.

How much farther? Aedan could not be sure. He did not know this territory as well as did the halfling scouts, but by the first gray light of morning—if one could truly call it light—he felt they should have covered enough distance to be able to emerge just beyond the borders of the Spiderfell. Morning could not come soon enough.

As he rode at a slow walk, Aedan kept thinking about the apparition they had seen upon the ridge. Just who or what was the Cold Rider? Could he be human, demihuman, or something else entirely? How much of what the halfling said was literally true and how much was merely his belief?

Halflings were a strange lot. Over the past eight years, Aedan had come to know the halflings who marched with them, but there was still a great deal about them that he did not fully understand. Their beliefs, for one thing. They swore by the gods—or at least Futhark and his scouts did—but Aedan had never seen halflings attend services at any of the temples. For that matter, there were many humans who never took part in religious services, but still had faith in the gods. With the natural tendency that halflings had to assimilate themselves into whatever culture was predominant in the places where they lived, it was difficult to tell what they really believed. And the halflings never spoke about it.

They were willing to answer certain questions about themselves, but only to a point. They had a way of turning aside unwanted questions by speaking in circles, appearing to give replies when in fact they were engaged in loquacious obfuscation. Talking to a halfling could sometimes be like trying to catch a will-o'-the-wisp, thought Aedan. They seemed outgoing enough and friendly, but there was still much that they kept to themselves.

For all the times that Futhark had guided them on expeditions through the Shadow Word, this was the first time he had ever made mention of the Cold Rider, and if they had not seen him—or it—Aedan was sure Futhark would not have volunteered the information.

If he was so afraid of this mysterious apparition, why keep coming back to this place? Why agree to guide them through the Shadow World? Why not simply stay in Cerilia, in the comparative safety of the world of daylight, and never return to this place that he and his people fled? Was it truly only a question of money, or necessity, as Futhark had put it? Halflings needed to live, like anybody else, but there were many halflings—the vast majority of them, so far as Aedan knew—who had found vocations for themselves as craftsmen, traders, merchants or entertainers in Cerilia and never went back to the world from which they had come. What made Futhark and his scouts so different?

Of course, they were paid extremely well. But could that have been enough? If the Cold Rider filled them with such fear that they had fled their world, why return and risk encountering him? Aedan tried to put himself in Futhark's place as he considered possibilities, the way his father taught him. Suppose something had made him flee his own world, the home that he had always known? Might there still not be, despite the dangers, a desire to go back? Perhaps. He could not imagine leaving Anuire permanently. It was the place of his birth, the city where he had grown up. He knew every street and alleyway like the back of his own hand. It would be difficult to leave, never to return. Always, he felt certain, there would be a pull back to his own homeland—and if something had happened to blight Anuire the way this world had been blighted, he had no doubt he would nurture a desire to see it returned to the way it once had been.

Here he was now, out of time, riding through a cold and misty world that always seemed more nightmare than reality, and he felt a desperate longing to be back in his own world, on familiar ground. Might not, then, the halflings feel the same?

Back home, he would visit the grave of his father every time he returned from a campaign or felt the weight of his responsibilities pulling him down. He would go early in the morning, when the cemetery was still deserted, and sit down on the ground beside the mound of earth that marked his father's resting place, and he would speak to him, unburdening himself and asking for advice and guidance. It was not the same, of course, as when his father had still been alive, though Aedan liked to think somewhere in the heavens his father could still hear him and send him strength and wisdom. He took great comfort in it. Perhaps it was like that for Futhark and the other halflings who periodically returned to the world from which they fled. It was no longer the same, but they still took some comfort in returning.

"Of all the humans I have ever known," Sylvanna said, breaking into his thoughts, "your silences speak loudest."

Aedan looked at her and smiled wanly. "Forgive me. I am not being a very good traveling companion on this journey."

"That was not what I meant," she said as she rode beside him. "I was not complaining. I was merely remarking on the fact that I can always tell when you are troubled."

"Have I become so obvious? That is a bad trait in an imperial minister. I shall have to correct it."

"We shall make it back; don't worry."

"It is my job to worry. The emperor has neither time nor the inclination. I must do his worrying for him."

"And who worries for you?"

"I worry for us both. It can be quite exhausting."

"If you like, I can worry for you. Then that would relieve you of at least some of your burden."

He glanced at her and saw that she was smiling. He grinned despite himself. "You know, sometimes

I think you're actually beginning to act human."

She sniffed disdainfully. "Well, you don't have to be insulting."

The screams were sudden and terrible. They cut through the stillness of the night, coming from behind them, at the rear of the troop formation. Aedan and Sylvanna wheeled their horses simultaneously, and Sylvanna's sword sang free of its scabbard. The men in the ranks immediately behind them stopped and without hesitation instantly turned to either side, prepared to meet anything that might come up on their flanks. Their battle-seasoned instincts served them well, thought Aedan, and it was a good thing too, as became frighteningly apparent within moments.

In the darkness, Aedan could not see what was happening back at the rear of the formation, but he could see the torches there bobbing wildly and erratically, some falling to the ground as the men dropped them to engage whatever was attacking . . . or else fell to the ground themselves. But before Aedan could do anything, he heard rapid hoofbeats coming up behind him and an instant later saw the emperor gallop past, sword in hand, heading full speed toward the rear of the formation.

"Sire, *wait!*" Aedan called out, but Michael was already disappearing into the darkness. He had moved so quickly that not even Lord Korven or any of his retinue riding at the front of the formation had time to react. Aedan swore. "*Go after him, you fools!*" he shouted, setting spurs to his own horse.

Sylvanna was right behind him as they set off at a gallop in the emperor's wake. And it was then that Aedan heard a sound that made his blood run cold.

An unearthly, ululating, keening sound that was half moan, half cry. He had heard it once before, on a previous expedition through the Shadow World, and that time over a hundred men had died.

It was the cry of the undead.

"Aedan! Watch your flank!" Sylvanna called out from behind him as they galloped headlong after Michael. Aedan glanced to his left, since the troops were on his right, and he saw the walking corpses coming, shambling through the twisted trees like drunken specters.

Some of them were wearing battle dress . . . or what remained of it. Rusting armor that squeaked and scraped as they moved; battered helms, some of which were cut almost clean through where a sword had split the skull; rotting tunics beneath chain mail encrusted with rust and covered with spiderwebs; greaves covered with dirt and mud; buckled shields with faded devices on them; tattered remnants of leather shoes and flapping breeches that were little more than rags. Others wore the rotting garb of peasants, through which decayed flesh and age-browned bones were clearly visible. Decomposing faces stared at him with eyeless sockets in which worms and maggots writhed. And as if the sight of them alone were not bad enough, every one of the horrific things was armed. Those that did not bear swords or spears carried pitchforks, axes, or make-shift clubs.

They had flanked the army, perhaps even surrounded it, Aedan didn't know, but the first attack came on the rear of their formation. Now the walking dead were pouring out of the woods on both sides of the trail. One of them came out in front of

Aedan, brandishing a spear. Without slowing, Aedan raised his sword and brought it down as he passed, cutting the shambling corpse's arm off at the shoulder. It fell writhing to the ground, but still the creature clutched at his stirrup as he went by. Aedan's horse dragged it along for several yards before Aedan managed to kick the damned thing loose.

The army didn't panic. That would have cost them their lives, and they all knew it. Tired as they were, they kept formation and fought the undead as they advanced. The wretched creatures moved slowly, but what they lacked in speed they made up for in relentlessness. And they could not be killed, for they were already dead. The only way to fight them was to dismember them completely, and even then they kept on coming, dragging themselves along the ground like snails. Blades rose and fell repeatedly, and tired as the troops were, they realized they could not pause in their grim work even for an instant. They had faced undead before, though not this many, and a lot of them had not survived to tell the tale.

Aedan saw the emperor. He had ridden to the rear of the formation, where the first attack occurred, and he was rallying the troops, whose formation had been broken up by the initial attack. He called out orders to the men as he laid about him with his blade, turning his horse this way and that to meet the shambling figures that came at him from all sides.

For a moment, Aedan had a memory from childhood leap unbidden to his brain. He recalled how he had tried to frighten young Prince Michael with lurid and horrifying stories of the Shadow World, spitefully hoping to give him nightmares like the ones he'd had when he was younger. And though Michael had dreamed of the Shadow World after being told those tales just before his bedtime, unlike Aedan, in his dreams, the prince had fearlessly fought the monsters and defeated them. Now, ironically and frighteningly, it was happening in real life.

And just as young Prince Michael had shown absolutely no fear in his childhood dreams, the adult emperor displayed none now. And that was precisely what alarmed Aedan as he saw him plunging his mount into the steadily advancing ranks of the undead.

Fear was a function of self-preservation, but it was an emotional response that was utterly lacking in the emperor. Courage, heightened strength and senses, regeneration, and protection from evil were all among his attributes, blood abilities that he had manifested after he had passed through puberty, and since his blood powers stemmed directly from the line of Anduiras, Michael possessed more of them than most. His blood totem was the lion, and like that noble beast, Michael possessed unrelenting courage and fearsome savagery in battle. However, his blood abilities did not render him invulnerable, though he often acted as if they did. And as Aedan saw him plowing like a juggernaut into the advancing ranks of the undead attacking the rear column of the army, his stomach tightened and fear-induced adrenalin hammered through his system.

As young Ghieste, Lord Korven, Viscount Alam, and the rest of Michael's mounted retinue came galloping up behind Aedan and Sylvanna, Aedan raised his sword above his head and cried out, "To the emperor!"

Without hesitation, they followed him, cutting their way through the staggering, animated corpses to Michael's side. However foolhardy Michael's heroics may have been, thought Aedan, they had galvanized the troops. On seeing him riding to join in their defense, they rallied, and their battle cry of "Roele! Roele!" went up, echoing through the darkness. Most of the torches had been flung to the ground, since the troops could not fight and hold them at the same time. Some of them had ignited the undergrowth, which was slow to burn because of the misty damp, but it nevertheless gave Aedan an idea.

"Torch the trees!" he cried out repeatedly as he laid about him with his sword, and in moments, men not in the forefront of the fighting began throwing their torches into the woods and snatching up those which had been dropped and tossing them, as well.

With so many torches soaked in pitch flung into the woods and undergrowth, the flames began to spread despite the dampness, and it gave them light by which to see. At the same time, it provided an unexpected bonus. The undead burned.

With all their bodily fluids long since dried up, the corpses caught fire like kindling. Despite that, they kept on coming, impervious to pain, burning as they walked. Men hacked away at flaming bodies that advanced upon them, but inevitably, the corpses succumbed to the fire and collapsed to the ground.

However, they were not the only ones who fell. Aedan saw many bodies lying on the ground, and among the burning or dismembered and still writhing corpses of the undead were many of the troops. Some were badly wounded, others had been slain, and dismembered corpses gnawed at many of them. Those still alive but too injured to move screamed horribly as the flames reached them, but there was nothing to be done. There was no time or opportunity to pull them back to safety, for there was no safe ground anywhere. The formation of the troops broke up into a wild melee. The undead kept pressing forward, rank upon rank, and the soldiers of the Army of Anuire hacked away at them like men possessed.

Aedan fought his way to Michael's side, with Sylvanna and the others close behind him. They tried to form a protective ring about the emperor, but Michael was not cooperating. He did not remain still for an instant, turning his horse this way and that as the animal reared and plunged through the grisly ranks as flame and smoke rose all around them. Then Aedan felt a strong wind come up behind him, and as he felt it plucking at his clothes, he heard Gylvain's voice within his mind.

"Futhark has opened a portal ahead," he said. *"The front ranks are passing through. Get the emperor and bring him back to the front while the rearguard fights a holding action!"*

The wind passed on, circling the fighting, fanning the flames away from the main body of the troops and blowing them back at the undead.

"Sire!" Aedan cried out. "We have a portal! Hurry, Sire, come quickly!"

"Not until the troops are through!" Michael shouted back.

"Sire! For Haelyn's sake, come *on!*"

A number of the men around them heard the exchange and shouted out for Michael to go back. Within moments, the cry was taken up in unison by everyone around them until the firelit night reverberated with the shouts.

"Roele back! Roele back!"

But before he could respond to the entreaties of his troops, disaster struck. As Aedan watched, horrified, Michael's horse reared up, striking out at several advancing corpses with its hooves, and one of them plunged a spear into the animal's belly. The horse gave out a shrill, whinnying cry of pain and went down hard. Michael tumbled from the saddle.

"*No!*" Aedan shouted, urging his mount forward, but several walking corpses blocked his way. He chopped at them frantically with his blade, trying to reach the emperor. The troops fighting closest to him saw it too, and the men surged forward, heedless of their own safety as they tried to reach him. But already Michael was encircled by at least a dozen of the undead, and Aedan could catch no glimpse of him as he desperately fought to reach him.

Suddenly, one of the undead near Michael was brought down, and then another literally went flying, hurled through the air with astonishing force. Another one went down, and another, and bodies were flying everywhere. Aedan reached Michael, who like a dervish lay about him with his blade, eyes wide, lips pulled back in a grimace of bestial rage, blood pouring from several wounds. He had unleashed his blood power of divine wrath, and Aedan knew there could be no reasoning with him till it was over.

It was beyond control, and in this godlike state of fearsome rage and bloodlust, Michael would smite friend and foe alike. The episode would not last long, for it called upon all the resources of the body, and when it had passed, it would leave him so exhausted he could barely move. But while he was caught in the grip of this overwhelming power, Michael was like an indiscriminate juggernaut of death, and Aedan did not dare approach him.

"Stay back!" he shouted to Sylvanna as she started to the emperor's aid. She glanced at him, startled, then realized what had occurred when she saw Michael laying waste to the undead around him, snarling and growling like a cornered animal, oblivious of his wounds.

Among all the powers that had passed down to the blooded from the old gods, divine wrath was the rarest and most dangerous, for once it was unleashed, there was no stopping it until it ran its course. Those few who had it used it only as a last resort, and only in the most dire extremities because it was a power that possessed its wielder absolutely, releasing the feral beast within and magnifying it many times. It turned a human into a raging berserker incapable of rational thought or self-control, bent only on mayhem and survival.

Blood powers were not a certain thing. It was known which hereditary blood abilities ran within each line, but there was no way of predicting which ones would be inherited by any given offspring. The potential for all the blood abilities that ran within the line was there, but some remained latent, to be passed on and perhaps manifested by the succeeding generation. Some manifested themselves shortly after puberty, while others could remain latent for years, dormant until they suddenly manifested without warning.

In most cases, this was no cause for concern, as the majority of blood abilities could manifest themselves without risk to others. Heightened senses could suddenly appear, or animal affinity reveal itself through communication with a totem beast, or iron will appear, or the power to heal. Such abilities did not expose anyone to danger. But others, such as the power to raise elementals or manifest divine wrath, or—in the case of those bloodlines that came down from the evil Azrai—commute decay through touch, could cause injury or death.

The first time Michael had released his divine wrath in battle, he had done so unintentionally. He was sixteen then, and the army had been attacked by gnolls one night after it made camp. The feral demihumans, a species that appeared to be part man, part wolf, attacked them while they slept, butchering the sentries so quickly and efficiently that they never knew what hit them. The only warning that the sleeping army had were the screams of the first victims.

Michael had come out of his tent, bearing his sword, and was immediately attacked. And that was when it had happened. Suddenly, it was as if he had become a gnoll himself in all but physical appearance. Though he was just sixteen, several years of campaigning had put plenty of lean muscle on his frame. Still, Aedan was not prepared for what he saw that night.

Michael had suddenly stopped being Michael and instead became some demonic force, unstoppable and unrelenting. His features had become almost unrecognizable as they twisted themselves into a mask of bestial savagery, and the sounds that came from his throat were growls that were not even remotely human. He killed every one of the creatures that came at him. Afterward, the soldiers who had seen it spread the word, and Michael's reputation grew. They all knew what it was. Many of them were blooded themselves, though in the entire army, no one else possessed that power. It was known to run only in the purest bloodlines of Anduiras, Basaia, and Masela, but only a few of the blooded ever manifested it. Aedan knew of only one other blooded noble who was known to have it—Arwyn of Boeruine.

This time, the soldiers recognized the state their emperor was in and did their best to move close enough to give him protection while at the same time keeping well out of his reach. In his state he would attack them as well if they got close enough. Aedan's problem, aside from trying to survive himself, was that with Michael in this state, there was no way he could get him to the portal Futhark had opened back into their own world. He had no choice but to wait until the wrath had run its course, and then whisk Michael away. Once the wrath had faded, Michael would be helpless.

There was no time to pay attention to it, but with a quick glance behind him, Aedan saw that the troops had been withdrawing gradually as the battle had progressed. The tide of it had carried them forward—backward the way Aedan was facing as he fought in the rearguard—toward the portal the halfling guide had opened for them. Ranks had formed on either side of it, protecting the opening as those in the middle moved through, and by now, most of the troops had already passed into it. They had formed into an inverted **V** formation, with the point of the opening of the **V** leading directly through the portal. Aedan was close enough to see it now.

All around them, the misshapen trees and scrubby undergrowth were in flames, fanned by Gylvain's wind as he circled round and round, keeping the fire burning while at the same time blowing the flames away from the troops and toward the undead attackers. There were fewer of them than there were before, and the ground was littered with dismembered, flaming body parts that writhed and jerked. The portal behind them appeared as a swirling, opaque opening in the air, outlined by smoke and flame. As the troops poured through, only a few warriors remained now, along with the emperor's mounted retinue, which would not leave without Michael. Aedan could not tell how much time had passed, but the sky was beginning to turn gray. The fire had spread outward from the battle, so that a wide swathe of forest was burning all around them, lighting up the area for a considerable distance and sending clouds of smoke into the air. As Aedan fought, with Sylvanna at his side, he glanced toward Michael every chance he got, when there was a moment's respite.

The emperor's movements were slowing now, the wrath fading. He had struck down all of his opponents and, in normal battle, his sword would have been red with blood. However, the undead had no blood, and all their blades had remained clean. Aedan's arm was tired from slashing and hacking for what seemed like hours. The muscles in his shoulder burned with exertion, and he was breathing heavily. But though the Anuirean numbers dwindled rapidly as the troops passed through the portal, so did those of the undead, falling aflame. Aedan cleaved one burning attacker from head to waist with a powerful stroke of his heavy blade, and the force of the blow almost made him fall from his saddle. Now there were no more of them within close reach, and he quickly turned back toward the emperor.

Michael had disposed of the last of his opponents, and though some still advanced through the trees, staggering on even though their bodies were in flames, there were none within reach of him. He saw Michael slump, supporting himself with his sword, and knew the wrath had passed. At once, he spurred his tired mount and rode to Michael's side.

"Sire! Sire, give me your hand, quickly!"

Looking dazed, Michael gazed at him dully, but he held out his hand. Aedan took his right foot from the stirrup so that Michael could use it to get up behind him. He pulled him up onto his mount and felt Michael slump against his back as he got on. He was too weary even to sheathe his blade. His left arm went around him, and Aedan sheathed his own blade, then grasped Michael's wrist to hold him steady. Immediately, he wheeled his horse and spurred it to a gallop, heading for the portal.

"Come on!" he shouted over his shoulder. "Pull back! We're going through!"

The others needed no encouragement. They turned and followed Aedan and the emperor, the mounted retinue pausing only long enough to allow the foot soldiers to run before them. As they passed through the portal, the ranks guarding its entrance collapsed their **V** formation and went through after them. The last ones shouted to Futhark, and the halfling raised his arms to close the portal behind them.

"Wait!" Aedan shouted. "Gylvain!"

He felt a breeze ruffle his cloak, then a familiar, lilting voice spoke in his mind. "*I'm here.*"

"All right!" shouted Aedan. "Go on, close it!"

Three more flaming corpses staggered through the portal, and the men fell on them, hacking them to pieces until there were nothing but burning body parts upon the ground.

As Aedan watched the portal close, the air folding in upon itself in surreality, the glow of the flames beyond it disappeared from view, and only the gray light of dawn remained. In fact, he thought, the troops guarding the portal had not been the only ones left on the other side. There had been many wounded they had been forced to leave behind. Aedan hoped the fire had gotten to the poor devils. Burning to death was an awful way to go, but there were some things that were worse.

He heaved a long and deep sigh of relief, then looked around and realized his relief was much too premature. As the sun began to rise, he saw the thick pine forest all around them and the heavy underbrush and realized they had not reached the safety of the open plains of Diemed.

They were in the Spiderfell.

* * * * *

"He's up to something, by Haelyn, I can smell it!" said Arwyn of Boeruine, smashing his fist down on the table and upsetting his goblet. The servants rushed to mop up the spilled mead, right the heavy silver goblet, and refill it. "Why has there been no word from any of our scouts or informants?"

"There *has* been word, my lord," replied Baron Derwyn calmly. He knew that when his father was in one of his surly moods, keeping a calm temper and demeanor was advisable. "Our spies reported that the emperor—"

"The Pretender, you mean," his father interrupted, scowling.

"Indeed," said Derwyn, agreeing indirectly, though he still could bring himself to use that detestable term. He *knew* the truth and would not be a hypocrite, not for his father's sake or anyone's. "They have reported that Michael left Anuire with his army over a week ago, but there has been no word of him since. And our scouts along the borders have reported seeing no signs of any advancing troops."

Arwyn gritted his teeth and shook his head. "They've gone into the blasted Shadow World again," he said. "The question is, where will they come out? And when?" He smashed his fist down on the table once again, once more spilling his mead. The servants mopped it up again and once again refilled his goblet. Arwyn paid no attention to them.

"Our garrisons along the border are on full alert," said Derwyn. "And advance parties of rangers have been sent out from Taeghas, Brosengae, and Talinie, in addition to our own complement, which departed to scout the border between our lands and Alamie. There is no way they can approach unseen."

"Unless he figures out some way to come out of

the Shadow World well within our borders," Arwyn said. "Perhaps even on the plain outside Seaharrow, itself."

Derwyn frowned. "I thought you said that was not possible, that they needed to employ a portal in the vicinity of Thurazor or the Five Peaks region, where the ley lines come in confluence."

Arwyn nodded, "Yes, and for a long time, I had thought so, too. However, our halfling scouts tell me that it *is* possible to create a portal where there is no confluence of ley lines, though it entails great risk and cannot be done reliably."

"How?" asked Derwyn.

"How in bloody bollocks should *I* know how?" his father replied irritably. "You try to get one of those miserable knee-whackers to explain anything and all that happens is you get lost in word salad. They'll answer amenably enough, but half of what they say makes no bloody sense at all! The point is, it can be done, but there is no guarantee they will be able to open up a portal when they want to, or come out *where* they want to."

Derwyn shrugged. "Then it amounts to the same thing, does it not? They cannot do it."

"But they can *try*," said Arwyn. "And however slim, the possibility exists that they just might succeed, despite the risks."

Derwyn leaned back in his chair, frowning thoughtfully. Yes, he thought, that was just the sort of thing Michael *would* do. The risk factor, no matter how significant, never seemed to bother him. It had been that way when they had played war games as children, and it was the same way now, when they made war in earnest.

As if echoing his thoughts, his father said, "I wouldn't put it past that miserable Pretender to attempt just such a thing."

Derwyn gave him a quick glance. His father had repeated the old lie so often, perhaps he actually believed it now. It was as if he thought that if he said it often enough, it would become the truth.

At first, his father had insisted that a strong hand had to assume the regency when Prince Michael was abducted by a goblin raiding party and taken back to Thurazor. He had appointed himself regent and vowed vengeance on the perpetrators of the hateful crime, but after Lord Tieran had outfoxed him by fleeing with the empress and her daughters while his father made at least a token effort—more of a pretence, really—at leading a rescue party into the Aelvinnwode, the story had begun to change.

As soon as he found out that Lord Tieran had absconded with the empress, his father had flown into a wild rage, smashing furniture and kicking the servants. Then after he'd calmed down, he had sent out dispatch riders across the empire to report that Prince Michael's remains had been discovered by his rescue party in the Aelvinnwode. What his knights, who had been on that rescue party along with Derwyn, thought of this was anybody's guess. Needless to say, they had never seen any remains, because the entire thing had been a fabrication, but they knew better than to contradict their lord. Derwyn's father had not seen fit to mention Aedan Dosiere in his dispatches, as he had not considered him important, which was fortunate for him, as it would have made later permutations of the story somewhat awkward.

After he made his formal alliance with Gorvanak, the goblin prince of Thurazor, his father changed the story once more. It would hardly do to vow vengeance on Prince Michael's murderers and then enter an alliance with them, so the goblins of Thurazor could not bear the blame. It was bandits who had killed the prince, renegade brigands from the Five Peaks region, as had been revealed by certain evidence the goblins had turned over to Lord Arwyn. Precisely what the nature of this "evidence" was had never been made clear. But that was not the final version of the story, either.

When Aedan and Michael had appeared back in Anuire, that had to be accounted for somehow, so Michael was accused of being an imposter, a look-alike or some boy whose appearance had been changed by elven magic so that he would resemble the prince. Since Aedan had never been mentioned in the original dispatch, that made the next variation easier. Aedan Dosiere, whose duty it had been to protect Prince Michael, was branded a coward who had fled his liege lord's side when the bandits had attacked, and to safeguard his own claim to power and the reputation of his son, Lord Tieran had cooked up the outrageous tale that the two boys had been rescued by the elves. The boy who called himself Prince Michael was a damnable imposter, a pretender, a tool to enable Lord Tieran to justify his claim to power. And then, of course, after Lord Tieran died, the story needed to be modified once more, and the final version had it that this "Michael the Pretender" had merely assumed Lord Tieran's place, following his plans, with "hidden interests" behind him to support his claim to the Iron Throne.

Exactly who or what these "hidden interests" were was never specified, but it was broadly hinted that the elves, those old enemies of humankind, were the ones behind it all.

Derwyn never thought people would believe any of these stories, but many did. Repeat something often enough and loud enough, and people eventually came to accept it. Or at least some people. And now it appeared as if his father had managed to convince himself, as well.

"With my own eyes, I saw the poor boy's broken body . . ." was usually more or less how the refrain went whenever Arwyn told the story, with subtle variations, depending on his audience. And now he apparently believed it, too. Derwyn had no idea what to make of that, but he knew better than to contradict him.

He had been there. He knew that no bodies had ever been found, neither Michael's nor Aedan's nor anybody else's. They had simply ridden out across the fields, headed down several forest trails without even going in very far, and then returned. It had all amounted to nothing more than exercising the horses. But none of the men who had gone out on that so-called "rescue party" ever talked about it, not even among themselves, so far as Derwyn knew. The archduke was the man who buttered their bread, and they all knew it.

Derwyn didn't like it. Not one bit. His father had always seen to it that he was trained properly and hard so that he could take his place one day and, to that end, as Derwyn got older, he eventually became his father's second-in-command. He had led troops in the field against Michael, the rightful emperor, his childhood friend. He had seen him several times, once fairly close, and had recognized both him and Aedan. Once, in one of the many battles over the years that had failed to resolve anything, they had almost crossed swords. The two armies had clashed, and it became a huge melee, dust raised like a cloud by churning hooves and feet, and it had been one of those occasions when suddenly, for a moment, one found himself in a small island of calm in the midst of a pitched battle. And there was Michael, mounted on his war-horse.

Derwyn had recognized the imperial symbol of Roele on his shield and tabard, as Michael had recognized the eagle of Boeruine on his. Derwyn had lifted his visor and Michael had done the same. For a moment, they had simply looked at one another, and then the tide of battle forced them apart. But in that one moment, Derwyn had seen the prince, the boy he had remembered. He had grown older, and his hair was longer, and a dark beard was starting to come in, but he had recognized his childhood friend. If he had ever harbored doubts about his true identity—and he had not—they would have been dispelled right there and then. It was Michael. No question about it. And the expression on his face had been one of sadness . . . and disappointment.

Derwyn felt torn. He was his father's son, and even if he had not loved his father, which he did, despite his harshness, he would have owed him a son's obedience. And the Duchy of Boeruine was his birthright. He had to fight to protect it. But to protect it from the rightful emperor, by whose ancestors' grace they had the holding? That was treason. Yet he was caught in a situation not of his own choosing, in circumstances he could not control. Be loyal to his father, and he would be a traitor to the emperor. Or else loyal to the emperor and a traitor to his father. Damned for a dishonored traitor either way.

Derwyn was tired of the civil war, though no one save the common people called it that. Michael called it a rebellion, which Derwyn supposed it was, in fact. His father called Michael a usurper and a pretender and called it a struggle against tyranny and referred to the forces under his command as "freedom fighters." He would never admit to the truth, that in his bid for power, he had underestimated Tieran. Though they had never spoken about it directly, Derwyn realized . . . now . . . what his father had intended.

Back when it all started, eight years ago at Summer Court, he had not really understood any of it. But now that he was older, looking back, he recalled how solicitous his father had been toward the empress, how he had tried to ingratiate himself to her, to charm her, taking every opportunity to do her some little service and express his sympathy for all she had been going through. He recalled being puzzled by his father's manner toward the empress. He had not acted that way with anyone else, not even Derwyn's departed mother. Back then, Derwyn had assumed his father was merely being a gracious host and doing his duty to the empress. Still, there had always been a tension in the manner of the empress when his father was around. Now, of course, Derwyn knew why.

His father had been trying to court her. Derwyn supposed he might have been able to excuse it if it had been love, but he knew his father did not love the empress, no more than he had loved his mother when she was still alive. Arwyn of Boeruine did not love women. He possessed them. What his father loved was power . . . and the fighting. That was where they differed. Arwyn of Boeruine loved war. His son was sick to death of it.

How things had changed since he and Michael were both children, Derwyn thought. He was only a few years older, but eight years of ceaseless campaigning had made a lot of difference. He had grown up hard and fast. He imagined Michael had, as well. That expression on his face when they had met on the field of battle that time had spoken volumes. They were no longer children who dressed up in toy suits of armor and played at war with wooden swords, thinking it was grand and glorious. They had learned the truth, that war was terrible and sickening and ate away at a man's soul. So why, then, did his father love it so? What made him different? Derwyn couldn't understand it.

They would never have thought that war was some noble and wonderful adventure if, as children, they had seen a battlefield in the aftermath of conflict. The ground torn up and littered with the bodies of the dead and dying, men with wounds so terrible that it made the gorge rise in one's throat to look upon the sight, the moans and groans and screams of agony, the horrid buzzing of the flies attracted by the blood and the smell . . . the *smell!* Nothing could possibly be worse, thought Derwyn, than the putrid smell of war. When a man died in combat, his bowels let loose, and after a battle had been fought, the smell of human excrement and bodies rotting in the sun was so overpowering it brought tears to the eyes.

All those times when they had "killed" each other in their play and clutched at imaginary mortal wounds, each trying to outdo the other in the dramatic manner of his "death" . . . Would we have found death so dramatic, Derwyn thought, if we had actually *seen* it? He had seen more of it than he could ever have imagined, and there was nothing even remotely dramatic about it. Except, perhaps, its ugliness and pathos. And the soldiers were not the only ones to suffer.

Derwyn had seen the tormented faces of the families as they waited on the streets along the route of the army's return, watching anxiously, fearfully, for their husbands and fathers and sons. He had heard the wails and screams of wives and mothers when the men that they were waiting for did not return, or came back maimed and crippled. He had heard and seen the crying of the children when they saw the broken bodies of their fathers or learned that they were never coming back. And each time he went through such a terrible experience, he felt as if another part of him had died. How could any man in his right mind love such an awful thing as war?

Perhaps, in some way, despite the horror of the reality, his father had somehow retained that part of boyhood that thought war was something grand. Or perhaps he had simply seen so much of it that its awful cost did not affect him anymore. Was that what he had to look forward to?

The first time they came back from a campaign, his "baptism of fire," as his father had proudly referred to it, Derwyn had been so shattered by the experience that he fled to his room at the earliest opportunity, bolted the door, and fell down and wept. It was not himself he wept for, but those who had been killed or crippled, and he wept for their mothers, wives, and children, whose torment had struck him to the quick. But over the years, each time it became a little easier, affected him a little less. And that scared him more than anything else. He saw himself gradually turning into his father, who saw only the prize at the end of the journey, and not the toll one paid along the way. Perhaps that was why his mother had died brokenhearted. When the capacity to feel the pain of others had been burned out of a man, the capacity to love was gone as well.

Why did it have to be this way? Why was it not enough to be Archduke of Boeruine, one of the most powerful and respected nobles in the empire? Why did his father have to have it all? The people were sick of war. Derwyn saw it in their faces when the army was on the march. He had seen it in Boeruine, in Taeghas, in Brosengae and Avanil, in western Alamie; everywhere they went, he saw the faces of the common people watching from along the roadway, or in the fields where they worked as the army passed, or in the towns and villages they went through. It was their toil that supported the conflict, their crops taken, their livestock butchered, their fields trampled. And they probably didn't care who won. They just wanted it to end. As did he.

"I grow weary of this waiting," said his father in a surly tone. He picked up his goblet and drained it, setting it back down on the table so hard that Derwyn thought it would break. "If Gorvanak had done his part, we could have ended this cursed stalemate by now. He promised he would take Dhoesone, then cross its borders and attack Tuarhievel, striking from the west while the goblins of Markazor attacked the elven kingdom from the east. Trapped between the goblin forces, the elves could never have prevailed. Once Tuarhievel and Dhoesone had fallen, we could take Cariele and the goblins could march through Markazor on Elinie. Then the Pretender's holdings would be encircled by lands that we control.

"It seemed a foolproof plan, but now Gorvanak complains that Zornak of Markazor refuses to cooperate. He fears to march in force upon Tuarhievel for fear that troops from Mhoried will move against his holdings while his forces are away. He will do it when Mhoried has been secured by us, but not before. And how in bloody blazes can I march on Mhoried when I have no idea where the Army of Anuire is? If I take Mhoried and they attack the garrisons at Brosengae again, or strike into our lands, we will be cut off."

"We should have seized western Alamie when we had the chance and held it instead of marching on into Avanil," said Derwyn. Then we would not have needed Zornak, and Avanil would have been flanked by territories we controlled."

"Oh, so you're a general now, are you, you young pup?" Arwyn said derisively. "If we had held western Alamie, it is we who would have been flanked, you fool. If we were cut off from the forest trails back into our lands, our forces would have been trapped between Duke Alam's troops and the Army of Anuire. We would have had to fight every inch of our way back home, with nothing to be gained. No, Avanil is the key to victory. Take Avanil, and we have Ghieste. Then press south and push the Army of Anuire right into the Straits."

"Only we cannot attack Avanil without marching through western Alamie once again," Derwyn replied. "And each time we try, Michael counters by striking at the garrisons in Brosengae, preventing our forces there from crossing into Avanil to support our attack from the south. And the distance we must cover through western Alamie leaves him plenty of time to break off his assault upon the garrisons and march north to counter our advance while Avan holds his southern borders. It is a no-win situation. The Seamist Mountains, which secure Taeghas from attack by Avanil, also work against us by forcing us to march around them every time. If we could only find a way to march across them—"

"And lose half our forces to the ogres before we even meet the Army of Anuire? You tell me how we can avoid the ogres and get our supply train across those bloody mountains and maybe I will try it. Until then, leave the strategy to me."

"I did not mean—"

"Who cares what you meant?" Arwyn drained another goblet. "That bastard Gorvanak won't move against Tuarhievel unless I support him with troops from Talinie, but I need those troops to keep the Army of Anuire at bay. Especially when I don't know where in blazes they are!"

"Perhaps if we used the Shadow World for transit, the way Michael does—"

"And risk having him outflank us while we are in there? No, we cannot afford to take that chance, and he knows it, damn his eyes. He has the advantage of mobility while we have the advantage of position.

And neither of us can give up those advantages. He has proven himself an able commander, though of course, he has Korven to help him. Besides, each time he travels through the Shadow World, he sustains losses that cost us nothing. He cannot keep that up indefinitely."

He's kept it up for eight years, Derwyn thought, but said nothing out loud. What kind of fanatical loyalty does a man inspire who can keep leading men into the Shadow World? At least one major campaign each year, with sporadic fighting here and there throughout the winters, when the weather was too severe to mount campaigns. During the rainy season in the spring, the roads all turned to mud, the plains were soft and damp, and the bogs became more treacherous than ever. It was impossible to march in force with supply trains and siege engines. The catapults and rams sank into the ground up their axles. Summer and autumn were the times for war. So during the past eight years, how many times had Michael led troops through the Shadow World? A dozen? More? And how many of his fighters had he lost in there?

Intelligence about such things was not all that difficult to come by. When soldiers returned from a campaign, they always talked about it in the taverns. But they always exaggerated, too. Numbers could not be trusted. However, one could get a general sense of the campaign by comparing stories. Their spies reported that the Army of Anuire had fought undead within the Shadow World, monsters like albino spiders, only even larger, big enough in some cases to drag off a cow, if the stories were to be believed. They had encountered deadly vines that lay dormant and withered-looking on the ground till stepped on, then suddenly snaked around a man's legs, rapidly climbing up his torso and sending root tendrils deep into the flesh to suck out the vital fluids. Cut the vine and the tendrils keep on growing underneath the skin, sending shockingly rapid new growth out through bodily orifices. Death came within hours, filled with excruciating agony. Derwyn shuddered at the thought. What would make men risk such things time and again?

His father could not command such loyalty. He seemed to know it, too. Arwyn ruled by fear. Michael ruled by inspiration. Perhaps his reasons for not taking troops into the Shadow World were strategic, as he claimed. Or perhaps he was secretly afraid his troops might mutiny if he attempted it. Indeed, thought Derwyn, it was a crazy thing to do. Maybe that was it. Even when they were boys, Derwyn had seen traces of that craziness in Michael, but at the same time, it was an infectious craziness. He could always get the other boys to do the most amazing things, things they never would have considered doing on their own. He was a natural-born leader, with a very special and powerful charisma.

Doubtless, it ran within his bloodline, as it did within Derwyn's own, but Derwyn had never manifested it. His father had it to a degree, but Michael possessed in abundance the blood power known as divine aura. His troops would follow him anywhere. And if a man were to fall in battle, Michael would see to it that his family was provided for. It had to be a ruinous expense considering the losses his army had sustained over the years. If we tried it, Derwyn thought, it would quickly bankrupt our treasury, but Michael had the advantage there, as well. The Imperial Treasury had built up a considerable surplus over the many years of the empire's history, and the Roeles had never been profligate spenders. Until now, of course, but the entire empire knew Michael dipped into his treasury to support his people, and so they contributed all the more willingly. Surely they were as tired of the war as the people in Boeruine or Brosengae or Taeghas, but they loved their emperor because he never forgot them. Still, there had to be a limit. If this war continued for much longer, it would break them both.

If it weren't for the considerable resources of the guilds in Brosengae or the merchant shippers in Taeghas, thought Derwyn, our own war effort would have stalled at least five years ago, and the interest on those debts was mounting steadily. The only way they would ever be able to repay the debt would be to conquer Anuire, seize the empire, and then bleed the country dry. He didn't want to think about the possibilities of what might happen if the guilds called in the loans. His father had the troops, of course, but the guilds had powerful alliances with other guilds throughout Cerilia. They could easily raise a mercenary army or else freeze Boeruine out altogether, isolating them and cutting off all trade. They could not afford to lose this ill-considered and seemingly interminable war. But then, Derwyn knew, as did his father, that if they did lose, they would undoubtedly be put to death, so there was little point in worrying about the debt. If they won, it would be paid off by taxing the people of the empire, who would certainly not love them for it.

Even his father was growing tired of the war. A

man who had always lived for the thrill of leading troops into the field on campaigns, Arwyn was showing the strain of the long fighting. He brooded about it obsessively, spent long hours with his advisors and field commanders, planning his campaigns, constantly sending observers out to report on the conditions of the border garrisons, which he expanded and refortified each spring. He so often complained about the goblins' failing to hold up their end of the alliance that Derwyn could recite most of his litanies by heart. How long could it possibly continue?

Given the continued support of the guilds, or some significant victories such as the seizure and garrisoning of western Alamie, the war could go on for years. It had taken over all their lives, and Derwyn was weary unto death of it.

Once, and only once, he had broached the subject of a negotiated peace. His father had flown into such a rage that Derwyn never brought it up again. Still, it seemed the only sane alternative. Assuming Michael would negotiate. And knowing Michael . . . well, he didn't really know him anymore, did he? Michael seemed to truly care about his people. Perhaps he would be willing to negotiate a treaty wherein Boeruine, Taeghas, Talinie, and Brosengae could form their separate empire, but the Michael he remembered would not give up on anything. And so it went on. And on, and on, and on . . .

"Milord," said Arwyn's chamberlain, entering the hall, "the wizard waits without and craves an audience."

"Send him in," Arwyn said in a sullen tone, gesturing for the servants to clear away the plates. "Perhaps he has some good news to report. I could use some for a change."

A moment later, Callador came in, walking slowly and supporting himself with his staff. Derwyn had no idea how old Callador was, but he looked ancient. As a child, Derwyn had been afraid of him because whenever he had misbehaved, his governess had threatened to have the wizard turn him into a newt or strike him dumb or make him "feel the fires." He had never been entirely clear on what it meant to "feel the fires," but it had certainly sounded unpleasant. Such impressions, gained at an early age, died hard, and Derwyn still felt uneasy in the wizard's presence. He shifted in his chair uncomfortably as Callador approached.

He was as bald as an egg and extremely thin, so slender that it looked as if a stiff breeze would blow him over. He had no hair at all, neither beard nor eyebrows, the result of some illness he had contracted many years ago, which had also left his voice hoarse and gravelly. Perhaps he could have cured these conditions with magic or gone to a healer, but he didn't seem to care. He was not very much concerned with his personal appearance, as evidenced by the threadbare robes he always wore, which were a faded brown wool, coarsely woven. Derwyn grimaced, hoping he would stop before he got too close. He smelled perpetually of garlic, and his body odor would have stunned an ox. His father, apparently sharing his olfactory sensitivities, spoke before the wizard got within a dozen yards of them.

"What news, Callador?" he said curtly.

The wizard stopped and stood, leaning on his long staff as he gazed up at the dais where they sat at the long table. "I bring word from our special friend at the Imperial Cairn," he said.

Derwyn raised his eyebrows and glanced from the wizard to his father. "We have an informant at the palace of Anuire?" he asked with surprise.

Arwyn smiled. "It has been a fairly recent development," he replied. "One that has taken some time and considerable trouble to arrange."

"And you never told me?"

His father shrugged. "There was no pressing need for you to know." Then, as if abruptly realizing he had indirectly spoken deprecatingly of his own son, he added, "Besides, I was not certain how reliable this source would be. Considering . . ." He let it hang. "Well, what is the report?"

"I was not given the report, milord," Callador replied. "As usual, our friend desires to speak with you directly." He glanced at Derwyn.

"Perhaps I should leave," said Derwyn stiffly. He pushed back his chair and started to get up. "With your permission, Father . . ."

"No, stay," said Arwyn, waving him back down. He turned to Callador. "Proceed. I have no secrets from my son."

You have secrets even from yourself, thought Derwyn, but he said nothing as he resumed his seat. He was highly curious as to who this source might be.

The wizard shrugged, then extended his staff and slowly outlined a circle on the floor with it, about nine feet in diameter, Derwyn guessed. It was difficult to tell, because the staff did not leave any mark upon the stone floor. However, even though the circle he'd just laboriously drawn was invisible, Callador seemed to know exactly where its boundaries were. Having drawn it with his staff, mumbling some sort of incantation all the while, he next proceeded to remove a vial of some clear liquid, perhaps water, perhaps something more esoteric for all Derwyn knew, which he proceeded to sprinkle around the edges of the circle, again mumbling all the while. He stoppered the vial, though it was now empty, and put it away within the folds of his robes. Then he removed a small, well-worn leather pouch tied with drawstrings. From the pouch, he took pinches of herbs, rosemary—Derwyn recognized the bright green needles—mixed with something else. Once again, he went around the outside of the circle, sprinkling the herbs upon the floor.

Now, at least, with a faint dusting of herbs outlining the circle, its boundaries were clearly visible. Callador took his time carefully pulling the drawstrings of the pouch closed and tying them, then put it away, reached into another hidden pocket of his robe, and took out several thick candle stubs. He placed four white candle stubs on the floor on the outside of the circle—north, east, south, and west, muttering under his breath as he did so. Finally, he reached into his robe once again and pulled out a piece of chalk. This time, he went inside the circle and outlined it with the chalk, then drew an arcane rune inside it.

Arwyn sighed and rolled his eyes with impatience. It seemed to be taking an inordinately long time. Finally, however, the wizard finished with his preparations, and he stepped outside the circle, surveying his handiwork and nodding to himself.

"Come on, come on, get on with it," said Arwyn irritably.

"These matters cannot be rushed, milord," Callador replied somewhat petulantly. "If the circle is not
cast properly and precisely, there is no telling what
manner of visitation may occur. These things do not
always work out as planned, you know. In case
some other entity should force its way into the
circle, for safety's sake, we do want to make sure it is
contained."

"Yes, yes, by all means," grumbled Arwyn, making little circles with his hand, indicating that the
wizard should continue.

Callador grunted and nodded, then made a pass
with his hand, and the four white candles stubs
ignited. Callador called the quarters, invoking the
spirits of fire, water, air, and earth to preside over the
circle. That done, he made a brief invocation to the
gods, then began to cast the spell. Derwyn couldn't
understand a word of it. He'd seen adepts at work
before, but increased exposure to magic did not
make him any more comfortable with it. There were
entirely too many stories about wizards conjuring
up some entity and then being slain by their own
handiwork. Callador was a master mage, the finest
in Boeruine, but even he admitted that magic could
be unpredictable. No wizard fully understood the
forces he dealt with. Those who claimed they did
usually had life expectancies that were very brief.

He felt the temperature increase subtly within the
great hall. The candles placed around the circle and
the braziers in the corners flickered. Through the
window, Derwyn could see the twilight fading fast,
but within the hall, it seemed to grow even darker.
The hairs on the back of his neck prickled and stood
up as the air within the circle became hazy. Some-

thing that looked like smoke appeared within the circle, except it wasn't smoke. It was more like a mist, but it didn't simply rise; it swirled and undulated, coalescing into a pattern that spiraled back into itself like a smoky whirlpool.

Derwyn moistened his lips nervously and leaned forward in his chair as the outline of a figure started to appear within the spiraling mist, or whatever that ethereal smoke was. As the smoke faded, the figure resolved, walking toward them slowly as if through some sort of tunnel. In a sense, thought Derwyn, that was exactly what it was. Somewhere in Anuire, in some locked room, that spiral had appeared, and their informant was walking toward it. If such a smoky spiral had appeared within his room, Derwyn wondered, even knowing where it led, very little could have inspired him to walk toward it. It was like contemplating entering the Shadow World. If the need were great enough, he supposed he could do it, but it would take a lot.

As the figure started to come through, Derwyn saw that it was female. The long hair down almost to the waist and the slender curves were unmistakable. And then the smoke faded behind the woman as she stepped out into the circle, and Derwyn sucked in his breath sharply as he saw who it was.

It was Princess Laera! He had not seen her in some years, not since that last, fateful Summer Court when all of this had started, but he recognized her at once. She was, after all, the woman who would have been his stepmother, even though they were almost the same age. She had grown even more beautiful since he had seen her last, and despite the cold anger in her gaze, Derwyn couldn't take his eyes off her. He was stunned, and not just by her beauty. The emperor's own sister was spying for Boeruine! He glanced at his father with disbelief, but Arwyn just sat calmly, sipping at his mead and watching her.

"Welcome, Your Highness," he said, his lips twisting into a slight, ironic smile.

She glanced angrily at Derwyn. "What is *he* doing here? I told you I would speak to you alone!"

"Since when do you dictate conditions here?" his father replied coldly. "Need I remind you, Laera, that it was you who came to me? If I choose to have my son present, that is my prerogative."

She glared at him, but accepted it. "As you wish," she said. "I suppose Derwyn can be trusted." She spoke of him as if he weren't even there. "It is just that I am taking an enormous risk in contacting you like this."

"Risk?" said Arwyn scornfully. "What risk is there to you? If you have left your bedroom door bolted, as you doubtless have, who would force his way into the chamber of a princess of Anuire? And if someone came knocking while you were here, you could easily claim to have been asleep. The chances you are taking here are negligible, so don't speak to me of risk. You took a greater risk in sending word to me by messenger when you first contacted me with your kind offer of assistance." He grinned wolfishly. "Now, what word do you bring?"

She lifted her chin defiantly, but kept her temper in check. Her eyes, however, spoke volumes. "My brother has returned to Anuire with the army," she replied.

Derwyn noticed the corner of his father's mouth

twitch slightly when she said, "My brother." He did not like any contradiction, no matter how unintentional or indirect, of his claim that Michael was only a pretender, an imposter. "He's returned, you say?" He glanced at his son. "And none of our troops or garrisons reported any engagements?"

Derwyn shook his head. "No, not as of the last report."

"That is because there were no engagements," Laera said, "at least, not with your troops. They went into the Shadow World, intent on finding a portal to your coastal region, but something went wrong. They came out in the Seamist Mountains and were attacked by ogres. And then when they went back into the Shadow World, they fought another battle, this time with the undead."

"How unfortunate," said Arwyn with a grim little smile. "I take it the casualties were heavy?"

"Apparently," said Laera. "I do not know how great their losses were, but it seems they were significant. Michael came back very much depressed. I do not recall when I've seen his spirits sink so low. The troops looked utterly exhausted and disorganized. If there was ever a good time for you to march upon Anuire, then this it."

"Indeed, it would seem so," Arwyn concurred. "You have done well, Laera. Very well, indeed."

"Just remember your promise," she told him.

"I remember," he replied. "I shall keep my end of the bargain. See to it that you keep yours."

"You may count on it," she said. She glanced at the wizard. "I am ready now."

Callador raised his arms and spoke an incantation. The whirling smoke appeared behind Laera in the circle once again. She turned and went back through the misty tunnel. Derwyn watched her walk away, disappearing into the smoke, and then it dissipated, and she was gone.

Callador took his staff and held it out before him. He walked around the circle in the opposite direction to the one in which he'd drawn it, clearing it, then blew out his candle stubs, picked them up, moistened his thumb and forefinger and pinched the wicks to make sure they were out, put them in his robe, turned, and walked away.

"Wait," said Derwyn.

Callador paused and turned around.

"What about those herbs you sprinkled on the floor? And the chalk-marked circle?"

"A broom and a scrub brush should do adequately," the old wizard replied flatly. Then he turned and left the hall.

Derwyn snorted. "The least he could do was clean up after himself."

"Never mind," his father said. "The servants will see to it."

"If we can find one who will not fear to come near that thing," said Derwyn.

"They will fear me more if they do not," said Arwyn. "Forget the circle. I swear, sometimes I think you should have been born a woman. Haelyn knows, you're fussy enough. We have far more important matters to consider. The Pretender will be vulnerable now. As Laera said, the time is right."

"And you trust her?" Derwyn said.

"Oh, yes. I trust her."

"By all the gods, *why*? She's Michael's sister! Why should she betray Anuire?"

"Because she seeks revenge," his father said. "And I trust her desire to get it."

"Revenge? On Michael?"

"No, on Dosiere. She claims he raped her."

"*Aedan?*" Derwyn was shocked. "A rapist? I don't believe it!"

"For that matter, neither did I," his father replied dryly. "I never cared much for his father, but the boy was a good lad. One should always check one's sources, and I had some of our people in Anuire make a few inquiries. With enough drink in him, one of the Roele House Guard admitted knowledge that Laera and Dosiere had an affair. Right here, in fact, during the last Summer Court, under my very nose. It seems she had a habit of stealing into his room at night, wearing nothing but her bedclothes, and staying nearly until morning. That hardly sounds like rape to me."

"*Aedan and the Princess Laera?*" Derwyn said with astonishment.

"The passions of youth," his father said. "She probably seduced him. I had all the palace staff questioned, and several of them admitted knowing of it. They had no proof, of course, which they claimed was why they never reported it to me. It was merely palace gossip, and they feared recriminations. I reassured them I was not interested in either proof or punishment, just what they'd heard or suspected. Several of them admitted hearing of it from the guards. Two of the housemaids found stains on young Dosiere's bed sheets, which is not incriminating in itself, of course, but bears weight when added to the rest. And one of the grooms reported hearing quite a row between them in the stables. He claimed not to know what it was about. He was not close enough to make out what they said—or so he claimed —but it appears they had a falling-out, and she bears him a grudge for it. My guess is that Dosiere finally came to his senses and ended it. And there is nothing more spiteful than a woman who's been spurned."

"But to betray her own people . . ."

"She cares nothing for anyone except herself," said Arwyn. "She is selfish, willful, arrogant, and spoiled, a spiteful, vicious little twit. I never really liked her. I would have much preferred her mother. But in denying me the empress, Lord Tieran also spared me the task of marrying her daughter. I thought if I could not have the mother, I would bolster my claim with Laera as my wife. I was furious with him for interfering with my plans, but I suppose I should probably be grateful to Tieran, rest his sanctimonious, self-righteousness soul."

"This promise that she spoke of," Derwyn said, "what did she mean? Did she bargain with you to spare Michael's life?"

Arwyn snorted. "He didn't even enter into it. She cares nothing about what happens to him."

Derwyn frowned. "So then, what was the nature of the bargain?"

"She had but two demands in exchange for her cooperation. The first was that she decides the fate of Aedan Dosiere."

"And the second?"

"She is, of course, concerned about her own fate, as well," his father replied wryly. "She wanted to ensure rank and position for herself under the coming regime. Our little princess has no wish to step down in station."

Derwyn's eyes grew wide. "Surely, you don't mean to tell me you promised to honor your original betrothal?" he said with dismay.

"Of course not," said his father. "I promised her she could marry you."

chapter three

It had been a long time since Aedan had been back
to the Green Basilisk Tavern, but tonight, he felt in
the need of some strong drink and some company
outside the palace. At the Imperial Cairn, there were
always demands on his time, always at least a dozen
things that required his attention, from routine matters having to do with the running of the household
to correspondence and dispatches from distant
provinces—one noble or another making entreaties
to the emperor—matters of strategy and policy having to do with the war against Boeruine. However,
there was nothing so important that it could not wait
till morning. His staff was well trained to handle
matters in his absence, and if anything urgent did

happen to come up, such as the emperor's requiring his presence, he had left word where he could be found. He did not think the emperor would require his presence tonight.

They had returned to the capital late in the afternoon, as the shadows lengthened in the plazas of Anuire. The streets had all been eerily silent as the weary troops trudged back to the parade ground by the docks, where they drilled regularly and assembled to go out on campaigns. A lot of people had turned out to watch the army as it marched through the city. They lined the route all the way to the parade ground, but no one cheered their arrival. When they saw the condition of the troops, they just stood silently and watched with grim faces, many of them scanning the ranks as they went by, searching for loved ones. Too many of those faces would be twisted with grief tonight, thought Aedan. Too many wives, mothers, and children would be crying for the men who had not returned.

After the troops had been dismissed from the parade ground and they had broken up to go back to their homes or their barracks, Aedan had returned to the palace with the emperor and some of the other nobles, such as young Viscounts Ghieste and Alam, whose rank—and hostage status, though that was never mentioned—gave them comfortable quarters at the Carin. Michael had retired to his rooms, saying he did not wish to be disturbed. All the way back from the Spiderfell, right up until the time they disembarked the boats at the Imperial Cairn, he had spoken not a word, brooding all the while. In a war that had its share of defeats as well as victories, this campaign had been the most disastrous yet, and Michael blamed himself.

Aedan knew better than to try lifting his spirits at a time like this. Michael needed time to be alone, and Aedan needed to get lost in a crowd and take some time away from his responsibilities. So he had bathed and changed his clothes and taken a boat back across the bay, then headed through the dark streets alone toward the artists' quarter and the Green Basilisk Tavern.

He recalled the sinking feeling in his stomach when they came out of the portal from the Shadow World and realized they had not reached the plains of Diemed, but the depths of the Spiderfell. Of course, there had been little choice. Risk the dangers of the Spiderfell or remain behind in the Shadow World to battle the undead and try to outrun the fire. Their chances if they had stayed in the Shadow World would have been slim. Perhaps now, thought Aedan, Michael would finally give up this madness of trying to cheat time. Even by going through the Shadow World, the army could not be everywhere at once, and each time they had gone in there, the odds against them had increased. This time, their luck had finally run out.

There was no way, at present, of knowing how heavy the casualties were. Aedan would find out tomorrow, after the captains delivered up their muster rolls. Right now, he simply didn't want to know. He felt depressed enough. They had wasted no time in re-forming and getting on the march again as soon as they came out into the Spiderfell. The troops were tired, and many were walking wounded, but at least the fact that they could walk had saved them from being left behind.

That was the worst part of the whole thing, Aedan thought. He had no way of knowing how many wounded men had to be left behind because they could not make it through the portal. Some had been fortunate enough to have their comrades pick them up and carry them back through, but all too many had been left to the fire and the mercies of the undead. And the undead had no mercy. If they went back, they might once again encounter those poor bastards who had been left behind, only this time, they would be marching with the ranks of walking corpses. Aedan would not have wished such a fate on his worst enemy.

The Cold Rider. The halfling had been right. Terribly right.

There was no trail where they came out in the Spiderfell. They were in thick woods, and a squad of men had to be sent forward with the scouts to clear their way through the undergrowth. It slowed their progress considerably. It was not yet morning, and even in daytime, little sun penetrated the Spiderfell. The elves, however, had an unerring sense of direction, and they were able to point the way. They headed south, toward Diemed.

As Aedan rode together with Sylvanna, right behind Michael, he felt a prickling at the back of his neck. Viscount Ghieste had insisted that Michael take his horse, and he now rode behind Viscount Alam on his. Michael had wanted to march on foot, along with the troops, but young Ghieste had insisted, and Michael was too tired to argue. The divine wrath had left him spent once it had passed, and even riding, he slumped in the saddle as if wounded.

No one spoke. They marched in utter silence, only

the steady tramping of feet and the jingling of gear breaking the stillness of the forest. At some point, Aedan wasn't sure exactly when, he realized what sounded wrong. No birds. It was just like in the Shadow World. Dawn approached and the birds should have been chirping. But there were no birds.

"You feel it, too?" Sylvanna asked.

He glanced at her and nodded.

"What is it?"

He shook his head, scanning the forest all around them. "No birds," he said.

"I had noticed that as well," she said, "but that's not it. There's something else. . . ."

Aedan heard something scurrying through the underbrush off to his left. He glanced quickly in that direction, and saw fern branches moving from the passage of . . . something.

"Pass the word for the troops to be on guard," he said.

As the word was passed down the column, he took a deep breath and let it out slowly in an effort to steady his nerves. After what they had just been through, he didn't know if the troops had enough strength to fight off some new threat.

Again, scurrying noises off to the side. He looked again, but whatever it was escaped his notice.

"There's something moving in the brush," he said.

"I know. I heard it," Sylvanna replied, her gaze on the underbrush around them. "And not just some-*thing*. There's more than one."

Aedan saw Caelum Ghieste and Taelan Alam looking around them, as well. The sounds had not escaped their notice. What was more, they seemed to be increasing. There was more rustling in the underbrush around them now. Aedan glanced over his shoulder at the troops. They were aware of it. Moments earlier, the men had been simply marching at a weary pace, their faces drawn and haggard, their shoulders slumped. Now, they were all alert and glancing to their sides, watching the brush and keeping their hands close to their weapons.

Aedan spurred his horse slightly and trotted up to Korven and Michael. "There is considerable rustling in the brush around us," he said.

"I know," said Korven. Michael merely nodded. His earlier slumped posture had changed. He sat erect in his saddle, clearly tired, but scanning the area around them intently. Visibility was still poor, but the sky was getting lighter, and more light was filtering through the trees.

"Another few miles, and we should be clear of this place," Korven said. He sounded more hopeful than certain. "The brush is getting thinner. We must be approaching the outer edges of the forest."

Sylvanna came trotting up behind them. "Aedan, look at the trees," she said tensely.

He looked and at first he didn't see anything. Then he saw movement on the tree trunks that they passed. Spiders. Hundreds of them. Some were small, but some were fist-sized, and some still larger, like small melons. They were crawling up the tree trunks all around them, making them seem to writhe. Some were already in the lower branches and were dropping down on web strands, one after another after another. The sunlight filtering through the upper branches glistened off the web strands, hundreds of them, thousands, coming down on either side of their route.

"What in Haelyn's name?" said Korven.

Hundreds of thousands of spiders were all around them now, spinning a vast curtain of webs.

"It's the Spider," Sylvanna said grimly. "He's controlling them."

No one living had ever seen the Spider and survived to tell the tale. One of the most dangerous and hideous awnsheghlien, it was said he was once a goblin king named Tal-Qazar, who had led the goblin forces fighting for Azrai at the Battle of Mount Deismaar. What little was known of him came from ancient writings preserved in the library at the College of Sorcerers in Anuire, set down by those who had encountered him hundreds of years ago, while he had still retained some shreds of sanity.

Imbued with the god essence of the dark lord, Tal-Qazar had united several tribes of gnolls and goblins under his leadership and founded his domain within the forest north of Diemed, which came to be known as the Spiderfell. The god essence of Azrai had brought about a horrible mutation in his body, which had progressed the more he used his powers, which in turn gave him an appetite for bloodtheft unmatched by any other awnshegh, with the possible exception of the Gorgon. The upper portion of his body was said to be humanoid in appearance, but so grotesquely changed that he bore almost no resemblance to his original form. His lower half was the bloated body of a huge arachnid, with eight legs and a bulging abdomen. He never ventured from his nest deep within the Spiderfell, but he knew everything that went on within his forested domain through the eyes of the hundreds of species of poisonous arachnids that lived within the Spiderfell. And to feed his insane appetite for bloodtheft, the gnolls and goblins he controlled brought victims to him.

The woods on both sides of the army were quickly becoming shrouded with a huge network of filmy webs as the horde of spiders clambered over the strands they were spinning. It was a frightening and repellent sight. None of the spiders were attacking any of the troops. They seemed intent upon their spinning, building up layer upon layer of gossamer webs on both sides of the army's route.

"They're trying to trap us!" Aedan said as understanding suddenly dawned.

"With *spiderwebs*?" said Korven. "Ridiculous! We can break right through them."

"Any man who tries will become covered with the insects," Aedan said. "Enough bites, and he will become paralyzed, and then the Spider's minions can drag him off to their awnsheghlien lord." He pointed ahead of them, where the network of webs was growing steadily thicker as they advanced. "Look there. They are creating a corridor for us. See how it turns? They are trying to lead us back into the Spiderfell!"

"We shall burn our way through," said Michael, speaking for the first time since they had left the Shadow World. "Pass the order for torches to be lit."

"There are no more torches, Sire," Korven said. "We used the last of them back in the Shadow World."

"*Gylvain!*" Michael said, looking around for the elven mage. "Where is Gylvain?"

"I have not seen him since we left the Shadow World," Korven replied. "You don't suppose we left him back there?"

"No, Gylvain came through the portal," Aedan said. "But I have not seen him since. Sylvanna?"

She shook her head. The webs around them were almost as thick as cloth now, carpeted with spiders. The procession stopped as Futhark came running back to them with several of the halfling scouts.

"The tunnel of webs bends around sharply up ahead," he reported, "circling back the way we came. We cannot go on, or it will take us back into the Spiderfell. Do you wish me to create a portal back into the Shadow World, Your Highness?"

Michael's face was grim. "And if we encounter the undead once more? Besides, by now, the fire we started must have spread considerably, and it will take a long time for it to burn itself out. Still, we may have no choice. . . ."

The wind picked up suddenly, and the sky overhead grew darker. They looked up and saw the morning light fading rapidly.

"It looks as if a storm is moving in," said Korven.

"No," Sylvanna replied, as the wind increased, "it's my brother! It's Gylvain!"

Thunder crashed as clouds moved in a thick, black bank above them and lightning lanced the sky. The wind continued to grow stronger, shrieking through the treetops; thunder crashed repeatedly like cannon, echoing throughout the forest all around them, and it began to hail.

At first, the hailstones pattered softly through the treetops, but then they fell harder and faster, like stones fired from slings, sheeting down and ripping through the spiderwebs, smashing the arachnids to the ground.

"Forward!" Michael shouted, and the army raised

a mighty cheer as they moved ahead. But their exuberance was cut short when another cry was raised, at first blending with their cheers, then riding over them as the troops stopped to listen. The new sound was a mixture of doglike howls and screaming voices. While hail fell like grapeshot, these new attackers came running through the trees, screaming and brandishing their weapons.

The weary troops unsheathed their blades and surged forward to fight the gnolls and goblins of the Spider. They had been waiting in ambush for them, waiting for them to try breaking through the webs so that they could move in and finish off the ones the spiders didn't get. The hail Gylvain had conjured had ruined their plans, so they had charged.

Aedan only remembered raising his sword and bringing it down again, over and over and over, slashing all around him as the goblins and the gnolls descended on them. Weary from the battles that they had already fought, the troops rose to the occasion; their survival had depended on it. They had cut their way through the attackers, but it had been impossible to maintain any kind of ranks or formation in such overgrown terrain. The army broke up into small groups that fought their way through the forest and reformed several miles away on the plains of Diemed, but though they had made camp and posted pickets, waiting for three days to allow the troops to rest and the stragglers to catch up, there were many who never made it out of the Spiderfell.

As Aedan walked down the dark and narrow streets of the artists' quarter, the buildings on either side of him reminded him of the web tunnel, dark with countless crawling spiders, and he felt sweat break out on his forehead and start trickling down his back. His breathing grew faster and more shallow as he walked, his eyes wide and staring straight ahead of him. The people who passed him in the streets saw the haunted, wild look upon his face and gave him a wide berth. He could not banish the visions from his mind. Over and over, he saw images of the battle in the Spiderfell, men and goblins hacking away at each other, the wolfish gnolls howling and snarling, their foam-flecked jaws snapping as they fought with the soldiers of Anuire, who had called upon their last reserves to cut their way clear.

He kept seeing the undead staggering toward him through the mists of the Shadow World, the flames leaping up, the shifting figure of the Cold Rider watching from the ridge. He heard the screams of the wounded and the dying, and they sounded so real that he had to cover his ears, but that didn't help. The screams and images were in his mind, and he couldn't drive them away.

He lurched against a wall, his hands up to his head, and doubled over, gasping. He struck his head against the wall several times, and the pain helped distract him from the visions. He straightened up, breathing hard, and looked around. He had taken a wrong turn somewhere. The tavern he was heading for was one street over. Shaking his head to clear it, he breathed deeply several times, then headed down an alleyway to get to the next street.

Halfway down the alley, three figures detached themselves from the shadows and blocked his way. "There's a toll to be paid for going through this alley, friend," one of them said. "Let's see how much coin you've got in your purse."

Aedan saw the glint of a dagger. Alleymen. Oh, gods, not now, he thought, exasperated. "Get out of my way," he said, hoarsely. "I don't have time for this."

"Well, aren't we high and mighty?" the leader of the trio said unpleasantly. "I think we may have to take you down a peg or two, milord."

As they came toward him, Aedan saw that all three had long daggers in their hands. And the leader wore a sword and a vest of chain mail over his tunic. A former soldier, Aedan thought, one who had left the army and turned to crime. After what he had just seen the army go through, the thought filled him with cold fury. How many of them had laid down their lives or returned home cripples so that the likes of this one could prey upon the people of city they'd protected?

"Get out of my way, you filthy scum," he said.

"Kill him," said the former soldier.

As the men came at him, something in Aedan snapped. He screamed hoarsely and drew his blade, launching himself at them like an enraged berserker. With a powerful, two-handed blow, he struck the closest one so hard that he split him from the shoulder clear down to the middle of his chest. The man screamed and fell as Aedan yanked his blade free, but by then, the second one was on him. Aedan twisted around, deflecting the dagger lunge with his blade, then bringing his sword hilt up sharply to strike the alleyman in the face. Blood spurted as the man's nose broke and he cried out; then Aedan ran him through. Only the former soldier remained, and as Aedan made for him, he drew his own blade and took a fighting stance, his cocky attitude completely gone, replaced by a deadly serious expression. He managed to parry Aedan's first stroke, but Aedan kept at him, screaming all the while, as the man fought desperately to keep Aedan's blade at bay, never having a chance to go on the offensive.

Aedan backed him toward the wall of the alley. They locked blades, the alleyman with his back against the wall. As they strained against each other, Aedan dimly felt a blow to his shoulder. He raised his knee sharply into the alleyman's groin, and as the man grunted and the breath whooshed out of him, Aedan bore down on his opponent's sword and slammed his forehead into the alleyman's face. Blood spurted from a broken nose as the man slumped against the wall. Aedan disarmed him easily, then threw down his own sword and started pummeling him with his fists. The nearly senseless alleyman started to slide down the wall. Aedan seized him by the throat with his left hand, holding him up, and repeatedly smashed his right fist into the man's face, turning it into a mask of blood. Over and over, he pounded him until he felt someone grasp his shoulder from behind.

Turning quickly, he swung a hard right at the cloaked figure that came up behind him, dimly registering that the alleymen had worn no cloaks. The figure ducked beneath his punch and drove a hard jab into his stomach, directly into the solar plexus. He doubled over as the wind whistled out of him, and the figure caught him, supporting him.

"Aedan! Aedan, it's me! Sylvanna!"

The familiar voice broke through his berserker rage. "Sylvanna?" he said, weakly, as he fought to catch his breath.

She eased him down to his knees, then left him to check on the alleyman he had been battering. She bent over him, then straightened. "This one's dead," she said curtly. She quickly checked the other two, but their condition was obvious. She came back to Aedan, who was just beginning to get his breath back. "What's wrong? You didn't have enough fighting? You had to go wandering through the alleys in the middle of the night, looking for more trouble?"

"What . . . what are you doing here?" he asked.

"Lady Ariel sent me," said Sylvanna.

"Ariel?"

"She was worried about you. She thought you might have gone to the Green Basilisk, so she asked me to see if you were all right. I was just passing by the alley on my way there when I heard the commotion. Doesn't seem as if you needed any help, though. Was that you screaming like a wounded bear?"

He shook his head. "I don't know. I don't remember."

"Oh, Great Mother, you're wounded," she said.

Aedan glanced down and saw a knife sticking out of his shoulder. He remembered, vaguely, feeling a blow and realized the alleyman had stuck him. "Pull it out," he said.

She grasped the knife firmly by the hilt and pulled straight back. It came out with some difficulty. It had struck bone and stuck there. As she pulled it out, the blood began to flow. Aedan winced with pain, then closed his eyes and concentrated, calling upon his blood abilities of healing and regeneration. After a few seconds, the blood flow stopped and he felt the wound starting to close. Moments later, it had healed completely, leaving behind only a mild redness of the skin. He opened his eyes and took a deep breath, feeling slightly dizzy. The fight, together with the healing, had taken a lot out of him.

"Wish I could do that," said Sylvanna, pulling back his tunic to check on the healed wound. "It's a handy trick."

"Help me up, please," he said.

She assisted him to his feet, putting his arm around her shoulder so he could lean on her for support. "Are you all right?"

"I will be, shortly," he replied, breathing heavily. "By the gods, I need a drink. I need a lot of drinks."

"Come on," she said, helping him out of the alley. "Show me where this tavern is I've heard so much about."

After a few moments, he was able to walk without her assistance.

"What came over you back there?" she asked. "I've never seen you like that before. It was like Michael's divine wrath."

He shook his head. "I don't have that blood ability. I don't know what came over me. Pure rage, I guess." He told her about the visions he had started having on his way through the artists' quarter, and how he had become confused and taken a wrong turn somewhere, gone down the alley to reach the right street, and encountered the three thugs. "That last one was a former soldier," he said. "He wore the style of chain mail we use in the army. I don't know, perhaps he bought it somewhere, but I doubt it. He had the look of a soldier about him. I thought of all the men we'd lost, fighting for the empire while that bastard remained home, preying on the citizens, and I just went mad."

"A delayed reaction," she said. "It happens sometimes, after a long period of combat. It's difficult to leave all that behind."

He nodded. "I know. I just can't stop thinking about it," he said. "And if it weighs on me so much, I can only wonder what Michael must be going through right now."

"At least he's safe back at the palace, and not wandering the streets at night, looking for another war."

Aedan snorted. "I fear you've been among us humans too long," he said. "You're developing a sense of humor. I sometimes think I've lost mine. Well, this is it."

He pointed to the entrance of the tavern, marked by a wooden sign above the door with a green basilisk painted on it. They went inside.

Aedan had not been to this place for a long time, ever since he'd assumed his duties as lord high chamberlain. He had stopped going because he did not think it fitting for the emperor's first minister to frequent taverns and drink with the lower classes. But in the years since he'd first assumed his post, especially after so much time spent in the field with the troops, he'd lost that old rigidity of opinions. Still, he had not returned. This place had seemed like a part of his past best left behind. Even then, as Lord Tieran's son, he had never really been accepted as one of the crowd. As lord high chamberlain, he thought he'd only make the other patrons feel awkward and uncomfortable.

Tonight, however, he simply didn't care. Even the lord high chamberlain was entitled to a drink or two or ten, especially after the nightmare he had just survived.

The place hadn't changed at all. He even saw a few familiar faces, though they were older now, of course. It was still the same dark, windowless rectangular room with stone walls on which the shadows danced in the flickering of candles and oil lamps. Still the same rough-hewn wooden tables and benches with rushes on the floor, the same long wooden bar stained with rings of countless goblets. Bards still sang their songs upon the tiny stage while girls passed the hat for them . . . and the Fatalists were still holding court.

"Well, well, look what the wind blew in."

He recognized Vaesil at once, even though the years had not been kind to him. Or perhaps more accurately, Aedan thought, the drink had not. He had put on weight, and his once flowing, lustrous hair now hung limp and oily on his shoulders. His angular features and high cheekbones, which had once given him a dashing predatory look, had a rounded softness now, and his eyes had the glazed and red-rimmed look of a dissipated drinker.

"To your feet, my friends," he said, lurching up, "for we are singularly honored by a most stellar presence on this night, or do you not recognize Lord Aedan Dosiere, the emperor's high chamberlain?"

The others at the table turned toward him, and Aedan saw a few more familiar faces, but mostly new ones. He did not see Caitlin. Strange, but until that moment, he had not thought of her in years. As the others rose to their feet, Aedan waved them back down.

"No, no, resume your seats, please," he said. "I am not here in my official capacity tonight. I just came to get drunk."

"Well, you have come to the right place then," Vaesil said, sitting down heavily. His speech was only slightly slurred. He still had the bard's voice, and a control over it that only a man long in his cups could exercise despite the drink. "And who is that with you?" He squinted. "By the long-dead gods, is that an elf?"

"Her name is Sylvanna," Aedan said.

"So, you've turned your back on your human friends and taken up with elves now, have you?" Vaesil commented. The others sat in shocked silence, amazed that he should address the lord high chamberlain in so familiar—and so rude—a manner. "I suppose I shouldn't really be surprised," continued Vaesil. "You've both butchered your share of humans."

"Vaesil! Have you lost your senses?" one of the others at the table said in a shocked voice. "Remember whom you are speaking to!"

"It's all right," Vaesil said. "Lord Aedan and I are old friends, are we not? True, it has been years since we have drunk together, but then he's been a very busy man of late. Sit down and join us, Aedan, and your elf girl, too. You can regale us all with tales of your last campaign. I understand the body count on this occasion was particularly high, and you did not even encounter Arwyn's army. Just a sort of lethal training exercise, was it?"

Several of those present got up from the table and left without a word, their gazes sliding away from Aedan's as they departed. The others all just looked into their drinks, not knowing what to say or do.

"Oh, dear," said Vaesil. "I seem to have offended a few tender sensibilities."

"I should think you'd be quite used to that by now," said Aedan in an offhand tone.

"Oh, well struck!" said Vaesil with a grin. "An excellent riposte! I see your diplomatic duties have improved your wit. Or perhaps it's simply been emboldened by all your heroic actions in the field. You were never quite so forthcoming in the old days. That deserves a drink. Dierdren! Some of your best wine for my esteemed guests!"

To Sylvanna's surprise, Aedan sat down at the table with Vaesil. Frowning with puzzlement, she joined him.

"Speaking of the old days, Vaesil, how is Caitlin? Do you see her anymore?"

"See her?" Vaesil snorted. "I married the sow. Not one of my better judgments, that, but she got with child, and as I was reasonably certain it was mine, I felt it only right and proper to do the honorable thing. I haven't done all that many honorable things, you see. In fact, I believe that was the first and quite possibly the last, as well. I rather enjoyed the novelty of the experience. For a time, at least."

"So you're a husband and a father," Aedan said. "Frankly, I never saw you in either role."

"Mmmm, neither did I," said Vaesil, wrapping his fingers around his goblet. The serving maid brought their drinks, and Vaesil fumbled around his person, looking for his purse.

"I'll buy," said Aedan. He paid her, including a gratuity, and she thanked him with a curtsy and a smile, then left.

"So have you a daughter or a son?" asked Aedan.

"One son, two daughters, and another baking in the oven," Vaesil said. "I am beset with squalling children and a shrewish wife who has grown broader in the beam with the delivery of each new addition to our loving family. Ah, the bloom is off the rose, indeed. But if I get drunk enough, I can still fulfill my duty as a husband. For a few minutes, at least."

"I am surprised she lets you," said Sylvanna.

"Ah, you can speak! Capital! I was afraid I should have only Lord Aedan to trade barbs with." By now, all the others at the table had left as well, without saying a word. Vaesil took no note of it after his first comment. "Yes, well, the pathetic soul still loves me, you see, despite her constant harangues about my drinking. But you see, I *must* drink to support my growing family. The muse requires fuel. I can no longer compose when I am sober."

"Perhaps you will honor us with one of your recent ballads?" Aedan said.

"Perish the thought!" said Vaesil. "I do not perform them, I merely compose for others who have more appealing stage presence. The last time I tried to regale an audience with one of my compositions, I fell off the stage. Broke both my wrist and the harp. Can't play worth a damn anymore, not that it matters, the sort of drivel I compose these days. I couldn't sing the stuff with a straight face, anyway. If I wrote what I really think and feel, no one would pay me for it, and I have hungry mouths to feed."

"If you are in need—" Aedan began.

"I do not require your charity," Vaesil interrupted him. "In truth, I am obscenely prosperous. By my standards, anyway. Caitlin's father died a few years back and left us his blacksmith shop. I could not manage it, of course, so I took on a partner, a most industrious young chap who was fawningly grateful for the opportunity and has made quite a success of it. And my ballads, worthless, sentimental dog droppings that they are, are in considerable demand. I even wrote a few about your emperor, glorifying his wonderful accomplishments in fighting to unite the empire and his unparalleled heroism on the field of battle. If I had any shame left in me, I would die of it. But I continue to live, worse luck. Well, shall we drink a toast for old times' sake?"

"What shall we drink to?" Aedan asked.

Vaesil considered for a moment. "To the past," he said. "The future is too depressing to contemplate."

"To the past, then," Aedan said.

They lifted their goblets and drank.

"Well, I suppose I should be staggering back to my humble domicile," said Vaesil. "I would not wish to disgust you any further, and my wife is doubtless waiting for me, wondering if I shall make it home alive or if the morning will find her a rich widow with a handsome, muscular young blacksmith at her beck and call. If I were him, I would be building on my future by working at her forge. She's still a saucy wench, despite having lost her girlish figure."

"Please give Caitlin my warmest regards," said Aedan.

"I shall do that, and I am sure it will please her to be remembered." He lumbered to his feet. "You wanted her, as I recall. I can remember how you used to stare at her, like a moonstruck calf. You should have tried to take her from me. I know you never could have married her, but I would have been too proud to take her back when you were finished, and she would have been much better off. Well, good night to you, my lord chamberlain and lady elf. And

THE IRON THRONE

give my regards to your bloodthirsty bastard of an emperor. Tell him I shall continue to extol his noble virtues while I curse his noble name."

He lurched off toward the door.

"What a horrid, loathsome individual," said Sylvanna with disgust. "I have never met anyone so beneath contempt. I cannot believe you allowed him to speak to you that way. Was he truly your friend?"

Aedan sat silently for a moment, staring into his half-empty goblet. "I don't think that Vaesil was ever anybody's friend," he said at last. "Believe it or not, there was a time when he was quite handsome and engaging. Oh, he was acerbic then, but not to this extent. Back then, he seemed very daring, spirited and charming in a dangerous sort of way. I wanted very much to be like him."

"I find that difficult to imagine," said Sylvanna. "He is the most detestable person I have ever met."

"He has become bitter and pathetic," Aedan replied. "As a Fatalist, he had believed in nothing greater than himself. And when he lost his belief in himself, he was left with belief in nothing. I do not think you could detest him half as much as he detests himself."

"This girl you mentioned, Caitlin. Did you love her?"

"Oh, for a while, I thought perhaps I did," Aedan replied. "But it was really nothing more than an infatuation. Besides, she had eyes only for Vaesil. I was never one popular with the ladies. I lacked Vaesil's quick wit and good looks, and I would grow tongue-tied in the presence of a girl I found attractive. Aside from that, I was Lord Tieran's son, and that set me apart. It was one thing, I suppose, for a

293

girl to entertain the notion of a liaison with a noble, perhaps on the off chance that it might lead to marriage or at least a bastard that the noble might feel duty-bound to support, but the son of the emperor's high chamberlain occupied too lofty a status. I always sensed they were uncomfortable in my presence, watchful of their remarks—except for Vaesil, of course, who was always recklessness personified."

"Why did you come here then?" Sylvanna asked.

"For some relief from duties and responsibilities that I found oppressive at the time," he replied. "Michael used to try my patience in those days. You recall what he was like eight years ago, when you first came here. He has matured a great deal since that time. As have we all, no doubt. But back then, I felt the need for some companionship of people my own age, people who were not associated with the court. I suppose it made me feel somewhat daring to come here and spend my time in company with philosophers, bards, artists, laborers, criminals. For a time, it made me feel as if I were one of them." He shook his head. "Strange. I killed three men tonight and feel no remorse for it. They preyed upon the innocent and would have killed me if they could. And yet, I feel pity for Vaesil, for he preys only on himself. What a peculiar creature I've become."

Sylvanna reached out and touched his hand, reassuringly. "I have always found humans peculiar," she said, "but you less so than most." Her touch lingered.

Aedan smiled. "I will accept that as a compliment."

"It was intended as one."

Aedan waved to the serving girl and ordered a

bottle of wine. "I'm in a mood to get good and drunk tonight," he said. "When we finish this, just bring another."

"You shouldn't blame yourself," Sylvanna said. "What happened on this last campaign was not your fault."

"I wonder," he replied. "I have always thought that traveling through the Shadow World was far too great a risk. I know Michael better than any other man. He listens to me. Perhaps if I'd tried harder, I could have talked him out of it."

"I doubt it," said Sylvanna. "Once Michael makes his mind up, nothing dissuades him from his course."

"I wonder if he's getting drunk tonight," said Aedan.

Sylvanna squeezed his hand across the table.

"Does an immortal fear death?" he asked.

"Of course," she replied. "Just because we have a longer life span does not mean we have less fear of death. We can be killed like anybody else, you know. Everyone fears death."

Aedan shook his head. "No, not everyone. I do not think Michael does. I have never known him to be afraid of anything. He seems to have no capacity for fear. That is why he has always been so reckless. And that is a large part of the reason he inspires his troops. In that respect, there is something lacking in him that most normal people have. I have always marveled at it and wished I could have his courage. But this time, something's changed."

"In what way?" she asked, still holding his hand. There was an expression of infinite sadness on his face, and it touched her deeply.

"I realized something this time that I never realized before," he said, pausing to drain his goblet and refill it. He held out the bottle to her interrogatively, and she nodded for him to refill hers as well. "Courage is not fearlessness," he continued, as he poured. "Fearlessness is just a lack of fear. Courage is overcoming fear. Without fear, there can *be* no courage. It struck me back there in the Spiderfell, when those horrid creatures tried to trap us with their webs." He shuddered at the memory that was still so fresh. "It made my skin crawl. I have always hated spiders. That first time in the Shadow World, when you flicked that albino spider off me and told me how they get into your hair and lay their eggs . . . I had nightmares about that for weeks. I would wake up in a cold sweat, and it was as if I could literally *feel* them crawling on my head. I'd have to go over to the washbasin and scrub myself till I thought all my hair was going to fall out. And that was only from that one spider. This time, there thousands of them, hundreds of thousands, so many that the tree trunks were writhing with them and the webs they spun were covered with the damn things."

His breathing quickened, and he tossed his wine back in one gulp, then refilled his goblet once again. "I never felt more afraid in my whole life. I felt consumed by stark, unreasoning terror. The only thing that kept me from spurring my horse and bolting in panic was the certain knowledge of what would happen to me if I did. And even then, I was on the verge of doing so. Until I turned around and looked at the foot soldiers marching behind us. I saw their faces and knew they all felt exactly as I did. I could see their fear. I could *smell* it. And yet they kept their ranks, kept marching. . . ."

"There was nothing else for them to do," Sylvanna said. "I felt afraid, as well, but giving in to fear would have resulted only in our destruction."

"I understand that," Aedan said, "but that is not the point." He emptied his goblet once again and promptly refilled it. "The point is this: the army has campaigned for eight long years. Oh, it was not eight years of straight campaigning. There were the breaks between campaigns, and in the winter and the early spring, but each time the call for troops went out they came. No matter how bad the last campaign was, no matter how many losses we incurred, no matter the hardships we suffered in the field, still they gathered up their arms and came. This last campaign was the worst disaster we had ever faced. We never even got to see Lord Arwyn's army, but we fought ogres, battled the undead, were terrorized by a legion of spiders, and set upon by gnolls and goblins. . . . Those valiant soldiers went through more than any man should endure, and yet I have no doubt that when the call goes out again, still they will come. *That* is courage."

She nodded, watching him. He was getting drunk. He tossed back his wine and poured once more. This time, she joined him, but he was having at least three goblets for every one she drank. He was starting to slur his words.

"If Michael has any real courage, he will not take them back into the Shadow World again. The Cold Rider was a warning. We survived this time . . . well, at least some of us did . . . but I doubt we shall be so lucky next time. If there is a next time. That is where my courage must come in, you see. I must prevent him. I must find it in myself to stand up to him, something I have never done. Vaesil called him a bloody butcher. You wondered how I could allow him to speak that way. Because he was right, that's why. Michael *is* a bloody butcher. He sees only the goal he strives for and does not consider the costs ... the terrible, terrible costs. Let Arwyn *have* his damned Western Marches! What does it matter? So there shall be two empires instead of one. So what? Nothing is worth this. Nothing."

He put his head in his hands and slumped over the table.

Sylvanna flagged down the serving girl. "Have you rooms upstairs?" she asked.

The girl glanced at Aedan and nodded. "I believe we still have a few available for the night."

"We shall take one," said Sylvanna. "My friend is in no condition to go anywhere tonight."

She paid for the room, then helped Aedan upstairs, supporting him with his arm around her shoulder.

"Where are we going?" he slurred.

"To get you to bed," Sylvanna said.

"I'm perf'ly able t'go home," he mumbled.

"No, you're not," she said. "You couldn't walk twenty yards without passing out."

"Mmmph. Maybe not."

"Come on, pick your feet up."

They reached the top of the stairs, and she helped him down the corridor until they reached their room. She kicked the door open and helped him in, then put him down on the dilapidated straw bed. The furnishings were sparse. Merely a chair, a washstand with a battered metal washbasin and pitcher, some blankets, a few candles, and a chamberpot. Sylvanna lit the candles, then started to undress him.

She pulled off his boots, then unfastened his breeches and pulled them down. He lay back, breathing heavily, but still awake.

"Come on, sit up," she said, pulling on his arms so she could take his tunic off. "Hold your arms up," she said. As he did, she pulled off his tunic and tossed it aside. His arms came down around her.

"I love you," he said.

She looked at him. "I know."

She eased him back down onto the bed, then stripped off her own clothes and got in beside him. He snuggled up against her. She pulled the blankets over them and put her arms around him. He kissed her ear and whispered, "I want you."

She kissed his lips. "Then have me," she said softly.

And when they were done, he held on to her tightly and cried himself to sleep.

ANUIRE

chapter four

"You did not come home last night," Gylvain said.

"No."

"You were with Aedan."

She hesitated only slightly. "Yes." Her gaze met his, defiant, challenging. He sighed. This was not going to be easy.

"Do you have any idea what you're doing?" he said.

"I knew exactly what I was doing."

"Did you? Need I remind you that we are guests here, serving the purposes of a sensitive political alliance? Perhaps Aedan has forgotten. Eight years is a long time for a human, after all. After such a time, things begin to take on a sense of permanence for them. But when this war is over, we are returning to Tuarhievel, and it is entirely possible the time will come when the humans shall be our enemies again."

"Aedan Dosiere shall never be my enemy," Sylvanna said. "And when this war is over, I shall not be going back with you. Unless you plan to force me. I know I am no match for your power."

Gylvain sighed and shook his head. "I would never wish to force you to do anything against your will. You know that, or you should. But you are not thinking clearly."

"I am not confused. I love him. And he loves me. I can give him what he needs."

"No," said Gylvain, sadly, "you cannot. I sensed that this was coming, but I had hoped you would know better. You are an elf, and he is human. You could never give him what he needs. You could satisfy his desires in bed, but even if that was all there was to your relationship, it would be most unwise. Suppose he gets you with child? Do you know what it is like for half-elves in human society?"

"The soldiers accept us," she replied.

"Because we have fought with them, side-by-side, for eight long years and earned their respect," said Gylvain. "But do you recall what it was like in the beginning? Think how long it took for us to earn that acceptance, and we had to earn it with our blood. Bring a half-elf child into the world and it will be no different for him or her."

"You could prepare a potion for me that would prevent me from conceiving," she said.

"Yes, I could," he agreed. "And I shall, if you insist on persisting with this folly, but think what you are doing, little sister. Even if it turns out to be no more than an affair of short duration, it will be difficult if not impossible for the two of you to be discreet. Such things always have a way of getting out. Aedan is second only to the emperor in this regime. He is a blooded noble, and you are an unblooded elf. An affair between you would only bring him trouble. It would be cause for scandal. He must wed a blooded noblewoman one day and perpetuate his bloodline. He must sire a male child who will become the lord high chamberlain to the next Emperor of Anuire. A half-elf child would be unacceptable in such a post and would only taint the bloodline.

"You are just a child yourself," Gylvain continued, "but by human standards, you are old enough to be his mother. He may not care, but others will make much of it. You say that you can give him what he needs. Well, in that regard, the needs of humans when it comes to love, true love, are much the same as ours. They need someone they can grow old with. Together. And that is something you can never give him. If you bind your life to his, you will watch him age and die, and it will happen more quickly than you realize. It will only break your heart, Sylvanna."

"What do you know of such things?" she replied angrily. "You chose celibacy so that you could pursue your craft! Because you have never loved, you wish to deny me the chance to find some happiness, if only for a little while?"

Gylvain approached her and took her by the shoulders gently. "No, I would never wish to deny you anything. Except pain."

"Then prove it."

Gylvain sighed deeply. "Very well. I shall prepare a potion for you that will keep you from conceiving a child. If I cannot talk some sense into you, then the very least that I can do is help you take some sensible precautions. But I do not approve of this, Sylvanna, and I fear you will come to regret it. Both of you."

* * * * *

There was a knock at Laera's door. "Enter," she said. Maelina, one of the palace servants, came in hesitantly.

"I have brought some news, Your Highness," she said, curtsying deeply and looking down demurely.

"What is it?" Laera asked.

Maelina was one of her paid informants in the palace. The girl had no idea Laera was spying for Lord Arwyn; she believed Princess Laera was merely trying to keep abreast of palace gossip and court intrigue. There was nothing unusual in that. Laera knew she was not the only one at court who bribed the servants to report on what their masters and mistresses were doing. Maelina would never suspect a thing.

"It concerns Lord Aedan, Your Highness. You said you were particularly interested in him."

"Indeed," said Laera, putting down her embroidery. "No one ever tells us women anything," she added. "We must strive to find things out for ourselves. We women of the palace must stick together. What have you learned, my dear?"

Maelina beamed at being included with the princess among the "women of the palace." It made her feel like a confidante, almost a friend. "Well," she said, lowering her voice in a conspiratorial manner, "he did not sleep in his room last night. When I came to change his bedclothes this morning, they had not been disturbed."

"Really?" said Laera, leaning forward as if enjoying some salacious bit of gossip. "Where *did* he sleep then?"

"I do not know for certain, Your Highness, but I made a few inquiries among the other servants and learned he left the palace last night to go to a tavern known as the Green Basilisk. He had left word he could be reached there if the emperor had need of him. That tavern is said to be a most disreputable place. I have never been there myself, of course, but one hears that it is a gathering place for all sorts of lowlifes—artists and the like."

Laera shrugged. "So he went out to do some drinking away from the nobles of the court," she said. "After the hardships of the campaign he just returned from, that would be perfectly understandable. He must have had too much to drink and simply took a room to sleep it off. Nothing much of interest there."

"Oh, but there is more, Your Highness!" said Maelina, clearly anxious to impart the news. "It seems Lady Ariel became concerned about him— she has always borne a great fondness for him, as you know—and she sent for that elf girl, you know, Sylvanna, the wizard's sister? She asked her to go after him and see to it that all was well. And do you know what?" She paused significantly. "Sylvanna did not return last night, either!"

"Indeed?" said Laera, raising her eyebrows. "Well now, that *is* interesting. You are quite certain of this?"

"Oh, yes, Your Highness. They both came back this morning. Together. In the same boat. Can you imagine!"

"Oh, I can, indeed," said Laera with a smile. "You have done well, Maelina." She handed the girl a purse.

"Oh! Your Highness is most generous!"

"I shall be even more generous if you are able to report further on this matter," Laera said.

"I shall try, Your Highness. Thank you. You may count on me."

After the girl had left, Laera leaned back against her chair and chuckled with pleasure. So that fool Aedan was bedding the elf girl! This was too delicious! The lord high chamberlain, the oh-so-very-proper Aedan Dosiere, was sleeping with an un-blooded commoner, and an elf, at that! And he had the temerity to call her a wanton slut! No one had ever spoken to her like that before. No one. And she had never forgotten it. She would have grown tired of him soon, anyway. In fact, she had already tired of him, but Seaharrow had been such a boring place and there was so little to do. . . . But the thought that *he* had been the one to break it off, and the manner in which he'd done it. . . . He would pay for that. He would pay dearly.

She didn't think this was anything Arwyn could use to good effect, for he was only interested in military matters, but it still had definite possibilities. Most delightful possibilities. She could completely ruin his reputation. But she would have to move quickly. Even now, Arwyn would be preparing to march on Anuire after her report of the previous night. Michael's army had come back from their campaign weakened and demoralized and Arwyn was not going to hesitate to take advantage of it. She smiled. It was so easy to find out what she wished to know. All she needed to do was show concern for the welfare of the troops, ask some questions of their captains under the pretext of finding out if there was anything she could do to help their families, and they would begin blabbing.

Meanwhile, her own reputation as a princess who truly cared about her people was being spread, so that when Arwyn came to conquer Anuire with his army and she was "forced" to marry his son, the sympathy of all the people would be with her. She didn't feel anything for Derwyn, but at least he was better-looking than his father. He lacked Arwyn's massive, bearlike frame, but his slender form was pleasing, and he had inherited his mother's looks, so that he bore only slight resemblance to his brutish father. There was a softness about him, and he would doubtless be a more giving lover than his father, who would have been impossible for her to control. Derwyn would be easy.

She knew he had always been attracted to her. She had seen him watching her and had seen the look on his face when Arwyn's wizard, Callador, had magicked her to Seaharrow. He had been shocked to learn that she was spying for Boeruine, she could plainly see that, but at the same time, she had seen the way his gaze traveled appreciatively over her form. She had been irritated that Arwyn had allowed him to be present, for she had wanted to keep her role a secret from everyone but him, but perhaps it was for the best. Seeing her again had served to rekindle Derwyn's desire for her, and she could use that desire to bring him to heel. Men were such fools. It was easy to make them do what she wanted.

She had learned her lesson with Aedan. Never let them know you want them. That gave them the upper hand. Give them a taste of passion, enough to make them want more, and then withhold it. Make them earn your favors. And whenever possible, make certain they have more to lose than you.

She had carefully practiced her seductive wiles over the years until she had perfected them. She had started with Leander, a young lieutenant of the house guard, who was putty in her hands within only a few weeks. She seduced him, and it did not take long before she was able to make him do anything she wanted. When she was through with him, she had induced him to desert, tearfully telling him that someone in the palace suspected their affair and that his life would be in danger if he did not flee. With warm and tender kisses, she had bid him farewell, telling him she would always love him, and he had fled Anuire for parts unknown, leaving behind a promising career and the girl to whom he had been betrothed.

After that, she had refined her skills, careful to select only those men who could be of use to her. One was the son of a prosperous leader of a merchant guild, who came to her under the pretext of displaying jewels and fabrics. It was through him that she was able to make other useful connections, which eventually led her to the mercenary whom she had used as her first go-between with Arwyn. That had been very risky, but the man was manageable. It was well known that she had been betrothed to Arwyn, and it was a simple matter to make the mercenary believe she actually loved the brute and was willing to trade her favors in return for having secret love letters passed back and forth. She had made him think it was he who was manipulating her, and after contact through Callador had been established, she had sent the mercenary back to Arwyn under the pretext of delivering a letter. Arwyn had obligingly disposed of him.

Her greatest coup had been Lord Korven's son, Bran, who was a captain in the army. When she had expressed an interest in his duties and professed concern about the war—and about him, of course— Bran had proudly told her not only everything that occurred on the campaigns, but all of Korven's strategies and plans, which she communicated to Arwyn at the earliest opportunity. Callador had given her a special jeweled amulet, which she wore on a chain around her neck. Whenever she needed to contact him, she needed only to pull out the amulet, stare at the jewel, and concentrate, "calling" to Callador. She would receive her answer when the jewel began to glow. When that happened, she needed to wait for only a brief interval before the swirling mist appeared within her room, a portal to Boeruine.

At first, this mode of travel had frightened her considerably. Portals of that nature opened out into the Shadow World, and Callador had halfling blood. However, the mage had reassured her that while the portal did open up into the Shadow World, it led only through another portal directly into Seaharrow, like passing through the two connecting doors of adjacent rooms. Still, each time she went through, she felt a knot of tension in her stomach, despite the wizard's reassurances. It would all soon be worth it, though. When Arwyn defeated Michael's army and took Anuire, he would control the empire. It might require a few small pacification campaigns to bring some of the more distant provinces into line, but that was the sort of thing at which Arwyn excelled. And once the Army of Anuire had been defeated, no one else would be able to field so great a force except Arwyn himself. He would assume the Iron Throne, and Derwyn would become the prince and heir to the throne. And as his wife, she would one day become empress.

She had been afraid Arwyn would insist she honor their original betrothal, and with him as emperor, there was no way she would have been able to refuse. It would have made her empress that much sooner, but she knew she would not be able to manipulate him. At least not as easily as she would be able to control his son. And then she would be forced to share his bed, as well, an idea that was repugnant to her. Fortunately, Arwyn no longer had any interest in the match. He had only seen it as a means to an end he would now realize without it. Derwyn would be a far more pleasant bedmate, and much more tractable. He lacked his father's strength. And by the time he became emperor, she would have him thoroughly beneath her thumb. She could gradually build up his ambition and drive a wedge between him and his father—which would not be difficult, since Arwyn treated him like a lackey—and then they could take steps to hasten the new emperor's demise.

But first things first, she thought. She would ruin Aedan Dosiere and get her revenge. She would make him suffer first, and then she would destroy him.

And if she hoped to do that before Arwyn marched upon Anuire, there was no time to waste. A word or two in the right ears and things would be set in motion. From there, they would gather momentum of their own accord. She would only need nudge things along every now and then. She smiled in anticipation. It had taken years, but at last, Aedan Dosiere was going to get what was coming to him.

* * * * *

Elation on the one hand, anxiety on the other. Aedan was torn between the two emotions. He had finally realized a dream he'd nursed for years. He and Sylvanna had become lovers. That night in the Green Basilisk. . . .

He had been drunk, but not so drunk that he could not remember, nor not know what he was doing. The wine had merely removed his inhibitions so that he had been able to say those words to her that he had never dared say before. And some physical effect of the wine, combined with the sudden flow of emotions that he had held back for so long, had energized him, kept him going long into the night. It had never been so good with Laera. He pushed that thought away.

When he woke up in the morning, suffering from the effects of the drink the night before, she had already risen and gone out to bring him back a potion that would dispel the headache, and they had made love again. He had never felt so happy. But at the same time, he felt concern.

How would Gylvain react to this? It would not be right to keep it from him. Besides, he would surely find out. They would not be able to conceal what they felt from him. He knew them both too well. But it would be wise to conceal it from everybody else. It was a delicate situation that could easily have nasty repercussions for them both. And Michael. What would Michael think?

The emperor had problems of his own. He had fallen into a deep depression after returning from the campaign and had retired to his chambers. He did not come out for three whole days, and the servants had reported that he did not eat the meals they brought to him. What was more, he had started drinking. And Michael never drank before.

For the first day or so, Aedan thought it best to just leave him alone, but on the second day, he had tried to see him. However, the door was bolted, and after Aedan had pounded on it for a while, Michael had yelled at him to go away. Finally, after three days had passed, Aedan's concern became so great he had the guards batter down the door, assuring them he would take full responsibility.

Michael was sitting by the window, staring out over the bay, dressed only in his nightshirt. His hair was disheveled and his beard in need of trimming. He had not washed, and there were dark bags under his eyes. He held a goblet loosely in one hand, and as Aedan came in, he didn't even turn toward him.

"Some people just won't take no for an answer," he grumbled. "What exactly is the penalty for breaking into the emperor's private quarters?"

"I don't know," said Aedan. "I assume you'll have to think of one and charge me with it."

"Why couldn't you just leave me alone?" said Michael. He took a long swallow from the goblet.

"Because I was concerned about you, Sire. The servants tell me you're not eating."

"I'm not hungry."

"You haven't eaten for three days."

"I've made up for it by drinking."

"A drunken monarch is not much use to anyone," said Aedan. "Look at you, Michael. You're a mess."

"Go away. Leave me alone."

"Wallowing in self-pity isn't going to solve your problems," Aedan replied. "*Our* problems."

"*Our* problems are primarily of my own making," Michael said.

"I have no doubt Arwyn would agree with you," said Aedan. "If you'd had the sense to abdicate in his favor, doubtless this war would have been unnecessary. No war is ever necessary, so long as one side surrenders. So is that what you want, to surrender? If so, let me know, and I will send messengers to Arwyn with a flag of truce to negotiate the terms. Then he can become emperor, and you'll have no further worries. Unless, of course, he decides to kill you. After all, you have been impersonating the emperor all these years. But then you wouldn't have to worry about the fate of all the people of the empire and all those men you led into the field who would have died for nothing."

"Damn you."

"No, damn you, for sitting here and feeling sorry for yourself and wallowing in guilt! What gives you the right?"

Michael stared at him. "What gives me the *right*?"

"That's right, you heard me. You are the Emperor of Anuire, for Haelyn's sake! You have neither the luxury nor the time for guilt. Your first duty is to your people, especially in time of war. I have known you practically from the moment of your birth, Michael, and you've always been a self-indulgent bastard. When this war started, you talked of fighting for your birthright. Well, fighting alone is not enough. You must live up to it, as well. You must think about the living and leave the dead to rest."

"They died because of me," said Michael.

"That's right, they died because of you," said Aedan. "Because they *believed* in you. But they also believed in an idea. They believed in order and in law. That is what you represented to them. *That* is your birthright, not this palace or your throne or your crown. Those are merely things. And people do not die for things."

Michael sat silent for a moment. Then he picked up his bottle, stared at it briefly, and suddenly flung it against the wall with all his might, making Aedan start with surprise.

"You are absolutely right," said Michael clearly, swaying only slightly on his feet.

Aedan stared at him and wondered, how much has he had to drink? He never drinks, but here he's been drinking for three days straight, apparently, and he just shrugs it off. He saw the slight frown of concentration on Michael's face, the intensity in his eyes, and he thought, of course. Iron will. Another of his bloodline attributes. And he suddenly realized it must have been what kept him going all this time. The strain must have been tremendous, and finally he had slipped. After all that had happened, who could blame him?

"Thank you, old friend," Michael said. "Thank you for reminding me who I'm supposed to be. I had forgotten." He sighed deeply. "And now, if you will excuse me, I must bathe and dress, then get something to eat." He glanced toward the splintered door to his chambers, lying on the floor. "And call a carpenter."

* * * * *

It was with a great deal of relief that Aedan returned to his chambers that night. Relief not only that the emperor was himself again, but that his own duties for the day were done. After the long campaign, many important matters pertaining to the business of the empire had accumulated and required his attention. He had to meet with his staff and discuss them all, receive petitions for the emperor, review reports of the army quartermaster and city council, endless stultifying detail. He was looking forward to a good night's rest.

He was so preoccupied that he did not notice her at first. She had been sitting quietly on a bench by the window and had said nothing when he came in. It was only when he took off his robes and started to unfasten the belt around his tunic that she cleared her throat slightly, and he started, glancing up with surprise.

"Ariel!"

She stood. She was wearing a dark green velvet gown and matching slippers, her long blonde hair twisted into a single, thick braid. An image came suddenly to him from eight years earlier, when she had come to him while he was working in the stables to tell him she had spoken with his father to tell him that she had knocked him senseless, so it was all her fault that Michael had been injured during play. She had worn green velvet on that day, as well. In other ways, however, Ariel had changed.

The awkward, coltish girl that she had been back then was gone, replaced by a grown woman, slender and curvaceous, no longer the tomboy, but feminine and every inch the lady. She had not grown into a beauty, but her rather plain face was set with green eyes, her most striking and appealing feature. There was an earnest directness in their gaze, an inviting innocence and total lack of guile. He had not seen her much in the intervening years, what with his duties and all that time spent with the troops out on the march, but her father, Lord Devan, was minister of the exchequer, so she lived with her family in the palace and spent most of her time with Michael's younger unmarried sisters.

"What are you doing here?" he asked.

She took a deep breath, gathering herself, and gazed at him directly. "Do you love her?"

"What? Who?"

"You know very well who," she replied. "The elf. Sylvanna. Do you love her?"

He tensed and hesitated. Too long. "What are you talking about?"

"You know perfectly well. She may not have told you, but it was I who asked her to go after you when you went into the city the night you returned from the campaign. I was concerned about you. I had never seen you so dispirited before. I stayed awake all night, waiting for you to return, so I know when you came home. I saw you. With her."

"Well, just because we stayed out all night, two comrades in arms, drinking—"

"Don't," she said. "Don't treat me like a fool, Aedan. Just answer my question."

"Your question is presumptuous, my lady," he said, retreating into formality. "As is your presence here at this late hour. It is most unseemly. You must consider your reputation—"

"My reputation be damned," she said, shocking him into astonished silence. "Answer my question. *Do you love her?*"

He exhaled heavily and looked down at the floor. "Yes."

She seemed to collapse inwardly. She stared at him with a stricken expression, then sat back down on the bench and closed her eyes. Laera's mocking voice came back to him, echoing in his mind. "*She loves you . . . loves you . . . loves you. . . .*"

"Ariel . . ."

"Be quiet," she said, not looking at him. "Just be quiet and listen. Laera knows. I don't know how she knows, but she knows. You realize what that means, of course."

"I don't understand. What do you mean?" He knew exactly what she meant, but he could not accept it. How could she know? How could Laera possibly know?

"I know what happened between the two of you at Seaharrow, all those years ago," said Ariel. "You and Laera."

"But . . . *how?*"

She looked at him with exasperation. "Do you think I'm blind? You think I didn't see the looks that passed between you? It was as plain as day that you were lovers. I was so frightened for you, it nearly drove me mad. I was afraid Arwyn would kill you if he found out. I do not know what passed between you when it ended, but I can guess, for she has nursed a hatred for you ever since. That, too, is clear to anyone who cares to notice. She looks at you with venom in her eyes. And now you have given her a weapon with which she can destroy you."

"But how could she know?"

"Are you that naive? Besides, what difference does it make? She *knows*. She probably has half the servants in the palace reporting to her. And she has begun to pass the word. She has not done it herself, of course, for she is far too clever for that, but rest assured it came from her. Already, tongues are wagging, and you know how quickly gossip travels in the court."

"What do I care about idle gossip? I have nothing of which to be ashamed."

"I did not say you did," she replied. "But instead of professing so much concern over how my coming to your rooms at night affects my reputation, you should give some thought to your own. Having elves among our troops was cause enough for controversy in itself, at least in the beginning. Since then, they have proven themselves our allies and been accepted as such, but this is something else entirely. If she were an ordinary, unblooded commoner, it would be bad enough, considering your position, but Sylvanna is not even human."

"Why should that make any difference?"

Ariel rolled her eyes in exasperation. "Don't be an idiot. I hold no prejudice toward her because she is an elf, but you know perfectly well that many people look upon race mixing as perversion. Even if she were human and a commoner, it would still be cause for scandal. Oh, I know that many of the noblemen have such liaisons, but you are not just any nobleman. You are the lord high chamberlain, second only to the emperor. Your honor and reputation must be beyond reproach. If nothing else, it calls your judgment into question, and as the emperor's first minister and advisor, your judgment must always be considered sound. It is not only yourself that you are undermining, but the emperor, as well."

Aedan could think of no reply to that, for she was absolutely right. He stared down at the floor, morosely. "I suppose I could resign my post. . . ."

"And leave the emperor to choose a new high chamberlain in time of war? He depends upon your friendship and your counsel. You have been trained for this from birth, Aedan. Who would replace you? In time, perhaps, an adequate successor could be found from among the nobles of the court, but if you resigned while Anuire is threatened, you would not only be utterly disgraced, but you would also weaken and demoralize the emperor at a time when he needs most to be strong and confident. You cannot afford to make the noble sacrifice, Aedan. You don't have that luxury. You don't have the right."

Ironically, he thought, she had used the same words he had spoken to the emperor earlier that day. And they were no less true applied to him than they had been when applied to Michael. He sighed and sat down heavily on his bed. "You're right, of course," he said. "But what am I to do? I suppose I could deny it, but the damage will have already been done. I knew Laera was spiteful, but I never suspected she would go so far."

"There is one thing that can be done, before the story spreads farther than it has. I am loath to suggest it, but I can think of nothing else that would serve to quell the gossip before it can erupt into a scandal. You must take a wife."

"A wife!" He thought quickly. Yes, that could work. And it would add further plausibility to the story that he and Sylvanna had merely stayed out drinking all night, comrades in arms unwinding after a long and difficult campaign. It would be a lie, of course, but a lie that people would find easier to accept with his being betrothed. His father had died before he could arrange a marriage for him, and what with the war, there had been no time for him to give any thought to marriage, even if he'd had the inclination. And even if people still suspected the liaison with Sylvanna, they would be unlikely to bring it up if he were married. Not without proof. Ariel was right. If he married, it would deflect Laera's plan for revenge, but that still left him with a difficult situation. Quite aside from the problem of finding a wife, he would have to marry someone he did not love. The marriage would be a lie. And how could he bring himself to do that to some innocent girl?

As if she could read his mind, Ariel said, "I will marry you."

He glanced up at her sharply. "No," he said, shaking his head. "Ariel, I could not possibly ask you to sacrifice—"

"What sacrifice?" she asked in a faintly bitter tone. "I have always loved you, ever since I was a child. And if I cannot have you, I do not want anybody else. I would almost rather die than marry you under such circumstances, for I know you do not love me, but good marriages have been made without love before. We are of the noble class. Such things are a way of life with us. A marriage based on love is rare among the nobility, and I have not yet been promised by my father. Nothing would please him more than to have you ask him for my hand." She swallowed hard, and tears came to her eyes as she spoke. "I will make you a good wife, Aedan. Who knows, perhaps, in time, you might even come to love me a little, but if not, I will understand and turn a blind eye to any liaisons you may care to have. Just don't flaunt them is all I ask. Let me keep some shred of pride. And one more thing. My father must never, ever know the truth of this."

"Of course," said Aedan. He got up and came over to her, then got down on one knee. He took her hand. "Ariel—"

"Don't," she said, shaking him off and getting up. "Let us not make a mockery of this. It is purely a political arrangement," she added stiffly, "between friends. Speak to my father in the morning. He will joyfully give his consent, and we will announce it to the court tomorrow. It would be best for the marriage to take place as soon as possible. The war provides an excellent excuse."

"Yes, I suppose it does," said Aedan woodenly. "Ariel, I—"

"And for Haelyn's sake, don't thank me. *Please*."

He looked down and nodded. He moistened his lips. "I must . . . tell Sylvanna. It would not be right for her to hear of this only when our betrothal is announced."

"No," said Ariel firmly. "You must not see her

now. It would only add fuel to the fire. I will go to her tonight and tell her myself. I will explain the situation fully and make her understand the necessity for this." She took a deep breath, and her voice broke slightly as she said, "And as I know you are too well mannered to ask it of me, I will also tell her that you love her. And I will try hard not to cry. Good night, Aedan."

She turned and ran out of the room.

chapter five

The wedding took place in the great hall of the
Imperial Cairn, with the entire court in attendance.
The floors had all been swept clean, white bunting
hung from all the galleries, jasmine incense added to
the coals burning in the braziers. The emperor himself officiated. Aedan looked strikingly handsome in
his family colors, with black hose, a black tunic, and
a vertically divided black and white tabard emblazoned with the Dosiere crest. Ariel looked stunning
in a pure white gown and matching satin slippers
with a girdle made of fine gold chain around her
waist and a garland of white and yellow wildflowers
in her long blonde hair. But had anyone looked very
closely, they would have seen a trace of sadness on

her face, about the eyes.

Women of the court whispered to one another about what a beautiful couple they made, and the men all nodded in approval of the lord high chamberlain's making a good match. A marriage between the daughter of the minister of exchequer and the lord high chamberlain would only serve to strengthen the internal unity of the emperor's council, and in a time of war, that was only to the good.

Gylvain and Sylvanna had both been invited to the wedding, and those few who'd heard the rumors circulating watched Sylvanna carefully, but saw no sign of anything except happiness for her comrade-in-arms as she stood next to her wizard brother. The married couple seemed very happy, and those few who mentioned it at all whispered that the rumors must have been nothing more than spurious, malicious gossip that deserved no credence.

Only Princess Laera seemed a little out of sorts. A number of the wedding guests commented upon her stiff posture, the lines of tension at the mouth, and what seemed like an uncommonly resentful look in her eyes, though she took pains to hide whatever it was that seemed to be troubling her. The theory was advanced and generally accepted that undoubtedly the wedding of the lord high chamberlain and Lady Ariel reminded her too painfully of her own thwarted wedding plans. She had, after all, once been betrothed to Arwyn of Boeruine, and that was a marriage that could obviously never take place now. And what with the war and the awkwardness of her situation, there had been no other suitors. None that would have been acceptable to a woman of her rank, in any case. Clearly, it was impossible for her to attend the wedding without being reminded of her own plans gone awry, and that was surely the reason for her seeming discomfort.

If the wedding seemed a trifle hasty, without an adequate period of betrothal, no one thought the worse of it. There was a war on, after all, and the young couple could not afford to waste any time. It went unspoken, though clearly understood, that circumstances could easily result in Lady Ariel's soon being a widow, and if the lord high chamberlain should fall in battle, it was important that he leave behind an heir to carry on his name and be raised to assume his duties for the future emperor. Aside from that, the word went around that Lady Ariel and Lord Aedan's parents had often spoken of a match between their children, but it had never been officially arranged because the war, and later Lord Tieran's death, had intervened.

The circumstances of a court wedding at a time of war also occasioned considerable talk about when the emperor would marry. It was dangerous for the empire to go without an heir when the emperor himself led his troops into battle. There was a great deal of discussion on this topic, and many young noblewomen's names were advanced as possible candidates, in many cases by their fathers, who knew an opportunity to maneuver for political advancement when they saw one.

When the wedding was concluded, the happy couple kissed, then turned and were cheered by the assemblage, after which they invited all their guests to sup with them at the banquet tables in the hall. The servants carried out platter after platter of roast venison and pheasant and baked fish of varying sorts, candied hummingbirds' wings and jellied lamb and roast boar and barrels of wine and mead. Dancers and acrobats entertained the guests, and through it all, through the laughter and smiles, no one would have guessed the true feelings of the bride and groom.

From time to time, Aedan's gaze would meet Sylvanna's across the room, and he wished it could have been her seated by his side, while at the same time he felt sorrow for Ariel, his wife, who had married him knowing that he loved another. Though she smiled on the outside, inside, Ariel's heart was breaking: she had dreamed of this day since she was a child, hoping against hope it would come to pass, but never like this. She had done it out of love for Aedan and a desire to save him, but she could not stop thinking her new husband must have felt he was trapped, and if she had not set the snare, she had at least come to collect the game.

She had not spoken with Sylvanna since the night she told her she and Aedan would marry, and why. It had been a difficult and painful conversation, all the more so because Sylvanna had tried to make it easy on her. Ariel had not known what to expect. She did not know Sylvanna very well. The elf did not associate with the ladies of the court, preferring the company of soldiers, and the few times they had spoken had been nothing more than a formal exchange of pleasantries. Outwardly, she had displayed no emotion when Ariel gave her the news and explained the reasons for it. There had been only a barely perceptible flicker in her eyes, but for Ariel, it had been enough. Sylvanna had listened silently while Ariel spoke, and when she was done, she had said, "You love him, too."

Ariel could only nod.

"So," Sylvanna had said, with no hint of emotion in her voice, "it is well. You will make him a good wife."

Ariel had felt a lump in her throat as she replied, "He wanted you to know that he loves you."

Sylvanna stared at her. "He asked *you* tell me that?"

"No," said Ariel softly, looking down at the floor. "He could never have asked me such a thing. I offered of my own accord."

"I see," Sylvanna said. "It would have been unconscionable for him to ask you. But it was very gracious and noble of you to tell me. Thank you, Lady Ariel."

"I . . . I hope we can be friends," said Ariel.

"I shall always admire and respect you," Sylvanna said. "But you do not want me for a friend. That would be too difficult for all concerned. I will stay until after the wedding. And then it would be best if I went back home to Tuarhievel. I have been away too long. But please do not tell Aedan. I do not wish to say good-bye. Good night, my lady."

As she watched Sylvanna from across the room, Ariel wondered how soon after the banquet she would leave. She glanced at Aedan, sitting next to her and speaking with her father. He will hate me, she thought. I love him with all my heart, and he will hate me. And then she saw Laera, sitting by the emperor and staring at them both with eyes like anthracite.

Suddenly, the doors to the banquet hall were opened, and the herald entered with a man beside him, a captain in the army. The captain nodded to him grimly, and the herald blew a blast on his horn, cutting through the noise of merriment. All eyes turned toward the captain, who went down to one knee and bowed his head.

"Sire, it grieves me to intrude upon this happy occasion, but I bring important news."

"What is it, Captain?" Michael asked.

"Lord Arwyn is on the march, Sire. He has gathered all his forces and advanced across the border into Avanil. There has been a battle. Our garrisons have fallen. He is but a day's march distant."

A dead silence fell upon the hall.

The emperor stood. "My lords and ladies," he said, "I crave your pardon for disrupting the festivities. All officers to your commands. Sound the call for the troops to assemble. We march within the hour. Those of you who do not bear arms with our forces, please stay and finish your dinner."

"Forgive me," Aedan said to Ariel as he got up, "but duty calls."

"Of course," she said, thinking, was there relief in his voice? As people started to rush out of the hall, Ariel quickly made her way to Sylvanna's side. "You will not leave now, surely?" she said.

"No, not now," Sylvanna said. "My departure shall have to be postponed."

"Please watch out for him," said Ariel.

Sylvanna simply looked at her. "I always have."

* * * * *

The army gathered on the parade ground as the temple bells throughout the town tolled the alarm.

As Aedan stepped out of the boat, his squire was already dressed for battle and had brought his mount and arms and standard. He swung into the saddle and rode together with the emperor to assemble the troops. Only a few days had passed since their last disastrous campaign, and yet they all came, as he had known they would. This time, there would be no battles with ogres, gnolls, goblins, undead. This time, they would face the Army of Boeruine. And this time, Aedan knew, it would finally be settled, one way or the other.

For Arwyn to attack in force now was too much of a coincidence. It would have taken him several days to gather his troops and march to Brosengae to make a push from there, supported by the troops manning his border garrisons. He must have started to organize his march as soon as the battered Army of Anuire returned from their ill-fated expedition. Somehow, he must have known they had fought several engagements and were weakened and demoralized. The timing was too close to be coincidence. His spies had done their work.

Well, weakened they were, perhaps, thought Aedan, as he gazed out at the assembled troops, but demoralized? There was firm resolve in every face he saw. They would be fighting to defend their city, and they knew that this, at last, would be the final battle. There would be no retreat. And if Arwyn tried to pull back behind his garrisons, they would pursue and attack with everything they had. They were all weary of the war. Now was the time to end it.

Michael rode up to his troops as their officers formed them up and called them to attention. As he started to address them, Aedan thought back to that day on the coastal plains by Seaharrow, when a younger Michael had stood before his "troops" of children, exhorting them to victory over the evil forces of Azrai. This time, however, there was a real sword in his hand, not a wooden toy. And this time, his voice was not high-pitched and squeaky, but it rang out clear and true. And this time, Ariel would not take part in the combat, but would remain behind, wondering if her new husband would return home safely. He glanced at Sylvanna riding up to join them with Gylvain and the other elves. There were fewer of them than had started the campaign, eight long and weary years ago. Their number had been reduced by half. Elves fighting and dying in a human conflict, he thought. Shades of Deismaar, indeed.

"Warriors of the Empire of Anuire!" shouted Michael, his voice carrying across the parade ground as he sat mounted before his troops. "Once more we march to battle! Many times we have assembled here over the past eight years. I see many familiar faces. And there are those, sadly, that I do not see. Our comrades-in-arms who have fallen in past campaigns. They all fought valiantly and gave their lives for the cause we defend. Today, they stand with us in spirit, and if they could speak, they would surely ask of us to ensure that they did not die in vain.

"For too long, this war has raged. The Army of Boeruine has struck out time and again, but never has there been a decisive engagement. They have plundered our lands. They have burned our fields and villages, slaughtered our livestock, trampled our crops, and murdered our fellow citizens. And for what cause? So that one man's ambition can be fulfilled! A man whose lust for power knows no bounds. Arwyn of Boeruine would sit upon the Iron Throne and call himself your emperor. He denies my birthright and calls me a pretender to the throne."

At this, a loud chorus of angry dissent rang out. Michael raised his arms for silence.

"Hear me!" he shouted. "If I were to lead you into battle merely to secure my place, I would indeed be that pretender he accuses me of being. If my palace, throne, and crown were all I cared about, I would be unworthy to lead you into battle. And if I truly believed Arwyn of Boeruine would make a better emperor than I, that the people of the empire would thrive and prosper under his rule, I tell you here and now I would step down from the throne and give it to him."

Almost as one, they shouted, "No!"

"We have faced much hardship together," Michael went on when they had settled down. "We have suffered the extremes of weather. We have gone hungry, tired, and sleepless on the march. We have faced the dangers of the Shadow World together, and we have grieved over our fallen comrades. Never before in the history of the empire has there been such a conflict. And never before in the history of the empire has there been such a true and valiant army! You honor me, but even more than that, you honor yourselves!"

The troops raised a cheer.

"If the gods meant for us to fail, we would have failed long since," said Michael. "If the gods meant for me to fall, I would have long since fallen. But this I promise you: I shall not fall!"

They cheered once more.

"There shall be no more expeditions through the Shadow World! There shall be no more retreat! There shall be no more burning of our fields or looting of our towns! And after this, there shall be no more Army of Boeruine!"

They all shouted themselves hoarse and raised their weapons, stamped their feet, and struck their shields with their swords. Words, thought Aedan. Simple words. And yet, he gives them so much meaning. It was because every sentiment that he expressed he truly felt.

"I was once told by a man much wiser in these things than I that there is no meaning in fighting for a palace, or a throne, or crown, that those are merely things, and things are not worth fighting for or dying for. We do not fight for the Cairn, or for the crown, or for the Iron Throne. We fight for an idea. The idea that in unity, there is strength that cannot be defeated. The idea that in law, there is order, so that men may live in peace and prosper. The idea that in courage, there is honor, so we may hold our heads high. And the idea that in resolve, there is purpose, so that we cannot be deterred.

"The empire has no true borders, because borders cannot encompass an idea. The empire is more than just our land, for land cannot an empire make. The Empire of Anuire is in the hands of the man who plows his field, of the woman who gives birth, of the child who dreams about the future. The empire is in all our hearts! And so long as there is breath within my body, I shall not allow those hearts to break! The war ends here and now! It ends today! It ends before we even see the enemy, for we shall win it with our courage, with our resolve, and with our purpose!" He raised his sword high over his head. "For the empire! And for victory!"

The troops raised a roar that could be heard throughout the city, crying out, "Roele! Roele!" as Michael rode the length of their ranks, standing in his stirrups and waving his sword over his head.

He used my very words, thought Aedan, shaking his head in admiration. Only he said them far better than I ever could.

"A wiser man than I?" said Aedan, when the emperor returned to his side. The troops continued cheering.

"Indisputably," said Michael with a perfectly straight face. "But because I'm such a self-indulgent bastard, I cannot for the life of me remember who he was."

* * * * *

It was almost sunrise when the two armies came within sight of one another on the plains halfway between the cities of Anuire and the castle of Dalton, visible in the distance. Each army had marched all night in an attempt to outpace the other. Michael had known he needed to maintain as much distance as possible between Lord Arwyn's forces and the capital. Arwyn had force-marched after rolling over the border garrisons in an attempt to gain the high ground on the hills around Anuire. It was a draw, and both met in the middle. Still, the first advantage had gone to the Army of Anuire. They had denied Arwyn the superior ground.

He did not expect us to mobilize so quickly, Aedan thought. Arwyn had counted on facing an army that would be tired, weakened, disorganized, unable to assemble in time to halt his advance upon the city. But he had not counted on the captain who had ridden like a man possessed to warn of his advance across the border. He had not counted on the indomitable spirit and resolve of the Anuirean troops. And he had not counted on Michael's ability to inspire them. In calling Michael the "Pretender," Arwyn had devalued him, and in devaluing him, he had underestimated him, as well.

Both armies took up position and settled down to wait for dawn. The soldiers took their rest upon the ground, with their weapons by their side, ready to form for battle on a moment's notice, but Michael did not rest. With Aedan by his side, carrying his standard, he rode among the troops, talking to them, asking about their families, calling many of them by name—it was amazing to Aedan how many of those names the emperor could remember—and Aedan watched their faces light up as Michael rode among them, encouraging them and speaking to them like a fellow soldier, not a monarch.

To one group: "So, a brisk evening walk, a short rest beneath the stars, and we're ready for the morning's work, eh, boys? We'll show them what we're made of, won't we?"

To another: "Well, are you boys ready to give Arwyn a sound thrashing? Shall we push him all the way to Thurazor and let the goblins have his liver for breakfast?"

And to some troops from Elinie: "What do you say, boys, shall we get this nonsense over with so you can all go back to Elinie and fish the Saemil? I hear the trout there grow this big—" holding his hands three feet apart—"and jump right out of the river and straight into your frying pans! I think maybe I'll go with you after we've taught these louts a lesson. It's been a long time since I've gone fishing."

He has the gift, thought Aedan. Seeing him now, relaxed and confident, bantering with them in a friendly manner, they would never have suspected that only a few days ago, he had been locked within his chambers, plunged into deep depression and drinking himself into a stupor. He was just as vulnerable to weakness as the rest of them, but he never for a moment let that show. His confidence gave them confidence. His refusal to feel fatigue gave them energy. And even Aedan started to believe. He felt his spirits rising and suddenly, defeat did not seem possible.

When dawn came, Arwyn's troops attacked. By then, Michael had Korven pass the word to all the officers. "We shall let Arwyn come to us," he said. "We shall let them make the charge, and see us standing here, implacable, immobile, like a wall on which his attack shall break. Let each man stand in silence. I want no battle cries. Let them see our faces—fearless, still, and resolute as death."

As the Army of Boeruine made their charge, the Anuireans stood firm, silent and motionless as statues. Aedan saw Michael anxiously scanning the charging ranks for Arwyn's standard. Yes, there it was, slightly to the left and in the forefront, as could be expected. Arwyn was a warlord in every sense of the word. He would not remain behind in safety, watching from a rise as his troops attacked. He would ride in the vanguard, with his standard-bearer by his side, so that his troops could see him leading them.

As Aedan watched them come, he thought, by Haelyn, he has brought them all. He has pulled back all his troops from the forest borders of Alamie and the Five Peaks, the forces from Talinie and Taeghas, and the garrisons in Brosengae. And there were goblin fighters with them, wolfrider detachments from the Prince of Thurazor. He must have left no one behind to guard the rear, thought Aedan. This time, it was all or nothing.

As the front ranks met, trumpet calls were sounded in the rear of Michael's army, and on cue, they quickly started advancing, moving to the left and right, reforming into wings to envelop the flanks of Arwyn's charging troops. Michael spurred his mount, and with sword raised, charged into them like a scythe cutting through wheat. Immediately, his staff set spurs as well, trying to form a protective circle around him, but trying to protect Michael was like trying to catch the wind. He had set his sights on Arwyn's standard, and his gaze had never left it. Now, he tried to cut his way through to his enemy, the man who'd take his throne.

The clanging of steel against steel filled the air, as did the shouts of men and the neighing of horses. In almost no time at all, the ground was churned up by many feet and hooves, the grass torn and trampled, and the choking dust rising. Holding aloft the standard in one hand and his sword in the other and controlling his plunging mount with his knees, Aedan had no benefit of shield, but Sylvanna stayed on his left flank, protecting it while he struck out on his right, trying to stay near the emperor.

The battle was a wild melee now, and in the tumult and the confusion and the dust, the fighters could know each other only by their colors and devices. Arwyn's flanks were being battered, but he had the advantage of superior numbers, and his center remained strong. Here and there, fighters penetrated deep into the body of the opposing army, on both sides, while in other places, the ranks held on for longer until there were men on both sides hemmed in by their opponents and forced to turn in all directions as they fought.

The noise was deafening. Men fell and were trampled by the surging bodies all around them. Spears were all but useless in such close quarters, except to those who held them up, seeking to unhorse a knight. Out of the corner of his eye, Aedan saw young Ghieste fall as a spear got past his guard and pushed him from his mount. Unbalanced, he went down into the milling bodies, and Aedan did not see him rise again. A moment later, the same thing almost happened to him. He saw a pike thrusting up at him, deflected it with his blade, then slashed down at his attacker, splitting his helm. The man had no time to scream.

None of the mounted fighters could maneuver very quickly now, hemmed in by the fighting foot soldiers all around them, and Aedan saw the emperor, perhaps ten yards away, hacking away like mad as he tried to reach Lord Arwyn. Arwyn, in turn, seemed intent on the same thing. The two were separated by no more than twenty yards, and yet neither could reach the other. Aedan tried to fight his way closer. His breathing was becoming labored, and he felt the soreness in his sword arm as he swung away at his attackers. The standard was an impediment, but he could not let it fall. As

Michael engaged a foot soldier who sought to slash his leg, Aedan saw a mounted knight coming up on his rear.

"Michael!" he called out. "Behind you!"

The emperor struck down the foot soldier and quickly turned his horse, barely in time to parry the sword stroke aimed at his head. For a moment, the two of them engaged in a flurry of blows, and then Michael's sword caught the knight a blow upon his neck, and he went down.

Gylvain fought as well, dressed not in his robes, but for battle. Magic was of little use in a melee, but Aedan noticed that no blade could reach him. As his attackers struck at him, their blades seemed to slide off the air around him, but Gylvain's blows struck home. Then there was no time to notice Gylvain as a mounted knight bore down on Aedan. They exchanged several blows before two Anuirean foot soldiers leapt up and dragged him from his saddle.

On and on the battle went, furious and bloody, with neither side giving way. Aedan fought more from instinct than will, only dimly aware of the dampness of the sweat trickling down inside his armor, the taste of dust in his mouth, and the smell of bodies surging all around him. From time to time, he caught a glimpse of Michael, and did his utmost to stay close to him, but it was all that he could do to fight for his own survival.

And then it happened. A momentary respite from the blades striking out at him, a brief island of calm within the storm, and Aedan saw Michael battling Arwyn, perhaps twenty yards away, their horses side to side as they engaged. In the area immediately around them, men actually stopped fighting so they could watch. Aedan urged his mount forward, trying to get closer.

The old warlord against the young emperor. Both had unleashed their divine rage, and everyone around them watched, mesmerized, as the two combatants smashed away furiously at each other. They seemed evenly matched, and they were battering each other with such force that both their shields had buckled.

Then Arwyn struck a blow that sent Michael's shield flying, and Aedan gasped as Michael seemed to lose his balance from the impact. He swayed in his saddle, and Arwyn raised his sword to finish him. But in that moment, Michael suddenly leaned forward as he swayed and lunged sharply, driving his blade point first through Arwyn's throat.

The momentum of his lunge carried Michael right out of the saddle, and as Arwyn fell back, Michael went with him, over his horse and to the ground. At once, Aedan and Sylvanna moved in to protect him, and then Gylvain was there, as well, and a group of foot soldiers who formed a ring around him. Michael got up. Arwyn never would.

Michael raised his sword with both hands and brought it down like an axe, severing the dead archduke's head from his body. Then he raised it high and cried out, "Arwyn is dead! Lay down your arms!"

Immediately, the cry was taken up by all the troops.

It happened like a spreading ripple in a pool, moving out from where they were to the fringes of the battle. As the cry of "Arwyn's dead!" was echoed over and over, slowly, the fighting stopped. The noise gradually died down, and the clash of blades diminished until everything was still. Men simply stopped fighting and stood where they were, dazed and exhausted, staring at one another, scarcely able to believe it was over.

As the dust began to settle and the only sounds upon the battlefield were the piteous moans and cries of the wounded and the dying, several mounted knights of the Army of Boeruine made their way toward where the emperor stood. Their horses came at a walk, and they held their swords by their sides. One knight rode forward and gazed down for a long time at Arwyn's decapitated body. Then he threw down his sword and reached up to remove his helm. Eight long, hard years had passed since Aedan saw him last, but he immediately recognized Derwyn, Arwyn's son, and Michael's childhood playmate.

His face was a mask of misery. For a moment, his glance met Aedan's, and he nodded. Aedan returned the gesture, and then Derwyn turned to Michael. For several moments, the two of them simply stared at one another as their men gathered around them. No one spoke. Derwyn held his head up high. Not in defiance, but in proud defeat.

"Derwyn . . ." Michael said, heavily. He could not go on.

Derwyn swallowed hard, then raised his arm and cried out in a loud and steady voice, "Long live Emperor Roele!"

There was a moment's hesitation and then the cry was taken up by the troops of both sides. "Long live Emperor Roele! Roele! Roele! Roele!"

"Thank the gods," said Aedan, wearily. "It is over at last. It is finished, Sylvanna."

But as he turned toward her, she wasn't there. He glanced all around him, frantically, but he could see no sign of her nor Gylvain. Nor of any of the other elves. It was as if they had melted away into . . .

"The air," he murmured, as the wind blew north across the plain.

BOOK III

THE GORGON

ANUIRE

chapter one

Seaharrow was a dismal place in winter, cold and damp and drafty from the fierce winds and storms that constantly blew in off the sea, and Laera hated it. During the summer, the weather was more tolerable, even pleasant, and the society much improved, since the annual Summer Court at Seaharrow was resumed. However, with each summer the old and bitter memories returned in force, along with boiling frustration and resentment, as her brother, Michael, once again arrived at Seaharrow with Aedan Dosiere.

She had come full circle. This was where it had all started. It was the ultimate ignominy that she should wind up here. There wasn't a place she could go within the castle that did not remind her of a secret tryst with Aedan. The hanging tapestry in the corridor, with the small niche behind it where she and Aedan had coupled passionately; the garden in the courtyard, where they had often met at night; the tower parapet where they had their first encounter; the stables . . . and the final insult, her own chambers, which had once been Aedan's when he came to Seaharrow for Summer Court.

Her husband had insisted that she take that room, and nothing she could say would sway him. He must have known. Somehow, he must have learned her secret, though she could not imagine how. The bed she slept in every night was the very bed in which she'd lain with Aedan all those times. It was insufferable. Maddening. But at the same time, it fed her hatred and resentment and firmed her resolve to get revenge.

At first, she couldn't understand why Derwyn had not denounced her. When she learned of Michael's victory over Arwyn, her first emotion had been bitter disappointment, for it meant her plans for Aedan and her own advancement had been thwarted. She cared nothing that Arwyn had been slain, but when she learned Derwyn had survived, panic seized her.

Except for Callador, who had disappeared after news of Arwyn's defeat had reached Boeruine, Derwyn was the only one who knew of her betrayal. When she found out Michael had spared him and Derwyn had declared his allegiance to the emperor, she was certain she was undone. Surely Derwyn would denounce her. She had almost fled right then. But the years and her experience had taught her to be calculating, and after her initial bout of fear, she had forced herself to settle down and think things through.

There was nothing to stop Derwyn from denouncing her to Michael, except he had no proof. It would have been his word against hers, and despite the fact that she and Michael were not close—they barely even spoke save for those times when formality demanded it—she was still his sister and a princess of Anuire. Derwyn's position was too precarious for him to risk making such an accusation. He had nothing to gain from it and a great deal to lose. And even if Michael believed him—and there was a possibility he would—he would still not thank him for putting him in the difficult position of having to execute his sister or, at the very least, send her into exile. Her disgrace would be the emperor's disgrace, as well. It would indelibly tarnish the honor and the reputation of the royal house.

However, there was a chance Derwyn might not have realized that. She barely even knew him, so she had no real way to estimate his character or intellect. It was possible that in an attempt to ingratiate himself with Michael, he might reveal her betrayal, thinking he was doing the emperor a great service. Or else he might do it to strike back at Michael for having killed his father. There had been no way to know for sure what he would do, but the more Laera thought about it, the more certain she felt that the situation, while it certainly posed potential danger for her, was not nearly as disastrous as it had seemed at first.

Derwyn would either denounce her or would not. If he did not, then all was well. But if he did, it would still be his word against hers, and the accusation would seem meanspirited and spiteful. And even if Michael did believe it, it would be to his disadvantage to act upon it. After due consideration, Laera had decided that while there was considerable risk in her position, the odds were still in her favor, so she would brazen it out. But she had not been prepared for what developed. Derwyn had surprised her.

In a ceremony on the parade ground of Anuire, where not only all the people of the city, but both armies had gathered, Michael had formally announced an end to the long civil war. The regions Arwyn had controlled would once more be taken back into the empire, and those who had taken up arms against him, so long as they swore allegiance to the empire, would not be penalized. The goblins of Thurazor, however, would suffer the wrath of Imperial Anuire at some point in the near future, which Michael did not specify. The armies had fought long enough, he said, and they deserved a respite from the trade of war.

This, of course, had brought him great acclaim as an enlightened and merciful ruler, but Michael's next decree had been as surprising as it was controversial. He had elevated Derwyn to the rank of duke and confirmed his hereditary ascension to his father's estate. This had drawn a reaction of absolute astonishment from the assembled multitude. Arwyn of Boeruine had rebelled against the emperor, and as such, he was a traitor. By all laws and traditions of the empire, his entire family should have shared his disgrace. An order decreeing Derwyn's formal execution would not have been unexpected, since like his father, he had taken up arms against the empire. At the very least, everyone thought he would be exiled. For him to assume the title and lands of the Duke of Boeruine was shocking and unprecedented, but Michael had yet one more surprise in store.

"My lords and ladies, valiant comrades-in-arms, and people of Anuire," he had said, his voice carrying across the parade ground. "I know that many of you are no doubt shocked and dismayed by my raising of Lord Derwyn to a dukedom when his father had plunged our nation into a long and bloody civil war. Many of you would doubtless call for his exile or even death."

At this, a loud chorus of assent was raised. Michael waited for a moment, then raised his hands for silence.

"Truly, either punishment would be in keeping with our laws and our traditions," he said. "However, there has already been too much dying. There are those among you, I am sure, who would want to see revenge exacted on Derwyn of Boeruine for the war that has long ravaged our country and taken so many lives. Yet I ask you to consider that the war was not of Derwyn's making.

"It was Arwyn who had allowed his blind ambition to cloud his better judgment," he continued. "It was Arwyn whose greed and lust for power led him into making an alliance with the goblin realm of Thurazor, and it was Arwyn who had used force of arms to induce Talinie, Taeghas, and Brosengae to join him in his rebellion. Arwyn has paid for his transgressions with his life. If I were likewise to punish Derwyn of Boeruine, would I not also need to punish Davan of Taeghas, Rurik of Talinie, and Lysander of Brosengae? And if, according to our past laws and traditions, these nobles were to forfeit their lives or be exiled for joining Arwyn in taking arms against us, then according to those same traditions, their families would likewise share in their disgrace.

"Where is the justice? Davan of Taeghas has two young sons aged six and ten. What offense did they commit? Shall we punish the sons for the crimes of the fathers? If we were to take that course, then if a commoner were to steal a loaf of bread, would his son bear the punishment, as well? And what of wives and daughters? What of grandchildren? Where do we draw the line? If, as Arwyn's vassal, Count Davan should be condemned for doing his duty to his feudal lord, then should we not also condemn all those troops who followed him? And *their* families, as well? If we were to proceed in such a manner, the empire would soon lack for a population.

"I say it is enough that Arwyn, who began the war, has paid for his mistake. There is no purpose to be served in further retribution. Boeruine and Talinie must present a strong, united front to defend their borders against incursions from Thurazor and the Five Peaks. Taeghas and Brosengae must now turn their efforts from the prosecution of the war to the pacification of the Seamist Mountains, for the ogres have grown ever bolder while we were in conflict and the dwarves can no longer contain them. Let us forget past differences and proceed with the task of rebuilding. Let us turn our efforts from planning strategy for war to the planting of crops and the raising of livestock.

"Henceforth, we shall be united. To strengthen that union, I propose to send permanent ambassadors from the Imperial Court to each barony and duchy. Each of those ambassadors shall take with him a staff with which to form an embassy that will communicate regularly and directly with the lord high chamberlain, so that the emperor shall have his personal representatives present at each holding.

"And to further cement the ties between us, I am pleased to formally announce on this day the betrothal of my sisters, the Princess Rhiannon to Lord Devan of Taeghas, the Princess Corielle to Lord Rowan of Talinie, the Princess Kristana to Lord Brom of Brosengae, and the Princess Laera to Lord Derwyn of Boeruine. Thus will those lands now be forever tied to our royal house by oath of fealty and bond of blood, and we shall quarrel no more. And in honor of these ties that shall reunite our empire, I hereby proclaim a festival that shall last for seven days and seven nights. Let the temple bells ring and let your voices raise in song and merriment. The war is ended! Let peace reign throughout Imperial Anuire!"

After the initial stunned reaction, the multitude broke out in wild cheering and, on cue, all the temple bells within the city began to toll. All present saw the wisdom and mercy of the emperor and all raised a chant to hail his name. "Roele! Roele! Roele!"

Laera had listened to her brother's final words with shock and amazement. It was the last thing she could have possibly expected. Had Arwyn won the war, as she had been sure he would, she would have married Derwyn, retained her rank, and eventually become the Empress of Anuire. Now, she was still going to marry Derwyn, only instead of standing to inherit the title of empress, she would be diminished in rank from Princess of Anuire to Duchess of Boeruine. Her lot hadn't changed at all from the days when she had been betrothed to Arwyn, only now instead of marrying the father, she would wed the son and live at Seaharrow, on the dreary, storm-lashed coast of a distant province. Fate was ironic, cruel, and fickle.

The one thing that had puzzled her was why Derwyn had agreed to the match. Perhaps Michael had given him no choice. He knew she had been a spy for Arwyn. Perhaps he believed it was because she had loved his father. Yes, she thought, that must be it, but she had soon discovered otherwise. After the Festival of Seven Days, which became an annual celebration, she had departed for Boeruine, where she had married Derwyn. And it was on their wedding night that she discovered his true feelings and motivations.

"Let us have no misunderstandings between us, my lady," he had said, his posture stiff and his voice extremely formal. "I know *exactly* what sort of woman I have married—and do not think to protest your innocence to me. My father had possessed a vast network of informants, and through them, I now possess a wealth of lurid detail about your past. You have changed lovers as a post rider changes mounts, and you have employed your wiles to destroy those whom you have seduced. Make no mistake, this marriage is nothing more than a political arrangement. I do not love you, and I never could.

"You may wonder why I did not denounce you to your brother as a spy," he had continued coldly. "Some of the reasons you have doubtless already inferred, but here is the chief reason of them all. It is up to me to rebuild the tarnished reputation of my house. An alliance by marriage to the House of Roele will do much to increase the diminished standing of the House of Boeruine. Your duty as a wife is to give me sons to carry on my family name. Two shall be sufficient, I should think. They shall be the issue of a union between our houses, and they shall once more raise the Duchy of Boeruine to its once preeminent status as first among all the nobility. The bloodline will be strengthened, and our kinship with Roele, the champion of Deismaar, will be reaffirmed. Beyond that, I want nothing from you.

"You shall sleep in your own chambers. Save for the purposes of procreation, I have no desire to share my bed with you. You shall have ladies-in-waiting to keep you company. I have no wish to be troubled with it. You shall be kept cloistered and under constant watch to ensure your faithfulness. Once you have given me two sons, you shall be free to choose whatever lovers you may wish, subject to extreme discretion. Bed the stableboys, for all I care, but if so much as *one whisper* of gossip should ensue, I shall have you exiled to the farthest reaches of the empire to serve as a priestess in the Northern Temple of Haelyn in the province of Ice Haven on the rocky coast of Talinie, where you shall have your head shaved, dress in simple robes of coarse black wool, and spend your days in constant prayer and solitary meditation.

"When necessity demands that we appear together on formal occasions, you shall play the part of the obedient and loving wife, deferring to my judgment in all things. Otherwise, you shall not try me with your conversation or your presence. On these matters, I shall remain as rigid as the rock on which this castle stands, so save your breath and plague me not with your entreaties. Such is your lot, and you shall accept it without question. Disobey at your own peril."

She had listened with stunned disbelief and mounting fury. Who was he to speak to her in such a manner? She was a princess of the royal house, and he merely some loutish provincial raised to the status of dukedom, even so, beneath her. And how could he know so much about her? Informants, he had said. Spies, he meant. Spies everywhere. She had been betrayed. Which of those servants in the palace had betrayed her? She had paid them well, the traitorous ingrates! And this was how they had repaid her kindness and largesse, by double-dealing and betrayal. If she ever found out who they were, she would have them lashed until the skin fell off their backs. Then she would string them up by their thumbs and roast their feet with coals. She would throttle them with her own bare hands! She wanted to scream and launch herself at her new husband, to scratch his eyes out, but some instinct of self-preservation had restrained her. That was not the way. Rebelling against Derwyn would only give him an excuse to rid himself of her—after she had borne him children.

Children! The thought of lying with him filled her with loathing now. He was much more handsome than his father, and when Arwyn had proposed the match, she had thought she could certainly do much worse. Derwyn was attractive, and his manner seemed to suggest he would be a gentle, thoughtful lover. But now this! Somehow, somewhere, he had found a backbone. She could see his method clearly. Exert forceful control at once, the better to maintain it. Well, she would let him think he had his way.

She had wept and cast her eyes down, meekly submitting to his will, playing up to his masculine power. And she had begun to form a plan that would reverse their roles. And as she considered how she would bring that about, she became filled with delightful anticipation. If Derwyn would use masculine force, she would employ feminine cunning. She would lull him into a false sense of security and then she would neatly turn the tables. It would take time, but she would thoroughly enjoy every moment of it.

That had been three years ago. Since then, her plan had progressed steadily and surely. She had accepted all of Derwyn's directives without question, at first merely acting sullen and stoic about it, but gradually, she had allowed him to perceive her mood begin to alter. This gradual warming trend she had timed to coincide exactly with the frequency of their efforts at procreation. The first time, about a week after their marriage—she could not tell if he was merely giving her time to get used to the idea or if he was working himself up to it—she had acted stiff and unresponsive initially, as if she were suffering in silence through an experience she could not avoid. But as he neared climax, she had begun to thrust against him slightly and had allowed a small moan or two to escape her lips, as if she were enjoying it despite herself. That seemed to both please and excite him, though he had tried not to let it show. She remembered laughing inwardly, thinking that men were so transparent.

The next time, as before, she greeted him as if what they were about to do was a trial for her, but once more, as their lovemaking progressed, she began responding, displaying a bit more excitement—but carefully, not too much. She couldn't let him think she was enjoying the act for its own sake. She wanted Derwyn to believe it was *him* she was responding to, that his male prowess was getting through to her despite her resistance. And little by little, she gave a little more, and then a little more, until eventually her entire demeanor had changed when he came to her.

After a few weeks, she greeted him with eyes meekly downcast, submissive instead of quietly defiant, but when she looked up at him, it was with hopeful anticipation. She always quickly averted her gaze whenever he noticed it, as if she did not mean for him to see how she truly felt. And out of the corner of her eye, she would see the smug little smile on his lips as he noticed what she had pretended to hide and she would think how easy it was.

They were really all the same. Cater to their sense of self, to their pride and illusions of power, and soon they all became putty in her hands. But with Derwyn, the game was more drawn out and considerably more elaborate, in part for its own sake, because she was bored and there was little else to do, and in part because the end result she planned for was ambitious and complex.

A month passed, and she had begun to act repentant, not saying anything outright, but letting him know through her demeanor that she regretted the way she had behaved before. When he came to her bed, she was tender and receptive, always careful not to show too much enthusiasm, allowing him to think he was bringing out the tenderness in her, the "true woman" who had slumbered for so long, that he was making her fall in love with him. And when he left her, she would always turn away and pretend to weep into her pillow. One night, when he hesitated, lingering by the door to her bedchamber as if he were about to offer words of comfort but managed to fight down the impulse, then she knew she had him.

Eight months into their marriage and she was still not pregnant. Doubtless, Derwyn was starting to feel frustration at their failure, but she wasn't pregnant because she had a supply of a special preparation, a potion she had obtained from a wizard in Anuire that would inhibit her fertility. She was not yet ready to give him a child. She had to build up his anticipation and break down his defenses. The timing had to be just right. With Arwyn, she knew, it never would have worked, but Derwyn merely thought he was as strong as his father ever was, when in truth, it wasn't Arwyn's strength that would have made her fail with him, but his complete indifference to anyone except himself.

A year passed, and she entered the next stage of her plan. She was, by now, playing the part of the dutiful and quietly submissive wife to the hilt, but now she added something else. She fell into a melancholy, and at times allowed him to find her weeping for no apparent reason. She began to go to temple regularly, praying every day, until even the priests remarked upon her piety. All of this, she knew, was being reported back to Derwyn, whose manner toward her by now had changed completely.

Convinced he had brought about a change in her, Derwyn was now puzzled by her new behavior. And one night, when she judged the time was right because he had seemed particularly tender with her, she waited until they were finished with their love-making and he lay upon her, spent. Then she started sobbing.

He looked up with alarm and moved to lie beside her. "What is it, Laera?" he asked, stroking her hair softly. "What's wrong?"

"Oh, everything is wrong!" she cried. "All wrong! *I* am all wrong!"

"But how? Why? I don't understand."

Still sobbing, she shook her head and turned away from him, as if ashamed.

"Tell me," he said. "Please."

"I am being punished," she said, sobbing. "Punished for the all wicked things I have done, for the selfish life I've led! That is why I cannot give you sons! The gods have cursed me and made me barren!"

"No," said Derwyn, "that cannot be true."

"I have tried to make up for my past mistakes," she cried. "I have no other wish now than to be a wife and a mother, but no child quickens in my womb! Each day, I go to temple and pray to be forgiven, to be deemed worthy of you, to be blessed with your son, but my prayers remain unanswered, for I have been wicked! Oh, how you must hate me! I wish I could die!"

Derwyn took her in his arms. "Hush, now, don't say such things. We must not tempt the gods."

"Send me away, Derwyn. Send me away to Ice Haven, where I may spend the remainder of my days atoning for my sins and trouble you no more! It is no less than I deserve!"

Inwardly, she held her breath. She thought the moment right, but if she had misjudged things, there was every possibility he would do just that.

"No, Laera," he said. "It is not you who must ask forgiveness. It is I. When I first brought you here, I was cold to you, filled with resentment. I thought to use you as nothing more than a means to an end, so it was I who acted selfishly. You were bitter because you had been hurt by Dosiere—yes, I know about that, too—and it was your anger and your bitterness that led you to do the things you did. Yet all that is in the past. You have been a good and faithful wife. I thought I could not trust you, but now I know I was wrong. You've changed, Laera. You've done everything I asked of you and more. From now on, things will be different. I promise, you will see. If the gods mean for our union to be fruitless, so be it. But I will not send you away. I could never do that now. I love you."

She looked at him, eyes wide with feigned disbelief, as if she had just heard the words she had always longed to hear, while inwardly, she laughed with scornful victory. The change had come. The tables were reversed. Now she was in control.

"Oh, Derwyn!" she said breathily. "I love you, too!"

A month later, she was pregnant, and the midwife decreed the child would be a son.

* * * * *

Almost four years had passed since the War of Rebellion, and the empire was united and stronger under Michael's rule than it had ever been before. For the most part, the nation was at peace, but there was still work for the Army of Anuire. Peace had to be maintained with strength, and there was never any shortage of those who would not hesitate to test that doctrine.

The ogre tribes in the Seamist Mountains had grown stronger while the war had occupied the humans, and periodically the emperor launched campaigns to assist the forces of Taeghas and Brosengae in holding them at bay. To the north of the Heartland territories, tribes of goblins and gnolls who made their headquarters in the Stonecrown Mountains continued raiding farms and villages in Mhoried and herdsmen in the southern part of Markazor, where the empire was attempting to expand its frontiers. Coeranys was subject to periodic raids from demihumans in the Chimaeron, and attacks from Khinasi pirates who plied the coast during the spring and summer seasons.

Rhuobhe Manslayer still remained a strong force to be reckoned with in the Western Marches, and his mountainous, heavily forested domain made a campaign to flush him out virtually impossible. During the eight years that the war progressed, he had taken advantage of the conflict to expand his domain into the forests of Boeruine, and he had pushed his eastern boundaries into the foothills of western Alamie, sweeping down into the valleys with his renegade elves to loot and pillage extensively. At best, the empire could do little more than pursue a strategy of containment by establishing strong garrisons along the western borders of western Alamie. The Five Peaks remained a lawless region, necessitating the establishment of outposts along the northern borders of Alamie to keep the bandits from raiding at their pleasure. And there still remained the punitive expedition into Thurazor, which Michael had been forced to put off time and again because his attention had been required elsewhere.

The outer reaches of Cerilia also occupied much of the emperor's attention. His dream was to expand the boundaries of the empire to encompass the wild territories to the far north, such as Rjuvik, Svinik, Halskapa, Jankaping, and Hogunmark, bringing the Vos tribes back into the fold. Ever since the Battle of Mount Deismaar, the Vos had been a law unto themselves, and Michael wanted to reclaim those territories and restore the empire to the glory of the days before the passing of the old gods. With the Vos territories under his control, he would then be able to mount campaigns from the far northern lands against the territories ruled by the goblin princes and the awnsheghlien, such as the Realm of the White Witch, Urga-Zai, the Giantdowns and, most challenging and dangerous of all, the Gorgon's Crown, the foreboding domain of Prince Raesene.

Beyond that, there were the territories of the Far East, made almost inaccessible by land because to reach them an army would have to pass through Chimaeron. It was the only practicable route to reach the Tarvan Waste and the lands of the Black Spear Tribes, the forests of Rheulgard, Rhuannach, and Innishiere, as well as the Northeastern Territories such as Kal Kalathor, Drachenward, Wolfgaard, Molochev, and the awnsheghlien domains of the

Raven and the Manticore. At one time, before the War of Shadow, which had culminated in the Twilight of the Gods at Deismaar, the empire had controlled almost all of Cerilia, and Michael's dream was to reacquire those lands, drive out the brigands, civilize the savage tribes who now controlled those territories, and defeat the evil awnsheghlien once and for all.

It was an impossibly ambitious goal, thought Aedan, and accomplishing it—if, indeed, it could be accomplished—would take at least a lifetime, yet Michael seemed determined to pursue it. He talked of little else. It was not enough for him that he had already accomplished far more than his father ever had, that the empire was reunited now and stronger than it had been in generations. He wanted to bring back the empire of the original Roele, whose name he bore, and to surpass all the accomplishments of the long line of Roeles who had preceded him.

Michael had become a driven man, and Aedan was concerned about him. He was obsessed with the idea of conquest. Despite the weariness he had professed at the end of the War of Rebellion, he could take no satisfaction in the peace he had achieved. The war had changed him. His formative years had been spent in warfare, and despite all the hardships it imposed, war was now in Michael's blood. He lived to lead troops into battle, and he became moody and restless when he was confined to the palace for any length of time.

That, thought Aedan, was the crux of it. Michael felt *confined*. The daily routine of governing the empire was something he found oppressive. He delegated most of his responsibilities so that, in effect,

Aedan ran the government while the emperor spent endless hours in planning strategies for new campaigns to expand the empire's borders or organizing expeditions to quell raids by bandits and demihumans on the frontier. He had become, thought Aedan, what he had fought. He was a warlord. He had turned into Arwyn of Boeruine.

The people loved him for it. To them, he was a hero, the warrior-king who had saved the empire. Under his rule, they had enjoyed more peace and prosperity than ever before. However, Aedan knew it could not last. The people of the empire hailed his expeditions to put down bandit raids and drive back invading tribes of gnolls and goblins from their borders. They cheered him in the streets when he led his army on the march, but Aedan wondered how long those cheers would last when the treasury ran dry— for it was already seriously depleted—and new and greater taxes had to be imposed to finance the continuing campaigns.

For now, farmers were pleased to contribute a portion of their crop yield to help sustain the Army of Anuire, and herdsmen uncomplainingly provided meat to feed the troops, but as the campaigns continued and the size of the army increased as it did each year, Aedan knew these attitudes would change. For the present, it was not a hardship for a farmer to contribute a tenth portion of his crops to supply the army, but what would happen when the empire demanded half? Parting with a few head of sheep or cattle did not greatly discommode a herdsman, knowing he was playing a vital part in keeping the empire secure, but when the army came and marched away with half his herd, he would be sure to feel resentment.

Michael couldn't seem to see that. The people loved him, and he could not imagine losing their support. For now, he had it, but if he maintained his present course, things were bound to change. Over and over, Aedan had tried to make him understand this, but Michael stubbornly dismissed all his concerns.

"You worry too much, Aedan," he'd say with a smile. "As we pacify our frontiers and continue to expand our borders, we shall make more land available for farming and grazing. And as we make more opportunities for farmers to expand their fields and herdsmen to broaden their range lands, our new acquisitions will attract people from the cities to the frontiers, where they will see the chance to prosper. And when people prosper, Aedan, they do not become dissatisfied."

"Indeed, there is truth in what you say," Aedan had replied, "but you have neglected to take several things into account. It is not quite that simple. As we continue to expand our borders—which will cost us—it will require more of our resources to protect them. We will have to build more garrisons, create new peers to oversee the administration of the newly acquired territories, and recruit more troops to defend them. Those troops will all need to be supplied and fed and housed, and the expense of that will counteract the growth in prosperity that you envision for a number of years, at least.

"Aside from that," he continued, "these constant campaigns, no matter how successful they may be, continue to impose a steady drain on manpower. We have already increased the number of mercenaries in our ranks significantly, and mercenaries do not have the same impetus to fight as do men who defend their homeland. In the War of Rebellion, most of our soldiers were family men. When they returned from their campaigns, they went to spend time with their families. Mercenaries, on the other hand, have no families to support, which means they have no responsibilities. When they return from the campaigns, they go into the city in search of entertainment. They go to gaming houses, brothels, and taverns.

"Since we have increased the number of mercenaries among our troops," Aedan continued, "there has been a marked increase in such establishments to cater to them. Along with them has come a marked increase in crime. Once quiet and peaceful areas of the city have become raucous fleshpots where taverns and brothels remain open till the early hours of the morning and men stagger drunkenly through the streets, accosting female citizens, getting into brawls, and generally creating a nuisance. They, in turn, have attracted a growing number of alleymen and cutpurses, and the city sheriff is too overtaxed to deal with them all. There have been numerous petitions from our citizens complaining of this situation and of the behavior of the mercenaries when they are on the town. We need to hire more men for the sheriff's guard, which will further tax our resources. To put it bluntly, Sire, we just cannot afford to continue on this course."

"As I said, Aedan, you worry too much," Michael had replied. "The empire is growing, and we are merely experiencing some growing pains. These are all matters that can be sorted out. We need no more men for the sheriff's guard when we can employ the

army to help police the city. A curfew can be insti-
tuted for soldiers on the town, and the city council
can pass an ordinance decreeing that taverns, gaming houses, and other such establishments may not
remain open past a certain hour. These are all matters that can be settled with a little thought and practical application. I leave them completely in your
hands, as I have utmost confidence in you. Work
with the city council to resolve them. I cannot be
bothered with such trivial affairs.

"As for the rest of your concerns," he added,
"these things will all be settled in due course. New
territories mean new wealth and opportunities and
more security for the citizens of the empire. If this
will tax our resources in the short run, the long term
gains will compensate for short-term losses. We
must look to the future. If that requires us to make
some sacrifices in the present, so be it."

Later that night, Aedan repeated the conversation
to his wife as they prepared for bed. "It just seems
hopeless," he told her when he finished describing
his discussion with the emperor. "He is wrong, and
he is trying to move too fast, but I cannot convince
him. It's no different than when we were children.
He is just as stubborn and obstinate as ever. The
trouble is, I have always been the sensible one, the
voice of restraint, and he simply thinks I am being
stodgy and overcautious. Of what use am I as his
first minister if he won't listen to my advice?"

"He needs a wife," said Ariel as she got into bed.

Aedan stopped his pacing back and forth across
the room. He looked at her, taken aback, then
chuckled and shook his head. "You women always
think that marriage will settle a man. Nothing short

of another explosion like the one on Deismaar all those years ago will settle Michael, and even then, I'm not so sure."

"Now who is thinking in overly simplistic terms?" she asked. "Or has it not occurred to you that a wife may influence her husband in ways his friends and advisors cannot? Aside from which, have you considered asking the emperor what will become of all his efforts if he does not produce an heir? Right now, he has nothing else to occupy his attention save his plans for the future of the empire. What about the future of his line? Has he stopped to consider that?

"And it wouldn't do for him to marry just anyone," she added. "The selection of a suitable bride for the emperor would take time and effort, much of which he would doubtless delegate to you, but his consultation would certainly be required, and that would give him something else to think about. Then there is the matter of reaching a decision. He would have to meet his potential bride and get to know her. I could not see the emperor blindly accepting an arranged match. He would naturally insist on forming his own opinion and making his own choice.

"Then there would be the matter of the marriage itself, of course, with all the necessary arrangements," she continued. "That, too, would take some time and effort. And following the marriage, there would be the customary period for consummation, after which a certain amount of his attention would be occupied by the production of an heir. If we could find the right sort of woman for him, one who is as intelligent as she is beautiful, one whom he could fall in love with and respect and not dominate completely, then it is doubtful he would spend every waking hour thinking about new campaigns. If a marriage would not settle him, as you say, then at the very least it would slow him down."

Aedan rubbed his beard thoughtfully. "You know, you're absolutely right," he said. "It would be the perfect solution. I cannot imagine why I did not think of it myself."

"I can," Ariel said softly. "Considering the circumstances of our match, I would not expect you to think of marriage as a desirable solution to anything."

Aedan compressed his lips into a tight grimace. He sighed heavily. "Have I been so inconsiderate a husband?"

Ariel shook her head. "No," she said. "You have been most considerate and kind and gentle. I could not ask for a more doting father for our daughter, nor a husband more attentive to my needs. I can complain of nothing. I know you have come to care for me over the past four years, but I also know that had you been able to choose freely, I would not have been the one you would have chosen for a wife."

Aedan sat down on the bed and took her hand. "It is true that I loved Sylvanna, but I have no regrets for the way things turned out. A marriage with Sylvanna would have been impossible, for all the reasons you gave me at the time. She knew that as well, which was why she left the way she did, along with all the others. We shared a brief moment of happiness, but we could not have made a marriage. I knew that even then. We were from two different worlds, and fate brought us together. We fought shoulder-to-shoulder throughout the war, facing death countless times, and when a man and woman

—even a human and an elf—are together in such circumstances for so long, I suppose it is inevitable that such feelings should develop."

"I wish I could have gone on the campaigns with you," said Ariel wistfully. "I am strong, and I can fight as well as most men, and better than some. I pleaded with my father to let me go, but he said it was not a woman's place to take up arms in battle, especially a lady of the court."

"Be grateful you were spared the horror," Aedan said. "I would not wish for you to share the nightmares that still plague me."

"I would share anything with you," she said.

"You have made me very happy, Ariel. You have become the nearest and dearest person in my life, more important to me even than the emperor, whom I have known and loved as a friend and sovereign since my childhood, and whom duty demands I place above all else. I could never have given Sylvanna what she truly needed, nor could she have done the same for me. You, on the other hand, have fulfilled all my needs and more."

"Had things been otherwise," she said, "and had you the opportunity to choose between us now . . ." She stopped. "No, I will not ask that. It is unfair and pointless. And I don't think I really want to know."

"But I did choose you," said Aedan. "And I have never had cause to regret my choice."

They blew out the candles and went to bed, but Aedan couldn't sleep for a long time.

ANUIRE

chapter two

The birth of Aerin of Boeruine was the occasion of
great rejoicing at Seaharrow. Derwyn had declared a
festival to celebrate the birth of his heir, and the bells
of the town tolled to commemorate the event. The
wine cellars of Seaharrow were opened, and barrels
sent out to the town, placed in the squares so that the
people could join the duke in a celebratory libation,
and a dispatch rider was sent to Anuire to inform the
emperor of the happy news that he had become an
uncle. A feast was held in the great hall of the castle,
and Derwyn had spared no expense to make sure
the celebration was every bit as lavish as those held
at the emperor's court. All present had remarked
that they had never seen him happier.

For Laera, it was an occasion of immense relief. She had loathed carrying the child. She was grateful to be free of the sickness in the mornings, of the immense discomfort that had only continued to increase as the child grew, of the pain in her back and the swelling in her ankles and the twisting and turning and kicking of the infant as it lay within her womb. She had known that birth was painful and precarious, but she had still been unprepared for the agony she felt as Aerin made his way into the world. It had felt as if she were being torn apart.

She had screamed and cursed Derwyn's name in terms so crude and vehement that even the midwives had been shocked, and she was later grateful her husband had not been present to hear how she abused him. It would have certainly conflicted with the new image of herself that she had worked so hard to build up in his mind.

Derwyn had obtained a wet-nurse for her, as was customary, for which Laera was profoundly grateful. She had suffered long enough in carrying the child. She had no wish to be burdened further by needing to care for it. That was why women of the common classes aged so quickly, she thought. Their children suck the life right out of them.

As it was, she had to bear pain in her bosoms for at least a week or more past the delivery and the discomfort of the compression bandage wound around her chest each day to catch the leaks and inhibit milk production. She knew that it would not be long before Derwyn wanted her to bear him a second son, and she was not looking forward to the experience. She would postpone it for as long as possible. She did not even want to allow him in her

bed, and in this, fortunately, she had the support of
the midwives, who had explained to Derwyn that
she was weak and needed time to recover from the
birth.

She thanked the gods the child hadn't been a
daughter. She hoped the next one wouldn't be. That
would mean she would have to suffer through the
entire process yet a third time, or even more, if
another daughter came. She still had a small supply
of her special potion left, but she would soon run out
and have to find a source for more. She would have
to find and cultivate some young woman of the
Court of Seaharrow she could trust. A servant
wouldn't do. She had learned her lesson. Servants
could betray her. She would need to find a girl of
some position who had a lot to lose.

For all that she had suffered, the birth of Aerin had
now made possible the next stage of her plan. She
had already begun working on it. As before, it
would be a slow process that would involve the
gradual manipulation of her husband, but she had
already laid the groundwork. Derwyn had intended
to be her lord and master, but by now, it was she
who held control. It had been such a simple matter
to convince him that he had made her fall in love
with him and that it was his prowess as a lover, and
not the subtle skills she had learned over the years,
that brought out the best in her ånd made sex so
pleasurable. She would now use it as a weapon to
get her way.

She had already planted the seeds for the next
phase of her plan. When Derwyn came to see her
following the birth, she had told him how pleased
and proud she was to have given him the son he

wanted and added, as if in passing, an observation as to the importance of the birth.

"He shall grow up to do great things, my husband," she had said. "I know it. I can feel it in my bones."

"I have no doubt he will," said Derwyn proudly.

"You now have a strong son to carry on your name," she said. "And he shall be an important person in the empire, for the emperor remains unmarried, and without an heir. As the firstborn of the eldest princess of the House of Roele, Aerin shall be the next in line to sit upon the throne. Of course, I am sure Michael will marry someday and produce an heir. It is just that he has been so busy with his campaigns of late that he has had no time to devote to such pursuits."

Still, that had set Derwyn's mind to thinking about the possibility. She could tell. Unlike his father, Derwyn revealed every thought through his expression. And the thought of his son one day sitting on the Iron Throne was something he had not previously considered. However, now that the thought had been planted, it would grow. And she would slowly nurture it until it bloomed into a driving ambition.

If Michael remained without an heir, and if something were to happen to him on one of his campaigns, Aerin would stand to inherit the throne, and Derwyn would become the regent until Aerin came of age. Once that had been accomplished, if some ill fate were to befall Derwyn, then as his wife, she would become regent. And she would rule the Empire of Anuire.

Each night as she lay alone in bed, keeping Derwyn

at bay until she had recovered from the birth, she planned as diligently as Michael planned the strategies for his campaigns. In her mind, she went over each aspect of her goal, refining it, contemplating every last detail. The one thing she could not control was Michael. If he were to marry and produce an heir, that could ruin everything. There seemed nothing she could do to prevent that from happening. But if, by chance, he did marry and the new empress, whoever she might be, bore him a son, she would have to find some way to make certain the child did not survive.

One night, as she lay in bed contemplating possibilities, she became aware of a subtle change in the air within her room. The candles guttered, and the atmosphere around her took on a certain thickness. It grew darker in the center of the room. As she sat up in bed, she perceived a smoky, faintly glowing mist that appeared just above the floor and rose in tendrils that began to swirl, spinning around and around until they formed a vortex, a misty tunnel in the air. Through that tunnel came a dark figure, walking slowly toward her.

She held her breath. As the figure approached, looming larger, she could make out the robes he wore and the staff he carried in his hand. Even before he stepped out into her room, she knew who had come to visit her.

"*Callador!*" she said.

He bowed to her. "My lady," he said, pulling back his hood and revealing his ancient, hairless features. "It has been a long time. I trust I find you well?"

"I am recovering from having given birth," she said. "Derwyn has a son."

"Yes, I know," the wizard said. "I have kept track of events. I still have an interest in what transpires at Seaharrow."

"Where have you been?" she asked. "You disappeared without a trace after the war. It is widely assumed that you are dead."

"That serves my purpose," Callador replied. "I had to take certain precautions. When I learned that Arwyn fell in battle, I feared the possibility of retribution for the part I took in his rebellion. For all I knew, your involvement in it might have been exposed, and the emperor could have taken it into his head to punish me severely for the part I played in it. Had you been revealed as an agent of Boeruine, I had little doubt you would try to save yourself by claiming to have been ensorcelled."

He held up his hand to forestall her comment. "Do not protest," he said. "That would have been the only logical course for you to take if you wished to save yourself, and I would not have blamed you for it. However, under the circumstances, I felt it prudent to remove myself from the possibility of imperial retribution, and since I had lost my patron, it was needful that I find another. I had not anticipated you might escape suspicion.

"I thought it likely Derwyn would denounce you in an attempt to save himself," Callador explained. "I never expected your brother, the emperor, would be so forgiving as to raise Derwyn to his father's dukedom and allow him to retain his lands. Nor had I anticipated you might become his duchess. Strange how things turn out. You appear to have emerged unscathed and done quite well for yourself, all things considered. Congratulations are certainly in order. However, knowing you, I expect you still have hopes of doing better."

"That I do," said Laera, "and I have already taken steps in that regard. But where had you gone? You say you went searching for another patron. Am I correct in assuming that you found one?"

"I have, indeed," said Callador. "And I must say, it took some convincing on my part to be accepted by my present lord. He is powerful enough in his own regard that he did not really need my services. However, I was able to make him see there would be certain advantages in taking me on."

"Who is this powerful lord?" asked Laera. "Gorvanak of Thurazor?"

Callador chuckled. "He is powerful, but not nearly powerful enough for me to feel secure in his service."

"Then who?"

"You will learn that in due time," Callador replied. "First, I wish for us to reach an understanding. You had expressed an interest in my tutelage once the war was over. Do you still desire to study the thaumaturgic arts?"

Laera's eyes lit up. Learning how to use magic would benefit her plans enormously. "More than ever," she said. "Of course, it would have to be done in secret. I could not allow my husband to suspect."

"That goes without saying," Callador replied, nodding. "I had an apprentice when I resided in Boeruine, but he lacked promise. You, on the other hand, possess the necessary attributes in rich abundance. You are clever, patient, quick-witted, and ambitious. I feel I could do a lot with you."

"When can we start?" she inquired eagerly.

"Soon," said Callador. "Very soon. I am growing old and would be grateful for the opportunity to pass on all my skills and knowledge. But there are certain conditions that would first have to be met."

"Name them," Laera said.

"Mages must protect themselves from unscrupulous would-be apprentices who would, under the guise of sincerity, enter into their tutelage only to steal spells," said Callador. "I do not for a moment suggest you would do such a thing, or even consider it, but prudence and tradition both demand a blood oath and a personal token to grant the mage security against betrayal."

"What sort of token?" Laera asked cautiously.

"A lock of hair would do," said Callador.

"Oh," said Laera, fearing it might have been something worse. "I can accept that. What are the other conditions?"

"As my apprentice, you would be bound by the same oath of fealty I have sworn to my new lord for so long as I remain in his service," Callador replied. "You would not be required to swear again, however. The oath you would swear to me would bind you to my lord, as well."

"I understand," said Laera, thinking such an oath would be of no real consequence.

Callador seemed reluctant to reveal the identity of his new patron until he was sure of her intentions. Doubtless, he wanted some assurance she would not reveal anything to Derwyn. No matter. Only foolish men gave any credence to such things as blood oaths. A little scratch upon the palm so that blood could mingle with blood and they thought it meant something. Besides, once her plans came to fruition, whoever Callador's new lord might be, it was he who would owe fealty to her.

"I can accept that," she said, feigning a somber and earnest expression.

"Good," said Callador. He tossed a sharp dagger onto her bed. "Cut off a small lock of your hair. It need not be much. This amount will do." He held his thumb and index finger about three inches apart.

She cut off a lock of hair, then handed it to him.

"Now, you must make the cut for the blood to bind the oath," he said. "Your left palm, the one closer to your heart."

She put the point of the dagger up against her palm, set her teeth, and made a small cut, just enough to allow some blood to flow. "Is that enough?" she asked, holding it up for his inspection.

"That will do. Now, hand me back the dagger."

She gave it back to him, and he made a cut upon his own palm. "Hold out your palm, like this," he indicated, holding out his hand, palm up.

She did as he told her, and he placed the lock of hair upon her bleeding palm, then pressed his own palm against hers, with the lock of hair between them.

"Repeat after me," he said. "With this token and my lifeblood, I do pledge my bond . . ."

"With this token and my lifeblood, I do pledge my bond . . ." she repeated, thinking this all foolishly dramatic.

"and do hereby give my solemn oath as surety . . ."

"and do hereby give my solemn oath as surety . . ."

"of fealty to my teacher, lord, and master . . ."

"of fealty to my teacher, lord, and master . . ."

"of support and loyalty to his designs . . ."

"of support and loyalty to his designs . . ."

"of trust he may repose in me with all his secrets . . ."

"of trust he may repose in me with all his secrets . . ."

"and obedience in all things he may ask of me."

"and obedience in all things he may ask of me."

"Thus do I swear, on this my token and my life-blood, to seal the pledge."

"Thus do I swear, on this my token and my life-blood, to seal the pledge," she said.

"Good. It is done," said Callador, breaking the contact and removing a small locket from his robe, into which he carefully placed her blood-soaked lock of hair. Then he turned and started back into the swirling portal.

"Wait!" said Laera. "When shall I see you again? And how?"

Callador paused. "I shall come to you."

"But what of my husband? Derwyn shall want to share my bed again before too long."

"When?"

She shook her head. "I can put him off a few more days, perhaps, but not much longer. He will grow suspicious."

"A day or two should be sufficient. Obtain a lock of his hair for me. Tell him you wish it as a keepsake. I shall come to you the day after tomorrow and collect it."

Laera frowned uncertainly. Suddenly, she had an idea that something had gone very wrong. "But . . . for what purpose?"

"So that I may devise a spell that will place him into a deep sleep at those times when I come to you. Never fear, it shall not harm him. And he shall awake recalling nothing of my visits."

He turned and started to walk into the misty tunnel. For a moment, Laera simply sat there, stunned, her mind racing. The lock of hair was more than just a token. If it could be used to cast a spell . . .

"Callador, wait!" she cried.

He paused inside the tunnel, his dark figure indistinct inside the swirling mist.

"This lord who has become your patron," she said. "Tell me his name!"

The swirling mist began to dissipate. But before the tunnel disappeared, she heard the wizard speak the name . . .

"Raesene."

* * * * *

The word spread far and wide throughout the realm that the emperor sought a bride. Dispatch riders were posted to all the holdings of the nobility throughout the empire, and before long, every member of the aristocracy with an eligible daughter was petitioning for her to be considered. Of those aristocrats with more than one unmarried daughter in the household, some put forth the names of their eldest, some proposed their youngest, while others still proposed them all, inviting the emperor to take his pick as if he were choosing puppies from a litter.

The higher-ranking nobles, mindful of the proper protocol in matters of this kind and wishing not to make a misstep, all sent representatives to court, some with written scrolls that they delivered, setting forth replies. Others sought a direct audience with the lord high chamberlain so that they could repeat verbatim speeches they had memorized, extolling the virtues of the young noblewomen on whose behalf they acted.

Aedan was soon swamped with petitions and appointments. Each day, he received envoys who came with prepared speeches, scrolls, locket miniatures, and full-size portraits of the women whose cause they were advancing. Dozens more had taken up residence in rooming houses throughout the city, all waiting for their turn. Other nobles, especially the lower-ranking ones whose concern for proper protocol was not as great as their ambition, had actually packed up their daughters and brought them to the capital, hoping to present them personally for the emperor's inspection.

It seemed every noble in the realm, from archduke to baronet to minor lords of small estates, had at least one daughter to present, and Aedan felt hopelessly ill qualified to choose from among them all. Even had he felt confident in his abilities to select a list of final candidates to present before the emperor, he could not handle it alone. He learned that very quickly.

There seemed to be no limit to the measures some nobles would employ to influence his choice. Many came with handsome gifts, while several offered outright bribes, and one viscount, who was as desperate for advancement as he was utterly unscrupulous, had even offered Aedan his youngest daughter for a mistress if he would advance his eldest for the emperor's consideration.

Aedan held audiences with nobles who came to parade their daughters before him, decked out in their finest gowns to show their poise and beauty or display their talents. He heard so many ballads strummed on harps and lutes and sung with widely varying degrees of aptitude that he began to hear them in his sleep, and he saw so many examples of embroidery and weaving that his eyes began to cross.

"I cannot bear it any longer, Ariel," he said one weary night, so driven to distraction that he couldn't sleep. "I never imagined there would be so many of them! This task is taking up all of my time, and I am falling hopelessly behind on other vital matters. This was your idea! You have to help me. Please!"

"Leave it to me," said Ariel. "You go on about the business of the empire, and I shall handle the selection process. Just put it out of your mind. I will present you with a final list of candidates when I am done."

"I really don't think you have any idea what you are letting yourself in for," Aedan said.

"Oh, I think I do," Ariel replied. "And what is more, I will be pleased to do it. I have longed for some task that would occupy my time and make me feel useful. Besides, a woman really would be better suited for this sort of thing."

"I don't know," said Aedan dubiously. "It is not that I lack confidence in your abilities, it is just that I am not sure you know Michael well enough to choose the sort of woman he would want."

"Perhaps not," Ariel replied, "but I think I can choose the sort of woman he needs. And that is really more important. If she is the right woman, she will make him want her, rest assured."

With considerable relief, Aedan turned over to his wife the task of screening the candidates, and Ariel set about it with methodical determination. She quickly assembled a committee of ministers and women of the court to assist her. Lord Dorian, chief clerk of the Ministry of the Exchequer, was appointed to her committee so that he could consult his records and keep her apprised of the landed worth of every noble who proposed a daughter as a candidate. Lady Arien was chosen to assist in making an evaluation of the social graces of those candidates who came in person. Old Rhialla, the senior midwife of the palace, was brought in to make determinations as to the health and constitutions of those applicants who presented themselves to the committee, the better to ensure that anyone chosen for the final list would have the fortitude to bear strong children. And several well-known bards who traveled far and wide across the empire and had a reputation for proper courtly graces were consulted in regard to those candidates who did not come in person, so that they could report on what they had observed when they had visited those holdings and pass on what they had heard, as well.

Within a few weeks, Ariel and her committee had eliminated most of the applicants who came in person, as well as a majority of those who had sent envoys to represent them, and had sent out invitations to those who sounded promising to come and present themselves at the Imperial Cairn. Each night, Ariel reported on the progress her committee made that day, and Aedan was impressed. A huge burden had been lifted from his shoulders.

On occasion, Michael would inquire as to how things were progressing, but by and large, he was content to leave things in Aedan's hands and let him oversee the work of the committee. He seemed neither anxious nor particularly interested, which puzzled Aedan somewhat. For as long as he had known him, which had been all his life, Aedan had never known Michael to show much interest in the fairer sex. If he had any experience in matters of the heart—or of the flesh—he had conducted himself with such discretion that Aedan was unaware of it. Of course, Aedan realized with some embarrassment, he himself had hardly been a good example to the emperor in that regard. Michael had known of his affair with Laera, and though he had never brought it up again, he had alluded to it once—when Aedan's betrothal to Ariel had been announced.

"I approve," he had said, nodding with satisfaction. "You had given me some cause for concern about your judgment in such matters in the past, but I am pleased to see you have learned from your mistakes. My congratulations, Aedan. I am sure the two of you will be very happy."

Mistakes, thought Aedan. Plural. It was the only time Michael had ever given any indication he knew of his involvement with Sylvanna, as well.

Ultimately, Aedan had decided Michael was simply too preoccupied with his plans for the empire to give much thought to women. He preferred the company of men, but not in any way that led Aedan to believe his appetites might run in that direction. He was polite but cursory with all his ministers except Lord Korven, whom he treated like an uncle. Korven was growing too advanced in age to serve as a general in the field, so instead had been advanced to the post of minister of war. And Michael dearly loved his troops. "My boys," he called them, fondly and with great pride. Each day, he drilled with them and always brought back a few, regardless of their rank or social standing, to share supper with him in the palace, so that he could solicit their opinions, which he often gave more weight than those of his ministers.

The energies and feelings that made most men's thoughts turn to women were, in Michael's case, expended in the physical exertions of combat, strenuous training, and making plans for further conquest. He simply had no time for women, became impatient in their company because he did not understand them, and was only interested in marriage because Aedan had convinced him of the necessity of producing an heir.

It made Aedan wonder what sort of woman would appeal to him as a bride. Through Ariel's committee, he would be able to make some recommendations, but the final choice, of course, had to be Michael's. Unless, perhaps, Ariel were wrong. It could be that Michael would be perfectly content to have the choice made for him. And if he was truly that indifferent, Aedan felt sorry for the woman who would become Empress of Anuire.

In an attempt to achieve some greater understanding, he sought an audience with the old empress, Michael's mother, Raesa. Having tired of life in the palace, Empress Raesa had retired to a walled estate on the east side of the city, where she lived with several of her ladies-in-waiting and was protected by a detachment of the house guard.

They met in the immaculate gardens within the walls of the estate, and Aedan was surprised to find the empress pruning the plants herself. She greeted him warmly and led him to a bench by the fountain.

Aedan had not seen her in quite a long time, as she no longer chose to participate in any official functions, and he was surprised at how young she still looked. She was not many years older than he, and there was no gray in her long golden hair, as there already was in his. She was still attractive, and her eyes sparkled with vitality. It was obvious her new life away from the palace agreed with her. He commented on that fact.

Raesa smiled. "It does agree with me. I never liked living in the palace. It was too cold and drafty. I was forever coming down with the sniffles. I much prefer living here in the city."

"Do you not get lonely?" Aedan asked.

The empress laughed. "Oh, hardly. I have my friends here with me, and there is no shortage of gentlemen who come to call. I am a woman of wealth and position, and still young enough to look reasonably pleasing to the male eye. My social life is busier now than when I resided at the palace."

"You have suitors, then?"

"None that I would seriously consider," she replied. "I enjoy the company of men, but at this stage of my life, I have no desire for any involvement deeper than friendship. I married very young and began to have children soon thereafter. And while Hadrian was a good husband and the experience of marriage had its own rewards, I am not eager to repeat it. I do not lack for companionship, and I desire nothing more. But then, you did not come here merely to inquire about my welfare, did you? You came to speak of Michael."

Aedan nodded. "It is true," he said. "I must admit I am at a loss to understand him sometimes. I came to you in search of guidance."

"You are overwhelmed by the task of choosing a wife for him," she said.

Aedan sighed. "You see straight to the heart of the matter. My wife has taken it upon herself to free me of the burden of the initial selection process, for which I thank the gods, but for the life of me, I just cannot imagine what sort of woman he would like. Or would put up with him."

"You know Michael much better than I do," Raesa replied. "He comes to see me on occasion, but you have spent far more time with him than I."

"True, but I lack the proper perspective when it comes to such matters," Aedan said. "And while a marriage can easily be arranged based upon a woman's rank and social standing and ability to bear strong children, I would like, if possible, for it to be based on something more. Compatibility, at least, or even love."

Raesa smiled. "That is something neither you nor anyone else could guarantee," she said. "Love cannot be planned. It may grow, under the right circumstances, but there is no predicting how or when. I came to care deeply for Hadrian over the years, but I was never in love with him. At least, not the sort of love a girl dreams of when she is young. There was fondness and affection, but never any passion. And for love to exist, there must be passion, at least in the beginning. A greater, gentler sort of love may grow from passion as time passes, but it needs that seed from which to sprout. If that is what you hope to accomplish, and not merely a marriage of political convenience so that Michael may sire an heir, you will need to bring him together with a woman he can feel passionate about, and one who will feel passion for him, as well."

"But what sort of woman would that be?" asked Aedan with exasperation.

Raesa smiled again. "One who is strong enough not to be intimidated by him," she replied.

"That is almost exactly what Ariel had said," he said.

"Then she is wise, and you must listen to her. But that alone is not enough. Michael is a driven man, obsessed with his plans for the future of the empire. It is all he ever speaks of. He is a great man, and great men are often ambitious, selfish, obstinate, arrogant, and even cruel. You seek a young woman strong enough not to be frightened of such traits and determined enough to wish to change them. Look for an expert horsewoman."

"A *horsewoman*?" Aedan said with incomprehension.

"Not one who merely rides well, but one who can control the most spirited of mounts," the empress said. "One who would not be afraid to saddle an unbroken horse and tame him, one who would regard it as a challenge."

"I see," said Aedan, slowly. "Yes, I think I understand."

"Seek also for a woman who is not afraid to express her opinions," Raesa went on. "Not one who is talkative or stubbornly willful, but who speaks when she has something of substance to say and is not easily swayed from her beliefs. Michael would not respect a wife who would defer to him in all things regardless of what she truly felt. He needs a strong-rooted mountain rose, not a shrinking violet."

Aedan nodded. "Yes, that makes excellent sense, Your Highness."

"Beyond that, look to your own knowledge of Michael," Raesa said. "Look for those things in him that make you prize his friendship, those qualities that inspire loyalty and admiration in his soldiers. Women have similar qualities, as well, though they may manifest them differently. Follow your instincts. And then let nature take its course."

Aedan thanked the empress for her words of wisdom and returned to the Imperial Cairn, feeling a bit more confident, but still anxious as to where such a woman could be found. That night, however, Ariel came to him in an enthusiastic mood to report that the work of the committee was done at last.

"We've found her, Aedan!" she said excitedly. "We need not even bother with a list of final candidates. We have found the perfect woman for the emperor!"

Aedan seemed a little dubious as he received the news. "Well, that is all very encouraging," he said, "but don't you think it would be best if we could present Michael with some choices?"

"If that is what he wishes," Ariel replied, "then we have narrowed down the list to five, and we could hold a feast, with dancing, during which he could meet them all. But I feel confident that the moment Michael meets Faelina, he will have eyes for no one else."

"Faelina?"

"She is the daughter of Baron Moergan of Aerenwe," said Ariel.

"I was not aware that Moergan even had a daughter," Aedan said.

"He has two," said Ariel, "but the youngest is only

twelve and already promised, by a long-standing arrangement, to Gaelin of Dhalaene."

"And how old is Faelina?"

"Sixteen," said Ariel. "But she possesses a maturity beyond her years. She is simply perfect. Wait till you meet her."

Aedan thought of Moergan of Aerenwe, whose holdings lay to the east, on the southern coast north of the Erebannien, near the Gulf of Coeranys. Moergan did not often come to court, only on important state occasions. He was a rough-hewn, taciturn man who brought to mind a stout and weathered oak, enduring and unbending. Aedan found it difficult to imagine that a brooding, plainspoken and even more plain-featured man like Moergan could produce a daughter capable of captivating Michael. He tried to recall what Moergan's wife was like, but found that he could not even summon up the name of the baroness, much less call to mind her features.

"Tell me about this girl," he said. "Is she comely?"

Ariel smiled. "She bears little resemblance to her father, if that is your concern. In her looks, she takes after her mother, but where the Baroness Vivianne is shy as a wild forest creature and takes pains not to call attention to herself, Faelina is vivacious and most attractive. She has poise, bearing, and a strength of personality that commands attention. The moment I met her, I was sure she was the one, and though her rank may not be high, all on the committee agreed she was the perfect choice."

Aedan raised his eyebrows. "Indeed? I am intrigued. When can I meet her?"

"Tomorrow," Ariel said. "I have taken the liberty of inviting her to breakfast with us in our chambers.

I thought that would give you ample opportunity to form your own opinion of her."

"I will be looking forward to it," Aedan said.

In the morning, after they had dressed and the servants came to set the table for their breakfast, Faelina of Aerenwe arrived promptly with her lady-in-waiting. The baron had accompanied his daughter to Anuire, and they had been given rooms at the palace, but unlike the other fathers, he professed no interest in directly championing his daughter's cause. He had served with the emperor in the War of Rebellion and had survived some of their most difficult campaigns, but socializing and political maneuvering were not pursuits for which he cared a great deal, if at all. He had an eligible daughter, and he had done his duty by putting her name forth and coming with her to the capital when they received their invitation. Beyond that, he was content to let Faelina speak for herself.

And she did so, frankly and directly, with disarming honesty. Aedan was very much impressed. She was, indeed, vivacious and attractive, but she was no great beauty. Most of the women Aedan had seen had gone to great lengths to enhance their beauty, and while Faelina was far from plain, she was pretty rather than beautiful and did not go to any trouble to enhance her appearance.

She wore no jewelry save for a thin girdle of silver chain around her waist and a small gold locket of her mother's. She came dressed in a simple yet taste-ful blue gown with matching slippers, and her long ash-blonde hair was arranged in a thick braid that she wore down the left side of her chest. Her skin, unlike the pale, creamy and flawless complexions of most young women of the nobility, was tanned from a life spent out-of-doors, rather than cloistered in her father's house. Her eyes were a startling, gorgeous shade of blue—frank and direct in their gaze. She had a slight dusting of freckles across her nose and was slim rather than voluptuous, yet appeared very fit. She was built along lines similar to Ariel's, which meant she was tall, long-legged, and small-breasted, close to Aedan's height, which would make her about a head shorter than Michael. Before she even spoke, Aedan found himself quite drawn to her. There was something about her, some indefinable quality, that made her quite appealing.

They made small talk over breakfast for a while, mostly about her life in Aerenwe, and she replied to Aedan's questions in a very self-possessed manner. She did not appear at all nervous or anxious, but seemed quite comfortable in their presence.

"What do you think of the emperor?" Aedan asked her finally.

"I love and respect him as my sovereign," she replied, "but as I have never met him, I have had no opportunity to form a more personal opinion."

What a contrast that reply was with others he had heard to the same question, Aedan thought. Most of the others he had spoken with had gushed about Michael's many virtues, his greatness and his bravery in battle, his handsome looks and regal bearing and so forth. And most had gone on at some length concerning what an honor and a privilege it would be to sit by his side as Empress of Anuire. Faelina's response was simple, honest, and refreshing. He approved.

"Why do wish to marry him and be empress?" he asked.

"I do not," Faelina replied.

Aedan raised his eyebrows in surprise. "You do not?" Ariel said nothing, merely sat there watching him, a slight smile on her face. "Why, pray tell? And why then have you come?"

"I came because it was my duty," she replied. "As to why I do not wish to marry Emperor Michael, it has nothing to do with him as an individual. I do not know him. I have never even seen him, save once, at a distance. How can I have a wish to marry a man I do not even know? Aside from that, I imagine life as Empress of Anuire would be much more confining than the life to which I have grown accustomed. I love the rolling plains of Aerenwe and the peaceful beauty of the Erebannien, where I can roam at will and spend my days schooling my horses. I can sew, but I have little taste for such things as embroidering and weaving and spending most of my days indoors. Given my choice, I would prefer a life that is more active."

"You are fond of horses, then?" said Aedan, seizing upon that.

Faelina's eyes lit up. "Oh, yes! I love them. There is no greater pleasure for me than to breed and raise them and train them to saddle. I do not even allow my father's grooms to touch my babies. I care for them myself." She held out her hands, palms up. "These are, I fear, not the hands of a great lady. But then, they are hands that do not shy from honest work. My father has never pampered me, for which I'm grateful. Perhaps it makes me a bit too common, but like my father, I find virtue in hard work and self-reliance. I say these things because I do not wish to pretend I am something I am not. In many ways, he raised me like a son."

"Did he take you hunting?" Aedan asked, his interest growing.

"I have gone hawking with him since I was a child," she replied. "And I have trained Chaser, my hawk, with my own hands. He goes with me everywhere."

"Then you have brought him with you?" Aedan asked.

Faelina nodded. "I thought, perhaps, there might be an opportunity to fly him, and I could not bear to leave my pet behind."

Aedan smiled. "Then we must go hawking after breakfast," he said. "I will ask the emperor to join us so that you may meet him and . . . form a more personal opinion."

* * * * *

Michael never missed an opportunity to go hawking, so he agreed readily when Aedan made the invitation. In passing, he mentioned that Baron Moergan and his daughter would be accompanying them and that they had already left by boat for the royal stables by the parade ground.

Ariel decided to come, as well, as she was eager to see Michael's reaction to Faelina and enjoy some time riding in the fields after all those long days spent indoors, conducting the selection process. It was unusual for ladies to go hawking because few cared for the sport; those rare exceptions generally did not dress in breeches when they did so, as Faelina did. She made no apology for not having worn a skirt, but explained she found such attire cumbersome on horseback and had never cared for riding sidesaddle. To Michael, that made perfect sense.

Her hawk was a handsome creature and Michael took time to admire it. As they spoke, Aedan and Ariel watched them and Ariel beamed with pleasure. "He likes her," she said. "I can tell. She can discuss with him the sort of things he enjoys."

"We shall see," said Aedan, cautiously optimistic.

Faelina's horse, which she had ridden from Aerenwe, was a handsome and spirited black stallion. Michael, an excellent judge of horseflesh, immediately asked if he could try him. Faelina hesitated and glanced at her father. Moergan shrugged slightly, indicating her response would make no difference to him.

"If it were anyone else, Sire, I would say no," she replied, "but you may try him if you like. However, I caution you that no one has ever ridden Midnight save me. He may not suffer you upon his back."

Michael smiled. "Oh, I suspect I can manage him," he said as if humoring her.

"Suit yourself," Faelina said. "But don't say I did not warn you."

With a smirk, Michael swung up into the saddle. Immediately, the stallion reared and started plunging wildly, bucking and kicking and leaping up into the air as Michael struggled to hang on. For a few moments, he managed to stay in the saddle, but it did not take long before he was flying through the air to land hard on chest and stomach. Aedan and Moergan hurried to his side.

"Are you injured, Sire?" Aedan asked with concern.

"Only my pride," Michael replied sourly as he dusted himself off.

"You should have listened to her," Moergan said. "I tried to mount that beast once, and he nearly broke my back."

Faelina seemed more concerned for her horse than for the emperor. She caught the stallion by the reigns and murmured to it, stroking its nose and apologizing for having let another rider mount him. Then she swung up into the saddle easily and reached out her gloved hand to the squire, so that she could take her hawk.

"Whenever you are ready, Sire," she said.

Michael snorted. "Well, she sits that hellspawn well enough. Let's see how well she rides."

They mounted up and set off for the woodlands around the coastal hills. Once they had reached the plains, Aedan flew Slayer, whom he had named after his favorite bird from boyhood. Faelina launched Chaser, and the two riders set off together at a gallop across the fields. Michael's horse, Thunder, was swift and strong, but Midnight was easily his match. The others had to ride hard to keep up as Michael and Faelina raced across the field, each trying to outpace the other. Faelina was every bit his match as a rider, and they hurdled over walls and post fences neck and neck. Their guard escort was hard pressed to keep up. Aedan and Ariel didn't even try.

"You were right," Aedan said to Ariel as they reined in to watch the others race across the field. "She's perfect for him."

"I think it remains to be seen if he is perfect for her," Ariel replied.

"I doubt Michael is perfect for anyone save

Michael," Aedan said. "But I think you were right. She may be exactly what he needs."

The royal betrothal was formally announced a week later. By then, it was obvious to everyone that the emperor was in love. And happily, it was a love that was reciprocated in full measure. No one seemed more surprised that Moergan.

"I must confess," he told Aedan privately after Michael had asked him for Faelina's hand, "I never thought to see Faelina fall in love. I always thought her a bit too spirited for most men. She's a good girl, and would have married as a duty to me, but it does my heart good to see her happy."

"They do seem made for each other," Aedan said. "And with such a couple, I think we may look forward to a strong heir." And perhaps to a few years of peace and quiet, he added mentally. For the first time, there was something else to occupy Michael's attention besides plans for new campaigns. He did not delude himself into thinking Michael would settle down and give up on his goal of expanding the empire, but at least for a while he would no longer pursue it with such single-minded determination.

The wedding would take place in the spring and would be celebrated throughout the empire. For a change, thought Aedan, there would be no spring campaign. And he would welcome the respite from going on the march, especially since Ariel was pregnant once again. This time, the midwife assured them it would be a son.

A new heir for Michael to carry on the rule of the Roeles and a son for Aedan to carry on the tradition of the Dosieres as standard-bearers and lords chamberlain to the empire. They had gone through much to reach this point. The empire was reunited and stronger now than ever since the glory days of the original Roele. There would be time for future conquests, but right now, the immediate future held a promise of peace. Aedan was looking forward to it with a great sense of relief. Everything had fallen neatly into place. It seemed now as if nothing could go wrong.

chapter three

Laera's life had taken on a surreal quality, fascinating and simultaneously frightening. For the first time since her childhood, she did not feel in control. Yet at the same time, there was a thrill to being balanced precariously on the abyss. It energized her and made her feel alive. In the past, she had looked to her sexual adventures to provide her with the stimulation of risk she craved, but nothing had ever provided her with the same dangerous edge of excitement she felt now.

When she had made her pact with Callador, the one thing she could never have anticipated was that the wizard would have chosen and been accepted by Raesene, the infamous Black Prince, known and feared throughout the empire as the Gorgon.

When Callador had revealed the name of his patron, it had sent her mind reeling, and she had almost given way to panic. The wizard had tricked her. He had allowed her to believe the token of a lock of hair taken from her head was merely that, a token and nothing more, to seal the oath between them, similar in principle to a favor given by a lady to a knight. She had known almost nothing about magic, so there was no way she could have realized the true significance of the ritual.

When she and Callador had cut their palms and clasped hands with the lock of her hair between them, it had been a great deal more than merely a symbolic mingling of blood to seal the oath. That lock of hair alone could have served to give him power over her, but impregnated with both her blood and his, it had forged a link between them for as long as it remained in his possession, and by practical extension, that same power would also be granted to his master, Prince Raesene.

At first, the idea had so frightened her that she had nearly succumbed to panic and the temptation to reveal all to her husband. However, common sense prevailed, and she soon realized that if she told Derwyn the truth, nothing would be changed. Callador would still hold power over her, and nothing short of killing him would cancel that. Such an act would incur the wrath of Prince Raesene. Even though she had Derwyn firmly under her control, Laera did not think he would be blind enough with love for her to risk taking on the Gorgon.

More likely, she thought, if she confessed the truth to Derwyn, she would lose her hold over him and he would banish her to Ice Haven, where she would be forced to spend the remainder of her life in constant prayer, solitude, and chastity as a temple priestess. Aside from the utter misery of such an existence, all her plans, everything that she had worked so hard for, would have been for naught. And there was no telling what sort of revenge the Gorgon might exact for her betrayal.

After several sleepless nights, she finally concluded there was nothing else to do but ride it out and hope for the best. The more she thought about it, the more clearly she saw that her situation, while precarious, was far from hopeless.

She reasoned that she was far too insignificant to attract the notice of the Gorgon. She was merely a means to an end. She was not certain precisely what that end was yet, but almost certainly it had to involve her brother, Michael. The Gorgon had some plan in mind, and she must have become a part of it at Callador's suggestion. Either that, or Callador himself had hatched some plan to increase his standing with his awnsheghlien lord. Either way, she would only be an agent, not the object of that plan.

Raesene's lust to control the empire was what had led him to betray his half-brothers, Haelyn and Roele, and sell himself to Azrai all those years ago. The illegitimacy of his birth had denied him a place in the royal line of succession, despite being his father's firstborn son, and his resentment and jealousy of his half-brothers had twisted him and eventually grown into a burning hatred.

After the Battle of Mount Deismaar and the defeat of the Dark Lord, Raesene had fled to the far northern territories and remained there ever since, doubtless brooding on his failure while he slowly built up his powers. Over the centuries, he had carved out his domain and established a stronghold at Kal-Saitharak, the castle fortress he had raised in a forested valley nestled high in the mountainous, rocky, and volcanic wasteland once known simply as the Crown. In time, the black stone castle became better known as Battlewaite, and the jagged cliffs and rocky escarpments that surrounded it came to be called the Gorgon's Crown.

Much of Raesene's history following his self-imposed exile in his remote domain was shrouded in myth and folklore, the accounts of the few travelers who had seen him so much embellished by the bards over the years that it was no longer possible to tell where truth ended and legend began. Most accounts at least agreed on a few basic points. Raesene had brought an unspecified number of his followers from Deismaar to Kal-Saitharak, and this force had grown over the intervening years into an army composed of the dregs of Cerilia.

He numbered gnolls and goblins among his followers, as well as dwarves who had been cast out of their tribes, trolls from the surrounding mountains, and ogres from the southern regions. In addition to the demihumans, he also had the descendants of his human followers at Deismaar, as well as bandits, escaped criminals from the empire, and mercenaries so savage and depraved that they no longer cared for whom they fought, so long as they had a patron to support them.

A walled city had grown up around the castle, and that city was now known as Kal-Saitharak, while the castle itself was called Battlewaite. Raesene never ventured outside his domain, and according to some stories, his power would be diminished if he did, though Laera doubted that. He had gained his powers through bloodtheft, and blood abilities were not bound to the land. More likely, Raesene had reasons of his own for remaining in Kal-Saitharak, though what they might be was anybody's guess. Perhaps the mutations in his body brought about by his powers rendered travel difficult, or he was dependent on the confluence of ley lines in his region for the energy required to increase his power. But whatever the reason may have been, it seemed to hold true for most of the awnsheghlien, who were rarely known to venture far from their domains.

By all accounts, Raesene did not look human anymore. He was said to be a massive, powerful giant with the head of a bull and the legs of a goat, which ended in sharp, diamond-hard hooves. His skin was described as dark and stony, and he was reputed to possess the power to slay with just his gaze, which could turn people to stone. At one time, Raesene was said to have been one of the greatest swordsmen of Anuire, and he had instructed his younger half-brothers, Haelyn and Roele, in the arts of combat. Legend had it that in the centuries since, he had perfected his abilities with every weapon known to man and periodically held death matches to keep his skills honed.

The most recent account of a meeting with Raesene was over a hundred years old and was stored in the Imperial Library at Anuire. It was the report of a trader who had traveled to Kal-Saitharak and met with him. This trader's account had described the walled city as an armed camp, a rough-and-tumble agglomeration of boisterous taverns, crooked gaming houses, and steamy fleshpots where the only law was whatever authority Raesene's lieutenants chose to exert at any given time.

To walk the streets at night, the trader wrote, was to take one's life into one's own hands, even if well armed. Kal-Saitharak was a melting pot of races, most of which nursed age-old enmities, and battles in the streets were not uncommon. It was, perhaps, the main reason Raesene had not expanded his domain much farther than the Gorgon's Crown. His army spent almost as much time fighting itself as raiding nearby territories.

The trader's account had confirmed the stories about Raesene's appearance, but disputed the claims that he had gone hopelessly insane. He wrote that the Gorgon, perhaps hoping to encourage other traders to visit his domain, had received him warmly and that they had engaged in polite and interesting conversation in which his host had referred to himself as Prince Raesene and had seemed intelligent and in full possession of his faculties. However, that had been over a century ago, and popular belief now held that Raesene had lost all vestiges of his humanity and was little more than a wild beast.

Laera found that hard to credit. If it were true, it was doubtful Callador would have been able to negotiate with him and reach an agreement for his services. Aside from that, a wizard of Callador's ability could have found another wealthy patron without a great deal of difficulty. He was too canny and had too strong a sense of self-preservation to sell his services to someone who had lost all sense of reason. If the Gorgon had gone mad, it was madness with a method that Callador could understand.

After her initial bout of panic, Laera had forced herself to calm down and think things through. She had followed Callador's instructions and obtained a lock of hair from Derwyn, saying she wanted to keep it in a locket so that she would have a part of him to carry with her at all times. He had been charmed—it was so easy!—and had readily agreed to her request. She had cut off a thick lock of his hair and kept a part of it to place inside a locket, in case he should request to see it. The rest she gave to Callador, who had used it to concoct a spell.

A week or so after her child had been delivered, Derwyn returned to share her bed. She did not think it prudent to put him off longer. However, she had no fear of Derwyn's discovering her relationship with the wizard who once served his father. When the misty tunnel started to appear inside their bedchambers, Derwyn would fall into a deep trance, a sleep from which no amount of noise or jostling would wake him. Laera would then pass through the tunnel and emerge in Callador's sanctum deep in the bowels of Battlewaite, where he would school her in the mystic arts.

She never saw any part of Kal-Saitharak beyond the windowless stone walls of Callador's retreat, and she never encountered anyone but him. Each night, she would spend several hours studying under his patient tutelage, then pass back through the tunnel once again and return to bed with Derwyn none the wiser. He would awake refreshed each morning, suspecting nothing, and the sleep that Laera lost each night she made up with naps in the afternoon.

She had made rapid progress in her studies, much to her surprise, and Callador took pride in her accomplishments, saying she possessed an uncommon natural aptitude for magic. Still, it was not a discipline that came easily to anyone. It required diligent study and concentration. She took care never to bring any materials back with her, because no matter how well she might hide them, they might still be discovered, and she was anxious to avoid suspicion. Callador shared her sense of caution. He was pleased with her efforts, but he never allowed her to forget she must refrain from practicing any magic out of his presence until he gave his approval. And he would not allow her to progress any farther in her studies than he deemed prudent. Magic, he reminded her, could be very dangerous, and mastering even relatively simple spells required patience.

Laera did not chafe under these restrictions, nor was she bored with the long hours of poring over ancient scrolls, committing spells and rituals to memory. If that aspect of her training lacked the fascination of the exercises she performed under Callador's watchful direction, she never minded because she knew that all those hours of painstaking study would result in her ability to gain power over others —one man in particular. The day of reckoning would come, and when it did, Aedan Dosiere would face not just a princess, but also a sorceress.

Meanwhile, Laera continued her campaign to build up Derwyn's ambitions for his son, Aerin. He still wanted another son to ensure the continuation of his name, and she used that, along with his desire for her, to lead him subtly in the direction she chose. Callador had provided her with a plentiful supply of the preparation to control her own fertility, and it wasn't long before she had learned to concoct it for herself. She would never again have a child unless she chose to, and she would make that choice only as a last resort. So long as Derwyn had only one son, he would pin all his hopes on him and continue to be driven by his desire to produce another. And that would help her keep her hold on him.

She went to temple every day, where she always made sure the priests knew she was praying for the birth of a new son. She always expressed a fervent desire to please Derwyn and become pregnant once again, stressing that it had to be her fault she could not conceive; surely there could be nothing lacking in *his* potency. Yet by raising the subject, she nevertheless planted a tiny seed of doubt in his mind, which she could use to good advantage as it grew. As Derwyn slowly came to fear the loss of his masculinity, he grew even more tractable and docile, which made him more vulnerable to suggestion.

Slowly and carefully, Laera played on his affections for her and Aerin, building up an idea in his mind that someday, if the right circumstances would prevail, his son might sit upon the Iron Throne and found a new dynasty bearing his name. When it was announced throughout the empire that Michael had married and an heir to the House of Roele would soon be forthcoming, Laera was not deterred. While expressing a feigned joy over the union and her brother's happiness, she kept reminding Derwyn of his son's importance in the scheme of things.

"When the prince is born," she told Derwyn, "Aerin will still occupy a vital role in the succession. He will not only stand to inherit your title and your lands, and grow up to be the most important vassal to the future emperor, but as the firstborn scion of both the houses of Roele and Boeruine, Aerin would be the next in line should any tragedy befall the prince—may the gods prevent it. Your father's claim to the succession may have been disputed, but as the firstborn of a princess of the empire and the Duke of Boeruine, none would question Aerin's birthright."

Aerin's birthright. It was a phrase she used judiciously, but often enough to start Derwyn thinking of his son's future in those terms. His right by birth to sit upon the Iron Throne. And once that possibility was firmly implanted in his mind, the next step was to manipulate him into a desire to do something to increase the probability of its coming to pass. It would require time, for she would have to proceed slowly, allowing Derwyn to think it was his own idea. However, it would not be very difficult. Derwyn was much weaker than his father had been, and her long experience with manipulating men made it simple. He thrived on her affections, and if she withheld them, he would bend over backward to regain her favor, assuming the blame for having done something to displease her. And so long as he still wanted a second son, he doted on her and catered to her slightest whim. Nor was he the only one at Seaharrow whom she had enthralled.

It took a while for her to pick out the right one, for she wanted to ensure that there would absolutely be no mistakes. However, after a few weeks at Seaharrow, carefully evaluating all the possibilities, she had settled on young Viscount Rodric, eldest son of Count Basil of Norcross, whose small holding lay to the north of Seaharrow, near the Black River and the border of Talinie.

Rodric, in the time-honored tradition of vassalage, had been sent by Count Basil to the court of Seaharrow to serve as a squire to his father's lord. At the next Summer Court, he was due to be elevated to knighthood. His father was getting on in years, and Rodric stood to inherit the estate. He was seventeen, and he had a promising future. In other words, he had a lot to lose.

It hadn't taken long at all. At first, she had merely noticed him, making sure he noticed her noticing him. Then it was a simple matter of eye contact, looking at him and then quickly averting her gaze, as if in embarrassment, whenever he noticed her attention. After that, whenever their eyes met, she had started hesitating before she looked away, allowing a fleeting but meaningful contact. To this, she gradually added subtle variations. A nervous swallow whenever their eyes met, a moistening of the lips, a few deep breaths to draw his attention to her bosom, then lingering sidelong glances, and finally, when she was sure no one else would notice, smoldering stares.

He started to find excuses to run into her around the castle and on the grounds. She studied his routine and made sure there were opportunities for them to encounter one another, as if by coincidence. When they spoke, it was with formal politeness, but he was always very attentive and solicitous. He started to take extra care of his appearance. The next step was brief physical contact. She would brush against him, as if by accident, and when they encountered one another in the garden, they would sit

and chat for a short while, their thighs or knees or
shoulders touching slightly. He had the fervor and
impatience of youth, which made things even easier.
When he took her hand and brushed it with his lips,
lingering just a bit too long, Laera would increase
her breathing and open her mouth slightly, gazing at
him with a dreamy stare. And when he kissed her
for the first time, he probably thought he was being
astonishingly bold and reckless.

She made him believe she could not resist him, no
matter how hard she tried. Her whispered protesta-
tions were punctuated by soft moans of encouragement, and soon thereafter, she "surrendered" to him,
as if no longer able to hold her feelings in check.
Then, as with Derwyn, she slowly began to tighten
the noose.

By the time the emperor's marriage was celebrated in Anuire, she had Rodric eating out of her
hand. She was conducting a torrid affair right under
her husband's very nose, and Derwyn did not suspect a thing. However, with Rodric, she did not
make the same mistake she made with Aedan. She
had learned that lesson long ago. She curbed her
appetite and always left him wanting more, carefully controlling the frequency of their assignations,
allowing his hunger for her to grow.

She complained of Derwyn's inattentiveness and
told Rodric her husband only pretended to love her,
that when they were alone together, he was brusque
and even cruel on occasion. While Rodric held her in
his arms, she speculated wistfully on what it would
be like if they could run away together, adding that
of course that would be impossible because it would
ruin both their lives. Yet, if only she were free. . . .

One more phase of her plan fell into place quite by accident, thanks to Rodric. Knowing the "miserable isolation of her existence," he took it upon himself to provide her regular reports of the goings-on in the town and its vicinity. He was a natural gossip, and most of his stories she found interminably boring, but one in particular piqued her interest.

A young teenaged girl in town, a thief and prostitute, had been arrested for stabbing a merchant. He had survived, but as he was an influential member of the community, the girl had been sentenced to hang. Privately, Laera thought it a fitting punishment. The lower classes had to be reminded of their place every now and then to keep them in line and properly respectful. But when she went to Derwyn, claiming to have heard about the incident from one of her ladies-in-waiting, she pleaded for him to intercede and save the poor girl's life. Surely, she said, this girl had been trapped in a life of hopeless misery, and only desperation had driven her to do the deed. She at least deserved a second chance. Laera offered to take the girl into her service, saying she was sure she could reach past the bitterness and the hardships she had suffered. And, she added, it would be a wonderful opportunity for Derwyn to display compassion and demonstrate to the people of Boeruine that he was merciful and truly cared about their welfare.

Derwyn had some reservations, but she wore him down, and soon the girl was brought from the toll-house in the town to Seaharrow. She was proud and haughty, but not so foolish that she did not realize she owed her life to Laera. Her name was Gella. She was fifteen years old, a peasant through and through, who had been orphaned at an early age and had learned to survive by her wits. There was a spark of stubborn wilfulness in her gaze, and Laera saw in her a kindred soul that could be molded to her purposes.

She told her other ladies she wished to be left alone with Gella, and when they had left, marveling at the compassion of the duchess to take a fallen girl under her wing, she confronted Gella severely.

"Well, let's have a look at you," she said, circling around her as if taking her full measure. "Hmmm. A bath and some clean clothes and you might even be presentable."

Suddenly, she reached out quickly and snipped off a lock of Gella's hair. The girl brought her hand up to the spot, startled, but said nothing as Laera came around in front of her, holding the lock of dirty, oily dark hair in her hand. "It could do with a trimming," she said, surreptitiously making a cut in her own palm as she spoke. "Let me see your hands."

Obediently, Gella held them out for her inspection. Laera took her left hand in hers, as if to examine it. "Rough, coarse, and dirty," she said. "But then, I suppose that's only to be expected."

With an abrupt motion, she seized Gella's wrist and sliced her palm. Gella cried out in alarm and tried to jerk away, but Laera moved with her, maintaining her grip. She dropped the little scissors and slapped the lock of hair onto Gella's palm, then covered it with her own. No blood oath was necessary; that was only ritual. The actual spell had been prepared in advance, as Callador had done, too.

Gella's eyes grew wide, and she stopped struggling. "You are a sorceress!" she said.

"What do you know of sorcery?" asked Laera.

"My mother was a witch," the girl replied. "They killed her for it."

Laera released her hand and pushed back Gella's thick, dark hair, revealing a slightly pointed ear. "A half-elf!" she said with surprise. "I never would have guessed. But now I can see it."

"What do you want with me?" asked Gella.

"I need you to serve me," Laera replied. "You shall be my personal body servant. I was the one who saved your life. It is now mine to command and do with as I please. Serve me well and faithfully, and you shall be well taken care of and rewarded. Play me false, and you shall suffer torments such as you cannot imagine, so that you will plead with me to take your life. Do you understand?"

Gella moistened her lips nervously. "I do, Lady."

"Very good," said Laera. "Then understand this, also. No one knows that I possess knowledge of sorcery save you. Not even my husband suspects. You seem to know something of the mystic arts, so perhaps you realize you are now bound to me for as long as both of us shall live." She took Gella's blood-soaked lock of hair and placed it in a small gold locket like the one containing Derwyn's, closed it, then slipped the chain around her neck. "You belong to me now. And by this token of your lock of hair, I can reach out for you, no matter where you go. Remember that."

"You want me to do something terrible," said Gella. "That is why you had me brought here. You have no need of a body servant. You require a criminal."

"The only law you need to fear is mine," said Laera. "And if you do precisely as I say, you will not be caught, and I shall make it worth your while."

"What is it you want me to do?"

"Learn, for starters. I will have you instructed in how to be a proper servant. And when the emperor arrives at Seaharrow for Summer Court, I shall have you assigned to serve the new empress." She went over to her jewelry box and opened a hidden drawer in it, from which she removed a small glass vial stoppered with a cork. "A few drops of this special preparation in her wine each week will prevent her from conceiving a child." Laera smiled. "It has no taste or odor and dissolves without leaving any residue behind. She will never know that she is drinking it."

Gella's eyes grew wide as Laera spoke, and she swallowed hard when she heard her final words.

"Your task shall be to administer the dose."

* * * * *

The journey from Anuire to Seaharrow for Summer Court took about a week of travel at the sedate pace the emperor's train maintained. They traveled with wagons bearing tents and supplies, a complement of infantry detached from the Army of Anuire, the mounted house guard, and all the lords and ladies of the Imperial Court. They averaged about twenty-five miles a day, with a rest period at midday, and they pitched camp at sundown.

For Michael, this type of travel was ennervating. He much preferred the faster pace he was accustomed to setting with his troops, and he felt restless on the journey, but Faelina's presence acted as a curb on his natural impatience. She had been looking forward to this journey, for she had never been to Seaharrow, and she kept Michael occupied throughout the trip, describing the countryside around Seasedge and telling her of his adventures in Tuarhievel.

Aedan regarded the journey with mixed feelings. It was a welcome relief to get away from the Imperial Cairn and have a change of climate and scenery. It was also pleasant to take a leisurely ride through the country without feeling concern about being attacked by enemy troops or fighting a battle at journey's end. And it was a much desired respite from his duties in the capital. On the other hand, Boeruine did not hold pleasant memories for him. And he would once again be seeing Laera.

Things had come full circle, in a way, and somehow it seemed a bad omen. He just couldn't shake the feeling that making this trip had been a bad idea all around. Still, having forgiven Derwyn for the part he'd played in his father's rebellion and elevated him to the dukedom, to say nothing of giving him his sister for a wife, Michael couldn't snub him now by canceling the Summer Court. It was something a great many people had looked forward to, both at the Court of Anuire and Boeruine, and symbolically it underlined the reunification of the empire. Politically, Summer Court simply could not be avoided.

Nevertheless, Aedan was filled with apprehension. He had not seen Laera since she had departed for Boeruine with her new husband, and relations between them had been strained for a long time. Perhaps her marriage to Derwyn would finally allow her to leave the past in the past, but Aedan doubted it. He knew Derwyn, and he knew Laera would walk all over him. Derwyn lacked his father's strength of personality. He was not a weakling, but he was too good-hearted, too eager to avoid conflict by accommodation. And Laera needed a firm hand on the reins.

Perhaps she'd changed, but Aedan had learned that people never really changed unless they wanted to and made a diligent effort. Judging by the rumors he had heard about Laera's behavior right up until her marriage, Laera hadn't changed at all. She had been very careful and had avoided scandal, but few things remained secret for long at the Imperial Court, and there were whispers concerning her libertine behavior. No one had ever said anything out loud, of course, nor were any accusations made, but Aedan had his sources—he could not properly fulfill his duties unless he knew what went on in the castle—and what he'd heard had given him no cause to believe Laera might have changed her ways. Quite the opposite, in fact.

He wondered, sometimes, if he might in some way be responsible for the way she had turned out. If he had not broken their affair off as he did, perhaps things might have been different. Perhaps it was anger and bitterness over the way he had treated her that led her to abandon all sense of morals and propriety. But then again, it was she who had seduced him and not the other way around. And he'd had no choice but to break off their affair. To continue it would have meant disaster for them both. And Laera seemed bent on flirting with disaster. It excited her.

She had never loved him. The words had never passed her lips. But Aedan could not blame her for that. He had not loved her, either. What they had between them was a hunger, a hunger that was obsessive, consuming, and unhealthy. There was something wrong with feelings like that, no matter how exhilarating and compelling they were. At the time, Aedan found making love with Laera an incredible experience, but he had only been fooling himself. They had not been making love. They were merely having sex. It had been thrilling, passionate, and intoxicating, but it wasn't until that night he had spent with Sylvanna that he truly realized what making love was really all about.

One night. That was all they had. And he had never been able to forget it. He had been drunk, but not so drunk that he couldn't function or remember, just drunk enough to lose his inhibitions. In that one night, something had changed in him forever.

They had known each other for close to a decade, and in that time, their friendship had grown and solidified until it became something much more profound. That one night, he later realized, had merely been the climax of a process that had been taking place for a long time.

When he was with Ariel, he never thought of Laera. But on occasion, while they were making love, he found himself thinking of Sylvanna. He had never told Ariel about that because he knew it would hurt her. And if she suspected, she never said a thing. He always felt a sharp stab of guilt whenever it occurred, for he had grown to love Ariel very much, but it wasn't something he could control. He did not love Ariel any less for thinking of Sylvanna, but it seemed if he truly loved her, he should not think of any other woman. And yet, he did. He knew no matter what happened, Sylvanna would always be a part of him. Love was much more complicated than the bards made it out to be.

He was enjoying their journey, but he was not looking forward to reaching their destination. Ariel knew about Laera, knew about their affair when it had gone on and had watched its effects afterward.

"I never loved her, Ariel," he had explained. "It was wrong. And what makes it worse is I knew it was wrong, but went ahead with it just the same. I was weak, I guess. I just could not resist her. But that is no excuse."

"It happened," Ariel replied. "There is no point in self-recriminations. You cannot change the past. You can only let it go. But I do not think Laera will ever let go. Be careful of her, Aedan. She hates you. I can see it in her eyes."

"She's hurt and angry," Aedan said. "Perhaps, in time, she will get over it."

"Angry, yes, but not hurt," Ariel replied. "She would have had to care for you in order to be hurt. What you did when you broke it off with her was even worse for someone like Laera. You stung her pride. You held a mirror up to her and showed her what she truly was. She will never forgive you for that. Never. But if she ever tries to hurt you, I swear I'll kill her."

"Don't talk like that," said Aedan. "She is married now and out of our lives."

"Don't be so sure."

"Derwyn is not his father," Aedan said. "She will doubtless have him at her beck and call, but he knows better than to make trouble. He lacks Arwyn's unscrupulous ambition and lust for power."

"Do not underestimate a woman's power to change a man," said Ariel.

"Ah," said Aedan with a smile. "I see. Is that what you have done to me?"

"Well, what do you think?"

He paused a moment, considering. "Yes, I think you have. And for the better."

"I am pleased you think so," Ariel replied, "but remember that you are much stronger than Derwyn. And if she can, Laera will change him for the worse."

* * * * *

On the second day of their journey to Seaharrow, they passed the battlefield where Arwyn had met his defeat, roughly midway between the cities of Dalton and Anuire. In the distance, they could see the Seamist Mountains, where the Army of Anuire had fought the ogres during their failed campaign to find a portal through the Shadow World to Boeruine. Just to the south of the mountain range, still invisible at this distance, was the line of fortifications where Arwyn had established his garrisons to protect the borders of Brosengae. And a bit farther east were the Anuirean garrisons that had been overrun by Arwyn's army on their way to the battlefield where the war had ended.

Famous battles were usually given names, most often after the place where they had occurred. This one was different. Though the fortifications in the distance and the nearby mountains could have leant their names to the battle, they did not. Michael himself had named this place, this killing ground that was simply a vast and grassy plain—grassy no longer, for it had been brutally churned up by the two armies that had fought here. When the rains came in late summer, the field would become somewhat more leveled as the gullies overflowed and water pooled and streamed in rivulets across it. The winter snows would cover it, too, and freeze the ground, further changing its appearance. Eventually, after snowmelt, new shoots of grass would appear next spring. Still, it would be years before all traces of the battle disappeared, wiped out by nature. And even then, the place would bear the name Michael had given it to commemorate those who had died here because of one man's driving ambition: Sorrow Field.

As they passed the battlefield, the traces of the struggle that had taken place here were still very much in evidence. The mounds where the dead had been buried where they fell dotted the torn-up landscape, and a hush fell over the royal caravan as they passed. Here and there, flowers had been planted on the mounds by relatives who had made the journey to the battle site.

As many of the graves as possible were marked, and some of the families of the soldiers who had fallen had replaced the crude little wooden markers with tombstones carved by the city's stonemasons. In many cases, however, it had been impossible to identify the corpses, and there were families who knew only that their loved ones had fallen here, somewhere. For them, Michael had commissioned the carving of a large memorial stone that identified the battlefield and bore a legend telling what had happened here. This memorial, too, was covered with flowers by those who had come out to say their last good-byes to loved ones who lay in unmarked graves.

This was the side of war that was anything but glorious, thought Aedan. There was glory in winning, heightened by emotions engendered by the act of survival, but glory was always fleeting. Death was permanent.

No one spoke as they went past the battlefield. And no one spoke for a long time thereafter.

They made camp that night near the abandoned fortifications on the border between Brosengae and Avanil. After the tents had been pitched and everyone had eaten, Aedan went in search of Michael. He found him a short distance from the camp, standing on a wall of an abandoned fort. A detachment of the house guard had accompanied him, for the emperor was not supposed to be left unguarded, but they maintained a discreet distance, giving him some privacy with his thoughts.

As Aedan came up behind him, Michael was staring out into the distance, toward the plains of Brosengae. The sun was setting in the west. It had almost completely disappeared, leaving a fading red-gold light illuminating the evening sky. Michael turned as he heard Aedan coming up behind him. He looked troubled.

"Is anything wrong, Sire?" Aedan asked him.

"No, I was just thinking," Michael replied. "About other journeys like this, in the past. Summer Courts of days gone by. One summer in particular."

"The last one before the war," said Aedan.

Michael nodded. He smiled suddenly. "I recall I said once that when I became emperor, I would do away with all this business of 'Your Highness this' and 'Your Highness that.' It irritated me that no one ever used my name."

Aedan smiled. "I remember."

"Well, I am hereby issuing a long overdue imperial decree. Henceforth, Lord Chancellor, whenever we find ourselves in private moments such as this, you will address me by my name. Not 'Sire,' and not 'my lord,' and most definitely not 'Your Highness.' But Michael. Simply Michael. I know you can do it, stuffy as you are. You did it at least once before, in battle on Sorrow Field."

"Yes, I recall you had given me that special dispensation, though I confess I had not thought about it at the time. The reaction was purely instinctive."

"Did you feel it, when we rode past the battlefield?"

"I felt many things," said Aedan. "Not all of which are easily put into words."

Michael nodded. "I meant the silence. Not our silence as we went by, but the silence of the place itself. The silence of the dead." He paused. "So very still. Not even the birds singing. The sort of silence that reaches out and envelops everything around it."

"They say a battlefield where a great struggle has been fought always feels different, no matter how many years pass," said Aedan. "There is always something about a place where many have given their lives in combat."

"I feel it here as well," said Michael. "They stood here, behind this very wall, watching Arwyn's entire army coming at them in the big push. Vastly outnumbered, knowing they would be overrun, yet still they stood. They stood for me."

"They stood for the empire," Aedan said.

"You imply I have hubris?" Michael said. "Well, be that as it may, I *am* the empire. It was my decision that put them here, and even if it was not for me that they stood, they still stood *because* of me. As a consequence of my actions. As the dead upon that battlefield fell as a consequence of my actions."

"Not just yours," said Aedan. "It was Arwyn who rebelled. It was Arwyn who made the war, not you. It was his army that was marching on Anuire, and that was why those brave men fell on Sorrow Field. They fell to stop them. Taking all the guilt upon yourself is not only unjust, but it detracts from their nobility of purpose. They fought and died for their wives and for their children and for their fellow countrymen. And for you. But not for you alone."

Michael sighed heavily. "Do you think I love war, Aedan? Tell me the truth. I shall not hold it against you."

"I have always told you the truth," Aedan replied. He paused. "And yes, I think you do."

Michael nodded. "Perhaps I did once," he said. "As a boy, I dreamed of leading troops in battle."

"I know." Aedan smiled. "We acted out those dreams often enough."

"How you must have hated it," said Michael with a grin, "having to play at war with children. All those times I made you 'die' over and over again because you did not do it dramatically enough."

Aedan chuckled. "I must admit, it tried my patience."

"A virtue you have cultivated well," said Michael. "I should benefit from your example. Perhaps I did love war. I don't know. I know I loved how it made me *feel*. It made all my senses sharper than the finest blade. It made the blood pound in my veins. It made me feel *alive*."

Aedan experienced a sudden epiphany. "The risk," he said, thinking of Laera. He had always been convinced that Michael had no fear, that he was incapable of it. Perhaps he had been wrong. Perhaps, like Laera, Michael simply found the fear, the risk, intoxicating.

Michael nodded. "You felt it, too?"

"Not in the same way," said Aedan. "Or perhaps not to the same extent. But I understand what you mean."

"I have been trying to remember when it changed," said Michael thoughtfully. "In the aftermath of our last campaign through the Shadow World, perhaps. That was certainly when it started, but as miserable as I felt afterward, I still don't think it ever truly struck home until I saw Derwyn ride up and see me standing there over his father's body, holding his severed, bloody head. I shall never forget the expression on his face. I see it in my dreams."

"It had to end with either Arwyn's death or yours," said Aedan. "Arwyn would have settled for nothing less. Derwyn knew that."

"Still. I killed his father, then made him a duke and gave him my sister for his wife, as if that could make up for it. And now we travel to Seaharrow, where he plays host to us for Summer Court." He shook his head. "It all seems mad. At least a dozen times, I have thought of forgetting all about this, turning around, and going back to Anuire."

"You could," said Aedan. "After all, you are the emperor. No one would question your decision."

"What about you? I don't imagine you're very

eager to see Seaharrow once again."

"I could do without it," Aedan said. "It holds unpleasant memories. But we both know this trip is necessary. If we canceled it, Derwyn would regard it as a snub."

"Yes, Laera would make sure of that," said Michael. "I did him no favor by marrying him off to her."

"By all accounts, she has made him very happy."

"So they say. I find that difficult to believe. It doesn't sound much like Laera, does it?"

"Perhaps she's changed," said Aedan.

"Do you really believe that?"

"No."

"Neither do I. She always was a mean-spirited little harlot. I'll never understand what you saw in her."

"That is because you can only look upon her as a brother," Aedan said wryly.

Michael remained silent for a moment. Then he asked, "Does Ariel know?"

"Yes. I told her everything."

"Did you? And how did she react?"

Aedan paused to consider his reply. "She was very understanding."

"What did she say?"

Aedan found this topic of conversation awkward, but he could hardly refuse to answer. "She said the past was in the past."

"And that was all?"

Aedan cleared his throat. "She said Laera would never forgive me, and if Laera ever tried to hurt me, she would kill her."

Michael chuckled.

"You find that amusing?"

"Only that it sounds like the Ariel I remember from our childhood games. She nearly killed you once, as I recall."

"It does not disturb you that my wife has sworn to kill your sister?"

"If she ever tried to harm you, is what you said," Michael corrected him. "And if it ever came to that, I'd kill her myself."

Aedan was nonplussed. "Well . . . I don't know if I should be flattered or alarmed."

"If she ever tried to do you any harm, it would be an act of treason," Michael said. And then, almost as if in afterthought, he added, "Besides, you are my best friend."

"You honor me."

"No, you honor me," said Michael. "As emperor, I can have no friends, only subjects. You are the only true friend I have. The only one I can really trust."

"What about the empress?"

"It is not the same. She is my wife, and I love her. I never expected that. I had looked on marriage as a duty, but I have found it to be a joy. And I have you to thank for it."

"I cannot claim the credit," Aedan said. "It belongs to my wife. Ariel chose her. She said she would be perfect for you."

"And she was right," said Michael. "You are fortunate in having such a wife, Aedan. I hope you appreciate her."

"I do," said Aedan.

"Well, we have been through much, you and I. We were captured by goblins and almost taken into slavery, we have fought a war and saved the empire, and we have found good wives. Now we must settle down and start having sons who will carry on for us and secure the future." He stared out into the distance. "I have decided there shall be no campaigns next year. Our army has fought hard and long. They deserve a rest. I shall send the mercenaries out to the frontiers to establish outposts to secure our borders. The empire is strong now. In time, we shall expand it, but I think my vision of one nation that stretches out across Cerilia from sea to sea is one my son shall have to realize."

"A wise decision," Aedan replied, nodding. "A builder must not rush to lay a strong foundation. You have already done more than any emperor before you. Your father would have been proud."

"As would yours have been," said Michael. "There is still much left for us to do. We must have our reckoning with Thurazor, for Gorvanak shall always think we fear him if we do not punish him for taking Arwyn's side in the rebellion. Aside from which, you and I still have a personal score to settle with those goblins. We have put it off for far too long. I intend to lash Gorvanak to a crude litter, as they did with me, and drag him all the way back to Anuire."

"I must admit, that is certainly something I would like to see," said Aedan.

"You shall see it before the summer turns to fall," promised Michael. "And after we have done with Gorvanak, there is still the Manslayer to deal with. Rhuobhe has grown ever bolder in his raids and has expanded his territory well into the forests of Boeruine. He has been a thorn in our side for much too long. I mean to pluck him out. However, after that, we shall cease our campaigning for a while and devote time to our families."

"I would like that," Aedan said. "Ariel is with child again and the midwives say it will be a son. In the coming years, I shall need to spend more time at home to supervise his early training and prepare him for the time when your son shall doubtless make him as miserable as you made me when we were children."

Michael chuckled. "Was it really so bad?"

"To borrow a term your sister used, you were insufferable," said Aedan.

"Talk about the pot calling the kettle black. Well, I shall make you a promise, Aedan. After my son is born, I shall take pains to instruct him in how to be more considerate of his future lord high chamberlain. I shall tell him that when they play at war, dying once is quite sufficient."

"It usually is," said Aedan. "I think that is a lesson best learned early. And now, with your permission, I shall take my leave and go back to my wife, before she starts to wonder what became of me."

Michael nodded. "Tell Faelina I shall be back presently. I feel the need to spend a bit more time alone."

Aedan hesitated. There was something in his tone. . . . "Is something troubling you?"

Michael shook his head. "I don't know," he said. "The war is over, we have expanded our borders and taken steps to secure them, and save for the future plans I have already mentioned, I cannot think of anything we have left undone." He paused. "And yet . . . I have a peculiar feeling something is not right. But for the life of me, I cannot think what it may be. I don't know. Perhaps it is merely restlessness on my part. Do not concern yourself. Go back to

Ariel before she starts to feel neglected. I will puzzle it out eventually."

"Very well," said Aedan. "I shall tell the empress you'll be returning shortly."

"Good night, Aedan. Sleep well."

"Good night, Michael."

Aedan turned and stepped down off the wall, then started heading back toward camp. The fires were lit now, and most of the lords and ladies had settled down for the night. Only the soldiers remained awake, gathered round the fires, gaming and talking quietly among themselves. As he passed the detachment of the house guard that had accompanied the emperor on his walk, Captain Koval moved to intercept him.

"Is everything well with the emperor, my lord?" he asked.

Aedan nodded. "He merely wants some time alone to think. He plans a campaign against Thurazor this summer."

"That has been the rumor, my lord," Captain Koval said. "But he has never been anxious about campaigns before. There seems to something else that troubles him. I have noticed it since we began this journey. Do you have any idea what it may be?"

Aedan shook his head. "No. But he has many responsibilities to occupy his mind. The Iron Throne is more than just a seat of glory. It can be a weighty burden, too. However, he told me he shall be going back to camp presently. We still have a long journey ahead of us, and he is not accustomed to traveling at so slow a pace. I think he is just restless and impatient to reach our destination. There is no need for concern."

"Thank you, my lord."

"Good night, Captain."

"Good night, Lord Aedan."

As Aedan left them, he wondered if restlessness was really all it was. Michael had always been restless and impatient. Perhaps the prospect of taking a year off from campaigning was something he was not looking forward to. Yet he seemed to have meant what he said. Faelina had made him genuinely happy, and for the first time, Michael seemed willing and ready to slow down. Perhaps it was just the idea of being back in Boeruine, at Seaharrow, that was troubling him. Aedan was not looking forward to it himself. But politics demanded it. And they would not be there long before the army came out to make ready for the march on Thurazor.

One more campaign, thought Aedan. Maybe two, at most, if Michael truly was intent on going after Rhuobhe Manslayer after he was done with Gorvanak of Thurazor. It seemed a tall order for one summer, but after that, a year without campaigning would be a welcome respite. He was looking forward to it.

He had seen quite enough of war.

chapter four

The preparations for the holding of Summer Court at Seaharrow had Derwyn in a frenzy of activity during the weeks prior to the arrival of the emperor's party. The years of war had seen most of the duchy's resources occupied with the campaigns, as well as the supplying of the army and the garrisons. The maintenance of the castle and the town had not been seen to properly in quite some time, and Derwyn was determined that Seaharrow would look its best when the emperor arrived.

Stonemasons had been gathered from all over the surrounding area and imported from as far away Diemed and Alamie to repair the cracking mortar that had loosened from the winter freezes of the past

nine years. They had erected extensive frameworks
of wooden scaffolding against the castle walls, clam-
bering over it like ants to repair the damage caused
by almost a decade of neglect.

The staff of servants hired from the people of the
town was tripled to ensure that the interior of the
castle was thoroughly swept and scrubbed clean. All
the rugs and tapestries were aired and beaten to
knock out the dust; worn furniture had been replaced; the arms displayed upon the walls were
taken down and polished. Stalls in the stables had to
be repaired, along with fresh posts and rails installed
for the corrals and new thatch for the roof. The wall
sconces for the torches were cleaned and the walls
behind them scrubbed to remove soot, and the braziers were scrubbed out and polished so that they
would smoke less. The bedding in every room of the
castle had been changed, the frames laced with
fresh, taut rope to provide good support, the mat-
tresses stuffed anew with fresh straw and pillows
with fresh goose down.

The uniforms of the guard needed mending, so
Derwyn had ordered new ones made and had insisted that every member of his castle guard clean
and polish his chain mail meticulously, replacing
any broken links. Armor was polished and weapons
rendered clean and sharp. Inspections were conducted every day, and the guard was drilled repeatedly to ensure that they executed their maneuvers
with perfection.

Classes of instruction were held for the servants
added to handle the arrival of the court, and the
cooks drilled their new assistants to make sure the
kitchens would run smoothly. An additional staff of

gardeners had been taken on to weed and prune and fertilize, making certain the gravel paths winding through the gardens were immaculate, and cleaning out nests of field mice and insects. Squads of grimy ratcatchers roamed the castle halls at night with their squirming sacks slung over their shoulders, and even the dungeons were cleaned out in case the emperor should decide to inspect them.

In town, the sheriff's men roamed the streets to make sure citizens had swept them and cleaned up any refuse. Wagons hauled garbage from the alleys out of town, and every shop owner, gaming-hall manager, and tavernkeeper was ordered to make his establishment immaculate. Not even during Arwyn's time had the town been so extensively refurbished. Everywhere one looked in the weeks preceding the arrival of the emperor, thatchers repaired roofs, carpenters installed new doors and shutters, and farm wagons brought in barrels of wine and ale, loads of game, and bushels of fresh produce.

Laera saw very little of Derwyn during this time, but that suited her perfectly. During the day, while he was running off to town to check on progress for the preparations to receive the emperor, she spent time with Rodric, a younger, more handsome, and better lover than her husband. At night, Derwyn came back exhausted and fell right into bed, fast asleep within moments. Then Callador's portal would appear, and she would pass through it into his sanctum at Battlewaite to continue her training in sorcery.

Even without Callador to tell her so, she knew she was making rapid progress. In all her life, she had never found anything to interest her as much as magic did. Her amatory diversions were merely that, diversions, something to add the spice of risk to an otherwise dull and dreary life. Once she had discovered sorcery, however, she felt she had found her true calling. She looked forward to the nights when she could go to Callador and resume her training, and in turn, the old wizard enjoyed having such a gifted pupil. But the night before the emperor's party was due to arrive at Seaharrow, there occurred a change in her routine.

Derwyn came to bed late, exhausted from overseeing the final preparations. Through his bond with her, Callador felt when it was the proper time to open the portal, and he could not do so until Derwyn was in bed, where he could safely fall into his trance. As it grew later and Derwyn still did not return, Laera started to feel anxious. All that day, she had felt a nervous anxiety, a presentiment that something would be different tonight, though she did not know what. She had even sent Rodric away, for she felt too preoccupied to spare any time for him. His attentions were becoming bothersome, in any case. Soon, she would have to figure out some way to be rid of him.

When Derwyn finally came to bed, they spoke for a short while about how all the preparations had progressed—or rather, Derwyn spoke, while Laera made appropriate noises feigning interest, nervously wishing he would shut up and go to sleep. Derwyn was concerned, anxious because he kept thinking there was something he might have overlooked. He wanted everything to go perfectly, to prove to the emperor and all the other citizens of the empire that the war was in the past and Boeruine was once more first in loyalty and standing.

He might have kept on talking, for despite being tired, he was keyed up and fidgety, but the misty tendrils of Callador's portal started to appear within the room, and Derwyn dropped into a deep trance.

Laera watched eagerly as the smoky tendrils slowly started moving in a circle, more and more of them appearing as they spun faster and faster, forming a swirling vortex that became the tunnel to the Gorgon's Crown. She got out of bed and walked toward the misty, swirling portal, disappearing into it as if into a whirlpool composed of fog.

She passed through the sorcerous tunnel and felt the temperature drop, as usual, and goose bumps broke out on her skin. Her hair was blown by the wind within the tunnel. It plucked at her nightdress as she walked against it. Then, at the far end, she saw a light. A moment later, she stepped out of the tunnel, and it collapsed and faded away behind her. But instead of coming out into Callador's sanctum, she discovered that, for the first time, she had emerged into some other place.

She glanced around, puzzled. Had something gone wrong with the spell? The walls of Callador's sanctum in the depths of Battlewaite were built of large, mortared blocks of stone, but the walls in this place were constructed of another substance. They were jet black and sleek, rough cut, yet with a dark gleam as if they had been polished with a jeweler's wheel. They seemed to absorb what little light there was, which came from large black, fluted iron braziers placed at intervals along the walls, emitting flames perfumed by some sort of musky incense. Obsidian, she realized suddenly. The walls were made from blocks of obsidian. She was inside the aboveground portion of Battlewaite, the castle fortress of the Gorgon, Prince Raesene.

She started as she heard a voice behind her. "You are late."

"Callador!" she said, turning toward him. "What is this? Why are we not in your sanctum?"

"There is no time for questions," the old wizard said, approaching her. "Come. His Highness does not like to be kept waiting."

His Highness? That could only be a reference to Prince Raesene. She realized she was about to meet her tutor's master, none other than the Gorgon. Her stomach tensed, and her mouth suddenly went dry.

She had never actually expected to meet Prince Raesene. She only came to Battlewaite at night, for a few hours, and spent all her time in Callador's sanctum, located in the subterranean chambers of the castle. During the time she had studied the mystic arts with the old wizard, she had stopped thinking about why he had returned to contact her in the first place. In all that time, he had never mentioned wanting anything from her, but of course, he did. His tutelage would not come without a price. Laera did not know what that price might be, but as time went on and he said nothing more, she had simply ceased to think about it. Now she was going to find out just what that price would be.

For a moment, fear seized her. What if the Gorgon wanted her? The legends did not speak of Raesene's having a wife. It was something she had never thought to consider. But now she thought about it. He had been here ever since he fled the battlefield of Mount Deismaar, centuries ago. The city of Kal-

Saitharak was old, but Raesene was older still. He had come here when there was nothing and had founded a settlement with his minions, raised this castle, and then over the years, the city had grown up around it. All that time, and he had never had a mate. What if that should be the price? What if, this time, she would not be going back? What if she would never be going back again?

As they walked down the corridor toward two mammoth, intricately carved ebony doors at the far end, Laera's pulse quickened, and she bit her lower lip. She had been repulsed by Arwyn when betrothed to him. Raesene would be much worse. It was said the Gorgon wasn't even human anymore. And if he wanted her, how could she refuse? He held the power. Laera felt a chill run through her, and it wasn't just the dismal, unearthly cold within the castle.

The two huge doors swung open of their own accord. A perverse thrill of excitement ran through her as flames burst from braziers along the walls. Her breathing grew rapid and more shallow. The fear was intoxicating, sensual . . . carnal.

They had entered the great hall of the castle. It was huge, cavernous. The vaulted ceiling high overhead shimmered with dark crystals. Black, winged creatures flitted between the sharply curved stone supports and buttresses, creatures she thought were bats until she noticed they made no cries and floated rather than flew, their shapes undulating like amorphous shadows, like primordial organisms floating in a waterless sea.

On the opposite end of the chamber, a large, frayed and tattered tapestry hung upon the obsidian wall.

Laera recognized the crest of the Roeles, but it had been modified. A single blood-red dragon, rampant, crimson dripping from its gaping jaws and claws, upon a field of black cracked with stylized, jagged golden lightning. Beneath the ancient tapestry, upon a raised dais of murky black and silver crystal stood a huge throne carved from a single giant block of obsidian. It was three or four times larger than the Iron Throne of Anuire, built to accommodate a giant, and from its back sprouted two huge horns carved from faceted blood-red crystal.

Callador stopped her in the center of the chamber, upon an inverted arcane rune of inlaid silver circumscribed by glazed red tiles set into the black stone floor. For a moment or two, they simply stood there, waiting. And then Laera heard the footsteps, and cold sweat trickled down her spine.

Nothing human could walk like that. The sounds came from somewhere in the shadows, through an archway to the left side of the throne. They echoed through the hall like fantastic drumbeats, and Laera held her breath.

Thoom, thoom, thoom, thoom . . .

A huge shadow loomed beneath the archway, and Laera felt her knees start to tremble violently. Her chest rose and fell as she breathed heavily through parted lips, her gaze riveted on that darkened archway. And then Raesene appeared.

Laera's chest felt constricted. He was *huge,* easily three times the size of a normal man, with a thick, muscular, bare chest; immensely strong arms with bony spikes rising from the elbows and the shoulders; a wide, powerful back that tapered sharply to chiseled stomach muscles; skin that seemed the color and texture of dusky stone; and the lower extremities of a satyr. Large, powerful, goatlike legs covered with thick black fur ended in hooves that gleamed like the black stone of the castle walls. But it was his face as he sat upon the throne and gazed down at her that made Laera's heart start beating like a wild thing trying to claw its way out of her chest.

Whatever Raesene may have looked like once, he was unrecognizable now. The face that stared at her with unblinking yellow eyes was a nightmare. The stories said the Gorgon had the head of a bull, but even that would have been preferable to the reality. There were gray-black bullish horns sprouting from his head, and he had bovine ears, but any resemblance to a bull ended there. The shape of the face and head was roughly human, but Raesene had no hair. The top of his head was covered with spiky, bony projections, like the shell of some tortoise armored for battle. The once-human nose had spread out until it was almost a snout, and the jaw was elongated, allowing for a gaping mouth with sharp teeth and prominent canines. From the upper part of his cheekbones and the lower part of his jaw, on either side of the chin, sharp spikes protruded, smaller versions of the upwardly curving horns on his head.

Callador was ancient, and he had used magic all his life without its altering his human appearance, so the only explanation for such a grotesque mutation had to be the divine essence Raesene had inherited from Azrai, the dark god. Augmented by centuries of bloodtheft, these powers had twisted and transformed him into a horror. Laera recalled the stories about Raesene's being insane and remembered doubting them. However, seeing him in the flesh made her wonder how anyone could possibly experience such a terrifying transformation and still retain his sanity.

Callador stepped forward one pace and went down to one knee, bowing to his lord and master. "Allow me to present the Duchess Laera of Boeruine, Your Highness."

Laera did not know what to do. She was numb with fear, but despite that, told herself she was still a princess of the House of Roele, and Gorgon or not, Raesene was a prince, albeit illegitimate, of the same house. Her relative. By rights she would not bow down before him. *I must not let my fear show,* she thought as she made an effort to stand erect and proud, gazing directly at him.

Raesene simply looked at her for a few moments, then spoke. Incongruously, his voice sounded completely human, deep, and resonant, well modulated and precise. The accent was Anuirean, but somehow slightly different. And then she realized it was not so much Anuirean as Andu, the way her people spoke centuries ago.

"Callador has told me much about you, my lady," said the Gorgon. "He tells me that you have made unusual progress with your studies, that you are very gifted."

"I try to apply myself, my lord," she said, choosing the formally polite yet neutral address.

"That is most commendable," the Gorgon said. He paused briefly. "Does not my aspect frighten you?"

"In truth, it is most fearsome, my lord."

"Do you find me repulsive?"

Laera swallowed hard. Where was this conversation leading? "I find you terrible," she said.

"You choose your words most carefully," he replied. "That, too, is commendable. I can sense your fear of me, yet you refuse to show it. You are proud and canny, both admirable traits."

"Thank you," she replied. Time to take the bull by the horns, she told herself, then suppressed a hysterical giggle at the irony of the thought. "You are gracious, my lord, but I do not think you have brought me here to pay me compliments."

Raesene's expression might have been a smile, but it looked more like a snarl. "Indeed. I have a task I wish you to perform. If you perform it well, there will be benefits for you in the near future. But if you fail, I shall take your soul."

Laera gulped. He meant bloodtheft. The thought of her death filled her with dread, but at the same time, there was an underlying sense of relief that he had apparently not brought her here for some more intimate purpose. She would rather have died.

"What is it you wish me to do?" she asked.

The Gorgon produced a tiny vial, no larger than a thimble, on a golden chain. He dangled it off one claw. "Your brother the emperor comes to your castle for the holding of his Summer Court. He brings his new empress with him. On the night of the summer solstice, you shall see that the empress ingests the contents of this vial. You may slip it into any liquid and give it to her. But it must be precisely on that night. You must not fail, else your life is forfeit to me."

"What will it do?" asked Laera tensely.

"It shall cause a child to quicken," said the Gorgon. "My child."

Laera gasped.

"If the empress is already with child when she arrives at Seaharrow," said the Gorgon, "Callador shall give you a special potion she must take. It will abort the child, and thenceforth, she must be given a preparation to prevent conception until one week before the summer solstice. At that time, you shall feed her the contents of this vial. The firstborn of Emperor Michael of Anuire shall be my son. And through him, I shall found a new dynasty and rule the empire that rightfully belongs to me."

The Gorgon stretched out his huge clawed hand, and the vial floated through the air toward Laera. She reached out and took it, then slipped the chain around her neck. The feel of it against her bosom made her skin crawl.

"Go now," said the Gorgon. "You know what you must do."

He got up and lumbered from the great hall, back into the stygian darkness of the shadows beyond the archway.

Laera stood motionless for several moments, stunned. Then she turned and slowly followed Callador out of the great hall. Once they had passed through the large ebony doors, which swung closed behind them, she turned to Callador and whispered, "This is madness!"

"No," said Callador calmly, "it is merely politics."

"Politics!"

"Yes, politics," repeated Callador. "Raesene has lusted for control of the empire for generations. He had failed once in supporting Azrai, and the specter of another failure still haunts him after all these years. For centuries, he has been building up his blood powers and strengthening his domain, increasing the size of his army—not an easy thing to do, since they keep killing each other in street brawls. If they ever had a common enemy, they would probably be a force to be reckoned with. The trouble with Raesene is that his lust for power has become virulently addictive. He needs more and more. He has become obsessed with it to the exclusion of all else."

"And he thinks by impregnating the empress with his child, he will accomplish his goal? That is insane! What sort of monster will the empress give birth to?"

Callador shrugged. "An awnsheghlien child. It will be killed, of course, but the spirit of the child will live on in the consequences of the birth. The firstborn of the emperor will be an abomination. Clearly, a sign from the gods." He smiled. "Or perhaps you can call it Fate."

"And what does that mean?"

"There are those within the empire who will interpret such a birth as an omen," Callador replied. "The inevitability of the ascension of the awnsheghlien. And Raesene is foremost among all the awnsheghlien. There are also those who do not believe in gods. At least, not in the new ones. They are a group who call themselves the Fatalists. They started as a small conclave of disenchanted bards, tavern philosophers—wide-eyed impressionable wenches and the occasional young aristocrat with artistic pretensions, but they have since grown into something of a movement. Blame the bards who travel frequently and bring such fads with them where they go.

"In a number of cities of the empire, these dilettantes have captured the imagination of the common people. The group has no real leader, and its dynamics fluctuate. That sort of thing can make them rather useful. They are ripe, to paraphrase the old maxim, for the picking.

"When the empress gives birth to an abomination, they can spread the word and place upon it an interesting interpretation. Fate, having taken a hand, has poisoned the seed of the Roeles. The god essence they inherited at Deismaar has corrupted them over the years, as it has the awnsheghlien. All the Roeles have ever done was plunge the empire into one war after another in the name of glorious expansion, increasing their holdings at the cost of rivers of blood. The War of Rebellion is still a recent, painful memory to many. Such memories can be exploited. Perhaps it is time for the Roeles to be overthrown and the people to rule themselves."

"You mean to start another civil war," said Laera.

"The empire is weak from the last one," Callador replied. "Another one would cripple it. And Raesene's forces could move in. With Michael unable to raise an army strong enough to stop them, defeat would be a foregone conclusion. Raesene would seize his blood abilities and increase his power. And the Gorgon would sit upon the Iron Throne."

They were descending a long flight of stone steps, heading toward the subterranean levels of the castle where Callador had his sanctum. A glowing ball of fire he had formed lit their way as it floated before them, casting garish shadows on the dank walls.

"*You* devised this plan!" said Laera, with sudden comprehension. "You gave Raesene the whole idea!"

"And why not?" said Callador. "Had Arwyn won the throne, I would have been the royal wizard to the emperor, with all the resources of the empire at my command. No more scouring for obscure supplies and ingredients for my spells, no more projects abandoned due to lack of funds; I could have pursued my art with no restrictions. But Arwyn lost, the fool, and I had to make new plans or face penury. I had grown accustomed to a reasonably comfortable life-style, enough that I developed a desire for more. When the empire collapses and Raesene takes power, I shall become the preeminent wizard in the land. And you, as my prized pupil, shall stand to become Cerilia's most important sorceress."

"You fool!" said Laera. "You think I care about so lowly a distinction? I had planned to ensure that the empress never bore a child! If Michael leaves no heir, my son would be the next in line to rule, and when Michael dies, I would become regent! I would have it all!"

Callador raised his eyebrows. "Indeed. And needless to say, you would take steps to ensure that your brother did not live long. But you forget, if your son were next in line and yet too young to rule, it is your husband, the duke, who would become the regent and . . ." His voice trailed off. "Ah, but of course. You have doubtless already made plans to become a widow at the proper time. I see that I have greatly underestimated you. Your plan is as sound and logical as it is diabolical. My compliments."

"Only now you've ruined everything," said Laera furiously. "If I do what Raesene wants and follow the plan *you* designed, I shall be left with nothing except whatever he chooses to bestow on me. And whatever that may be, it will be a poor substitute for what I would have had otherwise. *I* could have appointed you the royal wizard when I assumed the regency. If that was what you wanted, why in the names of all the gods couldn't you *tell* me?"

"Well, there was the question of trust," said Callador. "It is something I do not bestow very easily. Force of habit, I suppose. And I had not imagined you would plan something so bold and ambitious. I must admit, now that I have heard it, your plan has much to recommend it over mine. I wish I had thought of it myself. Unfortunately, it is too late now."

"Perhaps not," said Laera as Callador made a pass with his fingers and the arched door to his sanctum opened with a loud creak of its ancient iron hinges. "Perhaps there is still a way. . . ."

"How?" said Callador. "We cannot betray Raesene. As I hold power over you, he holds power over me. I had to give Raesene a token to seal my oath to him, just as I took one of you. There is now a bond between me and the Gorgon. If I fail him, there will be nowhere I can hide."

"Then you must get that token back somehow," said Laera.

Callador chuckled. "Easier said than done, my dear. You don't think he would miss it?"

"What form does it take?" she asked.

"A lock of my hair, the same as yours, which he keeps in an amulet around his neck."

"And if that amulet were empty? Would he be likely to open it and check?"

Callador raised his eyebrows. "I should think not," he replied, "but how exactly do you propose I reclaim my lock of hair? Sneak into his bedchamber while he sleeps? I think not. Discovery would mean my life, and with the bond between us, he would feel my presence if I drew so near."

"But he has no such bond with me," said Laera.

"You would risk such a thing?" asked Callador with astonishment. "If he awoke while you tried to sneak into his bedchamber, he would tear you apart."

"Not if I were welcome in his bedchamber," she replied.

Callador's eyes grew very wide. "You don't mean . . . ?"

"How long since he has had a woman? Does he still have the desire?"

Callador stared at her, mouth agape, absolutely speechless. For several moments, he was too shocked to reply. Finally, he said, "I . . . I don't know. But . . . you can't seriously mean you would . . . give yourself to him?"

Laera's mouth twisted into a grimace. "When you first brought me to him, I feared that was precisely what he wanted, and I thought that I would rather die. But with all my plans at stake, if there is no other way, I suppose I could overcome my revulsion for a short while."

Callador sat down unsteadily. He gripped the arms of his chair, shaking his head. "Even if you could, you would be taking a great risk. There is no telling what Raesene might do. I have never known him to be with a woman. I . . . I cannot guess his appetites. Nor can I imagine . . ." He glanced up at her. "He could hurt you. He might even kill you."

"I know," said Laera.

The thought of going to Raesene's bed filled her with dread. And yet, at the same time, there was that strange, inexplicable, perverse thrill engendered by the risk of it, by the thought that she would be the first woman he had known that way in centuries. And despite his horrible appearance, he was still, at heart, a man . . . or he had been once. And men could be controlled. She was a past master at the art. She would be the only woman who had lain with an awnshegh, the most dreaded and powerful awnshegh of them all. And to control someone like that, to conquer him . . .

"By all the gods," said Callador slowly, staring at her with disbelief. "The thought of it excites you!"

She had revealed too much with her expression, Laera realized. Callador must not know. "*Excites* me? Are you mad?"

"The look on your face just now—"

"If terror that chills to the bone can be called excitement, I suppose that is what I feel," she said, shivering to underscore her words. "What would you know about excitement? You who thrill to nothing save your potions and incantations? You are the one who got us into this! Because of you, I must do something . . . unthinkable! And if I should not survive or if I should lose my sanity as a result, it will be on your head! By Haelyn, if I were a man, I would strangle you with my bare hands! You have sold yourself to a monster, and in doing so have sold me as well! And now it is my lot to save us both! Damn you, Callador! Damn you for a fool!"

The wizard hung his head in shame. "You are right, Laera. I've been a fool, blinded by my own ambition. Would there were some way I could make it up to you. I truly regret I ever brought you into this. I am so very sorry."

"Words," she said contemptuously. "Words come easy when it is I who must made this awful sacrifice!"

"It is true," said Callador miserably. He brought his hands up to his neck and slipped off the golden amulet that held her lock of hair. "Here, take this. I release you from your bond. It is the very least I can do."

Laera smiled inwardly. Perfect, she thought, as she took the amulet. Right on cue. "Well, perhaps you really did mean it," she said, her voice softening. "You have been both a friend and teacher to me, Callador. You thought you were helping us both—you to find a better place in life and me to get revenge on an old enemy and on my brother for bartering me to cement a political alliance. I forgive you."

"I shall send you back," said Callador. "I cannot allow you to go through with this. I will take the brunt of Raesene's vengeance."

"No," said Laera. "There may still be a way for us to turn things to our favor. We may yet win our goal. But first you must be free of Raesene's power."

"You would still do this . . . for me?" the old wizard said with amazement.

"No, for us," said Laera. "Wait here for me. I shall either return with your token or die trying."

* * * * *

The corridors of Battlewaite were empty as she made her way back to the great hall. The braziers flickered dimly, their flames dying out. As Laera crossed the hall, heading toward the archway in the back, her heart pounded so hard she thought the sound of it would fill the hall, echoing off the gleaming black walls.

She had never been so afraid in her entire life. And yet, the fear excited her. She had to go through with this somehow. Not only because she still needed Callador, but because without him, her plans would go awry. The wizard knew too much, and so long as the Gorgon controlled him, Callador remained a threat to her. There was only one way to neutralize that threat.

She went through the archway and down a darkened corridor that led to a flight of stone steps. As she climbed them slowly, her terror mounted, and her excitement as well. This was the greatest risk she had ever taken. If she were caught, she would surely die. But if she succeeded, she would not only have taken the ultimate risk and gotten away with it, she would do what no other woman had ever done. She would have conquered the Gorgon.

No one would ever know of it, of course, but that didn't matter. She would know, and the sense of power and satisfaction she would derive from that would be intoxicating beyond anything she had ever experienced. The Gorgon, too, would know. Eventually. And there would be nothing he could do about it.

At the top of the stairs, she came to another, smaller archway. She passed through it into a darkened anteroom, illuminated only by several thick candles dripping on a table. The musky odor inside the room filled her nostrils and made her grimace with distaste. It smelled like the lair of some beast. She crossed the anteroom, headed for a curtained archway in the back. She tried not to look at the objects in the room: the bones scattered on the tables; the rats scurrying among the grisly remains of the Gorgon's last meal—she did not want to speculate what it had been—the human skulls, brown with age, arrayed upon the shelves, trophies of past bloodthefts. She tried to focus her attention on the task at hand. She tried to use her fear, to control it, to employ it as an impetus to see her through what she was about to do.

He was a man once, she told herself. Whatever he may be now, he was once a man, and men could be controlled. This would be her greatest challenge. Her skin crawled at the thought of what she was about to do, but there was something incredibly compelling about it, too. She moved as if in a trance, heading toward the sounds of snoring coming from behind the curtain. It was a rumbling sound, a growling that made her knees shake. She parted the curtain and stepped through.

She stood there for several moments, holding her breath as her eyes grew accustomed to the darkness. She could make out a huge shape lying sprawled on a bed big enough to sleep six humans side by side. An involuntary whimper escaped her throat. It was still not too late. She could still turn and run. . . .

"Who goes there? Who *dares* . . .?"

Lambent yellow eyes stared at her from the bed, like the gaze of some feral, predatory beast.

"Forgive me, my lord," she said, lowering her head. She didn't need to make her voice tremble. It did so of its own accord. "Please, do not be angry with me, I beseech you. I . . . I could not stay away. . . . Never have I beheld such power . . . such force . . . such terrible mastery. . . ." She moved closer. "I was unable to resist. . . . May the dark lord help me! I . . . I was simply overwhelmed. I do not even know what I am doing. Surely, this is madness, but it is a madness that has caught me in its grip and there is nothing I can do." She slipped her gown off her shoulders. "I sensed your power and was helpless and humbled in the face of it. I am lost. My will is not my own. I scarcely know myself. You may smite me down for my boldness, but I do not care. I had to come to you." She was breathing heavily, and she made her voice husky with desire. "Do with me what you will. You are too strong. . . ."

She crawled up onto the bed.

* * * * *

It was nearly dawn when she returned to Callador's sanctum, barely able to move. It had taken all her strength to stagger back to the old wizard. When he saw her at the door, his eyes grew wide, and he hurried to help her inside.

"May the gods have mercy! I was sure I would never see you alive again!" he said, easing her into his chair.

"Were I not of the bloodline of the Roeles, you never would have," she replied weakly. "It took all my strength to regenerate myself after that filthy beast was through with me. He nearly killed me. The pain was beyond anything I have ever known."

"Here," he said, pouring a liquid from a potion bottle into a goblet. "Drink this. It will restore your strength."

She drained it, spilling some of it onto her chin and chest. It felt warm going down and, within moments, the warmth began to spread through her body, suffusing her with invigorating strength. She took a deep breath and leaned back, shutting her eyes as the restorative potion did its work.

"Centuries without a woman," she said, her voice raw. "He was sure saving it up, curse him."

"I still cannot believe you did it," Callador said. "But at least you have survived. You tried. You did your best."

She looked up at him. "I did, indeed."

She reached inside her gown and held up the locket.

Callador caught his breath. "You took it!"

"He fell into a stupor after he was spent. It was a simple matter to remove it."

"But . . . you took the locket!" Callador repeated, with dismay. "You were only supposed to open it and retrieve the token! When he wakes, he will know that it is missing!"

"Then I suppose we had best be far away from here by then," she said. She let the locket fall back inside her gown.

"You have left me with no choice," he said.

"That was my intention."

"Give me the token."

"I think not. After what I've just gone through to get it, I certainly deserve to keep it, don't you think?"

Callador stared at her as the full import of her words sank in. "So, I see. It's going to be like that, is it?"

"That's right, it's going to be like that. I have my token back, and now I hold yours, as well. And that makes me the master now. I know how to use it. You have taught me well, Callador."

"As I have said before," the wizard replied, "I had greatly underestimated you, my lady."

"Form the portal," Laera said. "It is too dangerous for us to remain here long. Besides, it is almost dawn, and my dolt of a husband will need to be waking up soon so he can prepared for the emperor's arrival."

"As you wish, my lady," Callador replied. He began to form the misty portal.

"I will need some time to recover from this ordeal," said Laera, "and you shall need to find a place to stay. We will require supplies to replace those you must leave behind. I will make the funds available to you. Take only those scrolls and materials that are indispensable. The rest we shall replace as best we can."

As the portal opened in the center of the chamber, Callador quickly began to gather up those things he would be taking with him.

"It strikes me there is merit in both your plan and mine," said Laera. "The trick is in combining them."

"Combining them?" said Callador. "I don't understand."

"You will," she replied. "I will explain it in good time. I have suffered much to reach this stage. What remains to be done now is simple. It will merely take a little time and patience. But when all is said and done, I will sit upon the Iron Throne as regent of the Empire of Anuire. And as my first official act, I shall have Aedan Dosiere's heart on a platter."

chapter five

Laera's plan was made easier by the fact that the Empress Faelina was not yet pregnant when she arrived at Seaharrow. It was the first time she had ever met the woman her brother had chosen for a wife. Trust Michael to marry a tomboy, she had thought on meeting the new empress. She was pretty enough, in a rather common sort of way, but she had no conception of how to comport herself like a real lady, much less an empress. She walked like a man, with no grace whatsoever, and was much too direct in her manner. Subtlety was clearly something the poor girl would never understand, thought Laera.

Faelina was polite and friendly to the other ladies of the court at Seaharrow, but evinced little genuine interest in their pursuits. She had no skill at dancing, embroidery, or weaving and could not play a dulcimer or lute. She was unschooled in the courtly graces, and though she was amenable to conversation with the other women, she much preferred to spend her time with the horses in the stables or galloping over the fields with Michael. She enjoyed hunting as much as any man and took delight in watching the guards at their weapons practice. The men all seemed to find her captivating and delightful, remarkably earthy and unprepossessing. The women did not quite know what to make of her. However, it was obvious to everyone that Faelina and Michael were very much in love. They were birds of feather who understood one another, and everyone commented on what a perfect match they were.

Laera treated her like a little sister. Actually, she treated her much better than she had ever treated her real sisters, for whom she had had very little use. It wasn't difficult at all to gain her trust. Laera bestowed it freely from the very start. Manipulating her was not even a challenge. She was an innocent, completely without guile. Laera had nothing but contempt for her.

Faelina accepted Gella as her body servant without question, and from the day she arrived to one week prior to the summer solstice, Gella faithfully administered the potion that would prevent her from conceiving. Each night, she poured several drops into her mulled ale, which was Faelina's preferred libation before bedtime. She even drank like a man, thought Laera. Michael had no taste whatsoever, marrying such a common wench.

Aedan diplomatically kept his distance. When the emperor's party arrived, he had greeted her very formally and politely, with no hint upon his features or in his manner of what had passed between them. He apparently preferred to pretend it simply had never happened. Laera would have liked nothing better than to plunge a dagger deep into his heart, but that would have been too quick. Besides, his turn would come. He was courteous, but after the emperor's party had settled in, he avoided her as much as possible. That was fine with Laera. It meant he would not get in the way.

Toward the middle of the month, the army arrived, marching from Anuire for the long-anticipated punitive campaign against Thurazor, planned now for midsummer. There would be several weeks of preparation, and then they would depart around the middle of the next month. It meant that both Aedan and Michael would be kept busy drilling the troops in readiness for the campaign, which Derwyn would be joining with his knights and men-at-arms. Rodric would be going, too. The young fool wanted an opportunity to distinguish himself in battle. It was just as well, thought Laera. He was becoming tiresome in any case. With luck, he would fall in battle, and she would be spared the necessity of getting rid of him.

On the night of the summer solstice, Laera gave Gella the little vial that contained the Gorgon's seed. She did not tell the girl what it was, merely that it was a new and more efficient preparation of the same nature she had used before. Gella had accepted it without question, then returned later in the evening, as directed, to tell her that the deed was done. Now,

thought Laera, all she had to do was wait. The child
would quicken, and nine months later, when Summer Court was over and Michael and his party were
long gone, the birth would take place.

She felt confident no one would ever suspect the
truth of what had actually occurred. Aside from herself, only Gella and Callador would know, and she
held both their tokens, giving her power over them.
Still, thought Laera, would be best if Gella were
disposed of as soon as possible. Callador was old
and had too much to lose to think of betraying her.
He was too deeply involved himself, and he needed
a patron. Besides, she still had use for him. But Gella
was a loose end that would have to be accounted for.
She was the only one who could link her directly to
the birth.

After everyone in the castle had gone to bed,
Laera went to get the small bronze jewelry box she
kept beside her bed. In the hidden drawer it contained, she kept the lockets that held the tokens of
Callador and Gella, though she wore the one with
Derwyn's hair. She had given some of the lock to
Callador so that he could effect the spell that lulled
her husband into a deep trance each time the wizard
came to her, but she had also kept some for herself.
She used Derwyn's token now to make him sleep,
but at the proper time, would use it to effect a spell
that would make her a grieving widow. She imagined what it would be like.

When the monster child was born, any effort to
keep the birth a secret would be doomed to failure.
She and Callador would see to that, though indirectly, of course. The word would spread that Michael's
seed was cursed. The Fatalists would make sure.

They were already becoming known for spreading discontent and championing the cause of the commoners.

Michael still enjoyed the favor of the people, but they were growing weary of the years of constant warfare. It was a drain on the resources of the empire, and the long War of Rebellion, as well as Michael's campaigns of expansion, had left many widows and orphans. Nobles who were more concerned with the upkeep of their lands and their estates had become tired of Michael's constant demands on them to supply manpower and supplies for the Army of Anuire, and the commoners were starting to grumble that the emperor was more concerned with conquest than he was with improving the lot of his subjects. It would not take much to cause these seeds of discontent to sprout.

A royal birth that had been cursed by the gods would mean the people were cursed, as well, so long as Michael ruled them. There would be calls for his abdication, and if he refused, a rebellion would soon follow. The priests of the temple of Haelyn would support her cause. Her daily attendance at the temple had given Laera a reputation for uncommon piety and goodness. She had carefully reinforced that image by making lavish, regular donations to the temples in Boeruine, and she had sent money to the temples in Anuire and Alamie, as well, where the priests had the most influence. And she always took little Aerin to the temple with her so that the priests would see that the child was being raised in the favor of the god.

But there was still the Gorgon to consider. There was no way of telling what Raesene might do. He was

completely mad, of course, of that Laera no longer
had any doubt. For centuries, he had waited, slowly
but surely building up his powers and extending his
domain. He now controlled the entire mountain
range known as the Gorgon's Crown, and he had
pushed his boundaries north, into the Giantdowns,
east to the Hoarfell Mountains, south to Mur-Kilad
and Markazor, and west to the borders of Tuarhievel,
an area covering over five thousand square miles.

The traitor prince who had escaped Roele at the
Battle of Mount Deismaar was now an immensely
powerful awnshegh who controlled a nation in his
own right, one that might well be strong enough to
attack the empire. Moreover, Raesene would know it
was she who had stolen Callador's token from him,
and Laera did not think he was likely to forget it.

She would not wish to fall into his hands again.
That one night had been enough. It had been the
most terrifying and agonizing experience of her life,
and yet, despite the horror if it all, despite the pain
he'd caused her, despite her revulsion, there had
been an unnatural thrill to it all. What was it about
her that made her feel so alive and vibrant whenever
she risked disaster? What was it that made even pain
seem so exciting?

The thrill of her affair with Rodric, of all her past
affairs, which had seemed so dangerous at the time,
paled to insignificance after that one awful yet somehow strangely and perversely galvanizing night.
What thrill could possibly compare with what she
had experienced then? The deposing of her brother
and the seizing of the empire? Nothing less would
do. After it all came to fruition, she would wear her
widow's weeds and put on a show of grief and

lamentation over Derwyn's death at her own hands, and bravely allow herself to be persuaded to accept the regency for the sake of the people, who would have been primed by then to call for her ascension.

And she would reserve a very special fate for Aedan Dosiere. Over the years, she had contemplated countless times the form her revenge would take. But now that she was a practitioner of the sorcerous arts, there were new and more ingenious ways to make him suffer.

She had waited for this for a long, long time, and now, soon, it would come to pass. She would become a sorcerer-queen, with an empire to rule, and she would gather at her court the greatest wizards in the land to instruct her further until her power was matched by none. Then, not even the awnsheghlien would be able to pose a threat. She would bring even the Gorgon to his knees.

She reached for the jewelry box. It was time. By now, Gella had returned to the servants' quarters and was undoubtedly asleep. She would never see the morning.

Derwyn slept soundly in the bed, without the faintest clue she had placed him into a trance. He would not awake until she chose to wake him. She could do her work undisturbed. All she needed to do now was take the token locket, open it, and cast the spell. . . .

She froze as she opened the hidden drawer. It was empty! Her hand pawed at the silk lining, her eyes unable to believe what they were seeing. The tokens were gone! She had only Derwyn's, which she habitually wore around her neck. And she had enjoyed wearing it, too, because he always commented upon it with affection, never suspecting what it truly represented. The thought gave her no end of amusement. But the other tokens—Callador's and Gella's—were no longer in the secret drawer.

Stunned, Laera tried to think. Had she taken them out before and left them somewhere? No, she always kept them there, safe and secure. But not secure enough, as it turned out. They had been stolen. That was the only possible explanation. But who . . . ?

Gella!

It could have been no one else. Had the girl known about the secret drawer? Had she ever opened it in her presence? Yes, Laera realized, cursing herself for being a fool. She had. And Gella's mother was a witch, so she knew that without the token, Laera would have no power over her. She must have stolen it earlier that evening, when her back was turned, and now she'd run away, thinking she was free. But Laera still had the power of the Duchess of Boeruine. She would hide Derwyn's locket, which was nearly identical in appearance to the other two, and tell him the girl had stolen it. She had already been convicted as a thief, so no one would doubt the story. Laera quickly thought it through.

She would express sorrow over the way the ungrateful girl had repaid her for giving her another chance at life, and would tell Derwyn the whole thing was a sad misfortune but she could always get another locket and another lock of his hair to put inside it. It was only that she had grown so very attached to *that* one, because it had such special meaning. . . .

Derwyn would have his men-at-arms turn the city upside down searching for the girl. They would scour the surrounding countryside and announce a substantial reward for her arrest and the return of the missing locket . . . no, she would have to account for two, so that she could make certain they were both returned. She would say the second locket was one given her by her mother. It had held a lock of her dead father's hair. Yes, that would be perfect.

The girl had not had much of a head start. She would not get far, thought Laera with grim satisfaction. All she had to do was wake Derwyn and express such anguish and distress over the missing lockets that he would immediately send his men-at-arms out in search of the girl. She would be apprehended by morning.

Laera bent over her husband and made a pass over him with her fingers, whispering the words that would remove the spell that held him in a trance. Now all she had to do was cry out and he would wake, alarmed, and—

The sound of frenzied screaming echoed through the castle.

Derwyn sat up in bed. "By Haelyn, what was *that?*"

Laera was taken aback. The cry had not been hers. It had come from outside their chambers, echoing through the halls, and it continued, shattering the stillness of the night. It was a woman screaming, someone in terrible agony. . . .

Derwyn leapt from the bed and reached for his sword belt, buckling it on over his nightshirt. "By all the gods, it sounds as if someone is being murdered!"

There was the sound of running footsteps outside in the corridor, and an instant later, someone was pounding on the door. Derwyn threw it open to reveal one of the house guards.

"Come quickly, Your Lordship! It's the empress!"

"May the heavens preserve us!" Derwyn exclaimed.

"I'm coming with you!" Laera said. Meanwhile, her mind raced. This was too much of a coincidence. Gella had given her the Gorgon's dose only several hours earlier. Before the traitorous girl had stolen the tokens and absconded with them, she had reported that she had administered the content of the vial, as directed, pouring them into a goblet of mulled ale, and she had watched the empress drink it. It had to be the potion, whatever it was. Had the Gorgon lied to her? Had it been some poison meant to kill the empress?

Laera felt a thrill of excitement as she hurried down the corridor after Derwyn. This unexpected development could turn out to be even better than she'd planned. If the empress died, she could blame Gella for having poisoned her. No one would believe anything the girl said after she was apprehended. After all, she was a criminal. Had she not been arrested once before for stabbing a man? But what motive would she have for murdering the empress? It would make no difference, Laera thought. Perhaps the empress caught her trying to steal some jewelry. That would fit in well with her story of the stolen lockets. Or perhaps she was just insane. She would never escape now. And once she was caught, if she started babbling about having given some strange potion to the empress on Laera's orders, she would only convince everyone she was crazy.

Yes, thought Laera as she hurried toward the emperor's quarters, this could work out very well, indeed. Faelina's death would shatter Michael. And as the story spread, it could be slanted in a favorable way, as if it were all an omen from the gods. The empress had died because the emperor was not meant to have an heir. He had angered Haelyn and brought it on himself.

The door to the emperor's quarters stood wide open, and people had crowded in. Michael was standing by the bedside, frantic.

"The physicians!" he kept shouting. "What's happening to her? Somebody do something! By the gods, where are the physicians?"

Aedan was there, too, along with Ariel and several other members of the emperor's inner circle.

Faelina was in bed, thrashing like a fish out of water and screaming with pain. She was covered with sweat, and she had thrown the covers off. Laera immediately ran to her side, as if to comfort her, but Faelina was in such agony, she was unable to respond.

"Get out!" said Laera. "Get out, all of you, and let her breathe! Where are the physicians?"

As if on cue, one of the physicians came rushing in. "Everyone except the emperor and Duchess Laera, please leave at once," he said. "Lord Aedan, you have the healing blood ability. Can you assist me?"

Aedan was pale. "I have already tried. Twice. I was the first on the scene, but it was no use. She does not respond."

Laera hustled everyone else out of the room, then came back to the bedside of the empress, bending over her with a show of great concern. "What happened, Michael?"

"I do not know!" he replied. "She simply started screaming! I don't know what to do! You've got to help her! Please!"

"May the gods preserve us!" the physician said as he examined her. "She is about to deliver a child!"

"*What?*" said Michael. "But . . . that's impossible!"

"Look for yourself," the physician said. He pointed to her belly. It was swelling rapidly, growing right before their eyes, rising like a loaf of bread. The physician placed his hand upon it. "I can feel it kicking. Immensely strong."

"No," said Michael, shaking his head with disbelief. "It cannot be! She was not with child!"

"She is now," the physician said. He shook his head. "This is unlike anything I've ever seen. It passes all understanding."

"Send for the midwives! Quickly!" Laera shouted to the guards outside in the corridor. They would prove excellent witnesses for what was about to happen.

The Gorgon's child was coming. Only it was not taking the normal nine months to quicken and be born. It was happening right now, taking only minutes. Already, Faelina's stomach had swelled to the point where she looked like a woman five or six months pregnant, and it was growing still, visibly, expanding by the moment. If the midwives did not arrive in the next few minutes, they would not be in time.

"How can this be, physician?" Aedan asked as he stared in horrified fascination at the writhing empress.

The man simply shook his head. He was so baffled he was unable to respond. He could only watch, wide-eyed with astonishment and disbelief.

Michael seized him and started shaking the poor man furiously. "*Do* something! *Help* her, for Haelyn's sake!"

"Forgive me, Your Majesty, but there is nothing I can do!"

Faelina's screams continued as she bucked and thrashed in the bed. Her eyes were rolling wildly, and she was breathing in sharp gasps.

"Michael! Michael!" Aedan said, trying to pry the emperor's grip from the physician. "Let the man go! This isn't helping!"

"The child is coming, Your Majesty," said the physician. "There is no denying it, however incredible it may seem. We must make ready to assist the birth."

Michael released him just as the midwives came rushing in. They had already been told what was happening, but when they saw it for themselves, they cried out with dismay. Still, they overcame their initial shock and moved to help the empress give birth.

"You must leave," the senior midwife said to the physician. "This is no work for a man. All the men must leave, right now."

"I'm staying," Michael said.

"You will only be in the way," the senior midwife said curtly. "Emperor or no, this is no place for a man."

"Come on, Michael," Aedan said, taking him by the arm. "There is nothing we can do here now. Let them do their work."

Dazed, Michael allowed himself to be led outside. Only Laera, Ariel, and the midwives remained. "This is sorcery!" one of the midwives said. "Yesterday, she was not even with child, and now she will give birth at any moment!"

"Whatever it may be, our duty now is to the mother and her child," the senior midwife said. "Stop your chattering and hold her down before she injures herself."

Snapping out orders like a drillmaster, the senior midwife quickly took charge. Laera and Ariel assisted. It took them all to get the struggling Faelina into the proper position. She was delirious, but still the screams kept coming. Her stomach now was the size of a ripe watermelon.

"It's coming," the senior midwife said. "Hold her! Stop her thrashing!"

They held her down. Faelina was beyond being able to hear them. And there was no need to tell her to bear down. The child was coming, with or without her help. It was clawing its way out. The senior midwife positioned herself between Faelina's legs, then cried out with surprise as a gout of blood spurted out and splashed her. One of the younger midwives screamed with fright and bolted, but the older woman caught her and gave her a hard slap across the face.

"Back to your duty! Now is no time to be squeamish!"

Chastened, the woman returned to help hold Faelina down, but she was clearly terrified. Then the empress let out one drawn-out, throat-rending scream, and the child was born, ripping its way out. The senior midwife, for all her calm composure, gasped and recoiled from the sight. Faelina went limp, falling into a swoon.

"*Faelina!*" Michael shouted from the corridor. There were the sounds of scuffling as he was forcibly restrained.

"May the gods protect us!" said the senior midwife, backing away and staring at the infant with horror.

"Mistress! What is it?" one of the others asked. Then they looked, and they all started screaming. Two of them bolted from the room in wild panic. The third backed up to the wall and pressed herself against it, staring at the child with horror and whimpering hysterically.

"Oh, Haelyn help us!" Ariel whispered in a shocked tone as she beheld the child.

Like father, like son, thought Laera. The birth was an abomination.

Michael fought off whoever was holding him back and burst into the room. The first thing he saw was the blood-soaked bed, and he was brought up short. Then he saw his "son." He caught his breath, and his eyes bulged with horrified disbelief. Aedan and Derwyn both came running in behind him, and they saw it, too, and were shocked into immobility.

"Oh, gods!" Michael said. Then words failed him.

The child was dusky, gray-skinned, and twice the size of a normal newborn infant. It had the lower extremities of a satyr, goatlike legs with black, bifurcated hooves. Its hands were claws, and sharp little spikes protruded from its elbows and shoulders. Its mottled gray head seemed too big for its body, covered with bumpy, bony protrusions at the crown and two small, upwardly curving horns just above its temples. Its nose resembled a dark snout, and its mouth had all its sharp little teeth already in place at birth. It growled, snapping hungrily and instinctively at the air.

As they gazed down at the creature with horror, it opened its eyes. They were a bright golden-yellow.

Michael's knees buckled. Aedan and Derwyn caught him as he slumped, his eyes glazed with shock, and then something in him snapped. With an animal cry of rage and agony, he seized the hilt of Derwyn's sword and wrenched it from its scabbard, then brought it down upon the abomination lying on the bed. Again and again he raised it and brought it down, dismembering the obscene creature. Aedan and Derwyn seized him, but he fought them off, and they called for the guards to help restrain him.

He fought them like a man possessed, but finally, they got the sword away from him. It was slick with thick, dark green blood. They dragged him from the room as he screamed out Faelina's name over and over, but not before the guards saw what he had killed.

Excellent, thought Laera with exhilaration. They will never be able to keep it quiet now.

"Faelina!" Ariel said, bending over her and stroking her forehead. "Faelina . . ."

Laera stood at the foot of the bed, looking down at the limp form of the empress. "She's dead," she said flatly. "Just like her hellspawn."

Ariel looked up at her slowly. No words passed between them, but Laera clearly saw the look of sheer loathing in her eyes. So, she thought with sudden realization, she knows. In that one moment, all of Ariel's thoughts were perfectly transparent. Aedan must have told her. She gazed back at her, defiantly, as if daring her to say something.

"I knew you were a cold-hearted bitch," said Ariel softly, "but until this moment, I never truly realized how evil you really were."

"Evil?" Laera said. They were alone now with the

body of the empress, and there was silence in the corridor outside. "If *I* am evil, then what do you call *that?*" She indicated the remains of the thing Faelina had brought into the world. "How else can you explain such an event except to say it was willed directly by the gods? What portent shall we read from this, my lady?"

She turned and left the room, passing the physician as he was hurrying back. Laera paused, then stood against the wall by the open door, listening. She heard the physician's voice.

"Oh, no. Is she . . . ?"

Ariel's voice was leaden. "She's dead."

There was a sharp intake of breath as the physician saw what it was Michael had killed.

Ariel spoke. "How is the emperor?"

"I have given him a sleeping draught. It is very potent. He was . . . greatly distressed."

"Take that . . . that *thing* and get rid of it," said Ariel. "No one else must see it. And then have all the midwives report to me. And the guards who were in here, as well. There must not be a word of this. Not even a whisper. The empress died in childbirth. The child did not survive. It was . . . a male."

"I understand, my lady. But to keep something like this quiet . . ." Laera could imagine the man shaking his head. "Someone is bound to talk."

"Nevertheless, we must try, for the sake of the emperor *and* the empire. If word of this gets out," said Ariel, "there is no telling what may happen."

Oh, yes, there is, thought Laera, smiling with grim satisfaction. Oh, yes, there is.

* * * * *

Aedan had not been drunk in years, not since that night in the Green Basilisk, but he felt like getting drunk tonight. He needed to get drunk. He feared for Michael's sanity. He had never seen him in such a state, not even in battle when he loosed his divine rage. He had not done so tonight, for it was not rage that seized him but agony and desperation. Nevertheless, it had taken Aedan and Derwyn and four guards to restrain him.

Aedan had him brought back to his quarters, where the physician had forced a sleeping draught down his throat while they held him down. Thankfully, it was very strong and had taken effect quickly. He would sleep till morning. And then, when he awoke . . .

Aedan didn't want to think about that. He knew he had to because it was his duty to think about such things, but not just now. For tonight, just one night, he did not want to consider possibilities. They were too frightening to contemplate.

Ariel would sleep with her ladies-in-waiting tonight, if she would sleep at all. She had sent for all the midwives and the guards who had seen the . . . the thing, instructing them they were to reveal nothing, on pain of direst consequences, but it was an empty threat. What were they to do if anyone should talk? Imprisonment? Execution? For what? For failing to keep to themselves something so horrifying and grotesque that to keep it bottled up inside would eat at them like acid?

It was a doomed effort, anyway, and he knew it. By now, the entire castle would be buzzing with talk of what had happened, and by tomorrow, the town would know of it, too. From there, it would spread throughout the empire, and there was nothing anyone could do to stop it. He signaled the serving wench for another drink.

How could it have happened? It seemed beyond all comprehension. He could still scarcely believe it, yet he had seen what had come clawing out of her womb, killing her as it was born. The empress had given birth to an abomination. An awnshegh.

A gorgon.

It seemed impossible. Faelina was a virgin when she went to Michael's bed. Ariel had assured him of that, and he saw no reason to disbelieve her. He simply could not accept the alternative. Faelina had never left her father's estate. She had grown up there, had lived there all her life. Her trip to Anuire was the first time she had ever left home in Aerenwe. How could she possibly have lain with . . .

No, it was unthinkable. And yet, what other explanation could there be? He could not believe it was Michael's seed that had produced that . . . *thing*. Unless, perhaps . . .

He moistened his lips as the serving wench brought him another drink. It was late, and the small tavern was nearly empty. Tomorrow night, it would be full as people met to discuss what they would doubtless have heard by then.

Had the gods cursed Michael? Had Haelyn punished him? For what? What offense could have been so horrible as to deserve a penalty like that? Michael had been driven to expand the empire and secure its borders. In so doing, he had fought one campaign after another, and the losses had been very high. Had the gods punished him for his arrogant pride and ambition, which had cost so many lives? Why then did Faelina deserve to suffer as she had?

He had known she was dead the moment he entered the room. No one could have survived such terrible wounds. There had been so much blood. . . . He had felt shocked, horrified, and painfully helpless. He had the blood abilities of healing and regeneration, but he could not reanimate the dead. Michael had known it, too.

He had changed after he met Faelina. The marriage had been so good for him. They were perfectly suited to each other, and they had both recognized that from the moment they met. Michael had doted on her. He had become a different man. Still mindful of the goals he wanted to accomplish, but no longer so driven or possessed. What would become of him now?

Aedan drained the goblet and signaled for another. There would be many more to follow, but he did not think there was enough drink in all the world to numb what he was feeling.

"Lord Aedan?"

He glanced up. A cloaked and hooded figure had approached his table. It was a woman's voice, and it sounded vaguely familiar. She sat down across from him and pulled her hood back slightly.

"It is Gella, my lord. Perhaps you may recall me."

The memory clicked. "Oh, yes," he said tonelessly. "You served the empress."

"I fear I served her very poorly, my lord. Forgive me, but I must speak with you. There is something you must know. It concerns the empress."

She is past all concern now, thought Aedan, looking down into his drink. Clearly, Gella was ignorant of what had happened.

"And it concerns Duchess Laera, too. It is she who is behind it all."

Aedan glanced up sharply. "What do you mean? Behind what?"

The girl leaned forward, speaking in a low voice as if afraid she might be overheard, though there was hardly anyone in the tavern—only a few old men deep in their cups. "I had to flee the castle, my lord, or else she would have killed me. I know this beyond all doubt. I hid outside the walls, waiting for someone I could tell this to, someone who might believe me, but I did not know who that might be. And yet, I had to tell. I had to. When I saw you, I thought you were the only one who might listen to my words and not dismiss them out of hand. You are known to be a fair and honest man. And I . . . I am but a lowly thief. Still, I swear to you, I swear upon my life, I am telling you the truth."

"Wait, wait," said Aedan. "Calm yourself and speak slowly. What are you talking about?"

"Duchess Laera is a sorceress, my lord."

"A *sorceress!* Ridiculous. Laera may be many things, and most of them unsavory, but she has never studied sorcery."

"I tell you she has, my lord. She is well versed in the art. My mother, rest her poor soul, was a witch, and she had taught me a few things before she died. I know a sorceress when I see one. Especially when she takes a token of my hair to use against me in a spell if I should fail to do her bidding."

"A token?" Aedan knew something about sorcery. His old teacher, after all, had been the librarian at the College of Sorcery in Anuire.

"She kept it in a locket, which she had hidden in a

secret drawer inside her jewelry box," said Gella. "This locket."

She held it out, dangling it from its chain.

"She likewise had another, which I stole from her as well." She took the second locket out and showed it to him. "I cannot say for certain, but I believe this is a token of the wizard who comes to see her in her bedchamber at night. She thought I did not know, but I spied on her and saw him. I think it must be the wizard who instructed her, and she had turned the tables on him, so the student became the master."

"Hold on," said Aedan, trying to take it all in. "Who was this wizard? What did he look like?

"He was a wizened old man," said Gella, "very old, with a bald pate. She called him Callador."

"Callador!" Aedan no longer doubted the girl. Callador had been Arwyn's wizard, and he had disappeared after the Battle of Dalton.

"She has a third locket, as well," Gella continued, "but she never takes it off. It is a token of her husband, the duke, whom I believe does not suspect its purpose. Through it, she keeps him in her thrall."

Yes, thought Aedan, that sounds like just the sort of thing Laera would so. She had always liked being in control. Of men, especially. "I believe you," he said. "Go on."

"There was a fourth locket, too," said Gella, "and I believe it was her own token. Perhaps the wizard held it and she got it back somehow. I saw it once, but I have never seen it again. I think she must have destroyed it. But I stole these. This one, which is mine, I shall keep and destroy so it may never be used against me in a spell. But this one, which I believe is the wizard's, I shall give to you. I looked inside. The hairs are short and curled. As he is bald, I gather they came from elsewhere."

Aedan took the locket. "I see. Go on. How does the empress fit into all this?" He had the sudden feeling of a pit yawning open beneath him. He sat on the edge of his chair, completely alert and sober now. His blood was racing.

"She planned to insure that the empress would not have a child, so that there would be no heir to the throne," said Gella. "And if the emperor left no heir—"

"As the firstborn princess of the House of Roele and wife to the Duke of Boeruine, it would be her son who would succeed," said Aedan. He pressed his hands down hard against the table to stop them from shaking.

Gella nodded. "She assigned me to the empress as her body servant and forced me to give her a potion every night from a vial that she gave me. I was to put several drops into her drink each night, and it would prevent her from conceiving a child. This I did, though I was loath to do it, but you must understand that I did not have any choice. So long as Duchess Laera held my token, I was helpless to resist."

"A potion . . ." Aedan said, his mouth suddenly dry.

"Last night, that is, in the evening, before the empress was due to retire, Duchess Laera gave me a new vial, saying I was to use it instead. She said it was a new preparation, more efficient. I was to empty the entire contents of the little vial into her drink tonight, and she insisted I return and tell her when I did it. I did not *want* to do it, my lord, you must believe me, but I had no choice. I was afraid.

When I came back to her tonight to tell her I had done as she commanded, she responded very strangely. She smiled in an evil way and nodded to herself, then turned to gaze out the window for a moment, as if deep in thought. I knew I might never have another chance, so I stole the lockets. I am very quick and light-fingered. It . . . it was my trade, you know."

"And you gave her this new potion tonight . . ." said Aedan, his voice came out hoarse through a constricted throat.

"I fear it may render her permanently barren," Gella said. "I hope there is an antidote. If that should be so, I pray that it is not too late—"

"The empress is dead," said Aedan.

Gella gasped and gave out a small cry.

"She died in giving birth to an abomination," Aedan said harshly. "It quickened within moments and tore its way out of her womb. It was a gorgon. The emperor killed it, and now I fear he may be driven mad with grief."

"Oh, what have I done?" said Gella in a shocked whisper. She broke down and started sobbing. "I do not deserve to live!"

"But live you shall," said Aedan. "You are coming back to Seaharrow with me. We shall deal with her ladyship, the duchess."

* * * * *

Derwyn couldn't sleep. He was too keyed up. He paced across the room, running his fingers through his hair, frantic with anxiety.

Laera sat on the bed, watching him and listening

to him, thinking things couldn't have gone more perfectly.

"It's horrible," Derwyn kept repeating. "Horrible. How could this have happened? The empress dead, the emperor raving, the child . . ." His voice caught. "Dear gods! How can one call that nightmarish thing a child? That poor woman! That poor, poor woman! How she must have suffered!"

"She is suffering no longer," Laera said. "She has found peace."

"Peace! *Peace?* To die like that?" He closed his eyes. "I can only thank the gods she never lived to see the monster she gave birth to! What a horror! What a horror!"

"It was an abomination," Laera said. "A gorgon child. An awnshegh."

"You think I don't *know?* You think I did not *see?* How could it have happened? *How?*"

"It must have been the gods," said Laera. "That can be the only explanation."

"*The gods?* You must be mad! You do not realize what you are saying!"

"How else could it have happened?" Laera asked. "You saw it with your own eyes. I saw it, too. When she went to bed, she was not with child. It happened within moments. Mere moments. We watched the monster child quicken. We saw her stomach swell. It was unnatural. Who else but the gods could have brought such a thing about?"

"But *why?* Why would they do it? Why would they make an innocent girl suffer so?"

"It was Michael," Laera said. "They punished Michael for his sins."

Derwyn stopped and gazed at her with astonishment. "He is your own brother!"

"Even a sister cannot turn a blind eye to the truth," said Laera. "How many lives were lost because of Michael's ruthless ambition? How many died needlessly in his campaigns of conquest? And how many died because he would not give in during the War of Rebellion? How many suffered because of my brother's obsession with power and his thirst for blood? Or have you forgotten that it was Michael who took your father's head?"

"No, I have not forgotten," Derwyn said heavily. "How could anyone forget a thing like that? Was I not there to see it? I do not need you to remind me!"

"And now you defend him."

"He is the emperor!"

"He killed your father."

"Yes, damn you! But it was my father who had made war on him, not he who made war on my father!"

"And you were your father's son. What of your duty to him? What of your loyalty? If you had so little loyalty to your own father, what loyalty can I expect as your wife?"

"Do not speak to *me* of loyalty, you who would condemn your own brother!"

"It is not I who have condemned him, but the gods," said Laera. "Or can you deny the evidence of your own senses?"

Derwyn swallowed hard. His shoulders slumped. "No, I cannot. Much as I do not want to accept it, I can think of no other explanation."

"I can," said Aedan, standing in the doorway. He had opened it and walked in, hearing the last part of the conversation. "Why don't you ask your wife how this awful tragedy has come to pass?"

"Aedan! What are you saying? What is the meaning of this intrusion?"

"Justice," Aedan replied. "Justice is the meaning. Your wife is a foul sorceress, and it was a potion that she gave the empress that brought about the birth of the abomination. I am here for justice."

"*What?*" said Derwyn. "Are you mad?"

"He must be," Laera said. "The lord chamberlain seeks to find a scapegoat for this tragedy, and he has chosen me because I once rejected his advances."

"*My* advances?" Aedan said. "It was you who seduced me, right here in this very castle. And it was your spite at me for breaking off our affair that ate at you like a disease for all these years that led you to this monstrous betrayal."

"What nonsense is this?" asked Derwyn, staring at him with astonishment. He glanced at Laera.

"He lies," said Laera. "He is desperate to pin the blame for this on someone, and I am his chosen target."

"Aedan, I cannot believe you would stoop to this!" said Derwyn. "Where is your proof?"

"Does this look familiar, Derwyn?" Aedan asked, holding up a locket. "It is much like one your wife wears, is it not? It contains a lock of hair, a sorcerer's token to be employed in the casting of a spell. One just like the token she took from you and wears around her neck, even as we speak. This one contains a token from your father's wizard, Callador, her instructor in the sorcerous arts. And this one," he said, holding up a second locket, "contains a token from the woman she used as a dupe, to slip her foul potion to the empress."

"*That* is your proof?" said Laera with contempt.

"Two lockets which you could have obtained from any jeweler?"

"I have obtained something else, as well," said Aedan. "Come in, Gella."

Laera's eyes grew wide as Gella entered.

"She will tell you that everything I've said is true," said Aedan.

"She is a thief and would-be murderer," said Laera. "A common whore whom I, in my misguided compassion, sought to help. Is this how you repay me, Gella? By bearing false witness against one who saved your life?"

"You would have taken it when you were through with me," said Gella vehemently.

"As she planned to take yours, Derwyn," Aedan added. "When her plot to see her son placed upon the throne came to fruition, you would be all that stood between her and the regency."

"Enough!" said Derwyn. "I am not going to listen anymore to these ludicrous accusations! I demand you leave Seaharrow at once!"

"You forget, Derwyn, I am the lord high chamberlain of the empire," Aedan said. "As such, I carry the authority of the emperor himself. And it is only by the emperor's grace that you have retained your life and lands. If you are too blind to see the truth, I need prove nothing to you, nor account to you for my actions. I am arresting Laera for high treason."

Derwyn grabbed his sword. "You shall have to come through me."

"Don't be a fool," said Aedan. "You never were a swordsman. I have no wish to kill you."

"Then you shall die!" said Derwyn, rushing at him. Gella cried out with alarm as he brought his blade down, but Aedan ducked beneath the stroke and seized his wrist. As they struggled, Laera snatched up a dagger from her night table and raised it high over her head, rushing at Aedan. But before she got halfway across the room, there was a soft, whistling sound, and a crossbow bolt buried itself in her heart.

Laera stopped and gasped with shock. The dagger slipped from her fingers as she stared with disbelief at the bolt protruding from her chest. She looked up to see Ariel standing in the open doorway, a crossbow lowered at her side. The duchess shook her head, then collapsed to the floor.

"Laera!" Derwyn cried, rushing to her side.

Aedan glanced at his wife with surprise.

Ariel lowered the bow. "I told you that if she ever tried to harm you, I would kill her."

481

ANUIRE

chaptef six

The Army of Anuire stood drawn up in lines at
the entrance to the Valley of Shadows. The valley
was over twenty miles wide, flanked to the north
and south by the steep and rocky mountains of the
Gorgon's Crown. Nestled in the foothills of the
mountains to the north and rising high to overlook
the city of Kal-Saitharak spreading out below it were
the obsidian towers of the castle known as Battlewaite, the fortress of the Gorgon.

They had marched all the way from Seaharrow
along a hidden forest trail once used by Arwyn of
Boeruine in his repeated forays against the duchies
of Alamie during the War of Rebellion, across the
northern plains of Alamie and the highlands of

Mhoried and Markazor, then through a narrow mountain pass in Mur-Kilad leading to Kiergard.

In the northern highlands of Markazor, where the goblin vassals of the Gorgon had swept down from the mountains and extended their domain, they had to fight the troops of King Rozgarr, who had been ordered by his master to attack the Anuireans on their approach. But Rozgarr's goblin forces had faced the mightiest army ever assembled in the empire since the Battle of Mount Deismaar, and they didn't stand a chance.

On his march through Alamie and Mhoried, Michael had picked up troops from Duke Alam, who had mobilized every available man, leaving behind only a skeleton force to guard his northern borders against incursions by bandits from the Five Peaks. Flaertes of western Alamie had sent more troops, as well, all that he could spare, and additional reinforcements had arrived from Avanil and as far away as Osoerde, Elinie, and Dhalaene. Moergan of Aerenwe met up with them near the borders of Markazor, having force-marched all the way from his domain on the southern coast with every able-bodied man within his province to avenge his daughter's murder. Avanil had sent more troops, as well as Ghieste and Diemed, and even the tiny city-state of Ilien, on the banks of the Straits of Aerele, had sent a detachment of mounted knights who had ridden without rest to join the march.

News of the Empress Faelina's death and the circumstances surrounding it had spread throughout the empire, carried by swift dispatch riders who stopped at every town and city that they came to and sent more riders out, so that the news could be disseminated as rapidly as possible. It had not taken long for the true story to come out. Aedan had ordered the army to comb every house in Seasedge and the surrounding area in search of Callador. They had found him in a rooming house in town, where he had been hiding in wait until Laera could manage to secure more suitable quarters for him and replenish his magical supplies. They took him by surprise, in bed, without a struggle, and he was brought before the grief-stricken emperor, to whom he confessed everything in a trembling voice. Those in attendance listened, horrified, as the story of his betrayal came out, and when he was through, they called for the most dire punishments that they could think of.

Some cried out for the wizard to be hanged, others demanded he be drawn and quartered, while still others called for burning at the stake. As Callador listened to these angry cries for his blood, a fierce tremor seized him, and he cried out in terror, clutching at his chest, and fell lifeless to the floor. He was an old man, and his heart could not take the strain. Michael ordered his body burned and the ashes scattered to the winds.

Derwyn of Boeruine had listened to the wizard's story numbly, unable to believe the extent of his wife's treachery. In despair, he prostrated himself in front of Michael and begged for his forgiveness, swearing he would lay down his life if need be to avenge the empress. Michael had forgiven him, for in truth, he was blameless in the matter, and Derwyn ordered that Laera be buried in an unmarked grave in the most remote and desolate place his men could find. He did not wish to know where.

As the story spread, the people of the empire responded, not only knights and warriors, but common people, too, who came with pitchforks, spears, daggers, longbows, and whatever other weapons they could get their hands on. As the Army of Anuire set off on its march to the Gorgon's Crown, villagers lined their route and stood watching silently, their hats removed when the emperor passed by. And as the army marched, it grew, every soldier imbued with a grim purpose.

In northern Markazor, where they met the forces of King Rozgarr, they rolled right over them. They sustained losses, but not nearly as severe as those that they inflicted, and Rozgarr's troops were routed. They fled in disarray and the army moved on into Mur-Kilad.

In the mountain pass of Mur-Kilad, they were attacked by dwarves, who fired down on them from the heights and rolled rocks down on the troops. But the mountain dwarves who fought them lacked the resolve for a serious engagement. They were a conquered people who were forced to labor hard under their awnsheghlien master, and they put up only a token resistance when foot soldiers swarmed up the steep slopes of the pass to drive them out. Still, losses were sustained, but the army kept on with determination through the harsh and broken land.

In Kiergard, the southernmost domain of the Vos, they passed within sight of the city of Esden, but the grim Vos inhabitants declined to offer combat, though their army had assembled to watch the Anuireans go by. They were no friends to the empire, but they had fought long and hard for centuries to protect their land against incursions by the Gorgon's savage troops. They would not help, but neither would they hinder.

However, as the army headed north through Kiergard, news of their march spread, and the taciturn common people of the Vos came out from every small village and farm, bearing provisions for the troops. For generations, these simple, hard-working people had lived under the Gorgon's depredations, and as they came out to feed the troops with whatever they could spare, they wished them luck and the blessings of their god.

Finally, the Army of Anuire stood on the high ground at the entrance to the Valley of Shadows. Battlewaite, with its obsidian walls and towers, loomed ominously in the distance above the Gorgon's city of Kal-Saitharak. As Aedan glanced at Michael, at whose side he had ridden all the way, bearing his standard, he saw that same grim, stone-faced expression Michael had maintained ever since their march began. And he was worried.

The punitive campaign against Thurazor, which had been the reason for the army's arrival in Boeruine, no longer mattered. All Michael wanted was revenge against the Gorgon. The Michael of old had returned, driven and obsessed, but to an extent Aedan had never seen before. The air around him seemed to vibrate. Michael was once more in his element, but this time, it was different. He barely spoke at all, except to issue orders. Lord Korven had asked to be included on this march, but the old man had served in his last campaign. He had gone lame, and his strength was failing him. He could still sit a horse, but no one believed anymore that he could fight. Michael had thanked him, but ordered him to remain at home with his grateful wife and children. Michael was the general on this campaign, delegating nothing. He personally saw to every last detail.

When they had marched halfway across Kiergard, he had stopped the troops on the outskirts of the forest and ordered siege towers built. Squads of men with axes had gone into the forest and felled trees for the purpose, fitting and lashing and pegging the logs together to form three wooden siege towers for the assault on Battlewaite. Large logs were sawed for planks with which to construct the wheels to move them. He also ordered the construction of two trebuchets to hurl boulders at the fortress walls, and large logs were stripped and fitted with handholds to make half a dozen battering rams. A score of scaling ladders were constructed, and archers took the time to make more arrows.

They did not rush unduly in any of these tasks, for there was no point to it. They would have no advantage of surprise. Raesene knew they were coming. They would meet on his home ground in the Valley of Shadows, on the plain outside Kal-Saitharak. Michael knew the Gorgon would be just as busy assembling his army and making preparations to meet the attack.

Now, they stood upon the high ground above that plain, looking down at the opposing army drawn up to meet them. Aedan knew Raesene would not order his forces forward to attack. That would give Michael the high ground. The Black Prince would wait until they came down to him.

There was a distance of several miles separating them, so neither Aedan nor Michael could make out individuals among the opposing troops. They could not tell at this distance if Raesene himself was leading them, but Aedan could not imagine the Gorgon remaining in his castle when the opportunity he had awaited for so long had come marching to his door. For centuries, he had nursed a deep hatred of the Roeles, his half-brother's descendants, and now it would be settled, one way or the other, once and for all.

As the two opposing armies faced each other, Aedan's thoughts turned back over the years to a time when two much smaller "armies" had faced each other on the plains of Seaharrow. At this distance, the bodies looked small, and he could easily picture them as children. For a surreal moment, that was how he saw them, in their little suits of armor with their wooden swords and shields, grim-faced and very determined as they prepared to reenact the Battle of Mount Deismaar.

Now they would reenact it once again, in deadly earnest. In years to come, the bards would sing the ballad of this battle, the Battle of Battlewaite. Or perhaps they would call it the Battle of the Gorgon's Crown. They would sing of all the brave men who were about to fall here, and they would extol the glory of the victor—whoever he may be.

Aedan wondered if Vaesil would compose one of those ballads and if he would survive to hear it. Strangely, for the first time in his life, he felt no fear before going into battle. Just a sense of nervous expectation. Perhaps that wasn't a good sign. Vaesil would enjoy the irony of this, he thought. If he knew the entire story, he would doubtless include it in his composition, the story of two boys who fought a play battle in their childhood and grew up to relive it for real. Only this time, there would be no arguments about who would play Raesene. Raesene was here himself to act out his own role, much more powerful and dangerous than he had ever been. There would be real goblins shouting their ululating war cries instead of children snarling as they played pretend. There would be real gnolls, with their wolfish teeth and snouts instead of little boys howling in imitation of beasts they had thankfully never before encountered. The only thing missing was the elf contingent, who would not be here to turn the tide of battle at the crucial moment.

The past had come full circle, with the dark forces of the traitor prince faced off against the lineal descendant of the original Roele. Only this time, there were no gods to intervene and shake the earth. This battle would be fought to the bitter end by all-too-mortal men.

The troops waited in expectation for Michael's traditional address before each battle, but Michael simply sat astride his horse, staring out at the opposing army. He had a faraway look in his eyes, almost as if he weren't seeing them but something else. Perhaps a row of armored children arrayed across the plain.

"Sire," said Aedan. "Sire?"

Michael turned toward him. There was a strange look upon his face—distant, dreamy. His eyes, so often angry and full of fire in the past, were calm.

"Sire, the troops are awaiting your address."

"Ah," said Michael softly. He rode his horse out in front of them, and a hush fell over the army.

For a moment, he simply sat there, his gaze scanning the ranks. Every eye was on him. He gave the shortest speech he had ever given in his life.

"It ends here!" he said, his voice ringing out clearly. He drew his sword and held it high over his head as he turned his mount. "*Advance!*"

Aedan trotted up beside him with the standard as the army moved off at a marching pace down the slope into the plain. Across from them, standing perfectly still, was the Army of the Gorgon. They were as motionless as statues, all dressed in black armor, pennants fluttering in the breeze. There was no sound upon the field except the steady tramping of feet and the clinking of armor and gear. Inexorably, they closed the distance.

Michael rode silently, staring intently straight ahead, his gaze scanning the opposing ranks for some sign of Raesene. When they had almost reached the bottom of the slope, Aedan noticed Michael stiffen, and his gaze locked on. He looked in the same direction. For several moments, he could not pick out what Michael saw, and then he spotted it and wondered that it did not stand out more clearly.

It was the first time he had ever laid eyes on Prince Raesene, and he saw that the stories they told about his size were true. He sat astride the largest warhorse Aedan had ever seen, a black Percheron with tufted hooves and a long, dark, flowing mane. But as large as the horse was, its rider dwarfed it. He was easily three times the size of a normal man, incredibly massive and wide, dressed in black armor like his troops except for the red dragon emblazoned on his breastplate. Next to him stood his standard-bearer, holding aloft the black and red colors of Raesene—a red dragon rampant on a field of black, surmounted by jagged lightning.

What Aedan at first took to be a helm he realized after a few moments was not a helm at all, but Raesene's head. The Gorgon rode bareheaded into battle, bony protrusions on his crown and two large black horns curving upward from his temples. He was still too far away to make out the Gorgon's features, but he was grateful for that. He wondered if the legends were true about the Gorgon's being able to slay with just his gaze. If so, how was it possible to fight such a creature?

Rank upon rank of goblins, gnolls, and ogres faced them, augmented with human mercenaries, for whom Aedan felt the greatest contempt of all. What kind of men would willingly serve an awnshegh? A creature who had once betrayed his own people to the Dark Lord.

Behind him, Aedan heard the steady tramping of feet and the rattling and squeaking of the siege engines at the rear as they rolled forward, drawn by teams of horses. They would not come into play at this stage of the battle, and perhaps might not come into play at all unless they could not turn the Gorgon's troops and break them, force them into a retreat back into the obsidian fortress.

The enemy waited as they advanced steadily. A mile. . . . A thousand yards. . . . Eight hundred . . . seven . . . six. . . . When they were about five hundred yards apart, the Gorgon raised his sword, and a loud cry went up from his forces as they charged, the cavalry leading the way as they thundered across the field toward them.

"*Charge!*" Michael screamed, and with their battle cry of "Roele! Roele!" the Army of Anuire surged forward.

Michael headed straight for Raesene, with Aedan galloping at his side. The hoofbeats of the horses made a sound like rolling thunder as they flew toward one another, the foot soldiers running behind them.

The mounted sections met first, and the field filled with the sounds of blades ringing upon blades. Michael met the Gorgon, but they had time for only a quick exchange of blows before they were separated by the plunging beasts around them. Then both armies met with a clashing sound of metal on metal, and the air was filled with the noise of battle—men screaming, gnolls howling, goblins keening, ogres snarling, horses neighing, and above it all, the ringing clatter of swords and shields and spears. Archers on both sides loosed several volleys into the rear ranks of the opposing force, and then there were no more rear ranks as both armies melded into a vast melee as wild as it was deafening.

Aedan tried to stay beside the emperor, but it was impossible with so many bodies surging all around him. His standard fell, the shaft chopped in half by a wildly swinging blade, and one of the foot soldiers picked it up and held it aloft as Aedan reached for the shield slung from his saddle and lashed out all around him, killing and maiming to survive.

The gnolls fought like the half-beasts they were, using teeth as well as blades. One sprang up behind Aedan on his horse, and Aedan twisted, feeling teeth snap on his helm as he brought his shield around and knocked the creature off. A mounted mercenary charged him, and they engaged, Aedan with unabated fury and hatred of this traitorous human, who had sold out his own people for a few pieces of gold. Controlling their horses with their knees, they exchanged blow after blow, each blocking the other with his shield until one of the mercenary's blows got through. The blade whooshed toward Aedan's head, but he twisted aside at the last instant, avoiding a stroke that would have split his skull right through the helm. The point of the sword grazed the side of his face, just below the eye guard, and opened up a gash from cheek to jaw. Aedan ignored the pain, screaming through it as he lunged at his opponent. His sword took the man just beneath the arm, and the mercenary fell, screaming, to disappear beneath the swirl of bodies all around them.

The rocky and uneven ground they fought upon made footing difficult for both men and beasts, but it also meant less choking dust was raised. Still, a small cloud formed over the field of battle as the bodies milled around, slamming into one another with a frenzy. Even in the chill of this northern clime, Aedan was soon drenched with sweat beneath his armor. His arms ached from wielding sword and shield, which grew heavier as the battle drew on, and the muscles of his legs felt as if they were on fire from gripping his mount's flanks and exerting pressure to turn it. His breath came in hoarse gasps as he fought, and every spare moment he could seize, he glanced around him wildly, searching for some sign of Michael, whom he had lost in the milling throng.

It was impossible to tell which way the tide of battle was running, whether in favor of the Army of Anuire or the Gorgon's troops. The only way the opponents could differentiate one another was by the color of their armor. Only at close distance could humans and demihumans tell one another apart.

Aedan's ears were ringing from the sound of battle, thousands of swords smashing away, clanging like a symphony of blacksmiths pounding on their anvils. Bodies of men and riders surged back and forth, many tripping over those who'd fallen, and those wounded unfortunate enough to be unable to rise to their feet were trampled to death within moments of hitting the ground. The screams of men and beasts mingled in the air, creating a sound unlike anything Aedan had ever heard before. No battle cries could be distinguished now, only snarls and growls and hoarse-throated screams coming from both human and demihuman throats. It sounded as if the earth were groaning.

As Aedan fought, twisting left and right and slashing out at opponents both mounted and on foot, he lost all sense of direction. But when he had a brief chance to glance around, he saw that the mountains to the north were closer now. In a flash, he realized what that meant. The Gorgon's troops, having the advantage of fighting on their own ground, were better able to orient themselves in battle, and they were slowly pushing the Anuireans to the edge of the plain where they had met, trying to force them back against the rocky cliffs, where they could surround them. Aedan glanced up and saw black-clad archers perched up on the rocks in the distance, waiting for the Anuireans to be pushed into range of their bows.

He cried out, "*Anuireans! Forward to the center! Avoid the cliffs! Beware the archers in the rocks! Push forward! Forward!*"

The cry was taken up all around him as the men realized their danger and redoubled their efforts to push the enemy back. In the distance, toward the center of the plain, Aedan saw one of the siege towers burning. The Gorgon's troops had separated Michael's army from their siege engines and enveloped them. Now they were torching and toppling them, rendering them useless. Aedan pitied the souls who had been manning them, but he could spare no time to dwell on their loss. He was beset on all sides as he urged his mount forward, trying to make headway and fighting off opponents as he searched for Michael every chance he got. But it was becoming impossible to see anything clearly beyond a few dozen yards or so. The rocky and volcanic ground on which they fought was being churned up by now, and a grainy ash was floating in the air, making it appear as if they were fighting in a thick, dark fog.

Aedan cut down a mounted goblin, then quickly glanced around. They had gained some distance from the cliffs, but only a little, and it seemed as if they were being forced back once more, within range of those archers on the heights with their deadly crossbows, which could shoot with enough force to pierce right through armor plate and chain mail.

Then, suddenly, Aedan's horse reared up with a cry as an ogre leapt upon it and fastened its teeth into his mount's throat. Aedan almost lost his balance, but regained it and chopped down at the loathsome-looking creature, severing its spine, but blood was streaming from his horse's throat. The ogre had severed a major blood vessel, and the poor horse was rapidly bleeding to death. In moments, Aedan would be forced to fight on foot.

He searched quickly for a mounted opponent that he could engage, in hopes of taking his mount, but there were none close by. A moment later, his horse wheezed and stumbled, then went down to its knees. Aedan had only an instant to dismount before the animal fell over, trapping him. He swung down out of the saddle just as the horse fell over with a gargling exhalation, thrashed its legs several times, and died. Holding his sword and shield, Aedan fought on foot, pressing forward against the tide of warriors trying to push him back.

He could not see Michael. He had lost the advantage of clear visibility and, on foot, he could see only those immediately around him. He ignored the soreness in his legs as he pressed forward, but kept being pushed back by the determined fighters in black armor. He fought despite the burning in his arms and shoulders, hacking with his blade at goblins, gnolls, and mercenaries alike. His shield was badly buckled from the force of all the blows it had taken, and his helm was dented on one side from a glancing blow that struck it and slid off the plate upon his shoulder. He felt blood trickling down past his left ear and did not know how serious the wound was. There was no time to heal it; all his efforts and attention were taken up by the task of trying to stay alive.

It seemed to him that they were losing. They were trying to fight their way back toward the center of the field, but they were slowly, inexorably being forced back against the cliffs. And then he spotted Michael.

The emperor was astride his horse, perhaps some twenty or twenty-five yards away, battling two mercenaries. And closing in upon him, moving relentlessly through the press of bodies, was Raesene.

Aedan fought like a man possessed in an attempt to reach him, but in the tangled melee, twenty yards was as good as twenty miles. He came face-to-face with a snarling gnoll brandishing a spear. As the wolflike creature lunged at him, he batted the spear aside with his sword and brought the blade up in a slashing motion across the creature's face. The monster howled with pain and went down, clutching its ruined travesty of a face. When Aedan next glanced up, he saw that Michael had disposed of one of the mercenaries and was fighting the other. But Raesene was moving closer. There were only about ten yards between them now, and the Gorgon was steadily cutting his way through to reach him.

"Michael!" Aedan screamed. *"Michael, look out!"*

But Michael couldn't hear him.

Grunting with the effort, Aedan hacked his way through the press of bodies around him, desperately trying to reach the emperor's side. He was perhaps fifteen yards away now, but the Gorgon was much closer. The second mercenary fell then, his skull split by a powerful blow, and Michael spurred toward the Gorgon, each intent on reaching the other.

There were no other mounted men around them, no one to protect him. Aedan gasped as a strong blow smashed into his shield and buckled it completely, starting a split in the top that reached almost a third of the way through it. Aedan smashed the shield into his goblin opponent, charging him behind it, and he knocked the goblin off his feet. He brought his sword up and finished him, then turned to meet an ogre who was rushing at him. The lumbering, drooling beast was carrying a huge club with spikes in it, and Aedan knew if even one blow connected, it would finish him.

He hurled his ruined shield at the ogre, and as the brute flinched and tried to block it with its club, Aedan ran it through. Then, using both hands to swing his sword like a flail, he slashed around him in all directions as new opponents pressed in, desperately looking for a shield he could seize. He cut down several goblins and one gnoll, then came up against a human mercenary . . . with a shield large enough for him to wield. He smashed at the man, who took the blow upon his shield, and Aedan ludicrously hoped his blow had not been strong enough to damage it. He blocked the mercenary's blow, taking it upon his sword, then launched a hard kick at the man's groin. As the mercenary doubled over with a grunt, Aedan cut him down and wrenched his shield from him. Then he looked up, searching for Michael.

An instant later, he spotted him. He was locked in combat with the Gorgon, dwarfed by his opponent, and they were smashing away at one another with a fury. By the movements of his body, Aedan could see that Michael had loosed his divine wrath. His blood abilities allowed him to call upon great strength, as well, which made him an unstoppable juggernaut in battle, but the Gorgon was three times his size, massive and powerful, with a sword twice as large as his. Michael fought furiously, but Raesene was his match, and as Aedan fought to reach him, he saw that Michael was being steadily forced back by the rain of blows falling on his shield, smashing it into a twisted, buckled ruin.

Aedan cut down three more opponents in quick

succession, plunging through the throng around him. He was about ten yards away now. He glanced up and saw that Michael's shield was gone and he was swinging his sword with both hands, trying to batter his way through the Gorgon's guard.

Then the unthinkable happened. Before Aedan's disbelieving eyes, the Gorgon brought his sword down in a vicious blow that Michael took upon his sword . . . and his sword was snapped in two. The blow continued down and cleaved him right through the shoulder, severing his arm.

"*NO!*" screamed Aedan as he battered his way through to reach him.

But he knew it was too late. Blood was pouring from Michael's wound, and Raesene's next blow struck him from his saddle. Aedan charged his way through the bodies all around him and reached Michael just as the Gorgon dismounted and raised his mighty sword for the killing blow, and the blood-theft that would follow. In that instant, Michael struggled to his knees and reached out with his one remaining hand, placing his palm flat upon the ground. He jerked, convulsively, and bits of earth and rock erupted from the ground where he had placed his palm, grounding his powers, channeling them into the earth and denying Raesene the ultimate victory of bloodtheft.

With a howl of rage, the Gorgon brought his blade down and cut Michael in two.

Aedan went berserk. With a wild scream, he charged Raesene, slamming into him with all his might, but it was like hitting a stone wall. He bounced back and fell, shocked by the impact, and the Gorgon raised his blade to finish him. If he could not have the satisfaction of bloodtheft from the emperor, he would take what he could get from his lord high chamberlain.

The sword came down, but Aedan rolled at the last minute. It struck the ground beside him with such force that Aedan felt the impact. He struggled to get back up, but the Gorgon was already raising his blade again for the final blow. But it never came.

There was a fierce gust of wind, and a funnel cloud came down, enveloping him and spinning him around, causing him to lose his balance. A new sound filled the air, rising above the din of battle. The sound of wailing horns blowing in concert mingled with the shrill, high-pitched war cry of the elves.

As in the Battle of Mount Deismaar, they had arrived to join forces with the Anuireans at the key moment of the battle, when it seemed all was lost, and they pitched into the Gorgon's troops with a frenzy. As Raesene struggled to rise to his satyr's legs, the funnel cloud swirled away from him toward Aedan, enveloping him, and Aedan felt the dizzy, falling sensation he had felt once before as his corporeal body faded, transmuted into wind that raised him high into the air, above the battlefield.

Gylvain!

Sylvanna would never have forgiven me if I had let you die, the elf responded.

You should have left me. Michael's dead. The Gorgon killed him. All is lost. I should have died with him.

All is never lost, the elven mage replied. *And you must live. It is on you now to assume the regency and hold the empire together. You must salvage what you can from this defeat and build anew. You must live, Aedan, for your wife and for your children, for your friends who love you and for the people who will need you. I share your grief and sorrow and regret that we did not arrive in time. But life goes on. It must. Even if it hurts.*

Below them, on the battlefield, the Gorgon's troops were in retreat, heading back toward the obsidian fortress. The Anuireans were still fighting them as they retreated, but they were tired and grateful to the elves, who forced the monsters back. There would be no siege, for the siege engines were destroyed. The towers, the trebuchets were in flames. At a glance, it seemed as if only half the army remained. The field was so thickly littered with bodies, it was impossible to see the ground.

It was over. The emperor was dead, and his troops had no will to fight on without him.

It does hurt, Gylvain. It hurts more than I could ever say. And I am so very weary. . . .

Sleep, my friend. Let go of the pain now. Everything shall pass in its own time. Sleep and take your rest upon the wind. . . .

ANUIRE

Epilogue

The Eve of the Dead. The winter solstice. The
longest night of the year. It was, indeed, a fitting
night to mourn. Aedan Dosiere, Lord High Chamberlain of the Cerilian Empire of Anuire, sat slumped
over at the table in his tower study in the Imperial
Cairn. The bottle of brandy he and Gylvain had
drunk stood empty, and a pleasant warmth suffused
him. He raised his head and looked out the window,
across the bay at the flickering lights of the city of
Anuire.

It was nearly dawn, yet every window in the city
was still illuminated with the glow of candles that
commemorated the spirits of those who passed on.

"A dying flame. An appropriate, if rather maudlin

metaphor," Aedan muttered with a sigh. The weight of his years rested heavily upon him. He had survived. Survived his wife, who had passed on and left him alone to bear the heavy burden of his responsibilities. Survived his liege lord, who had fallen all those years ago, leaving him to assume the regency and lead the people of Anuire as best he could. Survived Derwyn, who had returned from Battlewaite a cripple and had lingered on for several years before taking his own life in misery; survived Laera and Faelina and nearly everyone else he knew back then. He had survived them all and carried on, even though it hurt.

Now the flame was dying. He could no longer hold the empire together. Truly, it had died with Michael, and over the years, one by one, the provinces had fallen away, forming their own independent nations until there was almost nothing left of the glory that once was. The dream. The goal he and Michael had both fought so hard to accomplish.

"Everything shall pass in its own time," muttered Aedan drunkenly as he turned from the window.

"Yes," Gylvain replied. "Even the pain."

"Truly. It is little more than a dull ache now. An exhaustion that has seeped into my soul and drained me." Aedan folded his arms on the table and rested his head upon them.

"How is Sylvanna?" he said thickly without looking up. "Is she well?"

"Yes," said Gylvain. "She is well. And she often thinks of you. You had already asked that once before."

"I did?" Aedan muttered sleepily. "I had forgotten. But it is good she remembers me."

"She will not forget."

"I am so very weary, Gylvain. . . ."

"Sleep now," Gylvain said, rising from the table and gazing down at his old friend. Aedan's shoulders rose and fell several times as Gylvain watched. His breathing became more labored and heavy. Gylvain raised his arms and spun around, fading away as wind blew papers in a flurry through the chamber. Aedan Dosiere took one more labored breath and let it out in a final, long, sighing exhalation, and then he breathed no more. The swirling funnel cloud moved over him.

Sleep, old friend, and take your rest upon the wind.

He slowly faded away into the wind that bore him out the window and across the bay, over the flickering lights of the city and heading north into the first gray light of dawn.